PIN YOUR SOCKS TOGETHER

Michael Craddock

Published by Washwell Press

A CIP catalogue record for this book is available from the British Library.

ISBN 978-1-0685004-0-4

Typeset by Clare Brayshaw

Prepared and printed by:

York Publishing Services Ltd
64 Hallfield Road
Layerthorpe
York YO31 7ZQ

Tel: 01904 431213

Website: www.yps-publishing.co.uk

PIN YOUR SOCKS TOGETHER

'Tal vez hay que se busca una cosa y se halla otra.'
'Perhaps it is you look for one thing and find another.'

Sancho Panza in *Don Quijote*

'that things are not so ill with you and me as they might have been, is half owing to the number who lived faithfully a hidden life, and rest in unvisited tombs.'

George Eliot, *Middlemarch*

'There is a world elsewhere.'

Coriolanus in *Coriolanus*

'Lord, what fools these mortals be.'

Puck in *A Midsummer Night's Dream*

For My Mother and Father, My Brother Tim,
Porage the Dog;

And All My Pupils Who Taught Me
Far More Than I Ever Taught Them

PREFACE

This tale about a school and its teachers is a coming of age novel, one imagining a world through the eyes of a rather innocent beginner. Innocence is often key in fiction. It can refresh a world, make it more interesting, maybe even save it from its own assumptions; for we human beings are an arrogant lot, not least in how easily we get to imagine we are what it's all about.

One of the claims made of the novel as a genre is to tell it as it is. I don't know much about anything, but when you teach for a long time, even the most Quixotic of individuals like me, learn something. I hope, therefore, there is some truth in this fiction – not historical, biographical, but about an imagined rollercoaster of highs and lows, joys, inspiration, challenges, and pathos on a teacher's journey. I have tried to make that story entertaining, funny at times, but fundamentally serious; and given some of the writing a particular immediacy, for teaching is a kind of drama. I have also tried hard to create a hero and heroine who are not the stereotypes of typical media fictions- save us from those!- but likeable, if flawed characters in whom the reader can have some stake.

But this is not just a story about teachers.

I have always thought how school can be a metaphor for life, not least in how we never completely escape classroom and playground, how so much begins there. Likewise, the idea of looking for transcendence and meaning in ordinary life, work, relationships is part of the story: how, if ever, we might find them.

Much amazing work goes on in many schools, but teaching can be tough. There aren't always solutions, answers to the challenges that everyone encounters in schools, or any form of education, particularly in an increasingly complex world. Too much information can get in the way of real knowledge and understanding. Trust is beyond price. But there are sometimes better solutions, and especially ambitions we can have, when we keep our minds on a bigger picture, something better.

The novel's themes encompass education, growth, loyalty and independence, not least for its central character. The tale as a whole, like its ending, does not aim to reach conclusions, even if its main protagonist tries. That would indeed be a presumption. *Trust the tale not the teller*, wrote D.H. Lawrence.

It's easy to lose sight of important things when we get used to whatever it is we are about. The things we should truly wonder over, the 'something more' that is a theme of the story, may be elusive and precarious in practice, easily lost, even illusory. I've left them purposely vague, but they should matter in education. It's really about that: *better, not just more*.

Novels have a mischievous relationship with the imagination, often a critical, disillusioning one. Save us, however, from the true madness of the unimaginative! The best of education, academic or otherwise, must be about more than knowledge and skills, vital as they are. It should be about seeking truth, learning understanding, kindness, respect, looking for better ways of living and being, how we can grow into better people. Imagination is the heart of all that.

Lastly, I hope there is something perhaps more in this than the rattle of egos (including no doubt the writer's!) – something about service, responsibility. Pin your socks together.

Michael Craddock

CHAPTER ONE

FIRST LESSON

Dom Greaves's first day.

Dark, wild, soggy outside. A half-soaked examination form waits outside his locked classroom, at the end of an unlit corridor, in the depths of part of the school parents never see.

Him – or is it *he*? – *an English teacher!*

*

He had faltered coming down the stairs into the rather imposing school foyer, next to what was grandly called Great Hall, actually the canteen. Excited apprehension had been building for weeks. Here was his chance: to inspire, enlighten, uplift – change his charges forever. Months of training had already come and gone in a swift blur of rich promise, challenge.

Then, suddenly, on the way there, a strange smothering fear had mastered him. The unmistakeable smells of a school lunch just finishing, the scrape of chairs, clink and clatter of cutlery, jostling voices edgy with the confinement of a wet break, stirred uncomfortable memories of his own school days. Then he was remembering: how he had felt starting school; a pale, lanky thing, fearful of the unfamiliar, easily set back.

They had given him a small, stuffy room with lines of dusty, drab texts, and an old, torn map of Roman Britain he recalled from his own school days. Graffitied desks – 'I'm bored', 'School sucks', even the comical 'Pig hates me' – had shaken his enthusiasm. Some particularly dark memories had been disturbed; curling embarrassments, stinging laughter, humiliations: everything public for all to see.

For moments he had stood there, apart from himself, watching someone else it seemed. He had only to go back up to his study, ring the Head: he had made a mistake, this wasn't, after all, him.

*

He takes a deep breath, determines to show them, and himself; then some of the hardest steps he ever has: down, down to the end of the echoing stairs.

And there he is. No going back now.

*

'Afternoon', he said to his waiting flock, trying to sound brisk, business-like. 'I'm afraid you've got me.'

The class, who had fallen temporarily silent, glared unresponsively, began to talk again as he fumbled with a key, striving with a suddenly clumsy lock.

Someone laughed loudly behind his back. Others surrounded him, shoving each other. The rain outside had made the class a mess already: the smell of damp cloth, wet hair was everywhere. Inside the wind was pummelling the windows so that they rattled in their ancient, confining casements.

'Don't push!' he remonstrated. Then, remembering how he meant to be, 'Keen to get started?' he quipped smiling; but it came out wrong, falling dead.

They burst past him, piling in without being asked,

attacking the seats at the back of the room. He sent them out, meaning to be firm. They re-entered, sullen, staring.

He began talking at them, surprised at the sound of his voice.

A girl at the back had taken out a brush, was combing out wet hair. Should he admonish? Some of the others began digging reluctantly into bags, flopping folders onto desks noisily. One of the boys looked challengingly at him, then away and began talking to another who turned to look him up and down, smirking. In front of him, a gangly lad who looked as if he had outgrown himself stretched out with a loud groan, adapting the desk as a pillow.

He had a sparkling presentation ready for them, hoping that if they wouldn't listen at least he could give this to ones who wanted to learn; but the computer was stroppy too. It wouldn't open it. He tapped away, improvising comments.

The class had begun to chatter freely now, glad at delay.

A white-faced girl called Jane, who had just started that term, with mousey brown hair curling over her forehead like a screen, arrived late, not knowing where to sit.

'Sit down. Quickly!' he admonished, hoping to sound authoritative.

Her fringe hid tears.

'Where you bin? You're late already!' one of her peers muttered, mocking.

Dom was about to challenge, but there was a snort of laughter about something going on somewhere else.

Then another hand had gone up. Some boys were gawping at something on a device; a girl was protesting hers wasn't working.

Everything was happening at once.

He ploughed on, announcing his learning objectives, his desire to inspire and challenge, to change their lives....

'Who the hell *are* you?' came a voice, suddenly, followed by laughter.

Somehow, he hadn't had time to introduce himself properly, and there was a register he should take, but he had to get on now, telling them something important, rivet their attention.

'Knowledge is limited but the imagination is boundless – that's why books matter,' he announced.

The class looked nonplussed. The boys resumed their examination of something more interesting on screen.

'Steady on, Sir! We had Fossil last term. He just read all lesson, showed us dodgy stuff, crap online,' came another voice.

Dom smiled, uncertain, not sure what to say. Who was Fossil? Pig by another name? Was there someone on the staff called that he had not met?

The class, reading inexperience, had begun to find their feet, however. Curiosity for the new boy was piqued.

'We're not doing work today, first day back, are we, Sir?'

'I don' do readin', Sir,' another voice announced definitively, amidst escalating noise.

Then suddenly it seemed everyone wanted to be heard, no one to listen.

'Now, *listen* you lot!'

He was raising his voice, already.

'Today, our lesson objective is to look at *Pride and Prejudice* and...'

There was a general groan...

'...how relationships and gender are presented in the first few chapters.'

There was general mystification.

'What's he say?' said one of the girls not particularly quietly.

'It stinks in here!' someone protested.

Somebody had sworn, he was sure, and was that a phone out under a desk; but it was easier to pretend not to notice. Then a window was being thrown open to protests and a spattering of rain and a gale of fresh air blew into the room, fluttering his plan off the desk.

At that moment, before he could intervene, there was a loud crash followed by noisy cheering. A large lad sitting at the back emerged from a cloud of dust holding up the remains of a chair.

'Sorry, Sir, it broke!'

The class loved it.

Dom tried to look as if he were taking all this in his stride, but a late summer wasp, taking refuge from the wind and rain, had joined them, and the class, enjoying themselves now, thought it much more interesting to follow its lazy progress. Even some of the boys looked up from their screen.

He crossed nobly to intercept it, swatting wildly, cracking one of the panes.

There were cheers, laughter.

'You'll have to pay for that!' someone declared with authority.

The wasp sailed on.

'Sir, my brother swallowed one of those and literally ended up in hospital,' one of the boys told him, hopefully.

'Now come on you lot, settle down: you're here to learn. Today's group tasks will help you do well in your exams.'

The class greeted this sceptically.

Two of the boys who had been jostling had begun to fight; the noise was impossible again.

'You two, BEHAVE! The rest of you, LISTEN!'

For a moment there was silence.

He noticed tears brimming again from the eyes of the latecomer.

'Do you need to go to welfare?' he blurted. 'Can you see she's all right?' Dom said to a group of girls sitting near the front.

He knew how she felt.

Half of the girls in the class attempted to exit with her.

'She's just f-in started – hates it already,' jeered one of the boys.

'Did you have to read this borin' old stuff when you were at school?' inquired a girl, with no interest in an answer.

'Did you enjoy school, Sir, when you were young?' one of the class asked, grinning, probing weakness.

They all looked at him now.

Dom paused a moment. He'd suddenly remembered Miss Pitter at his own school, how the pupils had made her cry most lessons. They all, even he who was a quiet lad, mucked about in her hapless, incomprehensible maths sessions, done blow by blow from a textbook. When she was writing on the whiteboard, kids used to pelt each other with chewed up paper, even spattering it above her head. She droned on pretending to be oblivious.

What must she have felt?

'Are you all right, Sir?'

'No. No, I didn't, not at first, not for a very long time in fact,' began Dom, slowly.

Stronger, however, were the memories of a boy who had a long fringe of mousey hair he tried to hide behind. The boy had a hard time because he appeared slow at everything, always hung back, could be made to cry.

'But I did when I had grown up enough to understand that I was there for my own benefit,',' he continued, feeling angry then, *'and learnt to listen!'*

The class sensed something in his voice. They might have to pay attention. At least he wasn't banging on about *Pride and Prejudice*.

'That's partly why I'm here,' he said, forgetting his plan, his nerves. 'You asked. I'm going to tell you- a bit about school, just what you are missing if you don't listen, participate: why all this boring old stuff matters.'

So he found himself telling them about past cruelty to Miss Pitter who had ended up leaving. Then about a friend of his, who, one rainy lunchtime, goaded beyond endurance by bullies – inside and out, had taken a knife and scored into his arms because it was the only way of dealing with the pain of feeling he was never any good. A kindly teacher, finding out, had been there for him, told him she'd struggled at school: it didn't matter how he did, but only that he tried, respected himself. He'd started to listen in her lessons and learnt that the 'old boring stuff' in books wasn't boring, but about sharing ideas and feelings, secret, even magical worlds; that bad things could change and be better, and you could even learn to live with things you couldn't change. Above all, Dom explained, 'old boring books' could teach you important stuff, like nothing else: how important it was to understand others, what it is to feel, what it means to be alive, *if you listen!*

Listen, really listen- or life will have gone by before you've ever learnt, found out what really matters, begun to love the understanding that turns the world!

The class looked uncomfortable, or just bored.

He'd been warned about talking too much, feelings getting in the way, whatever that meant.

He must pull things round.

He told them a bit about himself, his likes and dislikes. Some of them continued to talk amongst themselves, ignoring him. He asked if they had enjoyed reading the book. There were a few laughs, but no one said anything. He asked them about their holidays, their hopes for the future.

'Never having to go to school again!' someone declared.

Most of the class just looked as if they were wondering why they had had to come back at all, dreaming of wide worlds and possibilities that reached beyond the steamy windows of some old classroom.

*

Near the end of the lesson, Dom tried to resume official pedagogy with some worksheets, but things seem to grind to a halt prematurely. He'd run dry.

Soon the bell was ringing, and suddenly they were all scrambling to get out, except for one impossibly slow girl who smiled at him, asking if he were all right.

Then the classroom was empty.

He was alone again, bemused. It hadn't been how he'd expected, what he'd planned. He hoped he'd made them think a bit; perhaps he had only unsettled them. He paced through the lesson again in his head, cringed a bit. Then he picked his plan up off the floor. One of the kids had trodden on it as they left. It bore a large, muddy shoe print.

One of the older teachers, a Mr Ian Walker he had met briefly the day before, a stooped figure, as old as time, peered in.

'Survived?'

Dom smiled uncertainly.

'I made a bit of a mess of it,' he said, thinking of the littleness of much of what had gone on.

'Don't tell me. They didn't listen? Ah!' Walker nodded his head, enjoying his moment. 'You'll get used to all that, of course – boredom, having to repeat yourself a thousand times: can't concentrate any more, children. And they never learn till *they* learn. I wouldn't be a teacher again if I were your age.'

He left to shout loudly at someone innocently running past.

Dom sighed, looking outside where the rain continued. He walked over to close the window still open, and stared out across the fields to where a little stream sloped away like a question mark skirting the rather odd solitary hill that dominated the school campus, from which it took its name.

Hillview.

Not much to see today.

The girl, Jane, who had left in tears came sheepishly back in to collect her things with one of the other boys from the class. Was his name, Tim?

'Enjoyed the lesson today, Sir,' he said.

'Really?' said Dom, warily.

'Yeh, it was interesting – I didn't think anybody cared that much about old books, what we felt. Our last teacher just gave up. Our class are awkward, Sir. You should see what we're like with Mr Walker. He's been here since the Middle Ages.'

'You all right now?' said Dom to the girl, still behind her hair.

'Sorry, Sir, she said. 'It's just- my first day. Everyone else seems so sure, and I felt… lost-' she tailed off.

Dom heard her.

He looked at the smudges under her eyes, her mousey hair tumbling across her face, remembered.

'Everyone feels like that sometimes, especially at first. You'll be all right. I think we both will.'

She looked at him, puzzled, but managing a smile.

'School's tough, but we all go through it. Give it time – you'll find yourself,' he said gently.

She nodded slowly. Then her face clouded again.

'D'you know where maths-?'

'I've got maths next. My name's Tim. I'll take you,' said the boy kindly.

Then they both rushed off.

Another bell was ringing now, and, before he had time to gather his thoughts, or think how on earth was he to get through the rest of the afternoon, or all those days ahead, another lesson began for Dom.

CHAPTER TWO

TRIP UP

Everything mattered to Dom, for life must be some kind of art in the end. He believed things should be more than they were, and not just for himself. Living was nothing at all, nor were people, nor was having a good time, unless there were some serious, deep purpose in what you did, what it all added up to.

Perhaps this owed something to a cynical, materialistic age: but he genuinely felt there should be something more, even if this power of vague longing, and a need to prove himself, might have identified him – to some – as boyish, naive. If he himself had been as serious as he believed, he would have been impossible. But he had some saving common sense, a rather endearing diffidence in a world constructed mostly out of brash media fictions, even a surprising sense of humour. Nonetheless, he must imagine intensely, take all to heart, especially what he read. And his job was nothing less than a mission, of course: teaching English, literature, all that exceptionalism – its wealth of words, its grand imaginative realities.

*

Hillview School itself had been a bit of a world apart, its own imagined special place. A private school until the 1970s, and a proudly independent one with its own ways of doing things, it had been largely happy in its differences, and gloried in its past. An empire of success and idiosyncratic traditions had kept it punching well above its weight in the world until economics, and a certain complacency, had caught up. Then, one of its enlightened former heads had had some vision, grasped practical realities, realised ever greater problems with money were on the way. He negotiated a privileged place for it in the state educational system. It meant opening its doors to all, but it secured funds for a future, a potentially better one in collaboration with others, not out on its own. It was allowed to retain some of its perks and advantages, keeping a small boarding provision for those whose family situation required it, and many of the benefits of its situation as a country school with some land and a handful of old, if dwindling, private assets.

Many of the old guard had felt betrayed when change came, complaining about loss of independence, erosion of identity, but those who had come to work there subsequently believed in it. They had also relished the opportunities that a hybrid identity gave the school, even secretly congratulating themselves on their luck in having things both ways: state funding, some private resources. True, the intake changed, but a country school in a pleasant rural area retained advantages.

For many years only money worries- there was never enough to pay the teachers properly, or improve the ageing campus facilities- cast much of a shadow: but that was a burden common to all schools. Pupils rolled in, and out; most of the urgent bills could be paid. All seemed well with the place, although it was not what it had been. Perhaps it had never had.

Under the surface, tension, however, was there and growing, alongside a more widespread exasperation that individual entitlement in the modern age made the lot of the teacher, even in a school like that, trying. There was, too, a feeling in the generalities of daily grumbles that teachers were more and more subject to external control and regulation. They were losing autonomy in the classroom; increasingly more time had to be devoted to ticking boxes, rather than lighting fires of inspiration. There was, too, resentment at change so often being foist on them without their active agreement, a sense almost of feeling colonised by external forces beyond accountability. A desire for more freedom, independence, taking back control welled, but as yet remained below the surface, unfocused-frustrations rather than any precise manifesto for change.

As for Dom, he knew only what bore on his opportunity in securing a job there, and would no doubt have dismissed quite a lot of the rest of it as a sort of littleness. Where the money came from for the school, or the whole idea of a school as in any way a business, was of small interest. That was the government's job: he had his heart and mind on higher things; even if, he was beginning to find, his hands were actually full of perplexing practicalities.

*

Later that same first day, Dom stood on the kerbside of the nearby town of Wellsway with twenty-five still mostly unfamiliar pupils. He had found himself in charge of a trip to the theatre.

He was glad his first day was done; it would get a lot easier from now on he told himself.

It had been the pupils who had saved him, somehow.

His mentor and subject leader, one Mr Charles Royal, a man he was rather awe in of because he seemed to know everything, had suddenly fallen ill. He'd asked him to take charge of his trip. Apparently, this happened a lot. Dom had hardly had time to wonder how you could get ill on the first day after a long holiday, or why after seven weeks away it was necessary for some of Year Eleven, Twelve and Thirteen to go straight off out somewhere. He'd then had a frantic search to find someone to help him. You always needed at least one other adult on trips. He discovered, too, that there was endless paperwork involved; it had not been done – forests of it, all sorts of notes on the children that read like mini-novels. Did they all have some complex issue or other? He'd had to keep asking for advice when everyone was so busy, impatient already with inexperience.

There had been a lot of muttering about him that afternoon in the Staff Room, though no one had come forward to help, until another beginner, an English teacher, Emma Oakley, had taken pity, agreed to accompany him on the coach. She was new to it all too. That gave them a connection; but she was over twenty five, really old, and had, she told him, worked in some mysterious marketing world in 'the city' before coming into teaching. Unlike him, lucky thing, she lived off the school campus in a flat in town.

She was assured and confident in ways Dom envied, and, despite her age, he had to admit, attractive, striking in looks and manner in ways you could not ignore. Indeed, he'd not met anyone quite like her before.

The children were surprisingly eager to get away from school already. They were also amused that he and Miss Oakley, newcomers, had been entrusted with them. Speculation about the two of them together, new and young-ish, was soon rife. It might have embarrassed indeed, had he known their thoughts, but Dom, consumed in procedure, was quite innocent.

At least the rain storm that raged most of the day had mostly blown itself out, but heavy, wild showers alternated with spells of warm sunshine. The local town pavements, stained wet, blazed a blinding gold when they shone with the last elixir of summer.

Dom's spirits, dampened by his lessons, could not but lift. He loved the theatre: drama was a world changer. He thought of what a play would do, transporting them all to some other, richer reality.

But this practical business of it all!

The coach driver, who seemed to resent the service he was providing, had grumbled all the way there, remonstrating peevishly with anything that moved, let alone shouted, on board, then about pupils who had been slow to get off and pestered to get back on to find things they had been too busy talking to remember.

He wasn't going to wait, he warned Dom. *They could all walk home as far as he was concerned if they kept him waiting* and *NO! he hated theatre, could not see any point in anything make believe, prats showing off on stage, definitely did not want a spare ticket. Rather open a vein in a hot bath, thank you.*

He had driven off in surly mood to park the coach. Dom had been glad when he had gone. The pupils seemed to find his verbal demolitions of Sir's educational outing cool.

How many pupils were there – twenty-five? It seemed many more; all their new names and faces! He kept trying to check but they seemed oblivious to his efforts to reckon them up. Couldn't they keep still?

Finally, they were off together, a little snake of humanity, worming its way into the town's evening, Dom self-consciously at the front, smiling to see himself their leader, the adult in command.

They passed a homeless woman sheltering in a doorway, almost buried amidst cardboard cuttings, half asleep, head swathed in hats and scarves, a tin tray by her side full of small change, lots of foreign coins. Dom shook his head to himself. She muttered something in a foreign accent to one of the kids. He could hear one of the pupils openly laughing at her, talking in a loud voice without embarrassment or consciousness until Emma, bringing up the rear, shushed him.

'Sir, can we go for a quick drink before the show starts? The Head always lets us when we are out on trips; now we're sixth form,' said a cheerful looking lad.

What was his name?

His idea was seized on by the rest of the group.

'Honestly, Sir, don't worry,' joined in a striking girl. He remembered her name, Rachel. There was something rather decided about her. Dom noticed she was heavily made up –surely that infringed school rules, even on a trip?

'Mr Waseley says it's part of our education learning how to handle alcohol as long as we're over eighteen.'

There were broad smiles, much agreement.

'You're not all sixth form,' Dom began.

'I'm nineteen!' cried a very small lad cheekily. He was playfully attacked by his mates.

'Go on, Sir!' said the first boy, sensing advantage. 'We've ages before it starts.'

A chorus of support broke out.

Dom looked at Emma for a moment as an expectant sea of faces beamed at him. She seemed to be shaking her head, but he was in charge, needed to show it.

Moreover, they would know how to behave at their age: why, most of them would be voting soon.

'All right then, but absolutely no alcohol, most of you are underage,' instructed Dom.

Momentary protests broke out, but they would sort that later. With astonishing speed, before Dom could think where on earth they might go, the group took command, tracking across town, disappearing down some rather sleazy-looking stairs nearby into the dark depths of somewhere labelled *Dates*.

Emma, who had been bringing up the rear, caught up before he descended into what waited below.

'Not sure this is a good idea. There's plenty of them need watching.'

'It's only a few minutes. I'm not letting them off on their own. There's nowhere to wait – we've ages before it starts: the Head, Mr Waseley allows it,' said Dom, trying to look as if he were in control.

'I want to start by trusting them. There's not much they can do under supervision. I'll take responsibility,' he concluded.

Emma seemed to be raising her eyebrows, but he would show her – them.

Besides, whilst the staff might deliberate, the kids were already there.

*

Inside the building, some pupils had moved swiftly to the bar. Others were just standing idly around, rather self-conscious, or glancing amusedly over at the teachers. Some were texting away, already lost to anything else.

Were phones supposed to be so freely used on trips? He'd read something about that; but it was complicated.

One or two began asking loudly for non alcoholic drinks with cocky glances back at Dom and a non-commital smirk from a good looking young man who worked there. He had already caught the attention of some of the girls, and knew it.

Dom stared round, uncertain. Spent office workers, already a little too loud, mingled with other youngsters, perhaps from some local college. It was hard to tell the pupils from the townies when they were out of uniform.

The whole place smelt pungently of drink and stale humanity. Its dimly lit low ceilings and many corners and alcoves were just right for fun, or trouble: a little underworld, running to its own time and rhythms, so different from the formality of a school.

Dom's imagination must set to work. In a few hours it would be wild: vibrant, exciting, dangerous – the kids drawn across some threshold into darkness; stolen clinches in secret, dim alcoves; seductions; the toilets a hotbed of drugs, trauma, remorseful tears.

He wondered if he had done quite the right thing.

He tried to remember that he would have appreciated a bit of a treat after a first day back at school – some freedom, some escape. Anyway, he could get them all out in a few minutes if anything started, no harm done. But the more he thought about it-

They had better leave, with dignity of course, but under his orders and control – his pride intact.

Emma came over, wanting it seemed to speak to him, but another voice was breaking in on his thoughts.

'Did you always want to be a teacher?' said Tim, the kind boy from that afternoon's class.

He was not in the sixth form yet, but seemed mature.

'I'm enjoying it so far,' said Dom safely, not wholly accurately, his mind turning on how to get everyone out cleanly, without drama.

Emma laughed, then tried to get his attention.

'Reports are that you're quite cool about things, so far, Sir.'

Dom was not sure what to make of that.

A boy called James came up, arm draped around some girl.

'So, Sir, what's this *Wandering Heights* all about? It's not full of hidden meanings is it? Mr Royal said read it over the summer, but I only do the odd English lesson.'

He could feel Emma tugging his sleeve.

'It's all very romantic. There's a famous relationship between characters called Catherine and Heathcliff. It's about class and power and love,' began Dom forgetting his concerns now they were on safe, academic ground.

'Hot sex, Sir?' asked James hopefully.

Emma was nudging him, pointing towards the bar where Rachel, and a small entourage, were flamboyantly chatting up the barman. They seemed to be pleading for drinks – or more – the barman was round sitting on a stool amongst them; but then Dom's eye was drawn to another group of close-knit girls who were already noisily disinhibited, laughing outrageously, constantly glancing around challengingly to see the impression they were making.

This was not the right sort of behaviour.

'Can you explain, Miss so I don' have to read it. Just the sex- interesting bits,' pursued James.

'You should read it yourself. Don't be so lazy. That's how you learn,' Emma replied brusquely, then began, rather more sympathetically, to tell him something of the story. Dom moved to check on the group of noisy girls more closely, standing so he could see them clearly. They were staring frankly, even insolently back. When he averted his gaze he noticed they seemed to be passing something around, and surely, yes apparently generously sharing with each other what looked like a bottle of spirits.

Dom felt a lash of indignation, a hot sense of betrayal beat up. How could they? Who did they think they were?

But then came feelings of cold alarm – the ensuing scene… the consequences!

He would show them.

He strode purposefully over to his girls.

'What do you think you're doing? Put those drinks down immediately. What did I say to you when we came in? And look at what on earth some or you are wearing? You were told *smart casual*. How dare you behave like this? I want to see you all outside in two minutes sharp, lined up on the pavement.'

The effect of his words was, he observed, thankfully instantaneous. The girls froze, glasses arrested in passage, their faces a study in what looked like mortification. Some of them, no doubt the cheeky ones – he'd been warned about teenage girls – even dared to look surprised. They glared at Dom, rendered, he bet, in some cases for the first time in their existence, utterly speechless; but they had asked for this, and been told.

He turned angrily away, still hurt by their outrageous flouting of his trust. They would leave now, but understanding right and wrong, in good order, under control, having learnt a lesson. This Sir was no pushover, not to be messed with.

He regained his place next to Emma, sighing and shaking his head with all the world weariness of a whole day's teaching experience on him.

'We need to leave. Now!' he declared, rather unnecessarily.

To his bemusement, he saw that she and the boys she had been talking to were rocking with laughter.

'I don't think it's funny at all, actually,' he said, peeved.

'Nice one, Sir! You been teaching long?' said James who was looking at Dom with simple delight, as if he could not quite believe he were real.

Dom stared at him puzzled, irritated. Were none of them serious? Did they not see the heinous crime in front of them, understand how they had smashed a world of trust and faith in their disrespect and greed?

'You've certainly made an impression,' said Tim looking back towards the group. He alone seemed to be trying not to smirk. He appeared to look at Dom with something like pity.

Dom was genuinely puzzled.

Emma took over.

'They're not from school,' Emma explained gently, controlling her laughter, tears in her eyes. 'They're just some girls out for a good time, a laugh. Or they were. I think you've made their evening.'

For a moment or two, Dom could not take it in.

He looked back over to where the girls sat. They were talking, laughing again, looking across to where he stood, regarding him with unconstrained wonder, hoping perhaps he were going to come across, have another go. They would be ready this time. One of them had gone across to the bar, separating Rachel and her apparent target. She seemed to be giving the barman an account.

He'd never seen her in his life before.

He looked back at the group.

No, looking at them now, he did not recognise a single one.

For a moment, as the truth finally cut through him, he wanted to curl up, die.

Retreat was the only practical option. With Emma's still laughing help, he gathered his flock, sought the fresh, welcome air outside, hoping he were not too red faced, flustered, all the time trying hard not to look in the direction of the girls, or anyone else.

*

Back on the street, where rain had renewed, news of his public car crash had spread: their new young teacher was smack full of promise.

Some of the boys had lined up in pairs and gave him a cheer and a mock salute. It was probably already viral Dom winced, alongside his twisted tales of woe about self-harm in his own school days.

What must they all think? Emma especially.

Move! They must move! Off to the theatre with no more delay.

But new disaster struck when they reached the nearby theatre on discovering that neither James nor girlfriend, nor Rachel were amongst them.

James was found quickly enough, having slipped off down a dark alley for a few moments with his partner, encouraged no doubt by the relaxed but stimulating approach of the new Sir.

Rachel however was seriously missing. She had left the club with the rest, her friends maintained – but no one knew anything now, nothing at all. Of course, her phone was not answering.

Abuse of the public, leading the innocent astray, lost pupils. And we haven't got to the play yet. Some education thought Dom. A line from long forgotten reading came back to him.

We'll have the rest of the play at home.

But the pupils did not seem overly bothered, relaxed in fact. Who needed a trip to the land of dreams when Sir's outings were a laugh?

And so they stood on, outside the theatre, getting wetter and wetter, waiting.

Waiting for Godot, thought Dom.

Oh God, what next?

He wondered if he should phone her parents, call the police, or try another career.

CHAPTER THREE

WHY DIDN'T THEY JUST MOVE?

It was lucky for Dom that Emma was with him. She was sharper, more practical, guessed where Rachel might be, what kept her. Whatever her friends might say, she suspected that the girl really wanted a more exciting evening's romance than that offered by mere theatre, and decided to go back to the club where she eventually separated a deeply resentful Rachel from a disappointed young barman, but not before the school had attracted more attention, or Rachel had his number.

Dom spent the half hour this took blind with worry. He tried to keep smiling whilst they waited, but marshalling the group seemed even harder now. Although they had much to speculate over, not least Sir's antics and lurid versions of Rachel's fate (abduction by aliens or kidnapping were the popular bets) they were impatient with everything. There was not a second without something to deal with: minor squabbles; a lost phone; someone had forgotten their medication, a matter of life and death it was claimed – for thirty seconds until he found it. Dom wondered if he should ask for some.

Heavy rain kept falling.

By the time they could go into Wellsway's determinedly provincial-looking tiny theatre, they were all thoroughly soaked. Emma had eventually arrived with Rachel, indignantly and shrilly protesting her innocence. She had left her phone behind, 'just gone back to grab things' she was asserting loudly to anyone willing to listen, including some rather surprised local theatre goers who were expecting any drama to be during the play, not before.

But having been ages early, they were now late. In the foyer, they were admonished by a feisty usher coiled like a spring in anticipation of another misbehaving school group. She took the name of the school like a policeman making an arrest, demanded to know who exactly was in charge, looking Dom up and down dismissively and then speaking only to Emma. Eventually, she directed them brusquely out into the rain again, nearly incurring a riot from the children, up some steep back stairs, still shaking her head at them, and Dom most of all.

The way up was adorned with studio portraits of had been local actors, looking operatic, ominously fake, posed in black and white.

'Is the performance not in colour?' groaned a pupil.

They stomped their way indignantly to the top of the building, taking their frustration out on the stairs, Emma and Dom shushing them all the way.

Everyone was waiting as they made their noisy, disordered entry.

They were told to hurry, informed there was no interval – the play was long three hours on a good night.

This was shocking. Part of the reason for going on a trip was the action in the breaks.

'What's wittering mean, Sir?'

'It's wuther, dickhead. What's that mean, Sir? Did they talk funny back in the day?'

The usher shushed them – or tried.

Three hours? How would they cope? They would be bored, bored to death: no phones, nothing, the utter hellish darkness of no internet nor chat. Surely Sir had not dragged them all the way in the rain to something so desperate, first day back?

Dom, a little frustrated, wondered if some of them had ever been to a theatre before, but remained diplomatically silent. Perhaps long periods of silence for the rest of his career might be best.

*

At least as things began, Dom felt they were on the right ground at last. No more silliness, distraction, littleness, but high art, proof of how intense, passionate, alive the world could be. But no one seemed quite sure at the start, or indeed for the first quarter of an hour, what was going on, quite what they were watching.

Someone had said to Dom before he started teaching that the key requirement was to have a good sense of humour, and as he sat there, reflecting on the day's events and watching a truly excruciating adaptation of *Wuthering Heights* come slowly apart, he could not help agreeing. The director had felt it necessary to add a Greek chorus to spell out a story that was hardly modest in its passions. *Relevant, modern* were stamped all over it. But in practice it was a wild revenge on anyone daring to think literature might also be inspiring, elevating, or possibly entertaining.

Dom had dreamt of his pupils witnessing some world-stopping, heart-rending, life-enhancing vision of a richer imaginative world powering between the truths of heaven and hell. What they got was comedy: kid actors who could not act their way out of a paper bag.

Every so often a chorus of three buxom wenches, dressed to little advantage as trees of knowledge, would step forward and intone some blindingly heavy moral about victimisation, grievance, or exploitation. Meanwhile, characters talking in pseudo northern accents that a sensitive soul might have thought a tad patronising stepped in and out of role, not always intentionally, destroying any meaningful empathy.

The pupils gave it the benefit of a quarter of an hour's grace but then, uncomprehending, sympathies disengaged, untouched even by its hapless humour, began to talk, shuffle in their seats.

One day in, Dom reflected, and he'd already done in Jane Austen and Emily Bronte, perhaps literary appreciation forever.

At least he was sitting close next to Emma. She was valiantly trying not to laugh – though not at him, any more. He kept looking at his watch, remembering with a sinking heart there was no interval. Perhaps this was what school felt like from the other side he reflected glumly, remembering his first lesson.

But soon there was real drama. A whispered message arrived along the rows for Emma and him.

'Sir, Rachel's *dying*; she's really ill. She thinks she's about to pass out.'

There was a blood-curdling screech from one of the actors on stage.

'AM I CRACKED OR DID I HEAR A SCREAM?' intoned the girls, not entirely convincingly.

There was general incredulity. A few loud laughs escaped an audience shocked momentarily back into attention. A branch on one of the girls dislodged, clattering off the stage and into the audience.

'Oo, love, you've got woodworm!' commented some wag, getting the best response of the evening so far. A couple of pupils who seemed to have gone to sleep despite frantic gestures from Dom and Emma to at least look alert, stirred, looked up and around, but only for a moment before settling back again.

'Cathy must have died,' came an explanatory narrative voice.

Everyone laughed then, even Dom.

The actors on stage kept at it.

Please just stop thought Dom.

More urgent messages arrived about Rachel.

She was literally terminal, they averred, a hundred per cent. *Sir! Miss!...*

Dom and Emma conferred as quietly as they could, and Emma indignantly went off with her to the toilets, admonishing the sleepers as she went. The general public tut-tutted, more engaged by the school party than the farce on stage. The feisty usher rematerialised at the back, brimming with indignation, confirmed in all her prejudices. She remained there, looking down on them like a member of the Gestapo.

Dom wondered if anyone had ever had a death on their first theatre trip from school.

After another anxious quarter of an hour he was relieved to see Rachel and Emma return. Emma made a white-faced Rachel sit between Dom and herself- more audience upheaval – and a disturbed sleeper blurted out an unfortunate expletive when roused again. A radioactive pulse of disapproval emanated from the usher.

Rachel sat through the rest of the performance dramatically clutching her stomach and leaning forward every so often, as if she were going to be sick. During one lunge, Dom looked at Emma searchingly, who just rolled her eyes, whispering, 'Don't think she's taken anything. Tell you later.'

Dom tried to look as if this were all a matter of course for him, but he lived every moment.

He remembered a cripplingly boring talk given at his school once by local librarians, how they had ended up being laughed off stage to a slow hand clap. The staff had gone mad afterwards.

Eventually the play finished, as randomly as it had begun. The only reason anyone knew was because the lights died for so long. Someone felt they should start applauding. The youngsters joined in, noisily, slow hand clapping, adding some ironic cheering, particularly when the tree retrieved its branch from a helpful audience member. The house lights came up jerkily.

The audience couldn't get out of there quickly enough.

So boring, Sir, Miss! Was that what love was like back in the day? No action, no sex. Who'd believe that?

That's what Dad says it's like living next door to our neighbours.

One of the older pupils, whom Dom had been told was very clever, came up to him.

Why didn't they just move, Sir?

Somehow the comment summed up Dom's day. But there was more.

The theatre authorities had been spirited up by the usher. They were not amused by the restive audience, the chronic sleepers, a constant traffic to the loo, peals of laughter at high tragedy. Didn't they realise what they were watching was a classic. Had they no respect, love, for literature and drama? Why bring such badly behaved pupils out? Couldn't they control them – if not, what were they doing in the job?

Outside, they found that Rachel had disappeared once more off to the loos, sobbing uncontrollably. She had to be prised out again by Emma; so, of course, they were late back to the coach incurring more than a mouthful from the driver who had been looking for trouble all day. He took Dom aside and gave him a lecture about falling moral standards, especially the disgrace of poor punctuality, bred into them at school by useless teachers.

Meanwhile, Rachel's delay had just been dramatics over the boy in the bar Emma explained.

'Bit more exciting when I found them than *Wuthering Heights*. Good job I got there when I did,' she commented before announcing she was not accompanying them back to school but returning to her flat in town. *She* had strong ideas of work–life balance she declared and had had more than enough for a first day, whatever the rules.

Dom tried to argue: proper procedures, staff and pupil ratios, he protested; but Emma had a mind and it was made up. There was the coach driver, she asserted. She was off.

*

At last he had them all on board, even Rachel. His lists had got blurred and torn in the rain but he was past caring, and they were off, finally, home, goodnight, curtain down: thank God.

What a time things took with them all doing their own thing he thought.

Perhaps he needed to be a bit stricter.

Rachel grumbled loudly all the way back, phoning her parents, telling them how awful it had all been – and this new teacher who had taken no care of her when she was dangerously ill, literally dying. In the end, the coach driver roared at her for her incessant chatter. She fell into a deep silence, planning revenge.

As they travelled back the few short dark miles to the campus, Dom caught sight of his tired reflection in the coach window, eerily insubstantial. Most of the pupils, worn out like puppies at the end of long days of play, had fallen asleep whilst others texted in silence, their blue screens casting the darkness of the coach in a strange, flickering dreamy half light.

Unreal…

A mile out of town, one of the pupils shouted that James and girlfriend had just texted saying why had they been left behind? They would be returning by taxi. Would Mr Greaves cover the cost as they had no means of paying that much? Dom wondered if he went ahead and paid, would it buy silence.

No one mentioned the play

CHAPTER FOUR

PIN YOUR SOCKS TOGETHER

It was not that late when they finally got back to school as the performance had been mercifully shorter than planned, not that anyone in the audience had realised. But it was significantly later than the published time.

Irate parents awaited.

Someone called Mrs Tray introduced herself, Rachel's mother. She started onto him first about the trip, then launched into a wide-ranging attack on various aspects of the school: she already had a blow by blow account of how bad the play was, of a desperately ill daughter abused by new staff, assaulted, verbally by some driver. She was going to take this all up tomorrow. She looked Dom up and down, then drove off with her daughter crying again, although Rachel was busy texting her new-found friend amidst her tears.

Then someone lost their phone once more, which occasioned further delay, and as much panic as if a limb or vital organ had come away.

James's family had forgotten the pick-up time and their son and his friend, back ahead of time because of the taxi, had to wait another three quarters of an hour to be collected, standing there in renewed rain.

James and girlfriend found it all rather romantic.

When a parent finally arrived and the car filled, they drove off at sixty miles an hour crushing someone else's bag and its contents.

At least someone had paid Dom for the taxi.

'You'll never get a stroke of work out of him,' James's dad, or stepdad had grinned before leaving.

But the comment that lingered with Dom from the whole evening was someone's enthusiastic goodbye:

'What's up for our next trip, Sir?'

*

As the very last ones finally left, the rain finally stopped, but it had grown cold and campus looked chillingly empty and silent under scudding clouds and fitful moonlight.

Suddenly Dom was quite alone.

How quiet and still everything seemed, after all that battle and bustle.

Then he realised that he had misplaced his own keys and could not get back in anywhere. He sat on his mobile until he roused Terry the site manager, or caretaker as he still styled himself. He lived, like several staff, on site.

Dom had met him once and sensed that he was not, at the best of times, an easy man. He insisted Dom walk all the way to his cottage to collect a key.

'I thought you teachers was s'posed to be telligent!' he greeted Dom at his door standing wild-haired in the porch, wearing some extraordinary pyjama bottom and no top, exhaling like a brewery. Behind him Dom could see several members of what seemed to be Terry's enormous family who had been got out of bed especially to inspect him.

'Good job bloomin' Hemlock had me up to open one of them buildings for some bloody governor – otherwise I might never have picked up. We turns in early after a day here! Don' you forget it.'

Dom looked bemused. Could he be referring to their august Deputy Head, Dr Hennock?

'What was it tonight, summat brainy? Beyond that lot.'

Just give me the key thought Dom wearily.

'Why don't you take them to a pantomime; that lot'd get more out of it: they're used to it in this place.'

Tutting to himself and muttering that there was only two things wrong with schools –staff and kids, and staff were worse than the kids -he glared at Dom, and snorting slammed the door.

Dom retreated, wondering if everything he did at school was going to be this difficult.

But he was tired – so tired! Getting to bed and being fresh to try to begin over again tomorrow was all he could think about.

As he heavily mounted the stairs to his study/bedroom in one of the older parts of the school, devoted to its small group of boarders, he heard the stomp of feet and a tousle-haired bright-eyed resident appeared through a door, a grin as wide as the sea all over his face. It was one of a pair of twins, Joe and John, he had already met. They were 'characters' their housemaster Mr Jolson had boasted with an indulgent smile.

'What you doing up?' said Dom.

'Someone's sick, Sir. John put poo in his mars bar to see what would happen. Can you come?'

What more can they do to me?

'Have you decided what play we're doing yet? Heard about the trip, Sir! Nice one.'

'You should be in bed!' cried Dom. 'Who's on duty?'

'Don' know, Sir,' said the boy. 'We haven't seen anyone, not since last term. No one bothers much, evenings, so long as there's not a riot, Sir!'

And the boy pattered off leaving Dom to follow it all up.

*

Even later as Dom wearily mounted the final set of stairs to his accommodation at the top of the building, he saw a note stuck on the door. In large spidery letters it read:

PIN YOUR SOCKS TOGETHER

Impaled by the note were two odd mismatching socks that Dom recognised as his. It was from a Mrs Tombs, a woman who 'did for' the kids and the few resident staff. She had lectured him at length on the need to keep his socks properly paired up so that they did not have to be sorted after her wash. This was a matter of great importance: in detail, such small things, lay the essence of everything that really counted in a school, discipline especially. She had instructed at length.

It was the only really practical piece of advice he had had that day.

*

Home. A small, very small staff 'flat', if you could call it that, for weeks, months, perhaps years.

He emptied his pockets of all the bits and pieces, lists and notes, and a soggy, limp programme, even some Very Important Forms someone Very Important had given him, telling him absolutely not to forget to give them out: the world depended on it. He had.

He put them down in a messy heap on his desk: he could sort that rubbish in the morning. He ought to check his emails, but then he put his phone down too.

He had to admit it: bit of a disaster.

How everything he wanted to make so serious and meaningful, everything that really mattered had degenerated quickly into farce. You could make a funny story, several funny stories out of it, if you looked at it one way; but just now it seemed all rather pathetic.

He wondered if it was going to work. Did he even fit in? When he was down he often imagined he did not fit in. And he'd always been told he was rather serious, intense, took things to heart. Perhaps that was all it was now.

The room smelt damp. He crossed to the window leaving the light off, pushing the old-fashioned casement up with some effort. A draft of cold air came in and he stuck his head out finding, at last, some sense of relief in the silent, still, waiting world outside.

Suddenly the remaining campus guide lights went out leaving just one or two windows winking in the dark. A bell, scarcely heard in all the day's clamour, chimed, tolling twelve. Although the wind and the rain had gone, high in the heavens the whole sky seemed to be turning with the stars above, startlingly clear in the country dark. He gazed out at the wide rim of the great, brimming world, stunned by the mystery of it all, lifted out of himself.

There was something more, after all.

His thoughts turned for some reason to Emma. He had texted her to thank her for coming, but she had not replied. He hoped she did not think him too much of a fool.

He was about to turn away, pull the window down when he saw a figure coming from the direction of the hill that dominated campus. Whoever it was, was picking their way without much of a light towards the school. Instinctively he pulled back, but he could not be seen. Was this a pupil up to no good – more to deal with?

Then suddenly, out of the corner of his eye, he saw the door of one of the buildings open and out came the unmistakeable burly shadow of Dr Hennock the Deputy Head. He joined the other figure, a tall man. They were nearer now and, as the moon sailed out from behind the scurrying clouds flooding light across the scene, Dom could see them clearly.

He seemed to recognise the man: one of the school governors, but he could not remember his name. Remembering names and faces was hard. Wincing, he remembered the girls in the club.

He peered out, careful not to be seen. Terry's remarks came back to him. How strange, to be about so late having a meeting at night with a governor. He fancied something strangely sinister going on: deep intrigue afoot; a wild scandal that would rock the school, unearthed of course by him and, all a piece with this crazy, crazy first day.

Eventually, Dr Hennock bowed his head, the other man nodded; then the governor made swiftly off, swallowed up in the dark. Dr Hennock looked around for all the world as if seeing if he were observed, and then he too vanished into shadows.

The moon disappeared but the silent pageant of clouds and stars and all the turning great world continued to pass mysteriously by high overhead.

Dom lay down on his bed, puzzling, the events of the day circling in his mind, all turning into questions.

The bell tolled once more.

One o'clock! Nearly time for it all to start over.

Pin your socks together: the only possible answer.

CHAPTER FIVE

STAFF MUSEUM, PLAYGROUND

Hillview had a good staff, one that allowed for the eccentric and idiosyncratic as well as those capable of doing the things deemed correct. A few were idle, one or two out of their depth. Some just took the money, had given up. But most saw teaching as a vocation, had a heart, a heart for the school, a heart to serve. They did their best. They cared.

The question marks were over the leadership: the Headmaster and his relatively new first deputy Dr Hennock; the first, because, although he possessed immense charm and high intelligence, he was devoted almost exclusively to himself; the second, because he was something different altogether. No one had quite worked him out, what he was up to, there for. He was certainly ambitious; but staff wondered what world he wished on them.

*

Dom found himself alone in the Staff Room early next morning. There had been no instruction, but he had gone there instinctively. It seemed the thing to do; and he wanted company.

Despite the rollercoaster of yesterday, sleep and youthful hope had done their work. He determined to start afresh. He had risen early, revised for the nth time his lesson plans. It helped that today promised to be warm and clean: a clear sky and soft September air, after all the messy rain, beckoned through the large windows. He smiled at a reflection of himself in one of them. He looked like a Sixth Former primped in his new blazer and tie. Then he saw his shirt hanging out, tucked it in quickly.

He finally had time to look around properly, no one to distract. Here he was in the secret place at the heart of it all where no child ever trod. So far, whenever he'd been in there, he had been a bit in awe. But now, he reflected, the room actually looked rather tired and drab, if not a mess.

There was clutter everywhere from years old exercise books through unbelievably ancient-looking computer monitors to a stack of full school photos from another age, faded through long exposure, piled up ready for some tip, perhaps. Ripped open boxes lay all over the place, waste paper overflowed every bin: last year's efforts, rubbish now. The more he looked, the more debris he saw: dusty old texts, ancient course books, battered sports equipment, a stack of stuff so extraordinary it must be from some recent play, all intermingled with bits and pieces of staff and pupil uniform, even underwear, strewn about with random confiscated items.

Perhaps there were even decaying remains of old staff stashed in cupboards. *Fossil*?

Dominating the room was a huge board plastered with hard copies of urgent notices that had been flooding his inbox for days. The board was broken down at the edges and poised precariously on ancient classroom chairs, recent pressing additions pinned over other key bits of information in a vast frozen tsunami of instruction.

What mountains of paper, what a jungle of intentions and beginnings Dom thought, overwhelmed for a moment. How could anyone ever sort, get on top, of it, find a way through:

and look where it all ended. He pondered the mystery of it all for a few seconds. Maybe it all belonged in a museum. Perhaps school itself did.

But where was everyone else? He hoped he hadn't missed some meeting or other: there had been so many in the last few days.

Then he heard voices approaching, raised ones. He caught snatches, fragments of some debate. Argument? Already?

'*Trust!* It's crucial! How can we expect kids to learn to trust when we pretend so much to them, and to ourselves… Everyone can't do everything! *Education…it's not a machine, some instrument-*'

'All that's irrelevant here… what worked in the past…we need change!'

One of the voices was his mentor and subject leader's, Mr Royal's. The other was that of the Deputy Head, whom Dom had seen behaving strangely the night before.

They paused outside.

'Change, change! *Whose change?* Everyone believes in change – especially if it benefits them, until it comes and things don't change … I do my best with the pupils I have… I can't make them what they're not. That's not what this – or any other school should be about. *You can't teach intelligence-* First, you cherish the individual, find out what they can do and be-'

'It depends what you mean by intelligence; and you *can* change the way pupils relate to something, how they work. Equality. We're here to give everyone a chance, not just ones it suits.I'm here to facilitate changes to ensure we all enjoy a bright future.'

'*Facilitate?*'

Mr Royal impaled the word as if it were an expletive. Dom had never heard him cross before, even imagined it. He felt uncomfortable, as if he should not be hearing it at all.

'What future? *Whose future?* How can we educate properly if all we do is teach to results? The *result* of life is death! They need to learn to fail sometimes, appreciate difficulties, see things are not bounded only by obvious outcomes, or they remain childish: children, and prisoners of someone else's questions and answers. Results?! There are more important things we need to get across. We're infantilising them! *Betraying* them! Where's the honesty in that?'

'I'm simply talking about your outcomes, your results,' replied Hennock evenly. 'No one's bothering with your views on education. I've told you before: keep to school policy, it's not personal.'

'*Everything's* personal!'

They were entering the room now, perhaps expecting it to be empty this early. Dom could not decide where to put himself. There was a brief moment's consciousness on all three sides. Dom remembered meeting some of his teachers from school once, a bit the worse for wear, in a pub during a school holiday. They had been dressed in jeans, ripped jeans, despite the fact they must have been so old. They had parted quickly after a few clumsy words, embarrassment on all sides.

Dr Hennock and Mr Royal stared at Dom. The Deputy Head shook his head and frowned. Dom had begun to wonder if he quite liked the man, although he was determined to respect him.

Then Mr Royal laughed suddenly, breaking the tension, anger dismissed.

'Well, tiddly *pom,* here's last night's star!' he declared.

Mr Royal said tiddly pom a lot; he was also prone to sarcasm.

'I hear you had a most amusing time on the trip,' he continued relishing the moment.

Dr Hennock continued to frown.

'Spare, Dominic? You missed the meeting,' began the Deputy Head, but before Dom could reply he was adding: 'I need to speak to you about the trip. There have been, I'm afraid, complaints – Mrs Tray – you'll learn about her – and some disturbing story in a lesson. Book in to see me later: make an appointment; don't just turn up, I'm busy this week.

'Charles, I think we need to conclude our conversation another time. Better register your form or you'll be as late as young Dominic,' said Hennock crossing to the door.

'Meeting? Am I late?' began Dom, wondering what he had missed. 'I'm sorry about the trip.'

'Save your excuses. And it's a good idea to keep checking the diary. It's all there in black and white when we bother to look,' said Dr Hennock, and, with a small smile, swept from the room nearly colliding with Alison Tenace, and two other ladies who bustled in.

Suddenly, the room was alive with personalities. Katie Trippett – Dom remembered her from a staff meeting, she had kept interrupting, seemed to have something to say on every subject that came up. She was soon initiating the other lady in the mysteries of the noticeboard. The other lady stood nodding, smiling, quivering almost, in eager agreement if not comprehension. The words were not just going into her mind, but her whole body it appeared, vibrating like some exotic orchestral instrument in tune to instruction.

'Morning,' breezed Alison to Dominic and Charles, and began filling some staff pigeon holes, already overflowing with paper, with yet more. She was another school leader. There were so many in the place. But Dom liked the look of Alison. She seemed approachable, a kind, sensible woman, one with a ready laugh, a human touch. She was in charge of the pupils, all things pastoral as it was known.

The title made Dom think of sheep.

But she looked tired, and today was weighed down by mountains of paper, files she was embracing, overflowing her grasp.

'Shirt!' Alison said to Dom, glancing over at him, with a giggle this time.

'Sorry,' he said, tucking himself in again.

His uniform did not quite fit yet.

Mr Royal who had lapsed momentarily into deep thought looked up at Dom and laughed.

'Ah! Senior Prefect summoned for a conversation with our illustrious Deputy Head. Good luck with that,' he said. 'Tiddly pom! Indeed, I wish you luck.'

'Don't start disillusioning new young staff,' cried Alison continuing to cram.

'Mrs Dot, know what you're doing now this morning?' Alison said next turning to Katie's companion when there was a momentary pause in Katie Trippett's knowledge flow.

'Or any morning,' muttered Charles.

So that was Mrs Dot. For some reason, mention of her name seemed to provoke amusement, or despair, from his colleagues. But before Dom could say anything, Katie was upon him, a flood of instructions cascading.

'Give these to your form. Read the first three out, apart from the underlined sections – this page, where is it- yes, there -and take down these important details -anyone going on my half-term trip. They must have their deposit form in today, form 15B. Understand? I must have a list of who hasn't by break. Their parents should have signed this form as well as this one:17A. I need a list of who is missing too. Don't forget, read those out as well. Make sure they listen. Anyone missing needs to see me urgently: Room 4 at 1.45 on Wednesday.'

Dom was lost. If they were missing, how could they be there? He looked at her puzzled. Hadn't she sent him this already? But there had been so much paper, and that rain yesterday. She was a small lady, but formidable; he bet she were a dragon with her classes. She was standing very close to Dom, talking away, peering around his face in a way that made him feel uncomfortable, as if she expected incapacity.

She broke off suddenly.

'I suppose it's no use me reminding you, Charles,' she said to Dom's boss.

'Ah, Katie! I did not see you down there. Good lord, no, of course not my dear. All this paper. How many trees have died for your trip? I shall certainly forget,' said Mr Royal.

'Now, Charles, let's start as we mean to go on this term.'

'Are you reorganising the school secretariat as well as bidding for a Deputy Headship this week?'

Katie, looking as if she did not know quite how to react, stopped talking for a second or two, but quickly resumed on Dom. When she finished, him little wiser, she peered around his face once more, seemingly pregnant with long gestated dissatisfactions, then moved swiftly, returning to further enlighten a still quivering Mrs Dot.

'Have you noticed,' Mr Royal observed, seeming to address only Dom but quite clearly audible across the room, 'how some people, especially teachers, love the sound of their own voices? Bossiness. It becomes a habit so very quickly, especially amongst those in the iron grip of misplaced self-confidence. *Caveat Magister!*'

Dom was not sure what Mr Royal was on about. When he wasn't being ironic, he seemed given to deep pronouncements. You weren't always certain which was which.

He thought it best simply to smile.

Just then, however, there was a terrific crash and a squeal from Mrs Dot. The large noticeboard had finally met its fate, tumbling to the ground, with a myriad consequential papers fluttering in all directions.

There was a scrum of advice, none of which Mrs Dot seemed able to understand. Soon the ladies were all down on their knees all talking at once, each taking command, trying simultaneously to pin notices back on the board, disputing which should have priority, where they went, if they should put the whole thing back, leave it to Terry to secure, Katie giving it large about health and safety implications.

'Can I help?' said Dom, feeling he wanted to laugh, but shouldn't.

No one heard.

At that moment, Mr Jolson, dressed as usual in a tracksuit, the housemaster in charge of the school boarders, floated in looking for something.

'Missed our meeting, Dom!' he said, then seeing the chaos on the floor, turned and winked salaciously at Mr Royal.

'Staff First XI in action already I see. Panto time?' he quipped and was gone.

'First blood of the term to Mrs Dot as usual,' muttered Mr Royal laughing, and then addressed Dom, discreet now, shaking his head. 'Kindest of hearts, best of intentions, but you would not know what harm that can do.'

Dom wondered what he meant.

'But where did I put my keys? Never can find what I'm looking for.'

Mr Royal disappeared off into one of many large store cupboards around the room.

Dom checked his phone. Yes, there had been a meeting that morning, and he'd missed it; damn, but there were so many. And no, he wasn't late, so why had he been warned?

Alison had broken from the action on the floor.

'Those two!' she said, nodding towards Katie and Charles. 'Started early this year. I sometimes wonder if we ever escape the playground,'' she continued, looking at him earnestly for a moment.

A loud expletive came from the depths of the cupboard into which Mr Royal had departed.

'Not in front of the children, Charles!' Alison said more loudly, shaking her head but smiling.

She dropped her voice again.

'Don't end up like him, or her.' She glanced from the cupboard to the phone where Katie was now clearly locked in mortal battle with Terry whom she had summoned as if to some global catastrophe, not a bust noticeboard.

Alison stared hard at Dom.

'How's it going? You know, you remind me of Charles when he was younger,' she said, but without giving an explanation for this somehow disturbing remark. 'Remember: don't take any nonsense. From anyone!' and then she was gone with one last glance back, a roll of her eyes in the direction of Mrs Dot and Katie, the room in general.

How could he explain, even if anyone had time to listen, what it was like to be new here, to everything, everyone?

But Mrs Dot was approaching. Katie had told her to leave well alone before she made things worse.

She tripped over her own feet, or was it some of the rubbish left behind? Then she too moved in very close.

'Petra Dot,' she began. 'I'm cut. Nothing serious. Rog says I'd survive a nuclear war. You're Mr Drama this term aren't you. I'm costume. *Mistress of the Wardrobe* they call me- the polite ones- but our youngsters are lovely. Don't let anyone tell you otherwise. They didn't try to poison me last term in Food Club. Just fun and games! Anyone can do anything if they put their mind to it, that's my motto! Don't let them work you too hard!'

She stood back a moment, treading on something that broke instantly. 'People change when they've been here a bit. Don't change! You look like a Sixth Former! But I don't always see very well with or without specs. Rog says I need Laser Surgery. Like Jean.'

Suddenly, she shot to the door.

'My glasses,' she explained in a whirl, 'O bless you, you angel! You've helped me remember where I've left them. Welfare. Forget the silly paperwork, all this organisation, dear heart. I ignore it! Looking after others! That's all we need to do! I love it here-love being busy. Now I'm off. But any way I can help, just ask! Still registering for Vicky! Childcare's so expensive. Do you have children? They all gave me someone else's name yesterday! Dr Hennock did not find it funny, but so creative of them!'

She was moving again, gesturing a kissing action in Dom's direction, barging into the edge of the door, apologising to someone who wasn't there that she couldn't be with them later (she was helping with something else).

She left, still talking. Dom was not quite sure to whom. She accidentally slammed the door and a bit of plaster from the roof came down, showering the carpet with dust. Dom felt strangely exhausted when she had gone.

Katie was continuing on the phone deeper into a shrill and insistent argument with a reluctant Terry. Mr Royal appeared from the cupboard, noted the fallen plaster, looked over at Katie, pulled a wry face.

'Safe to come out? Dotty gone? Three people like that -I could destroy the world. Never be stationary when she is nearby. You'll learn!'

Katie finished noisily with Terry, addressed the room.

'Can you believe it? He's refusing – says he's not allowed in the Staff Room. Teachers' messes should be put right by teachers, not overworked support staff. What sort of attitude is that; and at that start of term? I'm going to tell Darren. I wish Petra'd just leave things alone. Everything she touches breaks.'

She passed Dom.

'Forms! My forms! Don't forget, my forms! There's a brush and shovel over there. You could clear that up if you're at a loose end,' she cried.

Then she was gone too.

'Teaching today!' began Mr Royal shaking his head at all the world it seemed. 'Demented staff, distracted pupils, bureaucracy, endless scrutiny and surveillance, and we still have chaos! You know the problem, young Dom: everybody talks too much instead of getting on with things! Everything to be justified a thousand times to absolutely everyone instead of just using common sense. When did the world lose its sense of reason?'

He looked round the room again.

'A mess, isn't it?' he added. 'Everything's a mess today. But I suppose it always has been!' He sighed deeply. 'We get through! At least we do here, until recently. I begin to wonder now. Don't get stuck here, not for long anyway, like me.'

Charles sighed again, brushing dust off his tie, wiping his hands. Then he turned, stared out into the warm sunshine where he could see all the hurry of pupils still arriving.

'Here comes the latest crop. Day One! The Survivors!' he shook his head. 'Now have you? I *am* sorry I missed your trip, I could have done with a laugh. I had the most awful migraine. I always get these terrific headaches at the start of term. Getting too old for it all. Doctor Mallin says it's stress.

Stress or a virus. *Doctors!* Doctors always say that. But they don't know much more than you or I half the time. *Nobody knows anything really.* Now, who said that?'

Mr Royal stared at Dom, then was chuckling once more.

'Do let me know of any further adventures, won't you? D'you know, I've forgotten what I was looking for when I came in. However. You and I must now to the great unwashed. *Tiddlypom!*'

And he was off, humming to himself, leaving Dom, who had a free first lesson once he had registered his form, quite alone again.

He stared out at the children gathering outside, ready to start their day too, but before he could indulge some earnest thoughts about all he'd seen, there came a sudden devastating knock on the Staff Room entrance, as if an explosion had gone off in the corridor outside. The door, reverberating, swung wide as if by magic.

Without invitation, three diminutive children walked boldly in.

'Are you teacher?' shouted a little boy with an angelic face, genuinely puzzled, looking apologetic. 'This Year Eleven, he said if you need teacher, go to Staff Room, knock very loudly or they won't hear – they're deaf – walk straight in.'

It was an old one. Dom could not help smiling.

'I'm not quite sure,' he began, grinning, tempted to shout back, but before he could get any further a voice really was booming up the corridor.

'How dare you! How DARE you! No child must ever, and I repeat *ever* cross this threshold.'

Mr Walker was upon them, and before explanations could be made, or anyone found out what the children might actually need, he was admonishing them for their outrageous and brazen behaviour with all the fervour and knowledge of his thirty years at the chalkface.

He drove them manically from the room.

Dom could ponder then, not least Alison's comments about people never leaving the playground.

But this was just a beginning, he reminded himself. Everyone and everything would soon settle, he was sure, into something much more grown up, serious. Yes, he was confident of that.

CHAPTER SIX

YOUNGSTERS TODAY?

The children now love luxury; they have bad manners, contempt for authority; they show disrespect for elders and love chatter in place of exercise. Children are now tyrants, not servants of their households. They no longer rise when elders enter the room. They contradict their parents, chatter before company, gobble up dainties at the table, cross their legs and tyrannize their teachers…

Mr Walker, perhaps others, would have agreed with Socrates – if Socrates ever said it.

Dom would not.

He had resolved never to let whatever professional experience he had begun to accrue blunt idealism. Earnest convictions, deeply held if not always precisely formulated, were what you stood by, even if you weren't sure where they came from, or why. If there were problems, it was your fault – you set things right: that was teaching. When doubts nudged, littleness intruded or distracted, you tried harder, took it on the chin, moved on. You held faith.

So something told him. To his credit, he believed it.

*

For some reason, Dom was being shown around the school by a pupil first thing that day. He really wanted to be back in the classroom. He had something to prove, especially after yesterday. He'd had a tour on interview, and then another when he first moved in. Quite a lot of things seemed to happen at the school for no particularly good reason except some precedent established so long ago that people had forgotten why. But no doubt it all had deep purpose and meaning.

To his surprise his tour guide, who turned up late, very late, was James, the James of yesterday. He looked different, but swaggered over, a proudly and newly appointed prefect it turned out, but one bearing a carton of coffee and a half eaten burger he had acquired on his way.

'Sorry, Sir!' said James, his mouth full, 'we were late in – your trip – didn't have time for breakfast.'

He looked sheepish when he also admitted he had forgotten. He'd been talking to his ex and then his latest, and well, you know, time, Sir. He finished his meal explaining.

Dom wondered what precise qualifications he had for the role, but it wasn't yet his place to question. He seemed an open lad, whatever else, proud of his school. James had a lot to say for himself that morning as they set off. Dom hoped the broad grin that kept appearing on his face was not solely there as a result of yesterday.

The boy was sporting an attempt at designer stubble and kept sweeping back his hair from his forehead as if posing. If Dom had been more at ease he might have teased, but he was still working out what he might and might not say to pupils, especially older ones. And, yes, he wanted to be liked, popular, for all his sense of duty.

'It's an awesome setting, Sir, for a school, this hollow in the hills with the Cloud making the background,' James began, officially. 'Our own stretch of river, well stream really. It's a bit of an exaggeration to say it's a river. Actually it's hardly a stream. Literally, one of the best locations for a school in the whole country.'

Dom could agree on that this bright morning. Landscape stirred, took him somewhere else.

'The place comes into its own in the summer, Sir. Hundred per cent – amazing then: like a holiday camp. We threw the Head Boy and Girl in the river there last June. Such a laugh, Sir!' he added.

'Weren't you all busy with exams?' said Dom wanting to laugh, wondering if he should;– and what really went on at the school.

James looked at him curiously.

'This way, Sir,' James said, sweeping his hair back again as he caught sight of himself in a window. Had he done something to his hair – was that why he looked different? Should Dom say anything?

'There's our technology hub – don't normally say this, but it's crap! They spent a fortune on it a few years ago so we could get connection anywhere on campus, use devices for everything. All out of date now. Even my dad says so.'

Dom looked at the rather shabby buildings as they passed. A boy was lingering outside, head down, as if he had been sent out.

'All right?' Dom smiled, feeling rather sorry for him: just starting, in the sunshine of a rural idyll. Trouble in paradise, that morning.

The boy looked sheepish.

'Got sent out, Sir. I changed all the computer screens to Mandarin. It was a joke – but they couldn't get it back and went mad at me.'

Dom wanted to laugh again, even if it was all wrong.

'What's your name?'

'Rymer, Sir. Tom Rymer.'

'A friend of mine did something like that at school: made all the lights turn off too.'

The boy smiled, but then looked sad again, his head down.

They walked on.

'Don't give him ideas, Sir! He's already been in trouble – his first day. He came from some crap place. Dr Hennock says we need to watch him. Some of these youngsters are so cocky. And what they get up to online, Sir!' said James with the tone of a veteran.

'Do you like it here?' Dom asked, genuinely curious about his guide.

'Apart from lessons, Sir, it's awesome, Sir – well, most of the time anyway, Sir, if you have to go to school.'

Apart from lessons. And James kept calling him Sir. He still did not feel like a Sir –but he wanted to: be a man of authority, a sage on all things, like Mr Royal.

But James was continuing.

'The Headmaster, Mr Waseley's easy. He's cool, Sir. He backed me for prefect when some of the old teachers wouldn't. I always go and see him if I have an issue; tell him what's going on in his school, set him straight. He listens to us, Sir. He knows every pupil's name. Not always those of staff. But the school, Sir, it's changing since the Doc, I mean Dr Hennock arrived: he's tightening things up, changing stuff. Some don't like that. Some of the old staff like Pig, Sir, who got sacked last year. Did you meet Pig, Sir? Such a laugh but a real psycho: he should have been locked up.'

Dom shook his head, remembering the carving on the desk. *Sacked? Psycho?*

'Change doesn't bother me. We're in our final year. You grow out of it all, but, I've had a great time. Social life's massive in the Sixth Form. Work's a drag. Sport's massive too here.– What's your sport, Sir?' But without waiting for an answer he continued. 'Mine's hockey. Cricket's a laugh with Jolson. He's so laid back. Wicked sense of humour. In the Sixth Form they mostly leave you alone, even if you don't work. I didn't do anything last year, just had a laugh. We're young, Sir! All this pressure! It's so stressful now – your final year – exams – your whole future. What's life for? All this study – it's not real life. It's not fair. I don't think people understand what it's like these days. It was all easier back in the day, when you were young, Sir!'

Dom could not imagine himself at that age being quite so direct with some relatively unknown grown up. But then he'd always been easily overawed at how confident, forward, other people appeared.

'What do you want to do with your life: when you grow up?' asked Dom, feeling this might recall them both to the seriousness of education – important matters, life's big purposes.

James grinned.

'What do you?' he parried. 'Mr Royal tells us: follow our dreams, but the Doc- sorry – Doc Hennock- says we should say something like brain surgeon, or a doctor or lawyer – if parents ask; but that's all fake. I *hate* fake stuff, Sir. I've actually no idea, no idea at all, except I want to have fun – make shed loads – and be famous. I might go and work for my Dad. My parents – all of them – are always hassled about work, money. I don't want that. And we'll all have to work till we're eighty. And with climate change and stuff, who knows about any future. Our generation have it hard, Sir. Our future's been stolen.'

Dom felt he could sympathise with some of that, but would not accept what James said. And he had views, perhaps old fashioned ones he sometimes admitted to himself: doing the right thing, working hard; value for value. Maybe this was not quite the moment to go into all that though: but something he must sort out with the pupils, when he got fully into his stride.

'Did *you* know what you wanted when you were young, Sir? I s'pose I'll take a Gap Year. Mr Walker says they're a waste of time: for thickies with no aim in life, or too much money. More dodging hard work or responsibility. He thinks we're all spoilt. Snowflakes. I don't think he was ever young, Sir! Did you hear about that guy who was only in his early twenties who's retired already, Sir? Mr Royal says we spend too much time doing, not enough being. Dad just says I'm lazy and what's he sending me to school for. He says people get money too easily these days. Parents are a pain, Sir, hundred per cent! I couldn't hack being a teacher – all the abuse. What made you teach, Sir?'

Fair question. Dom thought for a few moments. If he were honest, he'd never known quite what he wanted to do when he was at school apart from loving English, reading, perhaps because it seemed to answer some need for explanation, understanding in a confusing world. And it set you free from the trap of yourself. He'd had the luck to have been taught by a great teacher, loved his English lessons, never forgotten them. He wanted to pass that on.

His dreams had just about survived teaching practice in two tough schools. He remembered his father coming to pick him up one weekend when training; he had got in such a state, exhausted, trying to get them to understand, believe in what he thought they should. Managing the kids in one of the schools had been almost impossible, even for the experienced teachers. Everybody had been stressed all the time, or ill.

His dad had said, you live and learn.

'I suppose, and it sounds a bit pretentious, perhaps, I want to change things – try to show people there's something more, something better. That's why I am a teacher.'

'Good luck here!' laughed James. 'My Mum used to teach. She says you can't change people. She gave up,' he finished definitively.

They were almost out in open country now, the sunshine broadening with the day as they left the school behind. They did a circuit round the extensive games fields. Pupils were so lucky to have such space thought Dom. Hillview should be a little academic paradise in its lovely situation, an educational haven for the higher and better things in life. Just then, it was hard to imagine any meanness from the outside need ever encroach into such a world, if you got things sorted properly.

'We call this bit the Stray, Sir. It runs to the foot of the Cloud. It's out of bounds, but no one bothers; you can walk all the way round or over it to Wellsway, as long as you don't get caught.

'I was one of the few boarders still here when I was younger, that's probably why they made me a prefect: sticking the course. It's okay if you fit in, especially when you're young. My parents thought it might make me work but then they separated. You can be with your mates all the time. But when you grow older... It's so far from anywhere here – in the middle of nowhere, and in the winter... I hate the country, Sir. You get stir crazy. And there are too many rules in this school, especially if it's your home. No one wants other people's rules. I bet you get rules imposed on you: old staff always bangin' on.'

Here was a temptation to indiscretion. But as for the practical deprivations of professional employment so far, Dom hadn't thought about that much yet apart from some intuitive sense that he would lose some autonomy as an employee, just as he was gaining it as an adult.

'This one time, Sir, we had this massive midnight feast up there, Sir, when I was still a boarder with guys from another school. The teachers went bananas when they found out.

'The Cloud's steepest side faces the school, but the other side slopes down to Wellsway –its suburbs. The school owns some of it. The teachers keep saying some of the land's going to be sold for development – better facilities, but they've been saying that forever. To be honest, the school needs modernising, Sir. It's like our country: bit of a museum. Sir, I went to Dubai last summer with my stepdad. It was amazing. Makes our country look a dump.'

They were approaching the foot of the Cloud itself. Dom stared at the hill, its curious shape. He began imagining: relics of ancient kings, buried treasure. How could anyone dream of selling it for development. And as for Dubai, although he'd never been there himself.

'There's a story they dug up some antefacts once on the Cloud. There's nothing there, Sir. I can't get excited about old, dead stuff. It's not real. Like history. I don't get it. All the crap about the past. Our past's an embarrassment, Sir: colonialism and stuff, taking things from other countries. No one believes in England like that anymore. But I enjoyed English, apart from most of the literature. Sorry, Sir! But only because of Mr Royal. He's cool. He makes boring things interesting. He's a great teacher. So much of what we get taught isn't relevant to us any more, Sir; particularly old stuff. Half the teachers here don't get the real world. Some of the really old ones are almost like pre-digital, Sir; hundred per cent, Sir!'

Dom rather liked his new word antefact. It said something. But funny how you always knew everything when you were young. He'd been like that; but he was in his early twenties now so well on his way to complete understanding. Should he argue openly with what James was saying? He didn't agree with much of it. But people often didn't listen, except to what they wanted to hear. A lot of the time, people said all sorts, but they mostly listened only to themselves. Unlike teachers, of course.

James had turned his back on that entrancing landscape, checking his phone, preparing to return.

'You married, Sir?'

'No,' said Dom, just about coming back to the present. 'I think they want someone who'll work 24/7. I bet there's nowhere to put a married couple!'

He laughed. James looked incredulous.

'Mr Jolson's got an awesome flat for his family. You should ask Miss Oakley out, Sir. She's fit,' James nodded wisely.

'I'll bear that in mind,' grinned Dom.

They were returning across the games fields now: pupils and teachers appearing on the pastoral scene.

Sport. Now, that was serious stuff.

Mike Casle and Paul Workman, two of the other newbies alongside Emma and himself, were out coaching some of the younger boys. They came over.

'Sod this for a laugh. *Teaching!* They've given me ones who can barely move and who lack any hand-eye coordination whatsoever,' Paul began, half joking, half in exasperation, ignoring James. 'I can't do *anything* with some of them. How do you manage to get out of it; doing a play?'

'Stop whingeing. It'll keep you fit – put some weight on you,' said Mike to Paul, much to James's amusement.

Paul, who was tall and very thin, looked hurt.

'I think you'll find...' Paul began on a long list of changes and improvements he was going to make to the provision and organisation of sport, and numerous other aspects of the school. Dom had heard much of this before. Paul had views too.

'How come you've got the grand tour?' interrupted Mike looking at Dom. Then he stared at James. 'What the hell have you done with your hair?' but before James could react he returned to Dom.

'Heard about yesterday! Been sacked yet? And now you have a freebie when we're here slogging our guts out?'

Mike looked at James again, appraising his physique.

'You going to play for the seconds?'

James looked awkward.

'Not sure, Sir. I need to focus on my work.'

Mike laughed loudly.

'Work? *You!* Come on, get involved or you'll turn out like Mr Workman – or doing crap drama like Mr Greaves! What is there in life but sport?'

Paul rolled his eyes at Dom, but before he could find something withering to say back, a boy ran up crying, complaining that another had deliberately kicked a ball at his head.

'Aah,' said Mike sarcastically, whilst Paul tut-tutted, but then some of the others started fighting too and Mike and Paul had to go and sort things out.

'Sports department thinks it runs the school, Sir!' said James as they moved on. 'Look there's a real fight going on!'

There was, his colleagues struggling to gain control.

'That kid's always complaining. One day someone's going to beat the crap out of him.'

Dom was wondering why they wanted to fight on such a beautiful day. Then he was remembering one of his more eccentric mentors on teaching practice. He had gone on and on about how destructive and egotistical sport and its culture could be. It was divisive, trapped children in a demeaning cycle of aggression and competition. Teams were just packs by another name. If your face did not fit, you were no good, discarded. Education!

Dom wondered vaguely if there was a Whole School Policy for people who didn't fit into whatever it was someone else was trying to bash them into. He looked back at the sports field where the fight was subsiding, puzzling. Hillview was not grim like his teaching practice placements, but, well, some things didn't seem quite right. He'd noticed that far more on teaching practice, but put it down to the schools, and himself. Now, here again, was a rather confusing gap between how things ought to be and what actually went on. Was school being taken seriously enough? How was he to fix all this? Would it take long: even a year or two – before he got all sorted?

'Do you ever find that some things at school turn out a bit trivial, silly, kind of…little, mean sometimes in the end?' Dom said suddenly, struggling for words.

James looked puzzled then.

'Mean? People always go at each other, Sir, wherever they are, put each other down. You're older than me, you know that. Don't know about school. Lots of it's not for me, not for lots of us. But when you're here you get used to it all, whether it makes sense or not. Stuff happens. It's people in groups, Sir. We're all tribal at heart – we depend on binary thinking Mr Royal says: we all need friends, enemies, likes and dislikes. Something to do with identity, but I'm not into all that. It does my head in. Are you into deep stuff too, Sir? You'll get on with Mr Royal,' James concluded.

Dom wondered if kids would ever remember things he said, quote him. But he wasn't sure James had got his point, or indeed quite what his own point was.

Then he remembered how Mr Walker had been keen to tell him about some new teacher who had come to Hillview. He had been radical, fresh from college, keen to change the place, brimming with ideas. He had stuck it a few days, then packed and left, taking everything but his computer with him. Gone with no trace of his ever being here, Mr Walker had concluded, with an odd smile at Dom.

Thinking that only made Dom more determined, however. You couldn't ridicule the end of teaching any more than you could great books. It *did* matter that you tried to make sense of things, why things happened, understand your own story, for instance. Understanding, real achievement, should not be a privilege for the few whilst the rest just got by because no one offered them better, or good things got blown aside by little practical upsets. In fact understanding, its achievement, was the highest possible-.

'What you two dreamers doin' driftin' about? A mornin' stroll? Ain't you got work to do after six weeks' 'oliday?'

Terry.

'James is giving me a tour,' said Dom, glad he had remembered to return the key.

'Oh I say: 'ow posh! A *tour*? Sounds about right in this holiday camp! Don' you know where you are yet?' laughed Terry. 'You should be in my department. You'd see what really goes on. We does the heavy liftin' in this place, clearin' up after teachers who think they're above shiftin' a shovel, kids as daft as a brush. Never met so many thick people! That Trippett woman this mornin'… on and on! Mouth like an industrial vacuum cleaner! Complainin' to the boss! One day I'll walk then you lot'll find out what real work looks like! Got your keys, today?' he laughed, and took aim at James.

'Showin' 'im roun', eh? The blind leadin' the blind! Eh, it's your last year on the razzle here, isn't it? Y'll have to do some work when you leave! School won't save you then! Y' look older than him, you know – specially with that rinse!'

Terry chuckled with satisfaction. Dom made the mistake of trying to smile.

'What you come to a place like this for? Teachin' the likes of him? Them as can does, them as cannot- ', but before Terry could develop a favourite theme his phone went off.

'Can' they *f-in* leave me alone, today,' he muttered, but as it was Dr Hennock no less, he was forced to concentrate on the call, even attempt civility.

Dom and James turned away relieved, and started back to the main part of the school.

'He's always moaning. My Royal calls him Lenin, Sir! Says he's a vestige of a feudal age. I used to find him scary when I was younger. He's a laugh really.'

But Terry himself had not finished with them. He rushed past, coughing and blowing.

'Got some Chinese kids comin' have we? Aren't there enough twats in the place without importin' more? A delectation or something on a tour; nother bloody tour. Like a bloody cruise ship this place. What're they after? S'pose some dickhead'll want all the buildings steam cleaned again so as to big the place up. More work! Eh, the Doc says to remind you he needs to see you. Been a naughty boy, like 'im? Bein' sacked? Come and work for me – that'll teach you more'n you'll learn introspectatin'. I'm two staff down already: Ted's off for the term now, and Joan's hip's gone again an' it's only day two of bein' paid bloody peanuts for goin' bloody nowhere.'

He hurried off railing against the world.

'Chinese?' said Dom.

'We've got to show some round sometime soon. Doc Hennock has some plan to bring overseas pupils here. But you'll know all about that?' fished James.

Dom nodded not actually having a clue what he was talking about.

'That's pretty much everything, Sir. This is the main part of the school as you know. Part of the house is Elizabethan. The oldest bits are where you are and the boarders live. It looks grand from outside but it's freezing in winter. It needs rebuilding. Government cuts, Sir. Dad says all the money they've put in education hasn't made much difference with people like me so they're not putting any more in! Have you heard about the ghost? Some of the boarders say they see and hear stuff at night. Taps turned on. Lights. Locked doors suddenly open in some of the old rooms that were closed up after the last inspection. Bet they didn't tell you your wing was haunted when you started, Sir!'

It was a strange, rather rundown old place in parts Dom reflected. His rooms were certainly Spartan: stark wooden floor, clanking radiator pipes, high ceilings and an old metal-framed bed that reminded him of pictures of ancient hospitals; but the views across the grounds to the Cloud made up. There was no commute, board and lodging were provided, if he ate with the children that was, boosting what passed as a salary. Even his clothes were laundered for him, *provided he pinned his socks together* of course. A life of divine luxury and privilege Terry would no doubt assert.

'All sorts of stuff, Sir, they don't tell you at first!' James teased and then carried on in a sudden burst of confidentiality as if Mr Greaves had passed some security test. 'I have to go, Sir. I've got Old Tid – Mr Royal – now. We do English in the Sixth Form for some reason – and Maths: one of Dr H's ideas until he realised what some of the teachers were like when there were no exams to control us. I thought I'd got out of it. I mean, trips are fun, but I *hate* reading, except Mr Royal brings it alive – especially when he's had a bit to drink, Sir! You can smell it on him after lunch. We think he drinks like a fish some days.Have you met the Headmaster's wife, Sir? She's nuts. She's on all sorts of organic stuff for her mental wellbeing. She says she's being watched by the CIA – everyone is according to her. We think she used to be a crackhead. Mr Royal hates the Doc. He gives him things to teach he hates – makes him do pastoral stuff, which no one listens to. That sort of thing is such a waste of time, Sir.

Everyone's done all the things they warn us against by the Sixth Form anyway, apart from dying, and no one needs advice on that. Once you're dead that's it. They treat us like kids at times. We could teach some of them a lot. Sometimes I think life and education are upside down, the wrong way round. It gets in the way, Sir!

'And the problem with the school being quite small – everyone knows everyone else's business before it's happened. If you do anything, it's straight on social media anyway. Be careful, Sir! So much is made up, especially living on site! It's a pain. That and the fact that most of the stuff we get told here probably won't count outside. Sorry, Sir, but I really do have to go now. I've this essay to finish, well start really: Mr Royal says essays are never finished. That's certainly true of mine.'

With that he was off, leaving Dom amused, confused, disturbed.

Mr Royal drinking? The Headmaster's wife...

And James himself, his opinions, character, his school? For a moment, Dom's confidence wobbled. Was the place some kind of jungle behind a pretty facade, belittled in purpose, lacking in meaningful direction, irrelevant in practice to all the important, big things in life?

But here he was again perhaps taking things a bit seriously when it was all only new and strange, and he a shade young still.

*

Back in the Staff Room, a free Mr Walker and Mr Royal were waiting.

'*That* boy? *James? Taking you on a tour.* He should never have been made a prefect. Dreadful! Youngsters these days: him in particular! No respect for authority: idle, self-centred.'

'Oh, leave him alone, Ian! Just because he hated your lessons. James is all right. He pushes back against it all, that's all. He's young. Why should he work hard when he can't see the benefit in what he does. He doesn't want to go on with education, but get a job, get on with life. Give him his space,' countered Mr Royal.

'You didn't have to teach him all those years when he was younger. He's got charm I'll give you that, charms the birds out of the trees. I'm sure he'll end up earning far more than you and I, but he does nothing he doesn't want to, like most of them. He wants a good time; he's not interested in anything serious or concentrating on doing anything properly, buried on line... You'll find youngsters' sense of entitlement or victimhood is all their care these days! And this new Puritanism – over things like racism, sexism, the climate... as long of course as it does not affect what they want to do, the way they go on!'

Mr Walker waxed loud and long until he was finally called away to start his own lessons.

'He was all right. Nice lad,' Dom began to Mr Royal, stung into defending James now. Walker's blanket denigrations of youngsters, hurt. James was not bad, just, well needed something better to believe in.

But what would Charles have said if he knew all he'd been told?

Mr Royal shook his head.

'O he's idle certainly, but he's no fool. No more than the rest of us, less than some probably. The trouble with Ian: he's jealous – jealous of youth. It's so easy to get like that. I often think pupils know more and understand better than we do.'

He looked thoughtfully at Dom who was looking solemn.

'Don't take it all too seriously. James says what he thinks but that doesn't mean it's true, or he believes all he comes out with. Things are never quite what they seem. And don't be influenced by two bitter old men, young Dominic. Don't expect too much either, from anyone, young or old – or yourself, or you'll get pulled down by it all! Now, I must to the chalk face. See what I can stir in the tiddly poms today,' and he was gone, and Dom needed to be gone too.

As he walked to his lesson, Dom must be thinking over all he had heard. He sighed, pulled a face. He knew he had always been too quick to take others' words seriously, believe. It was easy to forget words were fickle things, talk a moment's exaggeration, quickly made up, rapidly forgotten, except by over earnest literature students of course.

The classroom in front of him now, however, was filling up – noisily, messily, so many voices, needs, so many different people, identities as the day decided. Soon solemn, deep thoughts were displaced by the constant new but hopeful beginning every lesson offered. Then every minute was crammed until the end of the day teaching; no time indeed to speculate about what lay ahead or behind, all the whys and wherefores of character and context, or the wide seas of understanding and mystery, just rooms full of expectant pupils, beaks wide open, clamouring.

Young faces all a question.

'Trick or treat, Sir?' they seemed to say.

CHAPTER SEVEN

FRIDAY

Dom was sitting in the dining area at the end of his first week. Many pupils, some of the staff were eating there: most, a traditional Friday lunch of fish and chips, salads or vegan fare for a few, one or two with limp, plastic-looking sandwiches. He was alone on a table with Mike and Paul and Emma; they sat together, a little island sharing a common language of inception, and sometimes incredulity, at what was about them. Other staff largely avoided them for now. They must find out for themselves.

Emma kicked off. Dom was learning she did not pull her punches,

'*This place!* The kids are all right but, the way it's run! I wonder if they've ever thought of knocking it down, sacking the leadership, half the staff, starting over! Alison's the only sensible one at the top. The rest!' she declared.

'The Head seems a nice guy, kind,' said Mike.

'A waste of space: he's a clown: no grasp of detail, no real direction, no substance. And he flirts with you if you're female. It's gross! A good example of why leadership in this country is so bad. Nice and kind are the two most dangerous words in the language: English for avoiding confronting anything, banging heads together, getting stuff done. And his wife!'

'Second wife! He must have hidden depths,' said Mike, laughing, winking meaningfully at Paul and Dom.

'He makes it up as he goes along- a showman, never serious- when he's here. He's been away since the first day back! How can a Head be absent at the start of term? This place needs a shake. It's so, so idiosyncratic! '

'Anyone translate?' Mike teased.

'Systems and procedures evolving like some exotic deep sea creature that has learnt to live under constant pressure without light and hope of ever surfacing!' pursued Emma trenchantly, rather enjoying herself, Dom thought, not sure whether to laugh or get worked up by what she was on about. 'A business like it would be closed in five minutes in the real world!' she concluded.

'I think you'll find Hennock's serious. He knows what's going on; he's the power behind the throne. He tells the Head what to do now, and he does it. Now, if I were in charge...' began Paul.

'You mean, *'Jump!'*, *'How high?'* Emma could not resist, interrupting.

They were getting used to Paul by now, those views.

'The kids respect him – unlike some colleagues, I've heard,' continued Paul.

Dom wondered. Everyone seemed to have decided opinions already. They seemed to speak with such authority. Should they not be showing more respect as newbies; but the conversation swept on.

'Your subject leader Royal is weird: Old Tiddly the pupils call him. He and Walker, their views, on everything and anything! Walker bores for England. The kids say Royal's a complete alcoholic,' added Mike casually.

'I'm not surprised, stuck here since the Middle Ages!' came Emma.

'Don't say that – you shouldn't believe what they say,' said Dom shaking his head, feeling they had gone far enough, whatever the truth.

'What's he know, incarcerated here most of his life? He's a brain on legs, I'll give you that, thinks his own thoughts, and good for Hillview: some grit in the oyster. But he runs our department like a little Switzerland, teaches English as if it is somehow separate from everything else, above the rest of the school, the rest of the world! Talk about iconoclastic!' Emma rejoined.

'But that's right!' began Dom. No one was listening to him.

'I can see why you're an English teacher,' replied Mike to Emma, not trying to understand anymore, 'Can you imagine him or Walker in a really rough school?'

'It's an open secret he and Katie don't get on. By the way, be careful what you say in front of *her*,' commented Paul as if sharing some deep confidence. 'Anything important goes straight to Hennock. She's the worst gossip on the staff.'

'Apart from you,' laughed Emma.

'The sort who eats male colleagues for breakfast if they cross her. So watch your step, Paul!' concluded Mike, then looked keenly at Emma. 'I'm going to see if I can wangle a second helping. Anyone else want more, except Paul, he's on a diet.'

Emma and Mike laughed. Paul did not.

Whilst Mike was charming one of the dinner ladies and filling his plate, Paul, who looked hurt again, took aim at Emma.

'Talking of staff gossip, apparently Waseley is winding down to retirement. And Royal told one of my form that the school was facing financial difficulties—falling rolls lower down, cuts. We could be in for an interesting time.'

'No one said any of that on interview. It's outrageous. I shall walk... And they need some decent female teachers here,' cried Emma.

'Walker says a lot of the female teachers here are useless, in it for the wrong reasons,' returned Paul.

Emma rose like a fish to the bait.

'Walker should be in a museum. How can you repeat such nonsense, and how would he know anyway?'

'If I were in charge-', Paul began.

'She's fit – the lady serving pudding,' said Mike returning. He smiled specially at Emma then settled himself comfortably to his carbs.

'Someone take him away,' said Emma half amused, half angry.

There began a lively argument from Emma, stoked by Paul, about how female employees were always belittled in one way or another. This school was a typical and terrible example of it all – old-fashioned, patriarchal: worse than the chauvinism of marketing or business men she had come across in the city. The conversation enlarged, swept on to all their colleagues' characteristics.

Dom had to admit the arguments, the banter built a sense of companionship. It was a release to make fun of what was still unfamiliar, making it less daunting. But something in him wanted to draw away from it. It was so easy to label everyone, criticise, belittle. It was not how he wanted things to be.

He let the others talk on, listening with part of his attention whilst the rest expanded to take in the sounds and smells and feelings that recalled his first day: the clatter of trays and scrape of chairs and tables; the lively chatter of pupils unbound from the striving of the classroom; the occasional cheer as someone dropped something; the smell of sauce and custard and steam; the little puddles by the water fountains, and the warm plastic glasses with their slightly soapy liquid. All mingled with the smells of young humanity.

He was inside it all now, he thought, not listening on the stairs, speculating on a tour. Even after just a few days, these things were becoming part of his identity, seeping into him, changing what was there.

Paul and Mike had to rush off for duties, so he had almost ten minutes alone together with Emma, quite a luxury he was beginning to realise, in an environment where every second seemed only for function, every day left you literally breathless.

'I enjoyed your trip at the start of the week, in a bizarre way,' laughed Emma.. 'It seems years ago already. Seeing the kids outside the place. They weren't that bad – apart from that girl! I've hardly seen my flat this week. Done nothing really. On campus you lose track of the outside world completely. Bit ironic isn't it since we're here to educate. I suppose at least it shows the job is absorbing. It must be hard for you here all the time. I couldn't hack it.'

Dom could only smile. He rolled his eyes.

'Don't mention the trip! I've still not seen Dr Hennock – I'm meeting him later. He's always busy whenever I go to see him, keeps insisting I come back.'

'That's rude – keeping you waiting. *He* wouldn't take it from us. I suppose somebody has to do the Head's job when's he's on some jolly...I used to wonder when I was on teaching practice who was really in charge in a school, the pupils or the staff: who it's for, what it's about,' said Emma sounding different for a moment. 'But that's life today! Some kind of wild west free for all, no real hierarchies, no binary opposites, rights and wrongs. Just getting by.'

Dom wondered what she was on about, although some of what she said resonated. She certainly had opinions.

Everyone did. Maybe hers added up to some kind of world view. She could be deep as well as direct; but he always felt a bit lost, cold when people began to discourse in terms of something that looked like a theory. Even their language sounded alien. Perhaps she was one of those really intelligent people he had come across before: way beyond him in her likes and dislikes.

Then he found himself studying her, thinking about someone else for a change. For some reason he did not get, he felt he wanted to know more about her. There was usually a chasm with people at first; so much unknown, other. People could seem hard, even cold and separate when you came across them initially, exclusive somehow. Emma was confident in that way; but she didn't seem remote. Indeed, it was almost as if he felt he knew her already in some sense. Yet in reality, he knew nothing of her, nothing at all: she was just part of this strange new world. But there was more – something more. He felt strange, then, carried out of himself. What was it – all that mysterious, other life she must have lived as herself, quite independent, quite apart from him, before he'd ever met her, knew the faintest thing about her?

Emma's voice was breaking into his thoughts.

'Not sure I take to Darren – Hennock: mind like a steel trap; intent on its business. I'd watch out if I were you. I've come across his type before: ruthless, ambitious. Don't look so worried! He can't give you a detention! Not yet anyway!'' she laughed suddenly looking younger, much younger, different again.

'He's all right. The sort of person kids will respect, look up to. They need authority. I respect him.'

Emma looked at him curiously.

Dom wondered what she would think of what he was going to do at the school.

'I'm directing this play later in the term. I'm looking for help. Are you interested?' he ventured.

She smiled, shaking her head.

'They've really got you haven't they? Living on site, doing a play, all that work. No. No way! I'd say yes if I weren't going to be busy enough – but I'm definitely not going to let this place take over. It'll be my former career – the city all over again.'

Dom found her references to the city jarring for some reason. It was as if she were telling him she, her past, were above this little world. Was he jealous in some way, of her confidence? Of another life she had had?

His thoughts returned to his week. In just a few days, life had contracted down to the engrossing but limited horizons of work he realised. Was that the problem?

But they were talking of his manifest destiny as director of the school play.

He pulled a face.

'I'm going to have to do this alone, I can see that.'

'You sound as if you're going to scale Everest or something. It's only a play. You said yes,' cried Emma, laughing. 'Don't take it so seriously. You can say no sometimes you know. *We're* not at school.'

'Are you sure?' Dom replied, grinning at last. 'It's felt like it at times this week.'

Emma studied him for a few moments.

'Mike and I are going for a drink later, and perhaps Paul, if he can tear himself away from the place. Do you want to come?'

Dom could not have wished for much more just then.

'You bet,' he said. 'It would be great to get out for a bit. I've done nothing but work all week,' but then he remembered. 'Although I have something called tea duty first – whatever that is, so it'll have to be later.'

Emma shook her head as if in disapproval.

Suddenly, there was a great crash just behind them. Derisive laughter and cheers broke out, and talking fell away almost completely as a hundred faces sought a victim. They turned to see the boy Dom had observed sent out of a lesson on his tour earlier in the week, a very red-faced Tom Rymer gingerly picking bits of his broken plate out of his fish and chips.

'Not with your fingers! Get a brush and shovel, boy!' boomed Mr Walker who was instantly on the scene. He always seemed to rise to a disciplinary opportunity, Dom reflected, as if waiting for things to go wrong. He felt sorry for the boy. Jeering mounted until staff hushed the children. Tom looked mortified, frozen over what to do now. Soon the chatter and clatter rose again. The eyes let fall their prey.

'Poor kid,' said Dom getting up.

Emma stared after him as Dom helped Tom pick up his food and his dignity from the floor.

'Very noble,' said Emma when he returned, 'but watch him. Hennock – Alison said he's trouble! Katie's been given him in her form. Someone who can handle him... I must go. Heaps of marking already, but I'm going to make them work in my lessons. They don't seem to have done anything at all last year! And how can you go through all those years in a junior school and be hardly able to write?' she pulled a face. 'See why I say I sometimes wonder what really goes on in schools! Don't let Hennock wipe the floor with you! Text later.'

And she was off.

Dom watched her make her way confidently across the dining room, out of the door, exchanging words with pupils or staff as she went, at ease with herself, everyone else it seemed. He wished he were older, experienced. Then he found himself wondering if she would stay at the school, or leave, go somewhere else, and if so what Hillview would be without her.

Meanwhile, tides of hungry or sated eaters swept on around him reminding him it was time to go. His thoughts became vague apprehension – the afternoon, Hennock.

Then, strangely, he knew that someone was standing behind him, waiting to speak.

He looked around. A still red-faced Tom stood there, looking embarrassed, awkward.

'Thanks, Sir,' he said simply, and was gone.

CHAPTER EIGHT

MANAGING

Everything in Dr Hennock's office was scrupulously tidy. This room was undoubtedly the smartest one he had been in. Dom noted the new low chairs around a side table: for earnest conversations about policy and principle no doubt; a trim, but grand desk with the latest desktop; and three phones, even a screen on the wall for deep conferencing. There were neat piles of paper everywhere, and more files than Dom had ever seen in one room before lined the walls, nothing a millimetre out of place. He had a momentary impulsive desire to ransack the place in a spirit of rebellious anarchy, tear open files, spill secrets, discover some deep, dark state behind the face of Hillview: Hennock's gateways to the secret administrative labyrinth of a school world, his doors to the heart of the education machine. The answers to questions that had been forming in Dom's head since he started might lie right here!

In one corner was a red, almost scarlet, padded sofa, one of its cushions bearing the large imprint of a recently departed guest. Dom imagined an angry Mrs Tray – or some such in full flow about hapless new staff, settled deep into her theme. Then his ear was caught by a coffee machine that was bubbling, hissing and spitting menacingly, repeatedly coming to the boil then dying away again. For Dom it became the angry spirit of some pupil helplessly trapped in the volatile, incomprehensible emotional rollercoaster of teenage life, pushing boundaries, then subsiding into a very temporary acquiescence.

His thoughts were overtaken with old-fashioned photographs of Hennock's family on his desk, his surprisingly attractive wife and two very young sons on holiday somewhere by the sea. Hennock looked quite different in it, much younger, slightly overexposed like in a picture from a pre-digital era, with longer hair and a rounder, softer face. He made a little story out of the picture in his mind of them somewhere exotic, another world before the weight of responsibilities had come down. How long ago was it he thought? How old was he? Everybody over twenty-one had always been just old till he started work. Now? Had Hennock a past, even a sex life, and not emerged from some womb already swarthily middle-aged, complete with smart suit, tie and agenda?

He'd like to be a Deputy Head, or a Head in the future, able to order everyone around, knowing everything, first in consequence and power, the person everyone came to for wise guidance, firm direction. He was sure Paul would be one day. So was Paul. You could make a real difference then, having power, wielding it to put the world to rights. Then he remembered Mr Walker telling him that being a Head was actually a nightmare; power always went to people's heads even in a little school pond. They began with principle, ended in expediency he'd declared.

The phone on the desk startled him out of his thoughts, then clicked on to some answering device. To Dom's further surprise he could hear what was being said.

'Darren! I've been trying to get you. Rupert here. Just to let you know there's progress at last with the council planning dept. You just need to square Waseley your end over the development proposal. Hope the plans for the Chinese visit are progressing: getting them onside is crucial. They're key to all we're aiming for. Call me when you get this.'

The phone went dead and a red light began winking. Dom wondered vaguely, as with the previous strange sight of Hennock moving about the campus at night, if he had stumbled on something actually secret and important, but his main thoughts kept coming uncomfortably back to what Hennock would say about his teaching, his fateful trip.

He looked at the photograph again, thought of holidays, seaside holidays with his parents when he was young.

The door burst open. Hennock.

'What are you doing in here?' said Hennock without any preamble.

'Sorry! Your secretary told me to go in, come in, wait,' said Dom, standing out of respect. He wondered why Hennock smirked, but, without words, he gestured for Dom to sit down, like an obedient puppy. There was no apology. Dom remembered his dad saying Important People always thought they had a right to be late – and never said sorry for anything.

'Now, I don't normally get complaints from members of the public, parents and theatre staff all on the same day,' Hennock began, sitting behind the desk, a world away from him.

'Who's complaining?' said Dom, remembering Emma's advice.

Hennock looked sharply at him.

'Does it matter!' cried Hennock. 'There's quite a list. The theatre authorities; because of the pupils' arrogant behaviour during the performance. Apparently you allowed the children to laugh out loud at the production. Mrs Tray,

Rachel's mother, says her daughter was lost, then ill, not looked after. The cast – upset at being openly mocked. Then there's the trip to some club! What were you thinking of? Verbal abuse of the public amongst other things. Someone there complained. And there's potential legal issues about underage drinking.'

'That's all exaggerated! I'm sorry,' began Dom, but Hennock cut him off waving dismissively.

'I'm sure you are very sorry, especially on your first trip,' he replied, 'but this is not a good start. We don't pay you for feeling sorry. Aren't you keen to make a good impression to begin with? Think where things could have ended up. '

'Nothing much did happen, they weren't drinking – I got muddled, told some off who weren't ours; and, anyway, they said the HM lets the older ones-'

'Please! Don't let's start making excuses, especially that sort. You can't be that naive.'

'But-'

'I haven't got time to go into all this now. I've told you several times this week to arrange to see me, but there's always been some reason why the meeting has not happened.'

Dom was quite at a loss at that.

'I'll have to take all this up with the Head, when he's back – Monday. Meanwhile, I've done my best to mend fences. All this – my first week back, as if I haven't enough to do. Make sure you book in to see him first thing next week. Don't keep putting that off either. I have spoken personally to Mrs Tray, mollified her as much as you ever can, but we've never had complaints from the theatre before. You'll need to write letters of apology of course. You can write a proper letter, I trust, not like half the stuff we receive here.'

'Yes, of course,' said Dom, taken aback again. 'I'm sorry!' Dom started again, before he could stop himself, 'but lots of the audience were laughing at the performance not just us. We didn't encourage it. It was terrible – the production. And Emma and I *were* in control of the pupils.'

'Not very effectively. You're there to set the right example. We can't afford to have our school's reputation trashed at this point in its history, and the merits of a production are nothing to do with behaviour management, you ought to know that. You might bear that in mind for your own little efforts…And why were you on your own there with Miss Oakley?'

'I thought you knew. Mr Royal was ill.'

'Ill?' Hennock shot him a look and then rolled his eyes.

'He had a migraine or something. Look, I'm really, I apologise, I've stuffed up, but it was my first day, first trip. I didn't expect to be on my own with a whole lot of pupils I did not know,' said Dom feeling anger begin to rise, 'it's my fault, but I think you need to keep this in proportion.'

But Hennock was shaking his head.

'Do you indeed? You aren't listening, are you? Arrogance, Dominic, one of the problems with youngsters, probationers: why they go wrong. Not accepting inexperience, thinking they know it all. And what about basic common sense? Didn't they teach you that on your course? This all looks very bad you know. It raises questions about your appointment before you've even got to the end of week one. I want this school to offer a first class education, world-class teaching. If staff are thoughtless… stupid…'

All sorts of thoughts and feelings welled in Dom, sore and tired at the end of his first week. He wanted to tell Dr Hennock that he indeed had ambition too, and a million other things about why and how it happened. And did he remember what it was like to be at the beginning of things, constantly confounded by the practical realities of it all?

But before he could find any words, Hennock leaned towards him.

'A word of advice. If you don't earn respect at the start, follow school policies, listen to those who are experienced, you're going to struggle, seriously. Respect – if you don't have it, you are in deep, deep trouble. Wanting to be popular were you?'

Before Dom could protest, Hennock was carrying on.

'By the way, didn't you notice James had dyed his hair when he was showing you around the other day? We don't allow that. I made a great point of it in the staff meeting at the start of term. Weren't you listening to that either? People your age…You're not one of those dreamy academic types are you, head in the clouds all the time? We had one a few years ago – always missing meetings, deadlines, behind with marking, too idle to manage the children properly, follow things up. He didn't last. Staff need to be on the ball, not showing off, or currying favour making friends with pupils.'

Dom was still catching up with Hennock's comments on James. Was he really supposed to police newly appointed prefect's hair styles, as well as everything else?

Hennock sat back in his chair.

'Which was it? Were you trying to show off in front of Miss Oakley or play to the gallery – win some kind of approval from the students so they'd think you were cool, not just weak?'

Dom was too astonished to reply.

Dr Hennock nodded to himself.

'I thought so. Both. Letters of apology, not emails, drafts please, don't send anything yourself. I can see I'll need to check them thoroughly – first thing tomorrow please. Yes. I know it's Saturday. I shall be working. By the way, I've put you down for a couple of extra lessons on Tuesday next week. It'll help make up for some of the mess you made. It may help you with the Head, your colleagues. It is your probationary year, remember. And don't get upset. I'm not punishing you, yet! It's hardly an onerous task is it? We all have to learn from our mistakes.'

'But I've already been asked to help with-'

'Best to say yes to everything in your first term, especially when you've had a car crash!' continued Hennock smoothly. 'We don't want to get into written warnings, not yet. That's how a community like this works, supporting each other, especially when we let others down. And whilst we are on the subject, I notice you have auditions for the school play next week. I told Charles I was not sure that was the best thing to take on in your first term. I'll be frank; I always am: if you can't cope, we'll take it off you, or pull it. *We* don't want a poor performance in front of our public do we? You above all should understand that now.'

He laughed.

'I'm doing it for the school! Everything I'm doing is for the school!' said Dom at last, almost mastered by Hennock. 'I didn't ask to take that trip alone. You can't expect me to know all the ropes yet. You must see that, really.'

Hennock looked at him for a moment, shaking his head.

'Now, don't let's get all emotional,' he said leaning back in his desk, putting his hands behind his head 'I've told you. It's common sense as much as anything. We mustn't underestimate our ego in all we do. I wouldn't say this in front of Charles who gets emotional over everything, but I sometimes think that's what your subject, literature encourages: emotionalism, escapism. Bit of an intellectual blancmange isn't it? A sentimental soggy pudding of hurt feelings, grievances! Come on. You and I know the dangers of self-pity, don't we: sob stories, everyone a victim! Drama fosters that too – all sorts of self-indulgence! Now, you're not really like that, are you? This must be a school where people work for the greater good, can take responsibility.'

Dom wanted to argue, push back, but all he could come out with was:

'Well, what would you have done, then?'

Hennock smiled again.

'Better. I would not have been in the situation in the first place, certainly not on my first day. You are going to need a lot of support, aren't you? If it were up to me, if I'm honest, we wouldn't employ staff straight from training, but that's for another time, not when you've made me wait all week to see you. You look tired already you know. It's hard work here:– not just trips, drama games, playing. Education is a serious business, not a walk in the park. You realise that, I hope.

'Now, run along – or you'll miss tea duty, and, no, they can't have alcohol with their supper – or smoke!'

He enjoyed his joke.

'Smile! We don't need long faces this early in the term. We'll talk more about the lessons to be learned from this another time; and your teaching! Pupils don't need to hear frightening stories of abuse these days to impress them. Stop trying to be cool and get on with some proper teaching. Off you go – I've wasted enough of my week on this already.'

Dom stood up and went to the door, trying to find words, master a flood of emotions, but he felt stricken, and could only say, 'I'm sorry' once more.

'Tea duty begins in five minutes. Don't mess that up too,' said Hennock who was already turning to his affairs.

Dom paused at the door trying again to find words, not let his feeling of humiliation, frustration show. But nothing came.

'Run along,' Hennock said, not looking up.

Dom had been dismissed.

*

Somehow, Dom got through tea duty: supervising supper for the school's few boarders. It seemed simple after Hennock.

The pupils were cheerful enough. It was the end of the week, nearly, and they were beginning to settle again into the steady routines of term. Dom was surprised. He could not think of anything worse than being stuck in school on a Friday evening; but they were with their friends they explained.

Some of them, who had begun to get know him, greeted him quite warmly. One even asked him to sit and join them, perhaps in earnest.

He wasn't quite sure what he was supposed to be doing as he walked around; but he was desperate not to make any more mistakes. Although there was a very long list of rules and policies and procedures in a monumental file he had been sent, nothing ever quite explained anything new. Somehow, however, before he knew it or realised it fully, he became absorbed in his roles as friendly policeman, older mentor, butt of banter, and sharer of at least a few years' more reach into some of life's larger ranges.

He had a bite himself, but he wasn't hungry. He couldn't quite get over Hennock, however much he told himself to man up. He hated to disappoint anyone, feel he had let them down. He knew it was partly hurt pride. But the man had made a meal of it. And he seemed so different now to how he'd been on interview. Dom resented his comments on his subject, as well. That stuff about self-pity cut deep. Perhaps there was a little dark corner of truth in it somewhere, but it all seemed unnecessary. No wonder he had heard Royal and him arguing. He supposed he must try to take it all on the chin, but it was hard to come out of it in a straight line. And now there was the prospect of another scene again on Monday with the Head, no less....

*

Towards the end of the meal, he noticed the boy Tom sitting alone and apart on one of the tables and went across to him.

'All right?' said Dom.

Tom nodded, but looked wary, pale.

'Look, Tom's found a friend,' said a solid, sporty-looking boy called Andy to some entourage who were sitting nearby.

They all laughed loudly, a pack now.

'This lad is new here, it might help if you made an effort with him,' said Dom sharply.

Andy smirked, stared back insolently.

The others watched the two of them closely. Tom seemed to shrink down into the table.

'Come on lads, let's clear, get a game in,' said Andy to his friends, suddenly ignoring him. They rose noisily and went out, arrogantly indifferent, Andy ruffling Tom's bushy hair as he passed by.

Dom glared at Andy but he grinned back. Tom dropped his head, looking mortified.

Dom sat down in the now nearly empty dining room opposite him.

'Where were you before coming here?' he asked, trying to be kind.

'Strensham Academy, Bristol. Hated it!' Tom mumbled, starting to stack things on his tray, looking for escape. Then he stopped. He seemed frozen. A tear released itself from his eye and ran down his face. He did not bother to wipe it away, but sat staring into the middle distance, quite rigid.

'Hey, come on, what's up? Look, if you're not happy, you should try to talk to someone you know. It's only school. Can I help?'

For a moment, Tom looked at him, a world of secret sorrow in his eyes, but said nothing.

Dom felt quite helpless.

'I'm new, too, you know. I know it's not easy. You'll get used to it.'

Tom only looked uncomfortable.

'It's not here – it's, it's me, and home, Sir. They hate me. They sent me here to get rid of me.'

'Don't be silly, I'm sure they sent you here to help you, do the best for you,' Dom said, suddenly aware he had no real clue about the boy, was out of his depth.

Tom shook his head.

'You don't know my dad, Sir. He – he, he keeps promising things and then he goes back on them. He's not there much, and when he is...They fight all the time, my parents,' said Tom with contempt. 'I hate being at home... I hate being here because of that.'

He looked at Dom a moment, then down at the table again. He wiped his face and stood up abruptly.

Dom was about to speak again, when Mr Walker who was taking over from Dom, came in and roared at Tom.

'Come on, boy! You should have cleared by now. Leave poor Mr Greaves alone and get off -prep starts in twenty minutes. I suppose you haven't got any?' Tom looked at Mr Walker with a kind of weary resignation and then moved off with his tray.

'I was talking to him,' Dom said annoyed. 'He's upset.'

'Oh you mustn't take their sob stories seriously. You'll make him more uncomfortable sitting down with him. He's got to learn to fight his own battles! That one's trouble, you mark my words, I know the type – one minute all tears, the next being a little b– in the classroom because he's bored. Don't be taken in by what they say. They've all got issues these days. The softer we are on them, the softer they get. I blame the parents.'

He went on for a good while once more.

As Dom walked back to his room, his mind busy with many thoughts, he saw Tom kicking a football. He was alone amidst the gathering September dusk. Dom waved at him and Tom smiled back, but then his head dropped and he gave all his attention to the ball, booting it as hard as he could into the back of the net, over and over again.

*

In spite of a stack of preparation, endless emails and a million chores to complete, as well as his letters of apology Dom needed company. 'Forget it,' he said to himself. Even new teachers must have a break. Emma's invitation. He wasn't going to miss that.

The White Hart, out in the sticks, midway between the school site and a village in the opposite direction to Wellsway had a welcoming, homely feel, partly because it was not school and partly, because it served a genuinely great pint. He'd been in there before on a visit to the school, Mr Royal had taken him for lunch, and a drink: more than one, he remembered now.

The pub had an open fire, roaring away it seemed, whatever the weather, and to pass through the grownups in the bar, a civilian amongst civilians, merrily grinding over the latest political disasters, or more earnestly talking sport or joshing each other was definitely reassuring.

Less so, however, was the sight of Emma and Mike sitting very close together, intimate. To his surprise, Paul was actually there, looked pleased to see him. Dom had wondered if Paul was at all sociable. He was consumed by school like Dom, but seemed content with its given horizons.

They were stationed near the fire that was cracking and popping greedily, all aglow in a pool of light, quite engrossed.

'What's the rest of your day done to you? Been on another trip to harass the local Wellsway talent?' cried Mike loudly as he arrived.

They all laughed.

'Don't!' said Dom. 'I've just been worked over by Hennock. I have to see the Head on Monday. Write loads of letters of apology like some naughty kid…'

He told them all that Hennock had said, glad to unburden.

'Waseley won't do anything. Hennock's a nob,' cried Mike simply. 'Anyway, if Hennock gets you sacked, Waseley's a human being – he'll write you a reference.'

'Thanks!' said Dom.

'Hennock's concerned for the school, its image,' declared Paul, annoyingly correct.

'At least you know where you stand with Hennock, but he is a b-. Forget it!' said Emma more sympathetically. 'It's not your fault if kids misbehave it's theirs, the school's. Stand up for yourself!'

'I blame Rachel, she's a nightmare, first to complain. She does nothing she doesn't want to, that girl. Her mother has some kind of lock on the place,' observed Paul.

'You sound like an experienced old hand already. Blame the pupil! She's great in sport,' said Mike.

'That's only what Darren says,' countered Paul.

'He didn't say that to me,' said Dom.

'Can we talk about something else?' said Mike. 'I'm sure our pupils aren't sitting around discussing us on a Friday evening.'

'I get on with both Waseley and Hennock..You should keep in with people who are useful, important,' declared Paul.

'Dom needs another pint. Whose round, Paul?' said Mike. 'I'll have a half for the road.'

'You're not going already, are you?' said Dom, 'I've only just arrived.'

They laughed.

'I'm dropping this one home,' said Mike, putting his arm around Emma, proprietorially.

Emma demurred, but she let her head rest on his arm.

Dom's face fell without him knowing it.

'Oh, Dom, stop taking it so seriously. Hennock's just being officious. He's nothing in the big world, some jumped up teacher. Honestly, you should have seen what went on where I worked! Everything's blown out of proportion in this hothouse!' Emma cried.

'Why are you working here if you think that?' asked Paul, looking at Emma and then at her and Mike with something that looked to Dom like contempt.

'You think too much you know,' continued Emma, addressing Dom, ignoring Paul. 'You should be more like Mike, here, a braindead sports teacher who lives from whistle to whistle.'

'Anyone heard the score?' cried Mike grinning.

Emma and he wrestled playfully for a few moments, then carried on bantering lightly, absorbed in each other.

Dom felt awkward, wondered how they had become so close so quickly.

Soon, Emma and Mike left together, Emma catching the attention of the crowd by the bar as she went.

'You know they're an item already. She's older than him,' said Paul with a parade of confidentiality as soon as they were gone.

Perfect, thought Dom, as Paul became engrossed in telling him in detail other staff gossip, and then what Hennock had said to him about the future of the school: how it must change, how he, Paul, would change it all for the better and one day would be a figure with the power and reach of someone like the Deputy himself.

Littlenesses! thought Dom, wondering why he should be feeling quite so down when he was supposed to be out enjoying himself. Perhaps it was something to do with Emma, some idea of some special closeness or connection with her: something he had only imagined, of course.

Paul talked on. Dom appeared to listen patiently enough, whilst inside he went over and over his week, the mistakes, perplexities over this and that: Hennock; a general frustration of feelings that things were not quite right; some disappointment over Emma that he could not work out. They piled in his imagination like logs on a hungry fire as he tightened the screw on his introspections.

Soon, however, he got to realising how silly, petty his own concerns were. He needed to get a life. This was all unreal, lacked substance. He was merely playing some bitter, poor part so far, treading much too narrow a role, his companions likewise. They were puppets, not the people he knew they themselves alone could be – if accidents could be overcome, when true chances came.

Nothing daunted, new resolve found him. He determined to be the teacher of his dreams, someone of substance, not consumed by trivia. That, after all, was not what life was all about.

CHAPTER NINE

STEP FORWARD

Monday found Dom up in front of the Headmaster, just like some naughty pupil he thought, but then, excitedly, about the business of starting to direct his play; some barnstorming, world stopping, life changing epic to show them all.

Colin Waseley Headmaster

King of his world, thought Dom as he approached the Head's office.

He faltered on the doorstep as he had faltered on his first day. He could not begin to see the man as an ordinary human being, whatever some staff or pupils might mutter. Heads were a breed apart, supermen or women. Dragons when crossed.

But so they should be, he thought, and took another deep breath.

'Good morning, good morning! Splendid!' cried the Headmaster as Dom was ushered in past ranks of assistants and secretaries who surrounded the great man, his Praetorian Guard.

Rumour had it they did all the work.

'Now, tell me, what has inspired you today?'

Dom had heard his gambit before, so he was not totally surprised. Waseley loved enthusiasm, irrespective of its object, especially when untrammelled by reality. He beamed over at Dom, emerging from some digital world, beckoning him to sit down. He was apparently already deep into several weighty tomes on leadership, headmastering in the modern age, and writing a book called *School and Country* in which he set out his way forward for both state, private education and, indeed, the UK, no less, as a whole.

'Couldn't organise a piss-up in a brewery let alone a school,' a colleague had groaned on hearing about it.

Mr Waseley smiled with genuine warmth. Younger staff were easier to organise, free from the disagreeable trappings of experience, open pages on which he could scribble. He tousled his mop of wild jet black hair in a gesture that made him look disarmingly boyish. Dom made some lively talk about the play he wanted to stage, its forthcoming auditions.

'Splendid, splendid!' nodded Waseley, listening only in part, vaguely wondering why this member of staff was there at all. 'The boys and girls respond to leadership, enthusiasm – then they'll follow you anywhere you choose to take them, anywhere at all. The sky's the limit when we inspire. Make it fun, and we'll take them for a real ride I say. A happy, busy ship – that's what I want!'

He roared with laughter.

Dom wondered if Mr Waseley kept laughing because of his misadventure last week. Would some killer blow land soon?

The conversation rambled around for a few minutes. Mr Waseley seemed to think Dom had chosen to put on Shakespeare's *Pericles* or *Coriolanus* as a school play, however many times he told him he was hoping to do a more modest *A Midsummer Night's Dream*.

'I used to act in my student days. Played Bottom myself at school! Seemed to think I was typecast! Bloody amazing too if I may say so. Forgot a lot of the words, but you can make Shakespeare up easy enough.'

Did Waseley recall why he was there?

In the end, Dom had to remind him.

'Oh, yes, yes, yes: of course, of course!' blustered Waseley, now thinking why was he being bothered with this when he had far more important things to deal with, not least the future of his school. But he had retained his sense of humour amidst all his heavy responsibilities. He roared with laughter again when bits and pieces of some earnest narrative Dr Hennock had banged on about finally came back to him.

'I'd love to have been there when you told the those, er, damsels off, ripped into the girls-if we dare call them that these days! *Madames*, eh?! Lot of those about these days! But good start, good start! A disciplinarian in the making I see. Can't use that word either can we! Strictly between you and me – some of the kids and staff here, they could do with a firm hand, a good putting in their place as well!'

Dom was not quite sure how to take this. He was often wrong-footed in conversation: he imagined people were as earnest as he wanted them to be.

'Don't worry. Sort of thing the children will always remember you by, eh,with delight?!'

He leant forward, tapping the table.

'It's personality, *character* that counts. Almost everything you teach them'll be lost the same day, before they're even out the door, but character, that's what impresses, what lasts! As for Wellsway, well, our reputation abroad, it's always been rather, shall we say, mixed given our unique identity. People don't quite know what to make of the place you see. *Expectations!* Always a problem. But what does it matter what the world makes of us? Self-confidence, self-realisation: that's what counts. As for the children, well, there are a few rogues of course, a few oddballs in our community- not just staff! But they're young. I was a tearaway in my day, believe me. Every successful child is; but we have no real disciplinary problems here. Mind you, I could tell a tale or two!!'

Waseley laughed again, then groped around for some thread, trying to remember details of a story which had never interested him much beyond its entertainment value despite Hennock agonising over and over it all in that way of his.

'Darren will be making a fuss out of things; he has to: that's his job! Jolly good at it he is too, jolly good. He'll be head one day; so will you – somewhere! Learn from it, absorb it all, Paul. Things go a bit wrong, move straight on like I do!' he was chortling again.

'Anything else, Paul?'

Job done. He leant back in his chair, seeming to expand as he did so.

Dom had been warned about the Head's getting names wrong.

'Dom!' he corrected.

'Who?' said Waseley, genuinely puzzled, then ploughed on. 'No, no problems – of course not, not in a place like this, young man like you: all enthusiasm. More important things, Paul, in life. Don't get trammelled in trivia. Far too many staff do you know end up cross eyed half of them, missing the big picture. Tell me more about this *Coriolanus*. I mean *Pericles* production. Good rollicking fun in it I hope as well as serious guff. What about doing it outside? Not that cold these days in November, all this global warming, has its upside you see. Always go for the upside, Paul. Exciting for pupils! Doesn't matter if the audience gets a little soaking; keeps them awake! Get staff involved – Trippett, Walker, even Royal would be an absolute storm on stage dancing the tango!

'Confidence is everything in a school, even if it's an absolute shambles. Don't want everyone bored witless, do we. They get enough of that in the classroom! Not yours, of course. There's enough doom and gloom in the country at large without adding to it. Cuts, austerity, all this nonsense about who we are, where we're going, what kind of country we're becoming. Same in education. I say get on with it: spend today, get things done now, take risks. The future will take care of itself! We only live once. Let's enjoy ourselves, do our own thing even if we go out on a limb like you did the other night! Now, if I were not discreet, I could tell you some exciting things about our future, Paul. Things to get the blood beating, the heart racing. Change, Paul. Plans, real plans I have for our own broad sunlit uplands!'

And he was off again, laughing away.

Dom, after joining in his general enthusiasm rather uncertainly, eventually excused himself, happy to get out of there. There seemed to be no more business, no great axe to fall on his crimes. He left, no clearer about anything.

He spoke to Mr Royal about it, before going off to audition.

'He was quite nice about it all,' concluded Dom.

'Oh, don't be taken in by that man. Everything's smoke and mirrors: *how it looks*. And he'll say anything to anyone when the mood takes him.'

Royal pondered for a moment, looking around to see if anyone was listening.

'Tiddly *pom*! If you want some genuine advice, my rule in life is: trust what people do, not what they say!' He shook his head, continuing, 'I sometimes wonder if there is much substance behind anything he says. All this stuff about plans – change. He's all optimism about Hillview, education, even the country, but where's the real grasp of things. And the devil is we're going to have to change one way or another – soon too, or we'll be in trouble. Things are not easy for any school just now, particularly this one. Let's hope, to quote the great man, *we are not for the dark!*'

And then he would say no more.

Dom wondered what he meant by gloomy comments about change ahead. Again, no one had said anything like this on interview. The country was in a mess with money. It always seemed to be; but why that should weigh particularly hard on Hillview he had no idea. As for Dom's mess up, that seemed to be that: so much for his own fears and Dr Hennock's sombre warnings about being sent to the Head.

For a few moments he wondered about Waseley, and Hennock – they seemed so different, and what plans they had – where things fitted together, if they did. Were Hennock and Waseley on the same page? And then there was that late night encounter and phone message. It all left you feeling as if what was going on all around you might add up to something significant, but actually it didn't yet, or you were too young to understand, or be trusted with such knowledge.

Bemusement once more!

But the play, beginning with the auditions now, that would be his way of making sense of things, and a positive mark, building a reputation, for the school, for himself, whatever else was up. If literature were his passion, theatre was going to be the practical mission of that – forgetting for a moment of course things like the cringe-worthy *Wuthering Heights* catastrophe they had all endured last week.

He had already persuaded the Head of Music, Mr Tring, to help. He had written some songs specially for *The Dream* in the past so that it would not just be a play but an all singing, dancing, feast of a production. Yes, he had heard some large stories about past ventures into drama at the school that had been, some said, less than successful, but Dom was not going to be intimidated by any of that sort of talk. He would go his own way, not listen to gossip, get snared in littleness. The Headmaster himself, after all, had said just that.

Even when Mr Royal told him he was brave, Mike that Shakespeare was dead boring, and Emma, more dramatically, that it would scar for life, he was not to be put off.

He cherished in his heart the wise words that education was about lighting fires not filling buckets...

*

That afternoon saw the first meeting called for those interested. The pupils arrived genuinely excited. Indeed, the shabby old room in which drama was done was soon crammed. There was far more interest than usual, had Dom known it.

He had been told that there never were formal auditions at Hillview. Apparently, in the past, people just wandered by, and got parts, sometimes as late as the dress rehearsal, or even, it was rumoured, the day of the show, but that was a very important element of the ethos of the school, its identity, its inclusiveness and diversity. Mrs Dot, without being asked, had already been recruiting expansively across campus.

Dom was going to change all that one day, make things formal, organised, but such detail must wait. First, prove it worthwhile.

It was hard to know who was more excited.

Dom was pleased to recognise that quite a few pupils he taught were there, although part of him could not help wondering if they had come to enjoy more pratfalls. Someone informed him that some, including Tom, the odd pupil he had met during his first week who had seemed so sad, had been waiting for a go, but they had been sent away already by the ubiquitous Dr Hennock to catch up on work missed, or do punishment. Katie Trippett had been along, too, raiding the ranks for extra classes, as well as issuing several other directives, including, apparently, advice on auditions and acting in general. She did know a lot.

He noticed James, his guide there, his hair a different colour once again. Should he say something now, he must have been seen by other staff; and Jane, the girl who had seemed so lost in his first lesson, and Tim, and then with mixed feelings Rachel and to his surprise, Andy, the awkward lad he had come across in the dining room. The boy had a reputation, did not seem a very likely thespian; but Dom was nothing if not an evangelist.

He wondered if they realised what an opportunity they had in front of them, and thought of how mean his own chances at school had been. How lucky they were to be in a school where all were encouraged to have a go, even if in actual fact there were perhaps rather too many in the room to deal with all at once.

He was quickly drawn back to the present, however, noticing Rachel was already in the thick of something, holding court.

As he was about to begin, she took over.

'Sir, we've decided we'd all like to do something other than Shakespeare.'

Dom was taken aback, but he was beginning to get used to pupils' forwardness. He looked around for Mr Tring for support, but, ominously, he was not yet there, so he launched into a hard sell on Shakespeare: how funny yet magical the *Dream* was; how relevant it stood in today's world, being all about relationships, control, power and gender. There were many excellent parts on all sorts of different levels. There were the added enticements of magic and mystery. They were lucky in having music specially written for it. Here were worlds of marvellous experience to unlock; and they were, of course, going to do it in a different and modern way. The uplift of taking part in a play, the rapport with audience and cast and crew – in the end – well, there was no comparing it.

When he had finished, Rachel simply said:

'We all want to do *Fame*: it speaks to our concerns, Sir.'

'Perhaps next year,' said Dom groaning inwardly, thinking of drug abuse, sexual misadventures, suicide, and then staff dismay, parental storms, nightmare scandals on social media.

There were some limits to his belief that life and art went hand in hand.

'It would need a lot of work."

Rachel disagreed, began outlining her cast.

At this point Mrs Dot appeared, with a bundle of military costumes under her arm, announcing that, after having spoken to the Head no less, she had found all this for *Coriolanus*. She had something for everyone; and there she was trying random things out on random pupils before he knew it. The whole thing degenerated quickly into an improvised fashion show, with Andy, amongst others, grabbing anything that looked vaguely cool.

Then, Mr Tring himself bustled in. Dom explained that the pupils were talking about doing something else. Before he could say any more the music director made an impatient, gesture towards all those gathered as if dismissing one and all as irrelevant, shot a brusque, 'What's she doing here? She needs restraining,' at Mrs Dot, and, sitting at the battered rehearsal piano, began thumping out one of his own songs loudly.

Mr Royal had said that Mr Tring was a very volatile character – he had the nickname Tinderbottom – so Dom was wary at first of intervening even though chaos was soon all about him. He waited patiently for him to stop, maybe venture an explanation, but Tring was not known for stooping to explanation, and he was soon leaping on with another piece of music.

'He's deaf, Sir!' said Tim sensing Sir's bewilderment.

'Typical Hillview: deaf music teacher!' piped up Andy.

'Are we starting *Fame* now?' persisted Rachel.

Thankfully, the music stopped suddenly for a moment. Dom was about to begin with a what they were going to do that afternoon, but Mr Tring resumed as abruptly as he had halted with a shatteringly dramatic *two, three, four!* This time it was a song for them all to sing together – with all their gusto, and more. Andy rose eagerly to the occasion. He was soon leading a group of boys in the delights of making an intimidating raucous counterpoint, as if rallying a bottom of the league football team to stave off terminal defeat. Beyond this cacophonous wall of sound, towards the quality of which Mr Tring seemed quite indifferent, and which Dom could not pierce with voice or gesture, one or two hangers on, bored already, including James, had begun an improvised game of hockey in a corner.

'Did you like my voice?' pressed Rachel once there was another second of quiet when Mr Tring momentarily lost his place, the sound droning to a halt.

'It would be great for *Fame*.'

Simultaneously, a small deputation of girls who had been hovering nervously on the fringe of things approached Dom announcing in a collective whisper, with frightened glances towards the temporarily distracted Mr Tring:

'We won't sing or act.'

Dom was not sure where to go with such a unilateral declaration; but they clearly meant it.

'Two, three, four!' came once more from a resurgent Tring and before Dom could introduce some attempt at structure to the afternoon, they were all plunged again into the symphonic psychodrama of the music director pumping out his compositions at maximum volume whilst the chorus

resumed its definitely spirited but also disturbingly abrasive arcs of harmony and discord.

Only when a huge pile of music on the piano wobbled and finally loudly crashed on the keys and then fell to the ground and Mr Tring, cursing wildly, had to stop, did Dom get his chance. While Tring dived under the piano to rescue the music, screaming at anyone who ventured to help, as if they were there to sabotage, Dom managed to assert some control. He explained what auditions were for, how they should not be shy.

'Everyone's got some talent. No one needs to be able to act, sing and dance perfectly,' Dom declared passionately, to any who were listening.

'Good job,' said Andy, who evidently was.

The group of girls looked resolutely unconvinced.

'There's your lead -an excellent Titania!' declared Mr Tring as he emerged from beneath the piano, pointing decisively at Rachel in front of all, as if the matter were already settled, and there were no need for any of this egalitarian nonsense about choice or inclusion.

'Beautiful voice, has experience,' affirmed Mr Tring, momentarily calm and devoted. Then he crashed down onto the piano stool again, hands poised ready for a triple forte, glancing back lovingly at his prodigy.

Rachel smiled around and then back at him so very sweetly.

*

After more heady music making, Dom finally insisted it was time for some acting auditions. Remembering his own reticence at school, he determined to give some of the shyer ones their chances, try to make it fun. He overacted the roles, did some wild flailing choreography for the rest to practise and keep busy with. He threw himself into it determined to make some mark, even if he felt self-conscious with all those watching him. It was definitely amusing, although one or two found a teacher moving that much faintly disturbing. This Sir was weird. But things settled for a few minutes. They seemed to be paying attention. In fact, some of them really were keen.

Progress.

He gave out some lines to practise: some of the easier and shorter bits. There was chuntering when it was discovered that it was in Shakespeare-speak, but he'd chosen wisely; and if a few of the words were hard to say, some of them verging on foreign, the clips were taken up because they seemed to speak a language, a truth of more than just some chance moment, even whilst they sounded quaint. Then he got all of the group doing some simple steps together – apart from those who were apparently either too shy, too lazy or too paralysed by the occasion to move at all. Soon quite a lot of them were actually moving at the same time, approaching a level of coordination, even if in a raw and clumsy way.

Slowly, slowly, something started to happen, even if Dom could not quite believe the huge effort it demanded– he was sweating himself, heart pounding away, out of breath half the time. The cast, showing signs of life, started to enjoy it, almost despite themselves. It began to mean more to them than they thought it would, something they could not quite put into words. It caught all up together, carried them into some enticing beyond. Dom felt it, although he was struggling to shout loud enough, keep even one step ahead of what they were doing.

Almost for the first time that term, he found himself happy, starting to forget the abiding newness, the still alien landscape of school, his own inexperience, the shifting sands of authority. He became simply alive in it all, littlenesses forgotten for the time being.

He might, just, be able to do this, after all.

CHAPTER TEN

STEP BACK

The auditions had turned a corner. But there were still practicalities to attend to; personalities to manage. It became another lesson for Dom in what he had to offer, had to learn.

First, one shy girl was spectacularly sick when asked by Dom to read something out in front of the rest. Luckily a pupil who knew her anticipated it and was adept with a bucket; but there was outcry and horror from the rest, windows thrown wide, wild flapping at the smell. Mrs Dot swept her away.

Dom momentarily imagined himself having ruined the prospects of some budding actor, but Mr Tring shouted across: *she always starts term vomiting, fainting or fitting. It's a syndrome: everything's a syndrome these days. Ignore it; just don't put her at the front any time on stage in case she erupts over the audience; or worse, the musicians.*

Part of Dom wanted to laugh. He could feel anyway something like a mild hysteria rising inside him, all these young people packed together, a step from anarchy, the poor kid being sick, Mr Tring mildly insane – himself on the same trajectory. He was sweating away even more, shouting ever more loudly, gestures increasingly extravagant, improvisations more desperate. Things were wobbling between success and disaster. One moment they were with him, the world at his feet; the next, everything seemed to break into shards: one second a chorus, the next a mob. How on earth was he to keep on top of it all?

Everywhere there was as well the counterpoint of personalities to the main event. Rachel had started to squabble with one of the new girls who was clearly very good, better than her. Two of the boys, the twins Joe and John, who were up for anything (and more), brilliant little comics in their own way, kept distracting everyone else, with antics of one sort or another. They were funny, genuinely entertaining, but Dom soon realised it was all improvised, on the spur of the moment, sucking attention away from anything else. He tried to make them centre stage, but then they could not remember what they had done that had given delight, let alone repeat it. Harness their talent! But they became director-proof when he tried to tell them what to do, to control something they had. Then the completeness of their incomprehension when faced with any simple external direction began to frighten him.

Finally Mr Tring, who had been shuffling around on his stool watching them, and others – with growing incredulity, impatient to attack the piano once more, stood up.

'Over *there* -where Mr Greaves is pointing: left; LEFT! THERE! THERE! *THERE!* Don't you know your left from your right: *MOVE!*'

He leapt at them, waving wildly in the direction they should go. They smiled sweetly back, not moving a muscle in any direction, rooted to the spot for all time.

Everyone thought it the best thing so far.

That amusement passed. Dom must reflect on the diversity before him. What could you say? Given the excitable state of Mr Tring, perhaps he had better keep the twins away from any significant musical contribution, or maybe restrained altogether, tied up and stashed somewhere with Mrs Dot, perhaps for all eternity.

But they were far from alone in posing challenges.

Some of the good ones were a bit too fulsome over their own abilities. Some, like Rachel, registered only their own interests. Jane and Tim were solid, worthy of parts but not outstanding. James decided, perhaps wisely, it looked too much like hard work, not cool enough. He slipped off, claiming he still had that essay to finish.

Despite all, however, Dom continued to be encouraged: chaos, yes, but a creative one. There were some who would perhaps always just be passengers; others needed micro-direction, a sort of painting by numbers acting: *breathe, move, stand, deliver.* But once he had made his way through the mazes of over enthusiasm, or painfully disabling self-consciousness, misplaced self regard, but also quiet yet real ability, he could see there was plenty of raw potential in the room.

But more than that: *some* were inspiring him.

One boy called Robert and one girl called Lucy were actually quite exceptional.

He had asked Robert to read Bottom's part as he woke from his dream. At first Robert made it predictably funny. Then Dom suddenly said, for no other reason than he was enjoying it:

'Make it more natural, perhaps even a bit sad, not as if he is just pleased with himself- as if he's really realising something more: he's been somewhere else, another world, deeper, one that has opened his eyes.'

'I've had a dream, and it shall be called Bottom's dream...' intoned Robert modestly, quietly, making his way through the words as if they were his own, said for the first time. Broad comedy became insight. Bottom woke up. A bragging buffoon stuffed with self-regard turned human as a moment of simple but world defining self consciousness took wing, creating nothing less than a self awareness that could imagine shooting a rocket to the stars.

Then the girl, Lucy, read a few of Helena's lines, articulating all the pathos of a lost soul moving through the dark woods of the world. She became the character, the words part of her.

For a moment, they all felt it, were there with the character, all with each other, with Dom and the actors, in that shabby old room, where no one important watched or witnessed.

Dom was over the moon.

But the auditions were not over. The play never was.

Two things happened simultaneously.

All of a sudden, Mr Tring, who had long lost interest and was reading a rather racy magazine confiscated from a pupil, erupted back into life with a loud random intervention:

'What day of the week is it?' he cried suddenly, looking round wild-eyed.

There was laughter from some. Those nearby were too wary to respond; he wouldn't hear any way.

'OH MY GOD! Shit, shit, SHIT!'

Mr Tring rose in wrath from the piano, magazine flung aside, and shot off like a bat out of hell.

At the same moment, Dr Hennock entered the room through another door in seemingly pantomimic coordination with Mr Tring's exit. Someone had propped an old stage flat that had been in the way against the entrance. It crashed dramatically down near some of the Very Shy, now trying to hide at the back.

The girls, and some boys, squealed, jumping aside, and then made such a fuss of their shock and peril that Dom first thought someone had been seriously injured.

'Ooo, look what you done, *Dr Hennock!*' jeered Andy, in mock horror. 'Come for an audition, Sir? Bit old for this kind of thing aren't you?'

Hennock did not reply immediately. He looked from the flat to the girls, then at Dom.

Andy and Rachel took their cue.

'Go on, Sir! Bit of a dancer on the quiet?'

'Dr Hennock, I've only got a small main part. We all want to do *Fame*,' Rachel repeated, moving in on him.

'Perhaps Mr Greaves could oblige?' Dr Hennock said in answer to Andy. 'Playing the fool. I hear it comes naturally.'

Everyone laughed, except Dom.

Then he addressed Mr Greaves, 'You have contacted the Site Manager, I assume, about health and safety issues in this room?'

Dom did not know what to say.

Dr Hennock sat down ostentatiously, at the back where he could surely feel nothing, let alone see or hear properly, and settled, to listen attentively to Rachel's expanding elaborations on all that was wrong and deeply unjust about her afternoon so far.

Dom could only carry on; but Dr Hennock's arrival had thrown everything. They were back at the start, the good things of the afternoon lost just as they were beginning to be found. The auditions became the difficult side of school then: assessment, judgement, comparison, all spectacularly public.

Fun was done. Moreover, an embryonic cast had lost its concentration.

Surely after an hour Sir had it all sorted. Give out the parts! Get on with it! We're ready to perform!

Dom soldiered on but he could feel things slipping more and more. Terry stuck his head and began a very long and contemptuous lecture on morons who moved fire extinguishers, wedged doors, or windows open, even if someone had chundered.

'Where d'y'drag this lot up from? Y' trippin' them up outside on the street and forcin'them in? Do a panto!'

'Y's'll be lookin' for another job,' he concluded shortly after that, departing noisily.

Only inexperience kept Dom digging his hole. His attention and missionary zeal landed accidently on one of those who had made definite her intention never to say or sing anything solo on stage, ever. He suggested she try a very simple line of very simple words -to boost her confidence.

The girl's determination to do nothing reached new bounds.

'I didn't think I would ever have to *say* anything!' she said, bright red in the face, looking terminally uncomfortable, finally forced to make some contribution, indignant at this ultimate betrayal.

Typical teacher treachery. He said we didn't have to. How dare they expect something so extravagant as sound. What bullies teachers were!

Unable alone to deal with groups and individuals all at once, anarchy flourished. Finally seeing Mr Tring come rushing back into the room he tried to rally them with one of the simple chorus numbers they had been singing with gusto earlier. That would impress Hennock surely.

'Oh, Sir, you haven't given us enough individual time to show you what we can do,' cried Rachel, clutching dramatically at her throat. 'You've made me hoarse. I really can't sing any more.'

'Well, just sing quietly then. You've been making enough noise up until now.'

Rachel looked black, but had her revenge ready.

'Have you ever directed anything before, Sir? Because you

aren't clear, everyone keeps mucking about,' she declared loudly to the entire room.

Luckily for Dom, as eyes turned on him, Mr Tring, who had only heard part of what was going on, and understood less, began to thump out a song from another part of the play. The cast set about one of the tunes with a poorly-remembered and different set of words and actions altogether.

Dom thought of the expression herding cats and briefly wondered if there were a simpler way of earning a living, like brain surgery. He pulled a funny face to himself wondering how to draw it all to an end without some final crash. Some of the bored boys seeing a smile, suspected he was on their side in spirit.

It was a laugh after all.

Singing away wildly, they pressed forward, a rough pack now, in love with their own silliness. Yet, Dom noticed, amidst all this, there were still some boys and girls at the back – nicely in the purview of Hennock of course, doing absolutely nothing at all, not moving, nor singing, just standing there like zombies. The rest had become a mass of flailing limbs, and shouting, ranting, ripping voices: animals not children; hooligans out for a smash. A great cheer arose from a number of Andy's entourage, as a section of them – mostly girls – was driven hard up against a wall, one or two of them still loyally and valiantly trying to do moves they had been given for another part of the play.

In the end, Dom shouted. At last. Really shouted. Loud and angry, surprising even himself.

But it was too late.

In sudden fury, perhaps born of too long experience, Mr Tring himself must erupt one final time. He burst upon them, feral.

'*MUPPETS*! THE LOT OF YOU! You lot! Yes – YOU!

You look and sound like a pack of ANIMALS!' he roared, exploding over the final word.

'Stressy!' came from Andy, followed by mocking calls and whistles.

A few of the boys started laughing quite openly.

Tring, madness whipped by derision, glared savagely around, opening his mouth as if about to lay some terrible curse on all. Then something suddenly seemed to snap inside him. He grabbed his music, slammed down the piano lid with the most spectacular, discordant, reverberation, and stormed out.

Amusement. Embarrassment. Awkwardness.

All eyes found Dom again.

Some kind of silence settled on the company.

'Sir, I told you we should have done *Fame*,' came from Rachel, turning to look triumphantly at Hennock.

There were a few titters. The cast stirred, began to talk.

Dr Hennock stood, frowning at Dom. He gathered his papers, began to make his way out. He still had a smile for Rachel as he passed her.

Dom sighed: all the broken glass.

'Okay. I'm sorry about that, but you must be sensible, not muck about,' he began. '*It started well*,' he tried, as much for himself as them. 'Now, you need to get along to lessons – whatever you have next. We'll let you know about the cast, when first rehearsals will be...Thanks very much. There's promise... lots of promise.'

He tried to smile, look cool.

Slowly, almost reluctantly, some of the cast began to drift away. They had been desperate to move on minutes before; now they seemed lost without direction.

Dom continued to stand at the front as if manning some redoubt. But battle was long over.

Mrs Dot burst back in bearing more military costumes.

'Girl okay- mother said must not fuss- fussing made it worse- when teachers fussed she was violently ill. How had it gone? Weren't the children marvellous? Everybody so excited –such talent!' she was saying, a book of words.

Dom tried, for a minute or two, to talk to her, or over her, bring her to some kind of a halt, but he had not the power. He walked away in the end, but she continued quite regardless of his retreat.

Lucy and Robert, some others still lingered. Had their interest been genuinely caught? A few came over. One or two thanked him.

Perhaps something had landed.

'When do rehearsals start properly?'

'When does the cast list go up, Sir?'

'Will Tinder...Tring be sacked, like Pig?'

'You should get him sacked, Sir, he's evil!'

'Is Hennock going to sack you, Sir!'

But 'Have I got a part?' was their real question.

The twins remained. They did not seem to realise that auditions had finished, and were doing some random scene over and over again in a corner.

Meanwhile Dom could still hear Rachel complaining.

'We need someone with more experience in charge. I said we should have done *Fame.*'

'She's such a drama queen!' came a voice aimed at Dom. Rachel heard. She turned on her heels, started to march out, but intent on making a grand exit, head held high in defiance, she tripped over her own striding feet, nearly crashing to the ground.

Everyone left laughed. Even Dom.

She quit the room, slamming the door behind her with such force that the stage flat, ruthlessly shoved to one side by the twins and perched precariously on end, wobbled, and tipped leisurely over, smacking the floor with a loud thump and a shower of dust.

Andy, who had lingered too, gave a mock cheer and then a slow hand clap before leaving, a wide grin all over his face.

He'd had a great afternoon, thanks very much.

When everyone else had gone, the twins, who were the only people left in the room, still at a loss, turned to Dom.

'Mr Royal, my memory isn't very good. If I get a big part, do you think I could sing the music of *Fame* to la – not bother with words?' said one.

'Were those auditions, Sir?' said the other.

*

Silence had fallen in the hall. A ray of the westering sun found its way into the room.

Dom was left to tidy up, picking up sweet papers, a phone, a sweater, even, incredibly, someone's school trousers, and endless sheets of photocopied music, some bearing the marks of being twisted in anxious grasps, some trodden underfoot with dusty footfall on them, now seemingly forgotten: dead notes on a page with no singer.

He left, intent on finding Terry to report further damage before he could be accused of wanton vandalism, and no doubt a thousand other violations of body, mind and soul.

The sun, emerging more and more from clouds as it dipped to the horizon, flooded the empty, silent room with warmth, catching the dust that was still falling, transfiguring it into sparkling lights.

CHAPTER ELEVEN

EMPIRICAL EVIDENCE

This time Hennock did not delay.

'I can't allow this to carry on. It's a matter of the school's reputation. And you need to apologise to Rachel; we can't afford to alienate pupils with talents like that. I phoned her mother, reminded her you are new to our ways.'

For a moment Dom was confounded; he had expected discussion at least, not something on Rachel.

'That's no way for her to behave.'

'She's right to be upset. My advice to you is apologise quickly; all that shambles. Let's not start making excuses once more. Staff need to accept responsibility -or what hope do we have with children? Respect, Dominic. What did I tell you just the other day?

'Pull the whole thing. I talked it over with the Head, spoken to Charles. They agree. I haven't time for this straight on the heels of last week's fiasco. You need to concentrate on learning to be a teacher this term – part of that is firm classroom management whatever venue. Leave the theatrics to more experienced staff. Mr Tring does that quite well on his own.'

'That wasn't my fault!'

'I've spoken to him. He's upset. He's been with us a long time, unlike you.'

'But-'

'Children use things like plays – an excuse to muck about, get out of real work, especially when they're disorganised.'

Dom felt the sweat pricking out on his palms, his heart beginning to thump.

'I'm sorry,' he said, 'but I think you've got this wrong. You can't judge just on what you saw. Drama's important. I'm trying to start it in the right way, make it fun, if it's going to be any good, get them on side, enjoying it. Give me a chance!'

Hennock had looked at him.

'Enjoyment, yes: anarchy, no. I'm afraid any inspector would only judge what they see: – empirical evidence, it's called. Do you know what empirical means? Personally, I've always thought drama's often a waste of time – boys fight, girls get emotional: we hardly want those stereotypes in school these days, do we? They can muck about in their own time. Your first year is a probationary one. Remember?' Hennock paused.

Dom stood up then, chastened, sorry, but angry too. He moved to the door, determined to say nothing more.

'I'm glad you've taken all that in and are moving on. Don't forget your apologies to Rachel. You've ground to make up.'

Dom had left.

He knew he had made a mess of the organisation, had beaten himself up about it almost to the point where self doubt had overwhelmed, but he had his own streak of stubbornness, perhaps arrogance. He was determined not to lose the play, nor to turn into another ranting Tring. He firmly believed that you had lost it when you started shouting. They'd certainly told him that on training even if he'd had to get a little bit noisy in the end.

Empirical evidence! How could you explain to anyone all the ups and downs of what he was trying to do. He held to the conviction that something had stirred, talent and interest that demanded an outlet, whatever messy impression Hennock wanted to keep, whatever improvements he needed to learn to make himself. For goodness's sake, he was only learning too!

He needed practical advice.

He went to Charles first. He seemed to find it all amusing, laughing off Dom's earnestness, his little crisis, then becoming loftily philosophical.

'Ah, crowd management!' he smiled wryly. A lot of teaching comes down to that in the end, or dealing with a minority who must always be agitating for their way. You can understand the whole history of the world when you watch a group of children at play.'

But he indignantly denied having spoken to Dr Hennock, assenting to the play's demise.

In the end Dom sought out Alison.

She looked at him thoughtfully for a while.

'Remember what it's like to be fifteen, sixteen, seventeen? You're a lot closer than me! All the ups and downs! Nothing happens quickly enough. *Everything* is personal, an issue, a crisis. Nobody else understands. It's your first time, your first go. It's the hardest thing we have to remember – they're *children* especially the older ones who *look* grown up.

'Actually, I know some of them really enjoyed the auditions. That new girl, Lucy was full of it, and Jane. You carry on – it'll be good for all involved. I know it's not easy. I'll talk to Darren. And Dom, do remember, it is only a play.'

Perhaps she had spoken to him. Since then Hennock seemed to leave Dom largely alone, apart from the painful induction sessions he had to attend, when the man insisted on every last detail on his agenda being discussed, then written up in laborious prose that must exactly square the empirical with the endless criteria and detail of the ordained teaching standards.

As for Rachel, he tried hard to see that it was his fault – his failings, at least in part. He shouldn't have laughed, he knew that, or at that girl who was sick all over the place, but, well...'

Then he tried to remember how teachers at school had often got him and his classmates wrong. You could so easily stereotype, forget a real person was there.

He took his deep breath, apologised to Rachel.

It was tough. She saw that. Did it confirm her in some advantage? Deep down was he storing up trouble for himself, if not with her, then with someone else as a soft touch? What a tricky game this handling of egos was. And your own was always there, he had to admit, overt or covert, ever intruding, self-justifying most powerfully usually when you were wrong.

Feelings demanded their slice of justice, whatever the rights and wrongs, and they were so much harder than facts to confront. But how easy it was for a world to run away from you, even with the best of intentions.

*

'Climate change!' Mr Walker had announced in the Staff Room some days later one darkening wet and wild afternoon, with all the satisfaction of someone who believes themselves above culpability or consequence. Another tempestuous and rainy day was beating Hillview. Everybody agreed it was seasonally unseasonal, but they were busy; too busy. Climate change would have to wait.

'Always watch out for trouble from children in windy and wet weather,' Mr Walker announced to Dom, as if he knew some secret dark consequence that would befall new staff alone.

Dom could only wonder what awaited now.

*

It was his 'favourite' group again – the one he had had begun work with. Didn't that day already seem an age ago? By now, however, he was getting used to most of his forms, even this one. On the whole, he was afloat, just. Despite all his bumps so far, he liked 'the kids' as he called them; well, some of them anyway. Sometimes he felt more with them than his peers.

Rehearsals had begun properly. There had been squabbles over the eventual casting and not just with the children. Rachel had not been alone in a sense of entitlement. Some parents had emailed their piece. He had been accused of bias and prejudice when he had finally put the cast names up. The range of accusations was wild. He believed he lacked guile, but there had been forceful pushback, questioning of his motives. Privilege, even in such a small thing as a play it seemed, was always to be resented by those on whom it did not land.

On the insistence of Mr Tring, who reaffirmed that Rachel had the best singing voice in the school, he had given her a consequential part that still left better things for even more deserving actors.

'*Have* you directed before, worked with pupils like these who need a lot of help?' Tring had said, when he bumped into Dom. He had had to appease him as well. He tried hard to ignore such dispiriting observations, wondering not for the first time how exactly you were supposed to be experienced when you were only starting but that was true of his charges the children. Wasn't he learning that at least.

But the complexities of people management, whatever their age, the compromises! Dom had vaguely imagined some more exclusive engagement with higher principles in his job, not these all too often complicated personalities. He needed to get through this learning business, then he could get on with the important things, the art.

As he hurried along in fierce wind and rain to his lesson, he reflected how his days were becoming ever busier. Every minute seemed taken, prisoner to some demand. There was so much to get your head around. You could never sit back, let things happen. The constant fall of jobs to do staggered. They never stopped coming: pupils needed endless blow by blow help; tsunamis of marking swept in if you set what you were supposed to. That devoured hours each day, deep into dark nights; it was never easy and what exactly were you judging?

Once finished, it all backed up again.

Colleagues required support with a million tasks. Management wanted anything and everything tracking, justifying. There were always lessons to prepare, new books to read of course. Another huge job seemed to be dealing with, sometimes placating parents, some of whom were only ever a one-sided text away from the latest action; the parents who bothered of course. Quite a lot seemed to leave it entirely to you, their offspring might be running quite wild, but you must set right the entire child even if only seeing them a couple of times a week.

And everything you did ended in some public domain. Talk about the Headmaster's wife and the CIA. Who needed scrutiny and surveillance if you were a teacher?

Nothing on its own was too difficult or impossible – it was all interesting, never for a second dull like some exciting live play, where you could change the outcome in any scene or line; but you could never guess even the next page. Sometimes everything together induced almost a sense of desperation if you had time to stop and think.

He remembered Mr Royal had warned him at the start in his rather grand way: everything was too quick these days for considered judgement or reflection.

'We live in a world of fragments, splintered awareness, a billion voices freely but irresponsibly speaking their truth to all the world. No one listens enought to the wisdom of experience, the better voices.'

But whose were the better voices? Experience, the empirical, had presumably created all this, but it often seemed not just difficult and complex, but muddled and confused. Maybe it was just this thing again about being young, new to it all.

Dom earnestly wondered.

But that class were waiting.

CHAPTER TWELVE

BACK IN CLASS

As he dashed inside, Dom could not help notice James, yet another hair colour, and girlfriend, arm in arm, strolling casually along, heading towards the stray it seemed, oblivious of weather, all else too.

Upside-down world!

He ran his hand through his wet hair, slipped off his soaking jacket. They were already noisily inside his room, all end of day, tired and frayed, last lesson of a wet afternoon; the result of the malicious timetabler again. Perhaps that was Hennock too.

He remembered what Alison had recently said about them being children, reaching back once more in his mind to what he had been like in his past. He had hardly been a total enthusiast for school. Seeing friends, enjoying the lessons usually only when pupils got at the teachers and work was effectively suspended, avoiding the bullies and murder mouths, looking forward to going home, but not the homework. That had probably been the best of it until he had matured a bit, seen the point of it all.

But he would do better for them.

'Open your books. Page two four five, and settle down. I want to-'

There were the now familiar groans and bangs, several pupils looking around for books to share, or grab, and that one lost soul (he could never remember her name, shame on him) – forever left behind by the simplest of instructions, putting up a hand to ask, and then to be laughed at by her fellows, starting another management rollercoaster.

'I haven't-' she began.

'Share,' anticipated Dom quickly.

That task would keep her busy for minutes, possibly the whole lesson, or even her life, he thought.

But then, he suddenly noticed that the boy Andy had joined the class, was sitting at the back chatting away.

Giving up on someone needy like Andy was no part of Dom's character. He'd even offered him a part in the play, despite a reputation for indolence as well as awkwardness. He was actually a good actor when he bothered, for he had confidence, presence.

Dom would turn him, even if so far he had yet to show for a single rehearsal.

No one had said anything about him being moved into his class: it might be just an omission. Random things happened all the time at school despite the endless timetabling and calendaring and rules and procedures and meetings.

Dom could sense the class were already conscious of Andy, watching Sir's reaction. Even characters like Jane and Tim, allies of a sort, would see this as a test.

Directing the others to sort their books and papers out, devices away, it was a reading session for the first ten minutes, they could manage that much surely, *please read the section they were to look at*, he crossed to Andy and, crouching beside him, quietly addressed him, trying to make it all look low key, non-confrontational, as he had been taught.

'Are you sure you're in the right class, Andy?'

Andy, leaning back on his chair, studied Sir with a smirk. Then he spoke, loudly.

'Ms Oakley kicked me out: said she couldn't cope with me in her group, said go to yours!' and then he paused looking around the room to promote the effect of his words. Slowly he smiled again, swinging back on his chair, legs spread-eagled, as sure as day.

'She said, no one does any work in your lessons anyway.'

There were sniggers. The class tensed, expectant.

For a moment, Dom was at a loss, but he was not going to give them what some of them wanted.

'Just remember, please, who you are talking to. I think you'll find that is far from the case. I'll need to check this with Miss Oakley – Ali, er, Mrs Tenace. I'll have a word with you at the end.'

He stood up, thinking quickly.

'Glad you've joined us for now. Make sure you earn your place then,' he managed, pleased with the slick reply he had pulled from nowhere.

As he turned away to email Alison and Emma, he heard Andy say to his immediate neighbours:

'Told you he wouldn' do anything!'

A particularly strong gust of wind blew and the lights flickered. The class's mind, at one moment on an incipient confrontation, was suddenly all outside on another.

'Sir, all the old teachers say the weather never used to be like this!'

'Sir, can we go home if there's a power cut?'

'Ssh! You know the form, first few minutes is reading.'

Alison had replied already.

I'll be along in a minute; just talking to Emma, dealing with something. Keep him with you at all costs. AT

'Sir, I've lost me book,' wailed a voice. Collective

concentration evaporated again as they tut-tutted in mock disapproval.

Andy was doing nothing, but he would not draw attention to it yet. Let them settle.

'Share with-' said Dom, nodding at another pupil. The other girl was still negotiating with her classmates. Poor kid; some of them were cruel, but if he intervened...

He looked around.

No one was really reading, he observed, but he would give them a chance.

'I'm not sharing with her,' the boy next to her muttered.

'Don't demean others: show respect,' said Dom.

'What's demon mean?' came a voice.

There was general laughter: baiting Sir was better than reading.

Some turned slowly to reading again, but there was still no real concentration. Smiles and smirks passed the parcel amongst a group of the boys. A crisis was brewing. He must not fuel it, make things go wrong just to relieve their boredom.

He pretended to read himself, set the perfect example, ignoring Andy's deliberately provocative restlessness. The boy had a way of seeming to do little but actually disrupt everything. He was a stroppy adolescent, pathetic really. But why, oh why, couldn't he and all of them just settle, read. He'd love to be back there, reading for fun, the end of a long rainy day, soon to go home, free to imagine after a day of drilling.

But then he wasn't reading either.

Had Emma really sent Andy to him, said that about him? He couldn't believe any of it. It was all a wind-up. The boy was so cocky. Perhaps he should have just sent him away. Was he frightened of him in some way?

He pulled back.

'Right, everyone read that section? Turn back to page 245 please.'

'Sir, we've done this-'

'What page?'

'Two four five.'

'Wha'?'

'Two Forty Five!'

'WHA?'

'TWO HUNDRED AND FORTY FIVE!'

'Stress!'

'Can we read please, Sir, only it's so borin' when teachers start-'

'Sir, please can we not do this book.'

The lights flickered again scattering the words to the winds.

Dom valiantly tried some of the fun starter activities he had learnt, but no one seemed much interested in them that afternoon. He wondered about showing them more of a film of the book: at least they would be quiet then, but he had not come in to teaching to placate, last lesson of the day or not, so he persisted, making them write down some thoughtful quotations they could find that captured a character.

He asked them to think about their own personalities and qualities, good and bad, who they really were. Surely they would be interested in themselves, then they could think about the characters in the book and find the writer's words for them: that would be useful, not too difficult, make them think.

'Sir, this is too difficult for last lesson. Can't we watch a film?'

'Sir, I don't know who I am.'

'Sir, are you just trying random stuff out on us here before going to a better school?'

He wondered if it were simpler just to give the answers to them. Then they learnt little for themselves; but get them to do it and they seemed to give up, or go wrong....

He hauled them back to the task.

For a few minutes some of them worked on, others pretending, quite a few sitting there just waiting for it all to end, go away.

And now there was something being passed around he was sure, but if he interrupted, then what work there was would scatter to the winds once more.

At least Andy seemed passive for the moment.

He noticed here was someone in front of him who had the wrong book completely and did not seem to notice why he could not find any of the right passages. Dom smiled to himself and then spoke to the child quietly, or tried to.

A few desultory answers were being written down as he went around helping and trying to enthuse them in finding useful comments.

It *was* hard he realised- and perhaps not that riveting. But he had to do something with them, or try to.

Dom wondered if any teacher, any human being would struggle with some of this lot that wild afternoon, that wild autumn.

A voice gained traction in his head. Was it really necessary to pick away at things like this if they did not yet get the feel and spirit of the story? Where was his big picture, the emotional sweep, the dream and theatre of literature with all its inspiring relevance, in this small scratching around for the right quotations to tick an appropriate box in some dreary exam?

He checked on Andy again, trying not to let him see he was.

Where was Alison? She had said she was on her way.

He regained his place at the front.

The class were watching, secretly, or not so secretly, waiting.

Andy was still doing nothing.

He imagined the scenario on teaching practice being worked through in some tried and trusted role play. Andy would be taken aside – there would be a man to man talk. Andy would be reasoned into trying and all would be well; or someone would go on about deploying a conduct ladder with its carefully modulated steps that covered everything except all the real nuances of personality in time.

The wind and rain came again, lashing the building. All eyes lifted – so quickly -away from the difficult letters to the simple elements outside. Perhaps their instincts were right.

'Sir, this is so boring!' said one of the boys.

'Look,' said Dom, 'I'm sure Austen did not write it to be boring, or torment future teenage exam candidates. Let's go about it in a different way, which does not mean,' he continued as some slammed the books shut thinking that was it for the day, 'that work is over. I want you to think about this novel. I love it. I know it's hard but she wanted to make sense of things, like we all do, clarify issues so that people could find something better. Look, let's talk about what it means to you. What do you want to do when you grow up?'

He was taking a risk, he knew. Open discussions were hard to master with even a good class, and could so easily tip off into silliness, but, he wanted them to think, learn, not stew.

The class was silent for a moment..The question was something almost inconceivably beyond the near present. It was difficult. Their future did not exist, yet. There was no future. They had little frame of reference to relate to the book, even if Sir made them see some connections. And no one wanted to be laughed at – especially with Andy there.

Then one chafing soul ventured a reply.

'Have fun and not read old books about dead people in oldie English.'

There was a bit of laughter.

'No change there then,' quipped someone.

More laughter.

Despite himself, Dom smiled. A couple of weeks ago it would have hurt. Perhaps he was learning. He must, must, must remember to listen to them. There was usually something in what they said. If you kept on telling and telling people what to do, what to think, what they should say and feel, even read, they would resist.

But they needed guidance or they'd give up on his better things.

'Okay, let's take the first one you mentioned. Have fun. How do you do that?'

'You need to get out more, Sir!'

'By not reading books like this.'

Dom made a mock groaning noise as if he had received an agonising physical wound, trying to make them laugh.

Some smirked back at him engaged for a moment. Others looked at him with vague concern wondering if he were ill, or just peculiar. He could see Andy, who had draped his head and shoulder on the desk, raising his glance, grinning, looking around for accomplices in dissent.

'Don't you think that the people in the book wanted the same thing?' he pursued.

There was a pause. What Sir said seemed unlikely, especially as the characters were fabulously ancient, and anyway, they never existed. What was he on about now. Wasn't it time for the end of the lesson?

'Why don't they just get on with it. All that stuffy politeness, faffing about,' came a more earnest protest.

'Life in that class was different then. They had to obey certain conventions, er rules, like you have to at school; they couldn't do just what they wanted.'

Then Andy spoke again, a voice of authority somehow.

'Things have changed.All this fancy language and stuff is just old. It's different today – from when you were young. No one our age gets information from books. This is where we get our ideas from,' said Andy holding up his phone.

It was a challenge, in so many ways a challenge. He must answer.

'Interesting point, but you know should not have that out in this lesson. Put it away,' said Dom.

Andy pointedly ignored him, beginning to flick through the screens as someone else ventured their opinion.

'Sir, he's right. Things have changed.'

'How old are you, Sir?'

Dom ignored the question.

'Put it away I said!'

'I'm looking at something,' Andy said indignantly. Then staring boldly at Dom, he laid it carefully on top of his closed copy of *Pride and Prejudice* so he could still consult its screen.

Dom carried on, hoping it was some kind of compromise.

'You see, Jane Austen wanted them to have fun too-'

Someone yawned loudly but he persisted.

Someone else made a very silly noise.

'She wanted them, especially the girls, er women, to say what they wanted for themselves more, find their voices – identity, that's important isn't it? So they could get on in a meaningful way. Women did not have many options them, but that did not mean they could not speak out, influence choices.'

Some of the class regarded him. They'd noticed this thing about him before: he seemed to care about whatever he was on about, but it all sounded unlikely, and heavy. What was Sir playing at – he still did not get it: this was last lesson of the afternoon. No one did any work then. No need for this old biddy, especially at the end of the day, when you were shafted.

Andy had put his head back down on the desk, seemed to be about to fall asleep.

Still no Alison.

Try again, Dom.

'How many of you have ever been in love?'

'Inappropriate,' came a lightning response.

'Sir, that's disrespecting us,' came another.

'Demoning us,' another mocked.

'Sir, some of the girls fancy you, it's disgusting.'

'Sir, why is it all the teachers in this school are really nosey about our private lives?'

'Sir, you should ask Annabel about hers.'

'Let's cut the backchat, shall we: show some respect!'

There was a snort from Andy. Then he spoke.

'Sir, why do adults always treat us as if we're like goldfish in a bowl, dropping bits of information in when it suits them, not telling us what really goes on pretending we don't know about sex and stuff-'

Dom was torn between being provoked, thinking it a thoughtful response. They were in their little bubbles. So was he. And was he now the adult conspirator keeping them there?

'That's a good comment!' Dom began, but Andy was intent only on dominance, not enlightenment, rubbishing anything, anyone else.

'Some of us have got a lot more experience than some of the sad teachers, particularly young ones, in this dump.'

'*Andy!*'

'I didn' say you, Sir. You're not sad, are you?'

Dom glared. Andy smirked back.

'Highly experienced, Jane Austen, was she?'

Dom ignored it, trying to sound light, easy.

'She wanted some understanding, decency in social affairs.'

'You're crossing boundaries Sir, asking questions about our social lives. It's out of order,' came another voice.

'That's what good literature is for, to break open our ideas of things in the light of experience: why we're teaching you this what you call old stuff, it's being grown up about what's important,' replied Dom, rather smug for a second in finding some answer.

Jane, timidly, raised her arm.

'Sir, I think love is when someone really understands and respects you, takes you seriously for who you really are not just what you look like,' she said.

There was a dismissive groan. Dom ignored it. Bless her.

'Good for you, well done,' he said. 'I like that. Look at Lizzie Bennet, bit of a rebel, doesn't get on with her mum, Dad's distant. She flirts with Wickham – she's quite cheeky in a sophisticated way with Lady C and Mr Darcy. All that's because she wants to be taken seriously really, not be a pushover. There's no one else to stand up for her. She's trying to defend, define herself. She wants something better. We all do. Her mum keeps trying to tell her what she should do. I bet your parents do! How many of you have rows with your parents?'

Almost all the hands went up.

Were they with him now?

'But why doesn't she just get on, marry Darcy. He's good lookin' 'n loaded.'

'Because, he doesn't take her seriously at first,' said Dom. 'D'you see? He looks on her as eye candy, with a bit of spirit not an independent character whom he really knows or respects.'

Some found his expression eye candy the funniest thing they'd ever heard from a teacher.

'O respect, that's really what you look for on a good night out!' Andy cried, still resting his head on his arm, flicking idly through his screen.

For a moment, things hung in the balance, but a chorus of protest from the girls, and some of the boys greeted him, and an animated argument began about how boys treat girls and how girls treat boys enlarging the discussion into something important.

Dom was relieved, pleased; for a moment, he had them: somewhere. Maybe they couldn't see the connection between Austen's world and theirs, maybe scratching around for quotations was a bore, maybe the text would always mystify, but they were in it, almost despite themselves, realising something similar hundreds of years later.

He indulged himself in a few seconds of self-congratulation. Covertly, like one of his pupils, he checked the clock. They were nearly there, had done some work. The lesson was just about through.

Then he noticed Andy again. He had closed his eyes completely.

Suddenly the lights flickered once more, but this time they died altogether for a couple of seconds, came back on, then went out completely, leaving the room in a strange monochrome gloom of shapes and shadows, drained colours, and the eerie glow, from out in the corridor, of some emergency lights.

There were a few cheers and a mock scream or two that Dom had to shush.

'Quite a storm isn't it?' said Dom, when order had been restored, looking out at the wild world beyond. For a moment, they all looked out, sharing.

Andy, however, was done.

'Power cut, Sir. Lesson over. We can't see to work,' he said, standing up, packing away noisily.

'Sir, what's the point in all this if our climate is f-, stuffed?' protested a voice.

'Might get some decent weather,' muttered another.

'Sit down, Andy, please! Let's draw together what we have all learnt.'

'Let's not. I haven't learnt anything, nothing useful,' cried Andy, still preparing to leave.

'Now's your chance then,' said Dom. 'Look at these comments I have put together that Lizzie makes. I want you to think how they show that Lizzie is looking for something better for women in her world.'

'Wha'?'

'Why?'

'Sir, it's too dark to see.'

'Or write.'

'Sir, it's the end of the lesson.'

'You're always on about something better,' began Andy. 'How is being a teacher in a crappy school like this anything better?'

The pupils looked at Sir, one or two, away.

'Andy, we're in – or we were in a good discussion about respect which I think we all owe one another. I'd ask you to remember that, please. Stop being rude and sit down!'

'I'm just asking a question.'

'I said *sit down!* We're here to listen to someone else's answers and questions as well as our own. They may be better than our own.'

'Says who?' jeered Andy continuing to pack.

'Mr Royal said to us this one time, ideals are dangerous,' began Tim.

Maybe he was trying to help.

Groans.

'That's brilliant. He's right, but great art takes us inside other people's heads, helps us understand things-'

'A *thinking adventure*!' said one of the girls suddenly, rallying, remembering something she had heard teacher say, now partially understood.

'*Adventure?*' Andy snorted. 'What adventure? I don't want to go inside other people's heads, have people poking around in mine. It's twisted and it don' get you anywhere unless you want to end up as some teacher. Life is for having a good time. You can take or leave this stuff. We'd rather leave it. I'm off.'

'I think we had better carry on this conversation after the lesson. I've told you: sit down!'

'I was only makin' a comment. You let others – praise them, ignore mine. You keep asking things, then rubbish what we say. You don' listen if we don' agree with *your* answer!'

'Sit down, I said. We'll discuss this later!'

'I'm busy later. I got better things to do than see you.'

'Right, that's enough, you need to calm down!'

'Just 'cos you can't control the class, you start pickin' on me.'

'Don't be ridiculous. I've told you to-'

Andy began to barge across the room.

'All righ', all righ'. I'm goin'! I don' want to be here anyway. I'm not learning anythin' – none of us are,' he moved aggressively through the silent room towards the door, every eye watching him and Greaves.

He shoved an empty desk roughly aside its feet squealing along the floor, lashing everyone's nerves.

Dom felt a blade of anger pass through him.

'Where on earth do you think you are going? I have not told you to leave.'

He crossed to block Andy's exit from the door, grabbing the handle.

For a moment, they were face to face, worlds apart.

Time froze. Seconds beat by, Dom's heart surging.

'Thank you, *Sir*!' sneered Andy eventually, slowly, twisting Dom's hand from the door. Instinctively, Dom grabbed his wrist.

'What you touching me for! *Stop touching me!*' jeered Andy.

He pulled free, yanking the door so that it suddenly flew wide open and crashed against the further wall shuddering on its rebound. Dom caught it, but Andy pulled the door away, shoved past.

On the threshold, Andy paused, turning back to address the class.

'F-in' borin' isn't it?'

He crashed out of the room, off down the corridor.

Dom, livid, about to follow, stopped, half in, half out. Mrs Tenace, Dr Hennock were at last coming down the corridor. But Andy beat his way past them too, ignoring Alison's pleas for a word.

'I need the loo. You can't stop me for that!' he shouted breaking into a run, off, away, past her, past Dr Hennock, leaving them all far behind.

Dom stood there, emotions boiling in his chest, some of his self-respect gone with Andy. Alison rolled her eyes, turned, set off after Andy down the corridor. Dr Hennock watched, then looked at Dom.

'You were told to keep him with you.'

Then he too hurried off.

Dom stood there, trying to master his emotions.

Inside, there was almost complete silence except the noise of wind and rain picking up again: some other world, beyond.

The lights flickered back on.

Faint cheers. Whispers, then general conversation rose.

Dom turned. He walked back in, trying to look calm.

But his lesson was over.

'You mustn't let him get away with that, Sir,' said one of the boys. They began to clear to leave without being told to.

'He's like that in everyone's,' came another comment.

'Don't worry, Sir, some of us quite like the book. I didn't at first but you make it seem real somehow,' said one of the girls.

Someone made a sucking noise. There were a few laughs.

But they were going, and the bell had not gone.

Dom tried to supervise an orderly departure of the pupils, salvaging, if he could, something. Dark thoughts chased themselves around his mind. The shocking thing was that, for a moment or two, he knew now, sharp and clear, that he had wanted to hit the boy, hurt him back, punch him as hard as he could.

Andy knew too. Did not care. Had won.

And a childlike lust for pure revenge dragged about Dom's heart.

Slowly, slowly, he began to register, perhaps for the first time at Hillview, an awesome responsibility for that world of which he had become a part, and for which he was now culpable.

The slow girl was approaching. How pale she looked, white even.

'Are you all right, Sir?' she said, looking near to tears herself. 'I'll see if I can find my book tonight, Sir. I think I left it at my stepdad's.'

Oh God thought Dom.

When they had all finally gone, he tried to shake free from a sort of stupor at what had happened. And he'd let them out early – a near capital offence.

He noticed several copies of the novel left behind. He picked one up, put it on his desk – ready for next time?The woman on the front cover had been given a beard and spotty face, and was now cross-eyed. Another time he might have laughed it off. He used to draw on his books when he was at school. He had even been pulled up for it. It had meant nothing.

He flicked through the novel. There were a couple of notes misspelt amongst the first few pages, then absolutely nothing. On the back cover *Greaves talks crap* had been heavily scored.

He was about to tear the cover off the back, rip it into little bits, feeling like burning it, but then stopped.

He put the battered book gently down, and left as the bell for the end of school began.

He closed the door on an empty room still being buffeted by wild weather, a ship far out at sea.

CHAPTER THIRTEEN

THE BIG PICTURE AT LAST?

It was strange how caught in it all you became. It was hardly the first time Dom had been crossed in a classroom; but how difficult not to take all personally.

He must understand Emma's role in it. Had she really sent Andy to his lesson? In the midst of all the mess of his feelings he found he cared about what she thought, more than other peers or his bosses. He needed to talk to her, but first report to Alison, then face Hennock, even if that meant another round of criticism.

Before any of that could happen, however, Dom's anger over Andy had been overtopped by events. Something really big was happening at Hillview.

Just after school finished that afternoon, it became widely known that there was to be an extraordinary staff meeting – a meeting all must attend, of the utmost importance. It had been called suddenly for late the next day after school.

This had *never* happened before. The news could only rouse the most fevered speculations, feed the wildest fancies. Old hands were quick to wind up younger staff – but they were genuinely perturbed themselves. Rumour ran riot.

Everybody dreaded it was going to be an inspection – but that idea was quashed by Mr Waseley himself when he announced, by email, he would be out of school for a few days later in the week (again). Even he could not go missing during that.

Nothing leaked, however, except that it really was serious, would affect the whole school. Those few who knew anything at all were tight-lipped. The rest had to wait.

Meanwhile, Dom made his report to Alison on Andy, still feeling as if his little world had fallen in.

She was far less bothered.

'It's serious. I will follow it up, swearing at a member of staff, rudeness, being in your lesson. We came as quickly as we could. But you need to know he's a very troubled young man. There are lots of issues – it's all much bigger, part of a pattern. Keep it in perspective. I'm sorry you got caught up in it. The Head's going to have to deal with this one.'

She had paused, looked hard at him, almost as if she wanted to say more, then smiled suddenly.

'It's not the end of the world; a teenage boy, walking out of a lesson, swearing. Something like this happens every day here, not always quite so serious, sometimes much more so. I was punched in my first term teaching.'

Dom learnt little more but his feelings would not immediately subside. He lived the episode over and over again. It wouldn't let him go even when the four newbies went down the pub together to try to escape a now febrile atmosphere on campus.

No one had had a good day. Paul had clashed with Tom Rymer during an IT language club. He'd been freely plagiarising, using AI, downloading inappropriate material, then shut down all the computers once more. Dom had hardly seen the boy much since the first few days, but knew he was always in some scrape or other. Rymer had claimed that Paul had been looking at the material. Paul, of course, had a million ideas for setting the boy, IT, the school and the world to rights; but he had been hurt too. That gave Dom some comfort, maybe even some satisfaction until he realised his own meanness. It was possible to laugh about colleagues' disciplinary tangles – not so easy your own.

Paul had gone to Hennock who was supposed to be dealing with it but he was too busy, caught up in tomorrow's drama, whatever that was. Even Paul's faith in the Deputy was wobbling that day.

Mike had taken a team miles for a muddy, messy ill-tempered match. There had been a dispute with the other school's linesman, who had blatantly cheated. It had come near to blows between staff and would have to be dealt with by Waseley. Even he was upset today.

Emma listened cursorily to their tales, but she was clearly impatient to begin her own. That was all Andy too. She could trump the rest: she had not only had a row with him, but also with Alison, then Dr Hennock. *That boy!*

'This place!' she kept repeating. 'But I'm not putting up with nonsense from anyone! I've worked in the real world. The things that go on.'

'*Did* you tell Andy to come into my set? I texted you, got no reply,' said Dom.

'Of course not, even you can't be that naive. No wonder he messed about. He belongs in a cage not a classroom. He dared to argue with me even before my lesson had started; had done no work. I sent him to Alison. That's supposed to be policy. No one to tell him off directly, upset him because he has anger management issues. Well, I'm not playing that game. I took him to see her myself, to see something was done. Can you believe it, he waltzed off. She went into this long spiel about how difficult his background was, then Hennock arrived, criticised me for handling him wrong, leaving my class. We're doing him no favours letting him get away with things. I told them. No one tackles anything head on, here.'

'I'd have given real money to see that particular meeting,' said Mike, grinning. Emma had to smile for a moment, but her blood was up.

'Andy's great at sport – a good leader, no trouble for us,' was his tactless take.

'Katie thinks Andy's actually really intelligent, good looking, charming when he wants. That's why he gets away with so much. We were talking about it,' said Paul. 'If I were running the school-'

'He told me how f-in' boring my lesson was,' Dom declared solemnly.'

'Probably right!' cried Mike.

'I'm going to raise the matter of classroom management at this staff meeting tomorrow. It's ridiculous what some of them get away with,' pursued Emma.

And she would thought Dom.

'It's only a minority. They're not that bad in this school. I should be careful what you say,' began Paul, backtracking for some reason. 'I hear there's trouble: financial, something about the school's funding from the state, its future. You know what a mess things are. Whatever you think, we're just beginners here. Last in, first out. The other staff won't take kindly to us telling them what they should do – challenging authority. If I were in charge-'

'You've just been banging on about that boy Rymer! The problem with everything here is some of the staff have never been outside the school's gates since the last century. Brown-suited dinosaurs half of them! One of them told me, yesterday, he had not been to London for *twenty years*,' cried Emma.

Paul's inside information, however, provoked more interest, but he could, or would not say more. Conversation swiftly returned to the pupils

'It all starts with people, things like dealing with Andy,' said Emma. 'Whatever financial stuff goes on in a school, whatever its identity, its ethos whatever they call it. It begins with the individual. I've experience. I'm not some wet-behind-the-ears, straight out of university, twenty-year-old cutting my teeth. Something needs to be done.'

Dom wondered if she meant him.

'If you have experience, you should expect this stuff,' returned Paul.

Emma gave him a withering look, then carried on deep in exasperation. The conversation went up and down little hills of frustration before it returned to the meeting tomorrow.

'It is serious. Look at this visit of all those Chinese students, planned, then postponed until later in the term. I heard that the Head knew nothing about it until it was about to happen and then he insisted on it being stopped. Between us please, I have also heard that… the Head's days are numbered. Hennock's just waiting to take over.'

Paul had held it back, then said it after all. He would say no more.

Dom remembered the mysterious message he had overheard in Dr Hennock's office, that strange meeting he had witnessed late on his first day. He wondered once more if Dr Hennock were already up to more than anyone realised. But he kept quiet: there was not much to share, and he must be brooding on his own disaster.

'None of it will affect us much. We're young, we've everything in front of us, whatever happens here,' declared Mike, suddenly bored with all the seriousness. Nonchalantly he put an arm around Emma.

That irritated Dom more.

Taking a swig from his glass Mike pronounced. 'This is how I see it. Dom will be sacked, the school reorganised by

Paul – to shut him up. Meanwhile, Emma and I are going to set up our own college.'

The others laughed, but Mike was looking at Emma knowingly. She looked uncomfortable.

'I thought you liked it here -apart from touchline judges at our rivals!' cried Paul.

'I do like it here,' said Mike. 'Paradise compared to my last place. The kids do what you tell them, most of the time; staff work hard, well fairly; not too many in the school; fixtures brilliantly organised thanks to our department, apart from the s-t today. What more do you want?'

'Then why start your own place?'

'It's the future, especially if places like this go tits-up. We'd start a tutor school. That's the way forward. All this group learning, it's the past. With tech, AI these days, there's far better ways of doing teaching. The way forward is individual, tailored to individual needs. Schools – the buildings, organisation everything, it's a nineteenth-century industry in the twenty-first century. That'd solve the time we waste on classroom management crap. Suit the kid to the teaching on their own: simple, no probs. And Em and I reckon you could make a mint out of a place like that.'

'That'd see the end to your beloved sport,' said Paul quickly.

'No way. We've thought of that. You'd have team activities still, but teach the kids to learn independently, teach them skills, equip them for real life. They don't need most of the academic information, knowledge we push into them any more: it's all online. Education needs to catch up with the modern world.'

'I think teaching and running any kind of school is a lot harder than you think. And you'll still have the same problems, people not wanting to learn stuff that doesn't interest immediately, management issues, kids going nuts over stuff on social media or on their mobiles!' opined Paul.

'That kid's really wound you up hasn't he. Rymer looking at something inappropriate? At least it shows he's normal,' said Mike.

'What's normal about it?' said Dom, rather primly.

'Sex and sport: that's life,' cried Mike. 'What is it, sixty thousand porn enquiries a minute on the web?'

'That's just you!' muttered Paul.

'He's a good example. That kid'll make a fortune out of IT. He'll be master one day. He doesn't need most of the stuff we're teaching him. He can learn himself,' continued Mike.

'That sort of power at his age frightens me; he'll be the victim of it all. I remember an old teacher at school saying we were all slipping away into some otherworld,' said Dom.

'Oh Dom, leave it!' groaned Mike.

'He looks like an alien being – those eyes, bushy hair. The creature from another planet like that freak who runs that social media group, what's his name?' declared Emma.

'Dom's a techno dino, like my grandfather, thinks we'd all be better off if the net hadn't been invented,' Mike laughed.

'Just look at you all now!' retorted Dom.

They all had their phones out except him.

The conversation continued, spiky with academic and practical frustrations. Dom wandered stubbornly back into a little maze of his own concerns, brooding on his busted lesson, annoyed with Mike, even Emma today. Something seemed to flip inside him, a fit of petulance welling up. His little concerns did not matter enough to the rest of them. They weren't taking him or his confrontation seriously enough, or the business of education. Tutor school! What silly distraction was this that Mike and Emma were on now with all these issues at school, some crisis meeting tomorrow. Typical. Everything dissipated, disappeared into littleness.

'Penny for them?' said Mike suddenly to Dom.

'You talk about tutor schools, but it's what we are and aren't teaching them now – and how – that gets me -all the elephants in the room,' said Dom venturing suddenly further than he understood, but itching to stir.

'What?' said Mike simply.

'All the big stuff like what's really going on in the world that gets lost in silliness in the classroom. How shabby, unfair and tight life is for most people, and what should really matter, what the point of it all is,' he ended.

'That all?! Deep, Dom!' mocked Mike.

'Lighten up, Dom. But you're right about one thing: we're being drawn in, turning into the job, stuck in the grind of it. Look at us! Ugh, I hate it! We should be having fun. Even Dom's old enough to be let out to play on his own.'

They all laughed, except Dom.

'You sound like Andy, now! It's got to be fun or we switch off,' cried Dom.

'I don't agree. Be practical. Kids aren't that interested in academic heavy stuff about truth or the human condition, most of them. Some oldie moralising about things – boring them rigid with social conscience. A lot of them are too young too stupid, or on another planet, or in some technopit fantasy for the most part like that Rymer guy. They want to have fun, enjoy themselves, not toil through all this heavy stuff. You didn't either at that age,' declared Emma. 'School's a pain, something to be got through. Look at kids like Andy. It's quite pointless trying to engage him in anything beyond basic information, and only then when it's useful to him. You're wasting your time trying to change him. He wants to be out there living not stuck inside old books.'

'This from an English teacher!' cried Paul

'I think you're wrong. I think they rise or fall by our expectations of what they will do and be, or even think about.

You can't teach skills or how to think, without exploring contexts, or information without understanding, feeling: they need some moral framework!'

There was a chorus of groans at that but Dom went on.

'No, *listen!* They need things like literature and drama to bring it alive for them, things they can feel and relate to, or it's all only skills and means – and no ends to them.'

'*Sir!*' went Mike with a mock salute.

'That's why some of them grow up twisted. A lot of them don't get stuff from their parents… they're too busy with the wrong things. We're not doing teaching right, or teaching the right things. It just keeps on and nobody stops and says think what you're doing.'

'He's just had a bad day,' said Mike mockingly to the pub in general.

They all laughed then.

For a moment, there was silence amongst them. The nearby fire roared up, a fine blaze. A loud, distinctive but careless guffaw came from someone amongst the small crowd at the bar, causing them all but Emma to look across to see who could author such a random, inexplicable, almost feral note.

'Do you really believe all that?' she said to Dom.

'Yes. I do!' he replied.

'Poor old Deep Dom,' said Emma, half in mockery, half touched by his earnestness. 'I know what you mean, but the reality of it-'

'Not poor at all, thank you very much. I want to teach important things, things that matter, not patronise them!' replied Dom.

He held her gaze, intensely, smiling no more. Here was a world in turmoil: billions struggling to exist from day to day, prey to famine, poverty, disease, war, injustice, age, corruption and environmental catastrophe. The small, fat, rich part, living on borrowed time, dancing to the sorry tune of some shallow fad or celebrity.Progress, rapid change, everywhere: overwhelming. Nothing steady. Authority leached out of old, dead things, not yet budded in new ones. Space-age technology, God's powers, in the hands of kids, thugs, even the soulless machine itself. Everyone greedy for more. Everyone breaking their souls on the wheels of materialism. Everyone, everywhere, every day, more and more a child, finding someone, something else to blame, do their work, take their responsibility. There were better ways of living. There was something more. They should be looking for all that inside the classroom and out.

'You look as if you need another pint or two- of whisky!' said Mike grinning at Dom.

They laughed, even Dom, but he sat quietly for the rest of the evening, frustrated with his frustration, realising over and over, and with something of a shock, how narrow his own horizons had become – all tangled up over some silly kid.

The others talked on about this and that. Emma seemed quieter now. Every so often she would look at Dom, then away as if she were trying to work something out, caught by something, something that had made her uncomfortable too, despite all his nonsensical seriousness.

But Dom was far too caught in thinking about his own hurt feelings to notice hers.

CHAPTER FOURTEEN

JAM TOMORROW

The very next afternoon, as they settled in their seats and waited for the great meeting to begin, much to Dom's surprise, Emma came and sat next to him. For a while they chatted away, easily enough, not about school, nor anything deep, but about friends, then each other.

The meeting was taking place in the Great Hall cleared of dining tables, doors to the kitchen area sealed, block floor newly cleaned and polished, still drying in places, so that the smell of disinfectant mingled with those of mealtimes. There was a cup of strong tea, too long mashed, and even stronger, bitter coffee alongside rows and rows of cheap, damp biscuits adorned with a bright plastic looking red cherry. No one was eating them, for it was rumoured Mrs Dot had baked. The last time she had done food, a number of staff had been out of action for days.

Whatever its content, part of Dom was intrigued to see how the drama of the meeting would play out, how the characters he had begun to get to know and who lived largely still in his imagination, would take their parts in whatever unfolded.

On the other side of him sat an always aloof, but today quiet Charles. As they waited, he took out a book, *Paradise Lost*, started reading it, soon ostentatiously absorbed. Dom, grinning, nudged Emma; she looked, rolled her eyes: only proximity held her back.

He looked around to see where his other close colleagues were. Mike was sitting at the back so he could circulate a sweepstake sheet on how long the meeting would last. Paul was eager on the front row. Dom wondered if he were going to tell the whole assembly exactly what they should all have been doing all those years to set the school right. Yesterday he might have joined in.

The important people arrived last, led in by Waseley. An expectant silence fell quickly of its own accord.

The house darkened; curtain up.

At first, Waseley was all smiles, congratulating everyone for everything being not just splendid, but better than ever. Dom puzzled. He had begun to find that no one on the staff ever sounded particularly content with things as they were. He looked at Dr Hennock next to the Headmaster for a clue as to what was really up, but he sat there, closed up in his own thoughts, folded in on his plans.

Alison's contribution to the meeting confined itself to sensible comments about some recently implemented policies, one or two brief thoughts on new pupils; but nothing was said about Andy, or Tom or most of the pupils Dom was beginning to have some stake in.

Emma kept trying to catch Alison's eye whilst she was speaking. Dom could feel her agitation. Finally, she interrupted asking directly what Andy's future in the school was to be. Open discussion of individuals was important she declared, however much the whole school's future might be the meeting's focus. She had only been there a matter of weeks, was concerned; pupils like that needed dealing with, swiftly, quickly, decisively.

The older hands smiled.

Alison looked uncomfortable but Dr Hennock broke in.

'Miss Oakley is, of course, new to our ways here, but this is not the proper forum nor is it appropriate to discuss individuals, nor one's own classroom management issues in public. If we could please keep to the agenda today. There is a lot of very important business to expedite.'

Emma was about to contradict but Katie Trippett launched, unasked, into a long spiel about the trip she was to lead over the half-term holiday. She went on and on, going into as much detail if she were planning a mission to Mars.

Emma must sit and seethe.

Random topics followed. The more trivial, the more staff seemed to get animated. Still the Big News was delayed. Dom looked around the room wondering if he were missing something. All this could surely be put in an email? Emma had subsided, was working her phone, apparently detached. Someone right in front of the Headmaster was conspicuously reading a newspaper advertising work in a local supermarket. Several colleagues'eyes had closed, whilst Mr Tring was clearly happily fast asleep, beginning to breathe heavily, a loud snore imminent.

Dom wanted to laugh. He began to pull his mouth around in an effort to control his facial expressions. In the end, fearing his irreverent smirk might be detected he had to look down. He noticed he was wearing odd socks.

Pin your socks together. It was telling him something.

Someone else was droning on now. He felt a wave of drowsiness pass through him, and stifled a yawn. His limbs were heavy, and the air in here was surely getting thinner. Now his eyes were starting to close, and a delicious, warm, sleepy world beckoned.

He jolted back. For a split second or two, he wondered where he was. Someone was going on and on on about some marking policy for exams later in the year: what blue meant on it. There seemed to be a lot of animation about the meaning of blue. Katie was challenging the use of blue... green she insisted would be better, better for those with learning needs. However did she know so much?

Charles whispered, 'They do this to waste time, break the spirit, so that there's less to spend on anything important or controversial.'

Looking surreptitiously at his watch, nearly half an hour had passed. Still nothing of great moment had been broached. The atmosphere continued to thicken.

But then, at last, Waseley took hold.

'Now, I don't need to remind you of this school's unique foundation, its special identity. We have some legacy endowments from our benefactors and founders, yet enjoy the support of the taxpayer for most of our work. As you know, all these diverse strands of our make-up were formalised back in the 1970s in a charter. We went from being what was effectively a small independent school into part of the state system, retaining certain privileges, features like our boarding.

'Now, however, we are facing, alongside all schools, whatever their nature, exceptional challenges, especially financial ones. Our relationship with the state has always been something of a marriage of convenience. We have enjoyed security through it, but there have been costs, some would say quite severe ones to our sense of ourselves. We have not been able to select or control completely who we take in, nor how we manage our finances as much as we would like. We have technological changes accelerating by the very day as well. But the biggest problem has been simple lack of money, falling rolls at the lower end of the school, and with our boarding. Further savings, more regulation and limitations are coming, one way or another. And the country's economic situation, well!

'Cuts! I don't have to remind anyone here what that means: staff numbers, pay and conditions! As things stand, we face a future of managed decline. Of course we're not alone in that.'

Everybody was awake now.

Waseley paused, looking almost serious for once, Dom thought.

'Now, you know me: I believe this is the best school in the county, one of the best in the country. But this great school faces a choice, a simple one really: more integration into the state system, more regulation, more control, and above all inevitable cuts to our provision,... or *maybe taking another route altogether.*'

Once again, Waseley let the words hang. His dear staff must listen today.

'We all want the best for Hillview, but we have choices to make, either be forced into some possible reorganisation, *repurposing,* perhaps contraction; or do the courageous thing and take some initiative ourselves. Now this other route, this departure on a new and exciting journey into the future, this bridge, if we take it, will require us all to be bold, be visionary. We may need to strike out in a completely new way....

He paused yet again looking round.

'And all this is connected with another theme. So many of you come to my office- a delight to see you of course; but the thread, the theme of your calls comes down to a sense that you feel you have lost autonomy as teachers! You can't pursue your own trade in your own way without having to follow so many rules, rules not made by us for us but by powers and forces far away. We all, staff and pupils, deserve better, much better: more freedom, more choice, and above all, more money!

'Now, in a moment, Darren, our details man of course, always our detail man, Darren is going to outline the substance of this route, bridge, or perhaps I should say *runway* to the future. Somehow, we need to grow, brush off financial restraints. The only way we can really do that is to *take back control*. Then, ladies and gentlemen, we can plan, manage ourselves with much more confidence, in fact *make, determine* our own future. In short, we can be free – free again, as our founders envisaged, to do the right things by our own school and its pupils: what we teach, whom we teach.

'I'm talking, as I am sure you have all worked out by now, about Hillview becoming a fully independent school once again as it was in its proud and glorious past!'

There was stunned silence.

Waseley sat back in his chair, surveying his audience, smiling broadly, delighted to be able to command such attention, irrespective of the merits of what he might be arguing.

'Now, I see this has come as something of a surprise, maybe even a shock, but I must emphasise that this is only a possibility, an idea, a proposal *for the moment*. This may all sound quite fantastic at first, but I ask you to think about what I am proposing, consider its possibilities, before leaping straight in with a thousand obstacles. This way, this *option*, if we take it, well; *what could we not do? What world could we not imagine, build for ourselves?'*

Staff were openly restive now. Dom could sense a million burgeoning questions, incredulity rising around him. His own feelings were mixed: excitement, surprise, concern. Nonetheless, at last someone was talking about big things. But this way? An independent school? Before anyone could say anything, however, Waseley ploughed on.

'I know! It sounds a pipe dream, and you will all have a thousand questions, concerns, objections; but let me paint a few pictures, fly a few kites, show you the stars for a moment.

'Imagine! Ladies and Gentlemen. *Imagine!*... a well-run independent school would have far more money for a start to do all the things we now only dream of. We could take in who we want, from where we want, improve our performance, our outcomes across the board at a stroke. At the same time, we could recruit the brightest and best staff: not that there's too much wrong with those we've got, of course!'

Waseley's jokes usually fell flat.

'Above all we can grow, ensure our provision becomes ever stronger not just fight some long defeat. We could even build – finally build-the facilities this school so desperately needs, has always needed, without worrying about borrowing, or spending limits imposed on us from outside!...

'Beginning to see, beginning to feel excited, beginning to sense possibilities?'

He looked round, beaming away at his flabbergasted audience.

'Think about it! We make our own curriculum, even set our own exams. Some independent schools are already on that; we could measure what really matters *on our own terms*! We'd be in control. *We'd be in control. NOT told what to do:* a free and independent Hillview offering a world class education with first class staff, all paid properly, no one left behind not even support staff, everything levelled up! Indeed, we would make our own way in the world going from strength to strength, head held high. *Education unbound*!'

The dam broke.

Uproar.

A thousand questions and concerns broke, but Waseley was holding up his hand.

'Ladies and gentlemen, ladies and gentlemen, please, *please!* Your patience – indulgence – for a few more moments. Before giving you time to voice all your concerns, Darren is going to present a detailed scenario: feasibility, transitional arrangements, funding, all that guff. Beyond me, of course, the financial minutiae, goodness! But that's not important is it? But believe me, we think it could work, and we want to share some of our plans with you. But the essential thing is, dear colleagues, we need to think big, *think big*, consider options in a completely radical way. So, patience, patience, dear staff! Listen to our inspiring plans before you judge! I'll now hand over to our details man, Dr Hennock, who has already been tasked with all the intricate ways and means that can take us all to the stars!'

'I and a select group of governors- we've spent many hours on this,' began Dr Hennock, swift to his feet.

'Please can I point out as the Head has said, that these are only *proposals, possibilities.* We envisage a period of full consultation before any final decisions are reached. More than that, you will all – the whole staff and support staff – for the first time in Hillview's history be allowed to cast a vote on our proposals. It goes without saying we feel this is the most important decision in the school's recent history. We need not just your consent, but full support in all this and an advisory vote in principle, even if some of you may not at first find all the detail straightforward, is an excellent opportunity to demonstrate how empowered we might all, everyone of us, become in a new *independent* future for Hillview. So, now… first slide, please!'

Despite staff bursting with questions, and simple disbelief from the majority to whom this was a total shock, Hennock went on for a long time in meticulous detail. It was mostly ways and means, but laced with plenty of promises too, substantial financial ones, and more than a sprinkling of exciting possibilities that must touch everyone there one way or another.

At last he stopped.

At last the staff could speak.

They began, unsparingly, with Mr Tring in trenchant outrage.

'I don't doubt the sincerity of Darren's presentation – we can all see the thought that's gone into this, but let's face it Headmaster, it's utter bollocks! Even by the standards of some of managements' and governors' recent ideas, it's total pie in the sky. Are you seriously suggesting the place will do better if we turn it into some kind of independent school again, a *business* in today's chaotic world and dreadful economic climate where such schools are under threat themselves?'

'It'll change the school forever! What about the school we signed up to teach in!' came more voices.

'How can we decide on all this? it's far too complicated for us to know what we're doing!'

'Why on earth should some wild idea of independence be a magic panacea for the problems that face us today. Surely it's the last thing we need, and the least practical?' cried Mr Royal. 'It'd be the end of Hillview as we know it for sure.'

Uproar.

When things died down a bit, he continued.

'If this gets the faintest traction, everyone's going to end up sleep walking into vague promises of some better future, because things are a mess now. That's change for you!' declared Mr Royal.

Hennock took that one comfortably in his stride.

'I know it's difficult when some, like you Charles, have been here so long, so very long, to think outside the box, or think the unthinkable at all. Groupthink!! We all get, dare I say, set in our ways, don't we? But, please, let's not jump straight to negative conclusions. We must not allow the dead hand of the past to smother discussion of the future. And I for one must object to your description, that Hillview's a mess. True we have issues, but where does not in these challenging times? We want open debate about all this, not closed minds from the start.'

Another storm.

Most were in dissent over something that seemed so radical, impractical, but confusion was as strong, and resentment at the way things already were turned into waves of concern over all that was wrong or not right about Hillview there and then. The possibility of a better future, or a disaster, started to get lost in a thousand current grievances. The lure of entitlement was potent. Whatever this was, they deserved better in a million ways.

Debate mounted, producing more smoke than light.

The Head intervened.

'Ladies and gentlemen you know you can trust me. I'm a listener, always have been. We have promised, *promised*, I repeat, full consultations. We've never done that before.'

'Shouldn't we have been kept better informed about all this, and what is the rest of the governing body's take on things? Is it a small group of them driving the rest who've been hijacked?'

'What does this really mean for the security of our jobs and pay and pensions? Who's going to prop all that up if things go wrong, let alone pay for us to go our own way in the first place?'

'Ah! Now I see what some of you are really concerned about! But we must think beyond ourselves, our own little future. And"*desperate*"is not a word in my vocabulary, never has been,' cried Waseley now, all mock outrage, 'Not the right word at all. And there is no threat, never has been nor will be so long as I sit here, to anyone's job or salary. Any threat is a long way down the line, and only if we do nothing. I'm an optimist, always have been. There is always a way forward! This is a great school!'

Then rather suddenly and strangely, the tide began to turn and besieged management began to gather support from the floor. One or two staff led by Katie Trippett were rallying to the Head's cause, coming out more or less in agreement with the proposals: *at least they should be considered*.

'We need to change. We need this wake-up call. I sometimes think this school is asleep, sleep walking along pretending it can ignore a changing world. Think of tech changes: we're so behind. And we could certainly borrow and invest independently – many independent schools do. We could set our own pay scales, reward those who contribute most, do extra- curricular things – like trips. My trip would be one of many in such a school.'

Then Mr Royal weighed in once more.

'But this is all fantasy: *if* we could be properly independent, *if* we could recruit, *if* we could somehow find money to build – *if the cow could jump over the moon*. I'm sorry, but everything, *everything* we have and are, all of us here, we owe to Hillview, funded by the state. To throw all that up for some dream of independence, the illusion of some fountain of easy recruitment, a wild punt on some dream sounds like self destruction to me. I ask you very simply, what certain gains are there in all this – how it is really going to benefit the tiddly poms to heap all this on them in our unstable world?'

But before Tring could explode in agreement again, or Katie leap to the proposals' defence, before Mr Waseley or Dr Hennock could venture some reply, Dom suddenly heard Emma speaking, beside him.

'Wouldn't it be better to try to change the things we don't do well or do wrong or unfairly first? Put our own house in order? It's capabilities that matter, not what type of school we are, state, independent, academy, comp, grammar. That would attract pupils, without all this constitutional or identity drama. It's people here and now that matter, that make things successful, not structures. I come from a business background.'

'What *do* you mean?' Dr Hennock fastened on her.

'We make more of the school as it is, its culture: the pupils we already have, get those right. Outcomes depend on improved performance all round and that starts with us, our expectations not how things might be or how they were. *We need a plan for today not a dream for tomorrow*. That would make a better school, a better business,' she said simply.

There was approval, much murmuring of agreement. There would have been more had she been there longer.

But management was management.

'If I may say so,' Hennock continued, 'whilst it's always valuable to hear from staff who are so very new, I think you are speaking rather vaguely, and, as even you must agree, from relative inexperience about the business of school. Hillview makes a great deal out of often quite modest pupils already – as you should be facilitating yourself. And as I have said before, there is not the time to discuss personal problems,' replied Hennock, smiling.

'Oh, that's not fair, that's not what she means!' Katie Trippett burst in, but without real focus, seemingly forgetting for a moment which side she was on. 'I mean look at the way some of the girls dress, and if you try to do something about it- I mean Charlotte Tatter, last night, coming out of a lesson wearing makeup an inch thick! Staff just turn a blind eye to all that; heels that are positively dangerous! Now, if we were independent, we would have more control!'

'Right into their hands,' muttered Charles to Dom; and it seemed to be true. From here it was an easy step for Waseley once again to allow pent-up anxieties about all sorts of current concerns, major and minor, to let rip, consume the remaining time.

'The Great Debate in Hell's Prison,' muttered Charles to Dom, brandishing his copy of Milton.

Dom's own feelings had danced initially at some of the ideas thrown about, even if the idea of fee paying schools made him uncomfortable. Bright visions glittered. Procedures and protocols that broke the heartbeat of trust and crushed the spirit would be swept aside. They would be free to do only the right things in the right way. The school would become a shining beacon of light in a darkening world, true to the best in education.

Why not?

Why not, indeed?

But as he listened more, it all sounded vague, as vague perhaps as some of his own dreams – if he ever dared to admit that. It even sounded selfish; going out on your own, to get one over on others, beggar your neighbour: that wasn't what education was about, surely? And then here he was just starting – hardly finding his feet – full of ideals, but knowing little really. What did he know about running a school?

He lapsed into confusion, thoughts, feelings all over the place.

Meanwhile, Mr Waseley was winding up the formal part of the meeting in his most unctuous tones, smiling, amused at the stir he caused.

'I would just repeat, there is no reason at all to be overly concerned, yet! A proposal is all it is at the moment! As for jobs, your pay, I know that's always top concern for staff, but worry not! There'll always be a Hillview! This will always be *your* Hillview!'

And that was that for now, or almost. The leadership team prepared to leave, all smiles except Alison. They had broached the idea of the seemingly impossible and unthinkable. Today's job done. Hearts and minds might take longer, but this was a first step down a road.

'The place'll become a skip – some awful finishing school for idle kids, whose parents think they can buy them a brain, or a dump for technocratic foreigners who'll return home to enrich their own country at the expense of ours; the school I know and love, a business park!' Mr Royal sighed to Dom and Emma as collective discipline in discussion broke down. 'Time for people like me to retire.'

'That's a bit reactionary – even racist, isn't it?' cried Emma, looking for somewhere to lay her own frustrations.

'And let's not stereotype independent or state schools, please. You can't just dismiss all ideas for change. This place needs a kick, even if this doesn't look remotely like a good plan on business grounds. Government never give schools or teachers enough.'

'Ah! There we have it. I'm glad to see you get real. You should know that this is all about money, very little to do with independence, or freedom,' Charles shook his head. 'Do we need to turn education into even more of a jungle? I despair.'

Emma was going to come back, but just at that moment a shrill screaming sound burst out and was suddenly all about them, tearing into everyone there.

It took a second or two – then they realised what was going on.

It was the fire alarm.

Its insistent shrieking summons defeated any kind of rational thought other than to move, somehow to move, get out, away from that splitting, splintering noise, its wild ringing and darker throbbing beat ripping away any remaining reason in the room.

Staff still sitting stood up, at a loss. Others were already moving, panicky, confused looking to each other, at the Headmaster, Hennock, and then to the exits, searching for leadership, a direction, a way out.

They had not prepared, practised for this.

What to do? Where to go? Who could help?

As the drill of the alarm bored relentlessly into the skulls of all present, half screaming for action, half numbing Terry himself burst into the Hall, looking more disordered than ever.

Then he began shouting, shouting as if a whole world were on fire.

'Everybody – ou'-, everybody get ou'side. The school's on fire. *The school's ON FIRE!'*

CHAPTER FIFTEEN

AFTER THE FIRE

The Great Fire of Hillview as Mr Walker called it, was all the talk of the school for a day or two, and even made a modest feature in the local paper, *The Wellsway News and Journal* by which time it was very old news indeed; but the truth of the affair was more prosaic, even though no one could quite escape the thought of what might have been.

Petra Dot's cookery class, Food Club no less, (Food Fight Club the pupils called it) – ran after school once a week. It tended to attract the greedy rather than creative, and it was widely known that most pupils went along for entertainment, rather than culinary art. The school's underground media described sessions as the biggest laugh on campus.

In her latest class, that included, Dom learnt, several of his friends, Andy, James, the Rymer boy – a food fight had really taken off. Andy had been bullying Tom, getting as much gunk as possible in his hair. Followers had joined in. James, and latest girlfriend of course – he was only there for her- had tried to defend the youngster: everyone was soon chucking ingredients about, first with a little effort at discretion, then quite brazenly, whilst Mrs Dot carried on at the front talking effectively to herself, issuing instructions on how to bake her famous rubber scones. Meanwhile other students had been experimenting with deep-fat frying, and there was another complementary unofficial challenge to see what really happened when you cooked a confectionery bar. It emerged later that one of the children had brought a dead mouse in, battered it and tried to fry that too (subsequently intent on offering it to one of their gullible peers). The food fight even went live on line: so those who had placed bets but were not present, could keep abreast.

The chaos had been fun at first, then disaster as the ragging, the fighting, the experiments escalated and an actual fire finally took serious hold.

Mr Walker and Mr Royal might see the fire as metaphor for the school's future in the light of the staff meeting, but fortunately the destruction was limited to the scorching of a couple of classrooms. It was soon brought under control with the aid of the local fire brigade. The rooms damaged were separated by a flimsy movable partition that was notorious across the school for its lack of proper cladding and sound proofing, meaning that lessons in either room usually carried on in simultaneous chaos. This double room adjoined Dom's own, and it was not long before he learnt that that too had been affected by smoke from the fire, not severely, but the lingering stench and blackening was enough to put it out of action for a while. It would be a nuisance: he would now have no proper base, and there were endless minor implications. But when he considered what might have happened, and he found it would mean he got to teach in some slightly better rooms, he had some consolation.

Most of the staff were simply relieved in the end that no one had been hurt, but they were familiar with the shortcomings of the school's infrastructure and Terry certainly was not letting anyone forget about many warnings about the state of parts of the building. Once over the shock, they were angry, wanted someone to blame, especially after the meeting yesterday, all it had stirred up. Most of that must fall on a management who had been told many times about Mrs Dot's wayward kindness, as well as the shortcomings of the partition – and done little in practical remedy. All agreed it was a tale symptomatic of the neglect of many current and urgent needs at the schools whatever idle dreams might be being peddled for some imaginary future.

Mrs Dot got a good pasting, but it was she who had gathered her wits enough to call the fire brigade in the end and, her resourcefulness in a time of crisis in getting her pupils safely out, summoning help, salvaged her some credit. She and the pupils had to face the wrath and a reckoning with Terry, however, which was more than punishment. But that was pretty much an end of it, except that one of the parents of one of the pupils who attended the club was threatening legal action on the school, and on Mrs Dot, for endangering his son's life. The fact that the boy had enthusiastically joined in the food fight was quite irrelevant.

The Headmaster contented himself with seeing the pupils involved, warning them of the dangers of fire, believing the real fright they had had was lesson enough. Andy once more seemed to slide out of his share of responsibility, or culpability for bullying Tom Rymer in the first place. Waseley was seemingly most concerned to avoid negative publicity, mollify the fire brigade. There would be weeks of tiresome inquiry, red tape, but Hennock could deal with that.

Meanwhile, Terry had gone home vindicated in his belief that teachers were mostly sausage-fingered retards with not a gobbet of common sense.They should be kept under constant close watch, if let out at all. He raged on for weeks after about injustices occasioned by defective infrastructure, out of control kids, woolly-minded staff.

'Teachers! Put donkeys in charge and expect nothing to go arse over tit?! Never met so many thick people as you do in *haducation*,' he told his wife and family many times that evening, and for days after, not without a good deal of satisfaction.

No one really listened to him, however, which only proved him right of course.

Mr Walker happened to overhear Terry chuntering in terms of donkeys in charge of lions and remarked that he felt like that about the leadership team after the meeting. The staff were donkeys if they went along with it. The fire incident, the school's future, even the country itself all manifested a complete failure to 'get a grip' he avowed almost as often and loudly as Terry cursed the teaching body.

Dom was chastened: the sudden potential upheaval of the school's future, the fire, the pupils' behaviour, the school's response. He could only wonder again where, and if ever, blame really landed for all the issues that constantly surfaced, and where on earth solutions began. How much responsibility the simple word teacher could come to comprehend!

Just now, trying to get his charges to learn their own language, and being responsible for a school play seemed quite enough.

*

'Never a dull moment in this place. Always expect the unexpected,' said Alison the next day, when she made a point of catching up with the four newbies after the drama.

She had had, she said, a deputation from senior staff expressing deep concerns after both meeting and fire. She'd spoken to the Head, Hennock.

'It's only proposals, possibilities at the moment, long term. The Head should have emphasised that even more. Nothing's going to happen without more discussion. It's years away. We'll keep you on board. You will be consulted.

All staff will. I don't want you four getting jaded and disillusioned....

'In my view it's the quality of staff that matters wherever you teach, whatever a school's make-up. You are all making a promising start, one or two blips apart!'

Was she looking particularly at him, Dom wondered?

'What do you really think?' said Emma, suspecting dissent amongst the leadership.

Alison looked at a loss for a moment.

'It's no secret, I have doubts. There are certainly many questions I want better answered before we go any further.'

She hesitated.

'I personally think there's no such thing as independence in today's world; better together I say. But in the end we have to do what is best for the school, to keep it viable frankly. We can't stand still – no one can in any profession. And our identity as a school has been muddled, falling between two worlds, as it were. But, I agree with you Emma, what you said. You see, we do listen, sometimes. It's what we do individually that counts; and I also agree with Charles: we need to remember everything we have, everything we are here, we owe to the school, its history, however difficult some things are right now. We're all apt to forget that.'

Dom was to remember her words over the following weeks.

Emma, still smarting from her reception at the meeting, angry at what she had heard about the causes of the fire, returned to her concerns about pupils.

Alison listened.

'I could see your frustration. I know classroom management, characters like Andy present challenges. I don't agree with Darren about us being able to pick and choose just the easy ones in future, if that ever were the case, and if there

-166-

are ever any easy ones. But, as I said to Dom recently, they're growing children not adults. We cannot make them into what we want them to be: any parent knows that; humility is the long lesson learnt when you have youngsters. You'll see one day, if you have children of your own. Yes, I know, I know, we should try to change them, correct them, bring the best out of them. We all believe – try to do that, but you cannot make them into something they are not. Very often it's our image of what we want, not them we're focusing on.'

Emma looked dissatisfied.

'Do you believe in God, Emma?'

Emma, surprised, bridled slightly, shook her head, as if she were about to challenge such an impertinent question.

'People are people. They're not products you manufacture – thank goodness. No one's perfect. You're shaking your head, Emma, but whatever we do, we cannot control things completely, whatever sort of school we are. After all, even God would not command that, would he?'

*

The youngsters carried on a more personal commentary later.

'No one mentioned any of this on interview! This place! And Is Alison God Squad? I thought she was the sensible one?' came from Emma.

'Hennock knows what he's doing. He has a plan. We should go with him. Independence'll give us chance to sort things out for ourselves not be stuck in a mess. I've sent them my ideas!' was Paul's response.

'I hope if things change, it's about the right things, the big things, not just lots of littleness again,' declared Dom; but no one quite knew what he meant, including himself.

'F-k it if it wrecks fixtures!' was Mike's only comment.

Predictably, Dom did not know quite what to think the more he thought. He looked to Charles for a lead, but he had become strangely silent since the meeting.

Money! Dom's family had never been rich, had much really, but they'd managed, with care. Now it seemed money weighed heavily even in the world of education, which was surely supposed to be beyond all that. He'd never thought of a school as a business, but he supposed it must be so in the end. Perhaps everything in life was a business – all the big things, birth, love, marriage – even death? Maybe they were all only transactions when it came to it.

His dad had always told him that there was no free money in life, that you had to work for anything. Maybe this was what he meant; that everything was a job to be done in the end, and paid for. But surely you put the end first, then the business of it all served that great point?

Why things were the way they were, and why when choices were offered they were so confusing, limited or the wrong ones, no one seemed to be able to explain easily to young Dom.

CHAPTER SIXTEEN

OBJECT TOM

One free period, a few days later, Mr Royal bustled up excitedly. Dom was expecting some lugubrious comment about the aftershocks of the fire, the meeting.

'Look! Look at this!' he declared, 'a boy's got inside his own head, found his voice, listen!'

Dom was in a hurry. He'd come to learn that teachers, himself included, recounting their lessons, could go on a bit, but Mr Royal was reading.

Teacher is standing just behind me. I dare not turn to see what he is doing, in case he shouts. Everything seems to shout at me today.

I stare at a blinding white sheet. Nothing answers. I am supposed to be writing but my head is a blur of words. I can't find the centre, the sense. I try again to put simple points down, but find only a mind's emptiness.

'A mind's emptiness- not bad for a fourteen-year-old. But listen how he ends.'

I'm standing, ready to leave the class, slip my bad work under all the rest's good − try to forget it. I want to look as if nothing matters, wear the smile of those who finish early because they're good; one over on the rest.

But I can't do it whilst everyone else can. I know then, as if I have always known: I'll never really leave this classroom. It'll always be with me, down all the long corridors of my life.

'The point is: this is from that boy Rymer, you know, recently joined. Everyone says he's trouble, hopeless, no one can get a thing out of him. It's negative, overdone, but there's feeling, insight, self discovery. That's what school's about. Not foundations, policies, systems. That's for the birds.'

'Show it to Dr Hennock, Alison,' said Dom. 'It might help his case.'

'I shall show it to Alison. That's if I can get in before Darren. The boy's in trouble again this morning; managed to shut down the computers once more. Can't say I entirely blame him, throwing the switch on what passes for civilisation. But there's something here, something worth persevering with.'

And Charles was off to see Alison, as excited as Dom had seen him.

Dom seemed to share some of Royal's mood that day, getting caught up himself, whilst hardly realising it, in a flow of passionate instruction. It could, indeed, have been a different school from the one he had been in a few days before with its confoundings, its confusions. Summer seemed to have come back too, lingering in a warmth and gentle breeze that drew across campus. His pupils, on the whole, set to whatever he asked of them. Before he knew it, the day was all but done.

As he wrapped up his last lesson, he noticed, with some surprise, the very same Tom Rymer hovering outside his room.

'Sir, can I have a word?'

'Sure, Tom. Come in. You okay? Hey, Mr Royal read me some of your work – he loved your writing –well done.'

Dom was kind enough, though part of him wanted to get on now, catch up with colleagues, other things. Tom wanted to stay, talk, however. He made certain the classroom door was wide open, sat down with him.

Tom looked shifty, pale. His head went down.

Dom waited. He had begun to be a bit wary about asking about difficulties; children, people – usually had plenty to say on that if asked.

'Sir, trouble. I'm in trouble.'

Dom wondered what was coming: confessions about internet activities, or some secret part in the fire, not yet fully revealed; maybe shutting down the system again. He rather hoped it was nothing he had to deal with directly: being friendly and sympathetic was easy at times, but they led on, usually into a management mesh. Then he checked himself. He thought of Mr Royal's generous words at the beginning of the day; then his own at the start of term, about needing to listen.

'How can I help?' he said.

Suddenly, tears were flowing down the boy's face.

'What's up?' said Dom, gently. 'Come on – I told you before. It's better to get things off your chest.'

'I didn't write it. I got it online. You see, there's a number of sites I use.'

It took Dom a moment to work out what Tom was talking about; then his heart sank.

'Oh. Tom,' said Dom, feeling both sorry for and oddly let down by the lad. 'Why – why do you do such things?'

Tom looked up at him for a moment, then down again.

'I don't know, Sir. I can't help it sometimes. I suppose it's there and I just feel- I feel mad sometimes and- I don't know-'

Dom looked at him, rather hopeless. At least he'd confessed.

'I s'pose-' there was a long pause. Dom wondered again what more might be coming. He had a lot to do. Emma would have gone home soon. She often lingered in the Staff Room at the end of the day.

Then he thought of Mr Walker.

'It's my parents. My mum at least-' began Tom. 'They were mad – because I was involved in the fire thing. They say it's a waste of time me coming here. This is my fourth school. If I get kicked out again...I'll have to go live back at home, with one of them. I can't stand that any more: rows, fights all the time. They're like children.'

'Have you spoken to someone about this? Who's your tutor?'

'Ms Trippett, Sir; but she won't understand. She's too old, Sir. Things were different in her day.'

He grinned suddenly at Dom, wiping his face.

'Sir, she smells funny!'

Dom shook his head. He could hear Dr Hennock's and Mr Walker's *told you so* coming, the boy taking advantage in some way.

'Have you told anyone else?' he tried, hoping now he had.

'It's not just that, Sir. I also... it was just a bit of fun. I hacked someone's emails – Dr Hennock's. It was a dare. That boy, Andy, the year above, he dared me- said they'd all got in trouble because of me. I couldn't take a bit of teasing. It'd be cool if-. You see, I can do all this stuff he can't.'

Tom was smirking now, but then, when he saw Dom's face, his expression changed, and his head was down again. Irritation beat up in Dom. Why couldn't the kid just steer clear of Andy and his kind. Why did he make things worse for himself by messing about so much? He wondered again why he was the one to hear all this, and what he would now have to do. Then a horrible thought occurred to him that Tom, in some way, was seeking approval, thought him cool, like Andy even. It could almost have been flattering.

Professionally it was all quite clear. But a teary human being messing up in front of you...

'It's just a joke, Sir. I don't want to read his emails: they're shit boring. And everybody mucks about with IT, Sir. The government reads everything, the Chinese and Russians and Americans and big tech companies.' Sir would understand.

Dom shook his head. Tom looked down.

He looked at the top of Tom's head, spikey with a gel that was frowned on in school. His world was feeding him all these possibilities without a scrap of responsibility, making money out of him, one way or another. Who would not be twisted up with even a half understanding of what went on? And his family, even the school, maybe, were letting him down. Perhaps his parents were irresponsible – did not care. It did not take much to see that it must add up to a picture of a fake, cheating world.

Object Tom he thought.

But feeling sorry wasn't enough. A child, but so quick to temptation, and with such power, such knowledge.

'I did Hennock's because he was horrible to me. He *hates* me.'

He looked hard at Dom again, searching for something.

The boy smiled.

'I looked at some of your emails too. Are you angry with me, Sir?'

For a few seconds, Dom struggled. It had suddenly become personal: all the world, only personal. He felt betrayed in turn, but there was also bemusement, bewilderment where to go next.

He fumbled for words, wondering what would come out.

'You -you know you can't do that sort of thing. In the real world when you're grown up you could end up in prison for that. It's – it's cheating, fraud – like the story. Little lies, they grow, and just because other people, things, lie-. One wrong does not excuse another. Tom, we have to own what we do – be responsible for it, you know that. I can't keep anything you tell me like this to myself. It's serious stuff you have done.'

Tom seemed to think then.

'Is it because I looked at yours, Sir? Don't tell them, Sir. Though I spect they will find out anyway. Everyone finds out everything here. But, it's always me. Like with the fire, and Andy. I always get the blame. My dad says – I'll end up in prison.'

Dom said nothing.

'I thought, maybe, well, you'd understand. You thought it cool what I did at the start of term, when I made all the screens go Chinese.'

For a moment or two, as with his involvement with Andy, Dom's imagination leapt in alarm at a sense of some twisted personal complicity. But duty was clear.

Tom was talking on. The conversation kept coming back to his dad.

'Tom, I think the best thing for you to do is come with me now, talk to Mrs Tenace – tell her what's happened,' Dom found himself saying.

'Sir! She hates me, Sir.'

'Don't be silly: she's trying to do the best by you, help you, whatever you have done.'

'Sir. I've told you. Can't we leave this now. No one else needs to know. You understand.'

Dom shook his head.

'Come on, Tom. Let's go and see her, and see what can be done. It's best to tell the truth, be honest. Come on. Come on now.'

He led Tom out of the room, down long corridors still full of pupils, most happily preparing to go home.

At least Alison would be understanding, Dom thought,

as he walked along, hands in pockets, trying to look relaxed, trying to chat away about football for Tom's sake.

It felt, absurdly, like betrayal.

Disaster. Alison could not be found. Alison, had been called away. Alison would not be back for at least an hour. Before he knew it her secretary was phoning Dr Hennock. Tom, who had kept his head down all the time until then, looked up white-faced.

'I told you because I trusted you,' he murmured to Dom.

Hennock was busy of course. They had to wait, ages, sitting in a little anteroom to Hennock's office, a secretary tapping away, her thoughts, too, all on her home time. The boy was more and more silent; something of the seriousness of all he had done settling on him.

When Hennock was finally free the Doctor summoned them both into his office, gestured impatiently for them to sit, as usual without a word, any kind of grace.

Dom felt as if he were guilty too.

'I hope this is important. I am very busy,' said Hennock.

'Tom has something to tell you,' began Dom, firmly.

Falteringly, Tom told his story. At the end he said once more he didn't know why he did things, but he was sorry, so sorry. It wouldn't happen again, ever.

A promise.

'You hacked staff emails?' Hennock said.

Tom nodded, tears again.

Without saying another word, Hennock reached down a file and started to leaf through it.

'This happened at your last school, one of the reasons you were kicked- asked to leave,' he said at last.

Tom said nothing but hung his head.

'Whose emails exactly have you been looking at?'

Tom looked at Hennock, then at Dom.

Dom said nothing.

'*Whose* emails?' he repeated.

But Tom would say no more.

'I think they may be some of yours,' Dom confessed reluctantly, not mentioning his own.

Hennock started. For the first time since he had known him, he looked discomposed. He turned to Tom.

'Leave the room. Wait outside whilst I talk to Mr Greaves.'

Tom looked up slowly. He stared first at Dom, then at Hennock, a strange expression in his eyes.

'I said, outside. I'll deal with you in a minute.'

Tom got up slowly, and walked to the door. As he reached it, he turned back and looked at Dom.

Then he left.

'Have you read any of my hacked emails?' cried Hennock.

'No, of course not,' said Dom, surprised at the question. 'He's only just come and-'

'Are you sure?'

'Yes, of course. I say, he's only just come to me.'

'Why *you*?'

'I think he wanted to get stuff off his chest,' said Dom.

Hennock sighed.

'To you? He must think you very naive. It's quite clear what he wanted: to get out of what he's done. Can't you see what's going on around you? You know what the boy's like, what he is. We have procedures. You should have gone through his tutor or Alison. The matter should have been properly investigated straight away, without you interfering. It's a very serious business. Don't you understand?'

Dom wasn't going to apologise.

'Alison's not here. I'm not condoning anything, but he did at least fess up to it all, and to me. I think he wants, in his own way to try to explain. I've no idea why he came to me but I came straight to-you.'

Hennock snorted at this point but Dom continued.

'I thought it best to come to you in the end. You were involved.'

'What do you mean, *involved*? What have you seen?'

'He did admit it all,' Dom repeated, feeling, despite everything he had had to do, he was on the back foot now.

'So, I repeat, what have you seen and why are you defending him?'

'Nothing, how could I? I'm not- not defending him, excusing anything. He has done something awful; but, well, I do feel sorry for the lad.'

Hennock shook his head.

'You would. You're sure you saw none of the emails?'

'How could I? Why should I?' replied Dom, exasperated, puzzled that this seemed to be Hennock's main concern. Surely there couldn't be anything that important in them, even if the boy's behaviour was disgraceful. It was only school.

Suddenly, Dr Hennock was sighing, waving him away.

'That will be all. I shall have to deal with this now. You'd better get back to your work- presumably you have preparation or marking or something to do – when not indulging excuses and sob stories.'

'I think he has a tough time at home,' replied Dom, stung, indignant.

Hennock snorted once more.

'He told you that, did he? And I suppose you believe it all- like Charles liking his essay. Well, I can tell you he's about to have a very tough time *here*. In the real world, this is crime we're talking about.

'You need to learn whose side you are on, stop falling for professions of victimhood that indulge selfishness. Can't you see how kids like that target young, green staff? Send him in. I've finished with you.'

Dom wanted to argue, tell Hennock that whatever the crimes, the lad needed some understanding, a proper chance to explain, that he must have been confused, hurt to behave like that, however wrong. But arguing would just fuel Hennock's prejudices.

He had probably made another mess of things he supposed, as he crossed to the floor to leave. But he could only hope that when Alison returned she would keep empathy with Tom, even whilst operating justice.

He opened the door, relieved to be able to get out of there, wanting in part now to wash his hands of it all, fed up that he had got caught in the middle of something that was no way his fault. Impossible really.

He shut the door on the infuriating man, who always seemed to deal with problems by demeaning someone. He wished he had the nerve to slam it. It might relieve a feeling that there was something unworthy in his own behaviour as well as Hennock's.

However, of Tom, outside, there was neither sight nor sound.

CHAPTER SEVENTEEN

NIGHT ADVENTURE

'You did the right thing,' said Mr Royal, nodding his years of experience.

For once he seemed to be giving Dom some practical support.

'Fancy plagiarising. I should have guessed but my vanity was gratified.'

'At least he was trying to present something decent to you. Look what he did to Paul! What will happen to him?'

'Who knows in this place. Some silly plagiarism: it goes on all the time. But hacking staff email, that's serious, especially if it's our esteemed Deputy Head's. Ingenious isn't he? Silly tiddly pom! Perhaps he's stumbled on Darren's secret plans for Hillview. That would never do.'

Charles stared at Dom for moment, then smiled mischievously.

'Don't worry, you mustn't let little favourites upset you. These things happen: *there's no art to find the mind's construction...* The real trouble is, they're never allowed to be kids these days. Innocence died with social media.'

Mr Walker, who was there and listening, as he always seemed to be, broke in.

'O, they'll always let you down you know, *always*. First lesson of teaching. Best not to care too much. I warned you!' he observed, smiling.

At that moment, Dom did not know whether he disliked Dr Hennock or Mr Walker, more.

*

But Tom could not be found. The parents were contacted, eventually, after a hard struggle to get in touch; but they knew nothing, and, Alison told him later, seemed resigned. It had all happened before. Now the police and social services were involved. Hennock was seen in earnest conversation with Alison and the Head at lunch time but nothing more filtered down to staff. A veil of silence descended. It was as if Tom had never been.

Dom taught a class who were in the same year group. They knew.

'He was weird, Sir.'

'He never fitted in.'

'He tried to set fire to Mrs Dot's wig, burn the school down.'

'We tried to talk to him.'

'No one spoke to him apart from the twins. They're weird too.'

'He was on something.'

'Bet he never comes back.'

'Did you ever run away from school, Sir?

'Lucky git's missed three tests today, including geog, with Tosser.'

Dom's friends did not have much more sympathy.

A couple of days later, better news came. Tom had been found – with distant family friends in Wellsway. He was safe. Alison was pretty sure he would not return to school, but did not know. It was out of her hands. Social services would deal with it in their way.

What a world of sorrow at home, or wherever he is, thought Dom when he heard, but then he too got caught up. The business of the days continued. School carried on, as it always did, returning to the safety of its routines as soon as possible, whatever dramas like uncertainties over its future, or fires, or little tragedies its individuals experienced. It had an independent existence of its own – its own biological clock that ran on automatic. If there were some terrible nuclear war, Dom imagined, still the bell would ring, the feet tramp on to the next lesson, always the next lesson, the clock still ticking....

There was something in it, some saving continuity, he thought; but it alarmed him too: he could not get away from the thought that it mirrored life, real life, in some disturbing way, if he could work out how.

For a long time he almost completely forgot about Tom.

*

A few nights later, tired from another day of tough but absorbing work, with a thumping head, feeling as if he were going down with something, Dom decided to go early to bed, retiring at an hour that would have astonished him a few weeks before. He remembered someone at university who had said that she had been in bed by seven-thirty twice a week when she started teaching.

He dosed himself up, even turned his phone off, burying himself under the duvet, sleeping soundly until he woke suddenly, feeling much better and ravenously hungry, shortly after midnight. He could not be bothered to get up to find something to eat but lay there, enjoying the luxurious sense of knowing he was getting better, on the blissful edge of sleep, amused as he turned all the recent crazy happenings around and around in his head.

Then he was startled to hear quiet voices just outside his door. He sat up, suddenly wide awake, wondering if he were imagining things. Perhaps it was the ghost James had told about. He hoped not; not tonight anyway.

Murmuring continued: had this been what had woken him? For a second or two, he thought it was some prank of the boarders, perhaps those twins. He was sure they were not quite right in the head; they were certainly cheeky enough. The pupils could come up to this floor in an emergency, but there was usually no reason as they could far more easily raise Mr Jolson by ringing a bell downstairs that accessed his, and his family's flat.

The rest of the floor, outside Dom's own door, that consisted of various storerooms and abandoned small classrooms deemed unfit for use after the last inspection, could only be reached by unlocking the door next to his own on the little landing at the top of the steep stairs that led up. No one ever went down there. He had been curious to explore at first, his imagination intrigued by the place's apparent emptiness. Terry had grudgingly shown him the corridor on arrival.

'Full of crap that'll burn like tinder. If the place ever catches fire, that wing'll go up like f-in' Guy Fawkes. Know who he is?' he'd said to Dom as he handed him a key. 'Tried to blow the King and all his ministers up. Could do with that today. Needs demolishin', rebuildin' like the whole place. The little shits get everywhere at night so it'll be your job to rescue any children cookin' down there if the balloon goes up.'

Dom had lost the keys in the turmoil of the start of term. He had yet to find a reason, or summon the courage, to ask Terry for a replacement. Anyway, there had never been time to venture down there on his own, but he had not forgotten the rooms he had glimpsed.

The voices outside were going on, even and serious. They did not sound like the little shits – the children he meant of course.

He was puzzled. He sat up listening harder, straining against the white noise of darkness.

The pitch of the voices was too low for kids.

This was irritating. It might even be serious, burglars. There had been intruders, he had been warned, on campus several times last year. Some old woman had even walked in on one of the Head's great assemblies he'd been told, asking where the loos were much to general amusement. It was all open country around after all – although they must be very stupid to come up here, expect anything of value, or anything that 'f-ing works' Terry had observed.

Dom slipped silently out of bed, his feet soundless on the floor, crept to his door, knowing well by now where the creaking floorboards were.

Pressing his ear against the cold wood, he could just make out, to his astonishment, that one of the voices was Dr Hennock's – talking quietly, yes, but there was no mistaking. Dom could hear fragments of what was being said, but it faded in and out, giving little real coherence.

'This lock, I asked Terry, but of course he hasn't; unless this is the wrong key.'

'Are you sure we won't wake-' murmured another voice that sounded familiar to Dom. Wasn't it the man who had left that message on Hennock's phone?

Then he started as he heard his name.

'Boarders won't hear...Workman said he's not feeling well, gone for an early night. And we can easily deal with him if he does. It's no one's business but ours. We- ah, there we are! We'll just have a quick look, talk about the-'

The sound of a lock turning and a door opening, footsteps,

then a door shutting with a neat click. Soft footfalls receding, all magnified in the wide darkness.

Somewhere in the distance, another door closed, Dom fancied; but there were no more voices.

Crazy, Dom thought, like something out of book.

It was cold out of bed, standing there in just his boxers. He began to shiver. His stomach rumbled loudly. Thoughts of hot food came to him; the draw of his warm bed pulled. He could so easily retreat, the duvet over his head. But his senses were too alert now.

Grabbing his phone as a torch, pulling on a t-shirt, Dom cautiously opened his study door, slipping it onto the latch without a sound and went and stood outside his room taking in the quietness of the little landing, all transformed into odd shadows and shapes by the dark.

Dom could hear the ticking of a clock, somewhere the distant gurgle of water running. Otherwise, all was quiet, so quiet he began to doubt himself.

He crossed the small landing to the door putting his ear to the wood with its flaky paint. Not a sound there either. His hand felt for the old fashioned brass doorknob, cold to the touch, loose from wear, and gently but firmly turned it, pushing, expecting resistance.

It was unlocked. The door swung slowly into a dark void beyond.

Suddenly, a light came on on his little landing, startling Dom, nearly blinding him, but then he remembered it was activated by a sensor, when it worked. After only a few moments, the light tripped off as the timer registered no more movement.

No one had appeared.

Dom could breathe again.

His eyes grew accustomed to the deeper darkness as he peered down the corridor and he risked flashing his phone light around for a few moments: he must have a glimpse of what lay beyond. There were old broken desks with inkwells stacked against the walls, even a portable old-fashioned blackboard. Then there were rows of little wooden chairs, under a funny old beamed roof. Stains down the sides suggested it let the rain in. The floor was thick with dust, and, covered, disgustingly, in thousands upon thousands of dead flies. Dom had never seen so many before.

One of the doors further along the corridor seemed to be ajar. He flicked his light out imagining Hennock and his companion might still be in there.

He shrank back for a moment or two. For a few moments, he hesitated, like some conspirator himself now he thought but then, aware of the absurdity of the situation, he pulled himself together. He was doing nothing wrong, just investigating a disturbance.

Crossing the cold linoleum floor, still silently however, he tiptoed along to the open door, and boldly pushed it open. If they were there, or it were kids up to some prank, he would give them a surprise! He stepped inside, groped for a light switch, pressed it.

Nothing happened. No one there.

He shone his phone around. There was a pile of forgotten library books, a mug brought in and never taken out, dark stained from contents long dried up, a couple of dog eared exercise pads, a pile of paper, yellowed and dusty. Right at the back of the room there was another door that looked as if it led into a small stock cupboard. There were old school photos heaped up.

Dom picked one up, read its label,1973. Many of the boys had big hair, like members of some ancient band. They sported broad school ties. There were fewer girls, and they were all together in a long line, as if they were somehow different. The teachers were wearing black gowns, and looked old, old and hard. Dom took it all in, imagining a school of long ago, a pre digital era, when education was a mechanical business of listening and copying, whilst the cruel eye of some beak bullied away at the front, relentless in judgement.

He wondered if Mr Walker had been there then; but it was impossible, so long ago, another world altogether. Sometimes the immensity of time and the littleness of a life terrified. There was something mortal about school he thought, putting the picture down quickly, wanting no more of it, turning its face away from the light.

Dom went to the stockroom door, tried it, but it was locked and there was no sound from within, not that he really expected it. Anyway, they would have hardly locked themselves in a cupboard: they must indeed have come and gone, even if he could not understand quite how. Only the past lingered in the air in dust, in a strange faint smell – acrid, bitter on the tongue.

Then Dom noticed something else.

Even in the torchlight and the thin moonshine that came through the windows, even though things had been moved, everything was covered in dust, shabby, dingy- except one item: a shiny folder on one of the desks, thick with papers, leaves and dividers glinting where the cold light caught it.

He knew that it did not normally belong there. Something told him he must look at it, open its covers, see inside. It contained the essence of some deep mystery he was sure; all the little mysteries that had been piling up since he started.

Heart pounding absurdly, Dom looked back down the corridor, listened again intently for a moment or two, then closed the door, crossing the room in a flash. He hesitated for a moment or two, hearing his own breathing, knowing what he was about to go and do, daring himself along, all the time thinking of what excuse he would now have to make if suddenly discovered there, in the dark, looking at something that did not belong to him.

Hands shaking, he grabbed the folder, using his phone light to scan the contents. At first he could see little, make less sense of what he had and there was, for a second or two, a sudden overwhelming sense of anticlimax, but then his attention began to steady. He saw lists of staff names with initials by the side, then some kind of building plans, a map of the campus that looked both familiar yet different. Further in, under another section, there were letters, emails, correspondence with Wellsway District Council and something that looked like the layout of a road with building plots alongside it. There was a photograph of a hill that looked like the Cloud from what must be the other side.

Quite what he had expected he did not really know, unless the plans were something to do with Hennock's schemes for development. But then attention was drawn back to a list of familiar staff names. Some had nothing by them. Others had initials that seemed to be linked to some sort of key at the bottom of the page.

With a start he saw his own name, and then Mr Royal's, but there were no marks by them. Then he noticed Paul's name and HM with a question mark by it.

For a second or two he wanted to laugh as all the maze of events and possibilities surged in his imagination. His mate Paul was to become HM, Headmaster, no less. No wonder he was always on about what he would do if he were in charge! But then sense returned. It could not be. It must mean something else. He looked in vain for clues, scanning names over and over, turning pages, guilty but greedy to know more.

He flipped back to the section where there was correspondence with the council. There was stuff about the Cloud, letters to and from the district council, planning permission, conservation. Dom remembered the references in the meeting to development. Thoughts raced in his brain: James, his talk of lights on at night, secret passages perhaps, and here he was in some secret part of the school, with this folder of secret plans; but, again, why any secrecy, why were staff creeping around so late at night. Everyone knew that the school was thinking about change.

Nothing made sense.

Then, suddenly, to his horror, he could hear distant voices, a jangle of keys.

Hennock, his companion were coming back.

They were almost here: about to break in on him. He was caught now, spying on things that were none of his business.

But there was no time.

He had looked into the folder. He must not be discovered.

Quick as a flash, he replaced it where he had found it, squaring it up neatly on the table so that it would look as it had been left. Desperate to leave it exactly as it was before, his fingers lingered, tapping its dividers, its pages all neatly and precisely back into exact line.

The voices were even louder. A key was snagging in the lock. They must have meant to lock it. Someone was trying it again.

Panic pulsed through him.

He could not get out of the room without being seen. Thoughts of detection, shame and guilt, ridicule and humiliation, the end of his career, avalanched.

Instinct took over. He dived down as quietly as he could behind what looked like an old teacher's desk at the end of the room, heart beating so loudly he was sure it would be heard.

For an agony of seconds, he lay there, pressed down against the cold linoleum and dusty floor, a few dead, dried out fly carcasses with their paper eyes staring at him, trying not to breathe yet insanely wanting to shout out, dispel this unbearable tension.

The door opened. In they came. A torch beam flashed across the scene.

Dr Hennock, the other man: they were in the room, almost upon him.

'It's all right, it is here. I told you I left it here,' came Dr Hennock's voice quiet but firm.

'And we didn't lock the door. We need to be careful,' came a reply.

Dom finally recognised the voice, clear now. Someone who had talked – at length-to Dom at some pre-term gathering- one of the governors!

He tensed himself for discovery as they made their way across to where he had found the file. Surely they would see him behind the desk from there?

There was another blind silence. He could hear breathing. What on earth were they doing?

'We'd better go, but you wanted to see for yourself!' continued Dr Hennock. 'This all has to be kept quiet for now. Waseley mustn't get suspicious.'

'Of course,' replied the other voice, 'you don't have to keep repeating that.'

'We can discuss more tomorrow,' said Hennock, 'But you can see the potential -if, as I say, we get the money.'

Their torch clicked off. He heard the door opening.

'Coast clear!' came Dr Hennock's voice laughing quietly.

The other man chuckled back.

'A right pair of conspirators, you and I.'

There was a pause.

The door clicked quietly shut. A key turned, a lock snicking into place.

Quiet steps went their way.

After a few moments, there was no more sound.

For what seemed hours, Dom lay perfectly still, half terrified that the men were really still in the room playing some cruel cat and mouse game. Had they really left or were they there in the darkness, grey ghosts waiting for him to materialise into their world so they could seize him, carry him away across their dark threshold?

Seconds became hours. A world of time and thought passed.

It seemed to him in some strange way that he had always been there, crouched on that cold floor, awaiting discovery.

Finally he could bear it no longer. Slowly, he raised his head, expecting at any moment the torch to come on, reveal Hennock and his accomplice standing there, gloating; but the room was empty, and only cold moonlight spilled across the floor.

His legs suddenly felt cramped, numb and deadly cold. He stood up slowly, crept across the room, one leg feeling dead, his whole body shaking. He reached the door and stopped, carefully waiting before trying it, knowing already with some terrible, dawning sense of finality that it would not open.

Fraction by fraction he turned the handle, pushed, gently but firmly.

But it was no use. It was locked.

Then the thought really came down on him.

It was locked.

He was locked in!

He was trapped.

CHAPTER EIGHTEEN

DELIVERY?

Dom stared wildly around, heart thumping again. He wished and wished in vain he had never come there, never woken up, that whatever he had discovered remained unknown, undisturbed.

Futile.

He crossed to a window, peering out. But even if he could wrench it open, the drop to the ground-. He stared down and saw a narrow ledge that ran just below the window frame along the building; some sort of skirting that bordered each of the floors of this crazy old place. There was a word for it. Even Mr Jolson knew it. He remembered Mr Walker telling him some tall story – a pupil sleep walking along one of these ledges, one night, out of his dormitory, right around the building. Impossible. Yet? Might he be able to get back to his room that way? He never completely closed his windows. But if things went wrong.

He undid one of the catches, praying that the casement was not as awkward as most of them. For a moment he hesitated, the whole mad situation spinning in his head. He flirted with the idea of phoning Paul, or even Terry, to arrange a rescue, but then his presence would be revealed, everyone would know and probing questions would be asked. Hennock, his accomplice, would guess.

The same consequences beat back into his brain.

There was no choice, no choice at all. He must at least try; if things looked bad he could always climb back in. And then?

Trying not to look down he swung his legs out into the cold night air, and felt for the ledge, clinging for all he was worth to the window frame. His feet found it. Cautiously, so cautiously, he tested it with his weight. The stone was hard and sharp, rough on his feet, but it seemed firm enough; yes, it seemed safe. Please God it was safe.

Still clinging to the frame, he manoeuvred around so that he was facing the wall, not having to look down at that dreadful drop. Reaching up, the other hand gripping the wall so tightly, he pulled at the window frame, until it suddenly sliced down, snapping shut with a noisy bang and rattle.

Now he had no choice.

Dom froze there clinging on for dear life, thinking if he ever came out of it, never again would he get himself in such a ridiculous situation, and if he only ever had one wish granted him in his whole life it would be to escape this.

Sweat trickling down his body despite the chill, he started shuffling along the outside of the building, groping for handholds of any kind, clinging, clawing, wrenching his fingers first on a drainpipe that ran above the ledge, and then on the curious neo Gothic friezes of stone that adorned the outside. A cold night breeze blew against his body. He wanted to be shaking, all over. But purpose held steady. Almost blind in the dark, his face and cheeks brushing the hard cold lichen encrusted stones, he inched along, every step an eternity.

Past one window. Past another. One more to go. Don't hurry. You'll make it.

He could see his room now, casement ajar.

Soon he was only a few feet away.

Then, almost as he was reaching it, and could, with just a bit more effort, have peered in, a part of the narrow, thin stone ledge, worn away with rain and wind, began to crumble beneath his feet, a shower of debris spattering and smashing to the ground feet below. He lunged wildly at another pipe to secure himself. For a second or two he seemed suspended in time and space, only his thumping heart could be heard. He thought he was safe, then he could feel the pipe itself beginning to come away from the wall, the slow, yielding scrape of metal on stone and mortar. A trickle of dust falling on his head spelt imminent disaster. With one final wild effort he lunged along the ledge, risking all, grabbing out for the bedroom window frame, more stone dislodging, cracking, more showers of dust and debris cascading, a scatter of stone pelting the ground with an impossibly loud noise that must rouse someone.

He wrenched, strained one last time -at his own window now. His strength and courage were almost spent; his hands wet with sweat, bloody from some scrape; his clumsy, aching fingers forcing at the sash, feeling a terrible but determined strain in his arms as he levered at it, frantic with fear.

Chest heaving with exertion, he felt darkness closing in on him, suffocating, blinding; and there was terror and the edge of a despair he had not known before. Then, eventually, just as he felt his strength of will would last no longer, the sash began to yield. He pushed on, never realising until then just what he could do to himself. Slowly, slowly, every moment threatening to jam completely again, the frame began to give, fraction by fraction, till, suddenly, squealing as it went, it juddered haltingly up, and properly open.

Dom took his chance, forcing himself up onto the sill, grazing his knees, tearing into his arm and chest muscles, his fingers anguish. Now he was precariously balanced, right on some painful impossible edge that dug into his stomach, half in, half out, clinging one hand on the window sill, another wrenching still at the sash. Then snaking the rest of his body forward, lungs tearing with the effort, he wormed through, scorching chest and stomach and sides, plopping ignominiously down onto his own floor.

The window behind him poised for a few seconds, then juddered down noisily behind him: in judgement, like a guillotine.

He lay there, frozen, bloody, torn between relief at getting in, and the numbing agony of wrenched fingers, strained limbs.

Slowly the full folly of where he had been, what he had done, and where he was now came at him.

He remained for some time, curled in a foetal position, panting like some animal, nursing hands and arms, without even the strength to find a way to get up, his mind circling his triumph, his madness.

Eventually, he realised he was shaking all over with fear and cold, shock and relief.

*

When he woke early the next morning, his first thought was it had all been some terrible dream brought on by his passing fever, but, as he first worked his fingers, then tenderly felt his bruises and scratches, the whole experience came kicking back.

He got up, crossed to the window, light headed, shaky. He saw he had knocked an old-style photo of his family off the sill. It lay on the floor, frame broken. There were a few bloodstains on the rug underneath. He must get rid of these quickly he thought- like some criminal intent on hiding his crime. When he dared to look out of the window he could see the small part of the ledge that had given way with a clearly new, clean crack in the stone. Far below, in one of the flower beds that abutted the ground floor, he thought he could see a few fragments.

But that was all. No trace of anything else. No vengeful Hennock awaited out there, or at his door. No policeman had come hammering at the school gates suspecting an intruder. Terry might pause and curse one day over some fallen masonry, but there was no clue to the causes of its break.

He had got away with it.

Awe at what he had done, the risks he had taken, embarrassment at his stupidity surged again but simple, simple relief was the overwhelming feeling. The rest he pushed out of his mind – for now.

Looking in the mirror, after he showered, he saw how white his face was. His fingers were stiff, more bruises appearing on his hands, both arms aching like mad, a bump and scrape on his forehead mostly covered by his dark hair. He cleaned himself up as best he could, washed away the marks on the rug, put his boxers, t-shirt to soak. He dare not give them direct to Mrs Tombs.

Pin your socks together!

What would she say if she ever found out?

*

'You all right, Sir? You look ill?'

'You been in a fight, Sir?' came from a couple of pupils later in lessons. But their curiosity was come and gone in a moment.

When his thoughts steadied, and the shock of what might have been fell back a little in the business of the day, he was able at last to think a bit more rationally about what he might have discovered. Clearly there was more going on than had been declared in the staff meeting. At the heart of it was Dr

Hennock ready with some secret plan for the school's future. There were clues in that file to something quite radical, not just building plans, but projections about staff futures that he bet they knew nothing about, restructuring on a huge scale. This must be some plot to deliver a new organisation entirely, however Waseley sought to present things.

So much for change being a long way down the line. He wondered if there had been any real staff consultation. But how-and why? And exactly how those two wandering around at night in a pretty derelict old part of the school fitted in he had no idea.

Whatever, Dom would find out- sooner or later. He was determined now: his battle had taught him that if nothing more. Despite what he had put himself through, he knew he had to find out more.

He ought to tell someone; but if he did, then it was his job, his career at stake. For all his trials so far, for all the clear uncertainties over the school's future, explicit and covert, he knew that mattered, really mattered to him more than he would have guessed even a few weeks ago. And he still had something to prove here- to himself, if no one else.

Then, with a sharp sinking feeling, it crossed his mind that he was behaving in some strange way like that boy, Rymer: invading privacy, taking secret possession of someone else's information, sneaking around and spying: childish really; but that comparison would only go so far. Tom was a kid, innocent, because of his age; Dom was, or was supposed to be, grown up. And in the cold light of day he had not a scrap of real evidence to hand, only his mad experience, and who would believe that, or if they did, take him seriously, trust him again.

*

Later that day, when he was recovered sufficiently, he hinted at things to Paul about the Deputy Head and his plans. He had considered tumbling out with the whole story, but something held him back from opening up completely. He remembered Hennock saying that he had heard from Paul that he was taking an early night. They were close those two.

Dom tackled Paul: what was really up in the school.?

'I hear rumours!' was Paul's cryptic reply. 'Hennock, Waseley – clashes – bit of a power struggle, I told you: Darren is angling on taking over. He's undertaking some kind of staff review, responsibilities and duties, all that, on a big scale. I had an interview on the subject last week, nothing formal. Hennock wanted a representative from the new staff. I was asked how I saw my future, what role I would like. I'm sure he'll get round to you in due course,' said Paul, patronisingly.

'I told him he should-.'

Paul was off once more, but as he talked on, Dom dwelt on his own conduct, both the night before and now. He hated the idea of hypocrisy, duplicity, people who kept secrets – all part of that littleness he claimed to despise; yet here he was being disingenuous with a so-called mate, hiding all sorts. And remaining still largely in the dark about what was going on.

He wondered if he dare broach the subject with anyone else. Mike would not take it seriously; Emma would think him nuts, would never keep things secret. She was too direct, open. He circled back to how little he could say without disclosing his own behaviour.

For the moment, he was stumped.

*

All too soon school routine, as ever, took over. He got lost once more in it all. In the days that followed, he saw little enough of anyone but pupils, had no time to do anything practical about his discoveries and conjectures, search for his lost key, contemplate another adventure as if he were in some crazy thriller. Indeed, as his strange adventure settled into uneasy memory, part of him was glad to be, as staff put it, 'under the radar' for a bit; busy with business, not excitement.

*

If his newly discovered role as some kind of detective could make no immediate advance, he was, without always realising it, making some progress as a schoolmaster, perhaps more so as a person.

He had to admit he had yet to earn a sense of authority, but he was enjoying some of his teaching and lessons more and more. And the job had its rewards. If he had been older he might have been able to reflect on the fact that what gave him most satisfaction was not the pursuit of some high ideal or mission, academic or even investigative, but simply helping, serving others.

It was a lonely journey, though, as recent events had underlined. But what did he expect in a job world? Had he imagined when he started, in a rather vain way, that they must somehow celebrate him with open arms- him and his arrival? Had there been a degree of arrogance somewhere in his behaviour, his expectations of what he could do? He even flirted for a moment, but not for too long, with the idea that the things in which he was involved were not exclusively about him.

But for all his broader reflections, he kept coming back to the realisation that he was on his own in a way he had not been in his life before.

He had been used to a close family, then the friendships of university that had become a second, solid community that still endured; he was catching up with his friends as soon as half-term came. In the past, companionship had been a given. He had even had his share of rather clumsy romances. So there had always been a net of support. At work, however, there seemed to be almost no time for anything like a private or social life. Had Dom underestimated the dedication he needed to master his roles? Was this what made the older and wiser Emma so critical?

Then there was this thing; he could only put it to himself rather vaguely: you felt a more overt sense of rivalry in almost every relationship at work in school. You had, he was learning, to cover your back. Perhaps that did not always include with all the pupils, but with the children you must keep your distance, even if, ironically, some of the best professional moments seemed to come when barriers went down. Mostly, you had to act, dissemble, at least to some degree to save something of yourself for yourself. Mr Walker was full of lurid stories warning of staff who had crossed the staff pupil boundary, sometimes in minor, inadvertent ways, sometimes spectacularly.

If he had had a partner, things might have been easier, but even with those who had paired up, the Mikes and Emmas of his world, had almost no time for themselves.

Sometimes he tried not to examine his feelings about those two closely. At least he had thrashed Mike in a game of squash recently.

Most of the staff, he saw, were married. Many had kids: so life, meaningful social life as well as meaningful work must be possible. But how on earth did you realise it all, especially when you wanted rather a lot – including that vague something more he told himself was important – and no imperfections on the way to it of course.

When – rarely – he had time, his precious downtime, Dom would reflect on such topics, but definitive conclusions remained frustratingly elusive.

Progress of sorts, yes, he felt that; but delivery of some of those dreams he had for his job, his life: they were still just dreams; and time was melting away.

CHAPTER NINETEEN

GETTING RESULTS

One afternoon, a few days later, came a clear professional drop.

He had had a trying lesson with a class who had been in a mood of resilient apathy despite his best efforts. Dom decided to attempt to find his way with Mr Royal. Maybe he could learn from the man's vast wisdom and experience, if he pushed harder. Had pride kept Dom from admitting just how confounded he could still be some days, he wondered? Surely, progress was defined by a straight line – not ups and downs?

'Charles, what can I actually do about boys, girls who simply won't, well, cooperate, don't want to work, do anything! Some of them seem, well just childish, selfish!'

Dom stopped. Words like that applied to children were discouraged – like calling someone stupid, or thick.

'They just go their own way in things,' he corrected himself. 'Some aren't interested, whatever I do. I try so hard, but-. Come on, Mr Roy- Charles. You been teaching forever. I mean years. Is it me? A beginner? Are they just trying it on because I'm new? What do I do, *practically*? There has to be a key!'

Royal regarded him for a few moments, smiling. Dom wondered where he would land.

'Ah, young Socrates sips the cup of hemlock,' he said in his way.

But Emma, who happened to be in the room marking, and was part of Dom's reason for being there, broke in.

'Dom's right. What do you do with pupils who do nothing! We have an educational philosophy of excuses here, *they're only children*. Aren't they supposed to be growing up? Look at Andy. Nothing was ever done about that business. What's the good of a final warning? It's like telling a serial killer to stay in for a few nights! When I do put them in detention, I get criticised – burdening the system, passing on my problems, not dealing with it myself. And the children resent it; and I still don't get a scrap of work out of them. *Nothing happens.*'

'They all work hard for me,' cried Mr Royal, grinning mischievously. 'You exaggerate, my dear.'

Dom could see Emma bridle. Charles rarely made things easy.

'Read your handbook? Listened in meetings? Remember, we don't have disciplinary problems here,' he added infuriatingly.

Dom was about to challenge, but Emma got there first.

'Don't you think that form of address is a little out of date, even here? And you know what they say about sarcasm. Come on!' Emma replied, continuing to tick and flick. 'What about more hard advice for us newbies? We don't know the kids like you yet. Aren't they allowed to get away with too much? The systems are slack. In the real world-.'

'Ah, Emma's real world. You mean the world of clawing adults on the make, ruthlessly excising anything that is not immediately efficient, mistaking productivity for creativity, devil take the hindmost. Is that the world you wish for; keep their noses to the grindstone so they can get those results, be someone else's unthinking masters or slaves in turn?'

'Very clever, but that's not what I mean, you know it. Everything should be better, tighter, in a small outfit like this.'

Mr Royal laughed,but Emma was not to be deterred.

'Aren't we supposed to be teaching fairness in holding people responsible for what they do? I'm not asking for world revolution: some justice now and again would be a start,' she declared.

'Like with some bankers, politicians, or, dare I say it, those who advertise, market things: more interested in the product, the sale, the money than people,' rejoined Mr Royal.

'That's not fair!' cried Katie Trippett who happened to be in the room. 'But we do need stronger middle management in this place,' she looked pointedly at Charles

Mr Walker, who was hovering as well, had to intervene.

'Ah! If only more women like Katie were in charge, or ruled the world, eh? Some of our problems, in fact, come from a feminisation of the classroom. We're all bleeding hearts today. Authority, integrity emasculated – for fear of ever upsetting children. We're frightened of their tears, frightened of the dears.'

There was the outcry he intended at his ditty.

'Here we go, Emma!' cried Katie. 'What Ian and Charles really believe is that education's failings come about because there are too many women involved today. They can't really cope, hack it -when they're not off having children that is. Actually, it's the female staff who do all the heavy lifting here: look at the trip I'm taking at half-term.'

'Now, Katie, no need to show your claws. I merely point out that not upsetting the children – as we call it, has rather eclipsed some of the more traditionally masculine approaches to education, and what it's about. Men are scared of going into teaching today, and vulnerable in a culture of little snowflakes. We're all mummies, today, if you'll pardon my pun,' Mr Walker replied much to Mr Royal's amusement.

'Oh, ignore them; they'll grow up one day. Men!' cried Katie, moving off to take a phone call.

Emma looked after her for a moment, then stared hard at Charles and Mr Walker.

'I'm sorry if we still have a sense of humour,' came from Mr Royal then. 'What a world if we can't make or take a joke or two. But Ian has *something* in what he says. If we lose a sense of reason, objectivity, and the world becomes only how we feel today – only teach wellbeing, and some pretentious ideal of social conscience dictated by modern ideas of fairness, we're in danger of losing the plot. The results are all around us. Can't people see connections? Education is not some giant dummy to suck on.'

Dom did not understand what Mr Royal was saying, but winced at the last remark. He looked at Emma. She had stopped marking, was frowning. Charles paused. Katie had put the phone down, was looking angrily across. She gathered her things.

'Darren. I'm going to see him now,' she said, looking meaningfully at Charles, and left the room abruptly.

There was an awkward silence.

'But what do we *do*, practically, when kids won't work, or won't do what they are reasonably asked, when they're just silly,' faltered Dom, trying to get things back onto safer ground, if there was any.

'There's not that much you can do, just *try to save the best, not let it be destroyed by the rest*,' replied Mr Walker, pleased with a second ditty. 'Look at the world about you, history. Look at all the wars, disputes, unfairness: the strong, the confident take what they want, the weak get trampled. Human nature. All the teaching in the world won't change that much. One generation after another. The world is hardly getting wiser. The results are always the same.'

'No, no, Ian. I can't agree with you there. Even I'm not that cynical! These youngsters,… another generation, new blood, Dom, Emma, maybe they can find a way. Let them try, see if they can do more, do better than we have done. Perhaps they can. Perhaps they can.'

'You've changed your tune. It was all going to hell in a handcart after that staff meeting.'

But Mr Royal ignored him, began addressing Dom and Emma.

'What do you do? Your best, for them all, of course,' replied Charles. 'Certainly be kind for a start. We're all here to learn to be kind to one another; that's a large point of education, understanding. And then try thinking, without going too far to appease them, why should they work for me? And do I work hard enough for them? Do *I* deserve it, have I earned their *trust*? And do I really care about them, respect them, not just their results, or as they function in my subject, my interests, but as people, individuals. And never never ever give up on anyone.'

'That's hardly practical. How can you possibly do all that for each and every one?' began Emma who had been shaking her head.

'And that's why it's a difficult but amazing job!' returned Mr Royal, but before he could continue, Mr Walker interrupted.

'You mustn't take it so personally. People give up all the time, too easily, especially young teachers. That's the consequence of having so many women in the profession: everything's got soft!'

Dom and Emma cried out at this.

'And that's the exact opposite of what Charles has just been saying, surely about sensitivity to the individual?'

pursued Emma. 'And if we're going down that ridiculous route, hasn't human history been all about male selfishness and aggression, male vanity and ego- a childish desire to dominate, be the centre of attention. Look at Andy!'

'We're all children,' sighed Mr Royal.

'But none so childish as those who put feelings above reason!' cried Mr Walker as if it proved his case.

'Which of course is never a male characteristic.'

'Not exclusively: extreme feminism has done its best to assert its equality in that department.

Emma rolled her eyes at Dom.

'I must go,' she declared gathering her things, 'before I get angry.'

She left, casting a withering look at both Mr Walker, and at Charles who seemed to have subsided into deep thought. Mr Walker hurried off too, realising he was neglecting a duty somewhere, winking at Charles as he went. His smirk was not returned.

Dom and Charles were left alone.

So much for finding a key Dom thought.

Unlike Mr Walker, however, Charles did not look pleased.

'Ian and I… we set each other off. Two old bigots. But I'm not going to be bullied into silence – not saying things that might have some truth in them because someone gets upset, might disagree,' Mr Royal began.

'I know. I'm an old man. None so foolish. Ian's worse, getting worse. Ignore us! But Emma, she always bangs on about girls, women, rightly – but the problems! It's bigger than that. It's our culture, our ways of living that are wrong – academic education alone can't stay all that. I used to feel sorry for the girls in education; but today it's a lot of the boys who are lost. They want to push boundaries, test themselves, lock horns with what they're told to do and think – and they need heroes, characters to inspire, to believe in, follow. All that's too easily seen as patriarchal, hierarchical, competitive, divisive or some such. Look what they get! They have to come alive in some virtual or social media world, endless mindless computer games. Sport is their only real release. Art, music, even drama used to be a way out: for the imaginative, but so few read or imagine now: it's all there in zeros and ones, digital, *virtual* – an ironic word if ever there was one. And people wonder why things are going wrong!'

'Don't people always blame the latest change – technology for what happens? And you don't believe all the things you come out with,' ventured Dom.

'Don't I? Ah, Dominic is beginning to learn, to challenge!' cried Charles smiling at him 'A heap of contradictions, aren't I?'

But then he looked more thoughtful, his eyes looking the way Emma had gone.

'But Emma, now. Forceful isn't she? Opinions! Good. I don't really mean to upset her. And I can see why you might want to defend her, whatever comes out of her mouth. I would certainly have been as delighted as you to have her as a colleague when I was young.'

Dom felt uncomfortable. A sudden surge of self consciousness at Charles's shift of tack might have led to a red face; but luckily Emma came back into the room at the moment looking for an exercise book she had left behind. He could turn away. Meanwhile, Charles looked from Emma to Dom, was about to say something when Katie returned with Hennock, a wide smile on her face.

'An urgent word with you, Charles,' Dr Hennock announced to the room, as if it were a class, and he were about to take a child out to dress him down.

Dom made to leave, but Hennock had no use for others' feelings. He gestured to Dom to stay put.

'This concerns your department. Emma, too. Come here.'

'Busy,' she began.

'This is more important,' replied Hennock evenly.

He waved a sheaf of print outs at Mr Royal.

'Summer exam remarks,' he announced, seeming to savour his moment. 'They have arrived.'

He paused again, used his light smile.

'All unchanged, Charles. Very disappointing isn't it?'

For a second or two, Mr Royal seemed at a loss.

'That's quick; but there you are you see: don't say I didn't tell you. The exam boards, they have got wise to students trying to up their marks by having them marked again.'

Dr Hennock said nothing, but looked down at the spreadsheet in his hand. He waited another moment then handed them to Mr Royal.

Dom could almost imagine he had seen Charles's hand shake.

'Oh, this is nonsense. The board is just trying to fob off its bad marking. David was far better than-'

Hennock cut him off.

'They have been marked twice. They can't all be bad markers.'

'They close ranks. You know that, when challenged,' cried Mr Royal. 'And half of them these days don't know whether or not what they mark is right or wrong. The exam board employs students, people as young as Emma, or even Dom. They were never a good group.'

'So disappointing. What shall you say to them now, their parents? I see you are free. We need to have a good look at these, formulate some strategy to move things forward. This level of attainment. After all your years of experience. You must be devastated.'

Dom noticed Emma looking awkward too, but Katie seemed all enjoyment.

'That happened on training at my last school with some of the English results,' Dom said; but no one was listening to him.

Hennock took Royal away. Katie followed, still smiling.

Emma and Dom both looked at each for a few moments, thinking the same thoughts but saying nothing.

'Education isn't about results,' began Dom, indignant on Mr Royal's behalf.

'It is if the results of what you're testing are shite,' replied Emma. 'I'd have more respect for him, and sympathy, if he didn't come out with nonsense at times, especially when Ian is around.'

Emma returned her attention to her search for the missing book.

'We all know he's a great teacher, but if results are crap, and his drinking – he leaves himself vulnerable.'

Dom just shook his head.

'Oh come on, it's an open secret. Typical of this place everyone knows. No one does anything. Haven't you noticed the aftershave. It's there to hide the smell on his breath.'

'We could do with some push back in this place, even if some of what he says is nuts.'

'Good, you're starting to learn.'

'At least he thinks for himself,' continued Dom, ignoring her. 'And yes, I had noticed; but, I'm not sure it's the drink that's speaking.'

'What is it then?' said Emma ignoring Dom's defence. 'Hennock knows, has that on him. Paul tells me he has been given an official warning. Katie said it was final.'

She would thought Dom.

'I think you're being a bit hard on him. We should be loyal. The kids love him,' said Dom.

'You're in awe of him aren't you? Too much in awe. People are never quite what you think you know: it's not a good idea to look up to them, or anybody.They only come crashing down.'

Dom rolled his eyes. Everyone seemed cynical today.

'I wonder what his problem is?' continued Emma to herself, then looking at Dom seriously for a moment.

Suddenly, she smiled.

'Mind you, I think if I had been here that long I would have taken to something stronger-... what's that horse stuff, ketamine? I can't find this wretched girl's book – I'm going to have to pretend I've left it at home, or accuse her of losing it, or eating it or something. She's been pestering me to know her mark since the second she handed it in. I wonder if they have any idea how long it takes actually to mark their masterpieces. Maybe she's sold her manuscript for a million pounds and I will appear one day on national media as the evil bitch who tried to destroy her love of English forever at that school which went bust when it tried to go independent. I must go- if you are going to observe me later, be kind. And it's not my fault if it's boring. I'm not having a good day, and I'm determined to take it out on the children.'

How could it ever be boring, Dom thought, grinning, with Emma around.

CHAPTER TWENTY

OBSERVATIONS

Later the same day, Dom was sitting in one of Mr Royal's lessons doing one of his scheduled observations. It had been a revelation. The man was a different person in his classroom, a lion in his domain.

'What you say is marvellous!' Mr Royal was enthusing to one pupil as they tackled Dom's own recent cross, *Pride and Prejudice*. 'Look what Lizzie replies when pompous Darcy presumes to propose. She demands he takes her seriously like the rational creature she is. Your reference is spot on: look at that word *rational*, reason, the great objective faith of Austen's world before truth morphs into romantic subjectivity. Everything becomes only about feelings and the potential for anarchy; what we might call our *my truth* world, takes over!' he said with a wink at Dom.

'Yet Lizzie is being true to herself as we all must be. And that of course is literature's and all great art's strength, but Austen shows the importance of feeling *and* reason. You can't just have a *my truth* world. You see, she was there centuries ago before all the flummery of today's debates.'

But Royal in performance sounded not merely deep, wise, his lessons were inspiring conversations, a master but no dictator of opinion, eloquent on all that mattered, and making what might seem dull interesting, transcendent. On he drew his pupils, up and out into new worlds, leading them beyond previous horizons with humour, energy and sheer delight. He opened it all out for them, simplifying without simplification, yet it was an entertainment too, never a collection of dull activities pushed at for the sake of variety.

At one moment Mr Royal had been teaching his class something about the upside-down nature of their world, how you needed to change perspective to see things freshly. Suddenly he was doing a handstand, much to Dom's surprise: an old man should be way beyond that. At another he was on about how literature, like all great art was really inspiring us to be different, to be creatively dissatisfied with anything and everything ordinary. This was delivered lying on his desk. Next moment he had the pupils up and moving around to see if they agreed with various propositions they had come up with, he had made concise, and posted at different points round the room to get debate going.

He acted, lived, loved, believed,what he was doing.

Most of all he kept finding the words Dom could only dream of to light all that old ink into living, blazing relevant thought and meaning.

Dom looked around the class. They were *listening*. Some were busy taking notes, without being nagged – indeed, two of the girls seemed to be at his altar, transcribing everything Charles said. Only a boy called Robin seemed in his own world, but even he would contribute at times: precise, sharp challenging points.

The class played out of their skins to the baton of his words.

Dom sat there wondering, could you bottle it?

About halfway through the lesson, Mr Royal made some excuse, went out of the room.

The group got on with a discussion, all on their own, without hassle or strife, taking up his themes, and their own.

'Enjoying it?' said the boy, smiling.

'I wish I could teach like that,' said Dom.

'He's cool, deep: bit weird!' said Robin.

The rest protested, rallying to Royal's defence.

'We all know where he's gone,' said the boy then, taking back ground.

There was an awkward silence.

One or two stole looks at Dom.

He pretended to be busy with his papers.

When Mr Royal walked back into the classroom, the smell of aftershave was strong.

*

Follow that, he thought, as he moved on to watch Emma.

He wondered at the wisdom of two observations in a day – and it was last lesson of the afternoon; but Dr Hennock had insisted he did two lessons consecutively to understand pupil experience better, just how hard it was for them, especially with young teachers, when they did not prepare properly.

He got there before her, sitting down as the pupils drifted in, looking vaguely at him. Then, when it didn't seem as if he were tooling up to teach them, or anything dire like that, they ignored him.

Dom felt odd, in someone else's room, neither teacher nor taught, neither one side of the desk nor the other. It was the limbo of the start of term once more.

He looked out of the window.

It was a glorious day. October had arrived with a return of summer. As he had walked across to where Emma taught, inspired, treading on air at what could be, he had been further moved by the waiting stillness of the gentle day. He wished today's tasks could have ended there and then in a quiet rapture of possibilities. How strange education was. He must remember not to tell pupils off when they stared out of a window. Why shouldn't they free their minds, now and again, from what they were being told; there was always more, so much more if you were open to it.

Maybe Emma would fire up her class as Mr Royal had, as he hoped to. But perhaps many lessons were bound to be just forgettable, not some earth shattering epiphany for one and all. What could he remember of so many he had been through himself, unless someone threw a strop, did something comical or ridiculous like Andy. Maybe some days, average days, looking out the window must be the best of it.

When Emma still did not arrive, the class actually began taking out books, settling to work she had left. Dom could not imagine any of his classes doing that.

Then a red-haired lad near him, who seemed rather at a loss as to what he should be doing, started staring at him.

The boy looked around as if it were all a bit beyond him, returned his gaze to Dom, regarding him, with a strange, intense yet blank stare. Dom wondered for a moment if the boy had any kind of real connection at all with what was going on. He pretended not to notice, avoiding eye contact. He sensed something disturbing, a quality in some curious way, quite unreachable.

Then the red-haired boy spoke.

'What *you* doing here?'

There were a few giggles, comments; but heads were soon down again at work.

Dom said quietly, 'Observing another teacher.'

'She's not here,' said the red-haired lad, still looking at Dom, almost through him.

'She's late. She's always late,' muttered someone.

'Don't you know how to teach? I told you. She's not here,' said the red-haired lad. 'She's not here. Why you here?' he repeated.

There were murmurs, laughter from some, but when the lad looked at them they seemed wary, turning back to their work as the boy resumed bold scrutiny of Dom.

'We're all here to learn!' quipped Dom. It sounded cheesy.

'*Two* teachers?' said the boy, intransigently, but more in a tone of incredulity than contempt.

Dom thought it best to ignore him, and studied the intricate observation form Dr Hennock had given him.

It didn't seem to have a box for this lad.

Out of the corner of the eye he could see the red-haired boy continuing to regard him, without response, without emotion, as if it were possible to look without seeing anything at all; but Emma was walking in then: the atmosphere changed except that the gaze of the lad remained riveted on him, confounded perhaps by the arrival of someone who only a few moments ago had simply not been there.

Dom, despite himself, felt his heart move when Emma appeared. A confusion of emotion swept through him. He looked past her, then back at her as if he were casually distracted by something beyond, but so his glance could rest fully on her, as if by accident. Then he must look away.

He chided himself for his silliness: what on earth was going on – just like a pupil with some crush. Grow up.

Emma was brisk, direct, telling them what they were going to be doing, why. It was to be a lesson on *The Merchant of Venice*. Soon, she was talking animatedly about heroes and villains, the strange character of Shylock, who might belong to both worlds. Dom sat there, quite entranced, not wholly for professional reasons.

'Right!' Emma said a few moments later. 'Anyone know any famous British Jews?'

'The Pope,' responded a girl in the front row, all seriousness. Those who were listening and understood the mistake, tittered, and then came groans of disapproval directed more at the girl than her error. Emma jumped on the perpetrators, told the girl off. There were names up on the board, some punishment system that seemed to have them. The girl looked mortified. Emma did not care to notice.

She gave a swift and sure – footed definition of Catholic and Jewish religions, followed by a handout, a worksheet, but before anyone could catch breath, she was commanding silence, focus on the task in hand. A timer was ticking the seconds away.

Some of the pupils picked the piece of paper up, handling it as if it were faintly radioactive. Devices were the norm these days, what was this prehistoric offering? Perhaps if they left it alone it would go away. But it didn't. Most settled to the task. No quips, no banter, no red herrings: just focused work, even with this lot, all end of day-ish.

This was business.

Time passed. Even the red-haired pupil bent to his sheet but not before casting surreptitious looks around to see what others might be doing.

They were so quiet, so disciplined. Dom couldn't imagine any of his classes, remaining so silent for this long, not questioning, protesting, distracting.

'Is Shylock Jewish?' came a voice eventually, breaking the silence.

Another name up on the board.

For a while, then, it seemed, no one dared say anything.

Dom looked around the room, once more. In Royal's lessons there had been a sense of sharing, of conversation, of relaxed cooperation. Emma was clear, well prepared, firm, no nonsense. She didn't have the brightest and best as perhaps Charles had. But she was efficiently ticking all the boxes on the sheet prepared for him.

His eyes found the window again, the soft light, the impossible colours of the trees outside, smudged in golden misty autumn air and the gentlest imaginable sunshine. From somewhere on campus, smoke was rising: Terry burning leaves perhaps, or effigies of staff, pupils, Mrs Dot.

Dom found himself having to force his mind back inside.

The red-haired boy kept breaking off from his worksheet, boring a nib deep into the woodwork of his desk, going back to his laboured, scratchy writing, patiently returning over and over to the digging of a tiny tunnel. Dom thought of that boy Tom kicking away at a football, Mr Royal's comments about boys in school. Terry would have something to say about the damage.

Emma was wrapping up this part of the lesson. She pulled the threads of the thoughts they had been gathering together with swift, simple clarity. There was a lot to take in, but she made it clear, straightforward, almost matter of fact.

Now she was getting them to act a scene at the end.

Would she ask the red-haired lad?

Perhaps he could be a master actor after all. Dom could have him in the next play, make something of him, bring him alive, back from wherever he had gone.

Emma became impatient. They mangled words terribly. She jumped on them so they dare not laugh at each other. They seemed glad to stop, as if dropping a burning baton, when it was no longer their turn.

Not teaching himself, Dom had time to imagine the dark side of their plight: the text only an obstacle on some long and difficult road to the horror of an examination. For now they could walk round the play, trying to avoid it really-tongues labouring, minds fumbling. Some dark tomorrow, it would be back: a weight on the shoulders, making slaves of them. Best for now just to try to ignore it altogether.

His night adventure came back to him then for some reason: the simple relief when it was over.

Dom felt every moment of the last ten minutes of the lesson.

The red-haired lad, he had noticed, before the bell finally rang, had shut his eyes: unseen, unseeing, quite closed up in some nothing of his own.

'Sir, can you teach us instead? They say your lessons are a laugh,' said a boy to him later as he wandered away after thanking Emma rather sheepishly for the lesson.

*

Emma and Dom caught up properly later by arrangement at The White Hart. Paul, and Mike were to join them later.

''nother good day at the chalk face?' grinned the landlord who was getting to know them, read their faces.

'You two teachers? Hillview?' piped up a bearded wag at the bar, looking Emma and Dom over. 'Teachin' teens? Couldn' hack it meself, teachin' kids who think as they know it all. Little s-s, I bet.'

'Just about sums today up,' began Emma, as they sat down in their favourite place, by the ever burning fire. 'Deadly dull, wasn't it? Don't be kind. I still can't believe how some of them react. They can't all be that thick – thinking the Pope was Jewish. So little general knowledge, no interest in what they don't know; that's what gets me. But you can't blame me for that. I've only just started. What has education done to them? Ten years in the system, and the outcome? They can barely read or write some of them-as for thinking! Perhaps Waseley trips them up on the street outside, forces them in.'

'That's what Terry says,' said Dom, laughing, not quite sure what to say about the lesson.

Emma was silent, unhappy with herself, her performance.

For a moment, Dom wondered if it were more. He thought how little he really knew about her still. He didn't want her to be sad.

'I don't think I was very positive at school, looking back. I didn't know much,' said Dom. But he couldn't agree with what she said about the kids, even if he felt it at times. It seemed some kind of betrayal.

But Emma was continuing.

'I wasn't that interested at school, but I had drive. And please don't say I was privileged, background – so on. I was a pain – typical teenager: moody, stroppy, always arguing, full of what everyone else should think and do, your basic nightmare; but I *cared*, wanted to do well!' she paused, looking sad.

'What's with that red-haired kid – I know you shouldn't use the term, protected characteristics and all that; but he seemed lost?' asked Dom, not knowing quite what to say.

'O, God, *him*, Declan! I've tried.Tried and tried over, kept him back after class time after time. Learning support told me: give him more help, then they criticised what I did, said he still didn't get it. Talk about space cadets. There's thirty pages of notes on him: dos and don'ts; but nothing gets through. I can't make things any simpler. But the lesson; no, it just died on me. Your being there didn't help. But I won't put up with them not trying, messing about, however hard it is for them. They're in for a shock otherwise when they have to work for a living, go into the real world.'

'I suppose it doesn't mean enough to them yet.You kept on top of them,' said Dom. 'I wish I could. You should hear what they say sometimes. At least Hennock wasn't there.'

'You're too soft. But they like you. What was Charles's lesson like?'

'Brilliant, absolutely brilliant. I know, experience and everything, but I wish I could teach like that.'

'Somehow that doesn't help. Maybe if I rolled in intoxicated or high-singing *somewhere over the rainbow* they would respond,' replied Emma.

Dom laughed. He looked hard at Emma. Her head was down, looking into her drink. She did seem out of sorts. He could not make her out: so confident, experienced, business-like – everything going for her, yet she was so hard on the school, pupils, now herself.

'Sometimes, sometimes, I wonder if I have done the right thing, teaching,' she said eventually.

'Don't say that. Don't be silly,'said Dom, but surprised, flattered by a confidence. 'I – we – the school needs people like you.'

Emma shook her head.

'No, you don't. You and Paul and Mike – you all fit. Not sure about me-if it's my thing.'

'It's just a bad day. The first year is supposed to be a nightmare; they told us that. You should see some of my-. The lesson was fine.'

Emma said nothing.

'If I'm honest, it was a bit of a relief seeing you with your class, not that it was bad or anything, but after watching Charles!' he said eventually, feeling a bit more honest.

Emma laughed.

'Because it was crap! But no, it won't do. They're going to come round, do well, or I'm off. I'm not going to let them get away with anything but doing better. No fifteen-year-olds get the better of me.'

'Competitive, aren't you? Success or bust. You want to be best, don't you?'

Emma looked at him and laughed.

'Quick aren't you? Yes, I want to be the best, or at least as good as I can whatever I do.'

She looked into the fire for a few moments, light shining in her eyes.

'Can I tell you something? You must wonder why I'm teaching, came out of marketing. That really was all about results, money. Not much creative or romantic about that. I got into it through family connections. Long story. But if this doesn't work I won't hang about. I've already proved that. Maybe I'm just tired, exhausted today. But I don't think people in the real world have any idea what a big job teaching is. I'm serious. I don't mind hard work. It's not my character to give in, but the money's dreadful, the hours never-ending. What's life for? Lessons like today when nothing comes back, the feeling you're banging your head against various brick walls: difficult kids, staff stuck in the past, specs designed by head in the cloud academics, no proper systems, dodgy finances, now all this malarkey about the school's future, and: it's *just a job*.'

Emma hadn't got it right there, Dom knew that much.

'Charles, all the old teachers, say it gets easier. Experience, getting used to it. Maybe, we need to give it time.'

'We?' said Emma. 'And getting used to things- sounds deadly to me.'

She looked up briefly, smiled, then looked down again.

'Perhaps it just isn't me. As I said, it's right for you,' she said. 'They like you.'

'You said that. Some of them don't: Rachel, Andy.'

'Don't mention him!'

She checked her phone.

'Where on earth is Mike? He's so laidback, never on time, casual about everything. I suppose that's what attracts people to him. We're so different really. I wonder why I am going out with him sometimes.'

'Come out with me instead then. I'm much more interesting, nicer, and better looking.'

Emma laughed, then looked serious.

'Ever feel you are watching your own life go by, playing a series of games, and you, you're not really inside any of it?' she said.

He could say much, but where to begin; but then Mike and Paul bustled noisily in, full of their day, the business of school.

A moment was come and gone. Emma was Mike's.

They all had to leave shortly. There was so much to be done now that term was well under way, not least, sooner than any of them could credit, reports, some due the very next day, tracking, measuring, justifying, explaining in as much you could explain.

Outside, it felt much colder. The year was getting on. Dom looked up at another magnificent sky in the deep dark of a country night. He'd rarely seen so many stars before. They glinted sharply down from other worlds, scarcely possible to imagine. How could such a spectacle not promise some ultimate sense to it all?

He had to give Paul a lift back to school whilst Mike and Emma were off to her flat in town.

The car windscreens were icy, opaque so that when they climbed in they were suddenly shut in little dark kingdoms of their own, their breaths steaming, curling like flags in front of them.

Even though Paul was, as ever, full of ideas for change at Hillview, and Hennock's plans for this and that, including some postponed Chinese students' visit, Dom's thoughts lay elsewhere, mostly round Emma: all the things he had not said. He could not forget their conversation, her openness, doubts, feelings.

Nor, for some reason, could he forget that poor, weird red-haired kid, though he'd forgotten his name already.

The stars above- perhaps what they promised was not there some days, many days even, for some.

It was only illusion.

CHAPTER TWENTY-ONE

BULLY

Time passed. Unbelievably quickly. Lessons, days, came and went, and then, almost before Dom knew it, eight weeks, two whole months, had gone by.

It was getting to half term when, one day, an email popped into Dom's inbox. The teacher in him, he noticed, as he scanned it, had become so much more sensitive now to mechanical errors, but the contents were not uninteresting.

Hi sir

I expect you are suprised to here from me at all but I wanted to say thank you. You tried to help me when I was strugling at hillview

My mum has sent me to this new school now I am trying to stay out of trouble but i don't like it. They would not keep me at hillview because of the way I was

I spose all you teachers herd

We had meetings with Dr Hemlock he said I had done all sorts like copied his emails and used his phone when he was out of office but none of that is true I did use his phone once when I was waiting for him I got his password. He made my mum cry about my future

He hates us

*The twins say your lessons are cooland the play is wicked I
wouldof enjoyed being in your play to. Theres nothing like
that at this school.*

I have conselling now

Thanks again sir

Tom Rymer

Dom read the email several times, touched, even though
he had forgotten the boy. *Conselling*!

He sighed. He hoped the lad would find someone,
something to trust somewhere: it was an awful world if you
did not have that. Maybe Tom would turn things, or things
turn for him. Perhaps he would become an e-genius one day,
confound them all, *Hemlock* too! Even Emma would approve
the outcomes in that case.

He replied kindly, wondering what Tom's parents
were like and why he were a pest: was it nature, nurture?
His thoughts returned to Dr Hennock, what he seemed to
represent. Hennock again, he thought, at the root of some of
the problem, squatting in the way, at the end of all chances
and choices, ruining things- just not getting other people as
people? But Dom supposed he had his job to do too.

And what had Dom really done to sort anything himself?

*

He and Emma were to meet later that day with Dr Hennock
himself for some regular progress review. They had had
meetings every few weeks. These were supposed to happen
frequently, but Hennock usually cancelled or postponed at
the last minute; something that was a bit of relief to Dom,
although he could have done with more of a forum, if only
to let off steam.

Their meeting was on classroom management.

The Doctor was ostentatiously locking a drawer as they arrived. Dom remembered his meeting in there with Tom, thought of the boy raiding the man's emails, even using the phone. He could not help wondering if the file were here, and what other secrets lurked in hard copy in that room, or on emails. Perhaps that explained why the man had been harsh.

But Hennock was pronouncing.

'Now, tactics for dealing with challenging pupils in lessons – not that we have that many really difficult pupils here. This should have been dealt with in your training. I can see there are gaps, deficiencies; your experiences mixed.' Emma seemed to stiffen at this, but he went on. 'We have a lot to learn, don't we? Your thoughts.'

Emma had come ready for a fight. She cut to the chase.

'The reason it's there in my review is because it's a school problem, not just mine. I can't speak for Dom. The issue is with the ethos and structures, systems here, not with me. For example, I put pupils in detention they don't turn up. Nothing gets done about it.'

Hennock was ready too.

'We're not here just to discuss *punishment* are we? That's not the essence of good management. You know our thinking on that. I always see that as sign of failure. And if you abuse a system, you won't get respect,' he smiled in conclusion.

'Some are just not interested in doing any work, whatever I try.'

'I have heard this before from you, haven't I? And who doesn't turn up for detentions? Are you sure you're not exaggerating? And, if I may, what have you done about it? Don't you mean, as I often find trainee teachers are really saying, *I* can't handle it – or will someone do it for me? Classroom management is first and foremost the responsibility of the subject teacher. If you're not organised, well prepared, inspiring and enthusiastic, well, you will have difficulties.'

'But everyone must have problems, sometimes. It's what to do then that's the issue,' Dom chipped in.

'That depends on individual circumstances. No one would surely order some kind of blanket reaction without considering the individual, would they? There are all the range of options we discussed when you started, all outlined in the handbook you were both given. Read it? I liked English at school, for all its drawbacks. You know; a lot is down to the teacher: present yourself appropriately from the start.'

Dr Hennock smiled as he looked at Emma.

'Incidentally, I wonder – just a thought -I wonder if it's hard to get respect from pupils when you are your age, and dress, shall we say, casually. The professional dress of staff: it can be an issue. Normally, I would leave such things to Alison, but comments have been made. Tight trousers that look like jeans, glamour above appropriate working dress, heavy makeup; not our way at Hillview, not professional. If you push boundaries, children will too.'

Emma was too taken aback to respond at first, but Hennock carried on smoothly.

'Authority comes from respect, respect for the whole person, certainly not trying to be on their level. You learn from *experience*.'

'But how can I we be experienced when starting. And no one else has commented on my dress sense. I am used to professional working environments.'

'So I was led to believe. You are sensitive about your image, aren't you? I thought so. But you are young, from a metropolitan culture where I suspect things are rather relaxed. And we're all inclined to vanity when young. Children are simple. They see through appearances very quickly,' affirmed Hennock.

Emma seemed either too angry or just lost for words to respond directly. She was forced back on the defensive.

'I spend hours planning my lessons-.'

'So I have observed, blow by blow. It does not come easily? We had one student here who practically wrote a script for each session. She didn't last. Couldn't cope. You were at Exeter, and after that in the city working for some small family marketing firm. Perhaps you would have benefited from being in a bigger, more corporate environment? Then teacher training at a college-.' He left the sentence unfinished, hanging on a tone of disapproval. 'Hillview is a very different world. We all have to be prepared to adapt, be flexible.'

Dom could see Emma's silent fury but before she could reply,the doctor continued.

'I can see you're stressed – then everything gets out of proportion, doesn't it? But that's part of all jobs these days. Teaching is no exception, I'm afraid we're all consumers these days – even the young who know their rights all too well-and they expect a lot. If we do become independent, charge fees, expectations will rise more. Not afraid of that either of you are you? We all have to cope with change. Strange you, Emma, have issues, with all your experience, especially, if I may say so, as you're quite long past the student stage. But I can see you might be struggling.'

He looked at Emma.

'Of course, it doesn't suit everyone you know.'

'What doesn't?' cried Emma, cold and hard now.

'Teaching,' said Hennock, and left it hanging.

Dom was about to intervene but Emma, mastering her indignation, wanted something definite.

'I'm sorry but some of what you are saying does not seem appropriate to me, but I'll leave that. Would you please tell me exactly what I should do with some of these exam pupils who are going to fail if something isn't done? Some, like our friend Andy, are lazy and arrogant, don't want to do anything, want me to do it all for them, or want to muck about all the time.'

'You really have a thing about him in particular, don't you?! I wonder, if I may say so, if you have ever considered that that might be part of the problem? He's fifteen/sixteen – a teenage boy, and you are much older. I've talked to Andy, sanctions have been applied, warnings issued. He's assured me he has mended his ways. But you persist in saying it is all so much worse when you have him, you cannot deal with him. *That* concerns me. Perhaps I need to come in much more,' smiled Hennock.

'I think that's a bit unfair,' cried Dom. 'I watched Emma, as you asked us to do, not teaching him but with others. She had them well under control. I think they're a bit scared of her!'

'Very gallant,' said Hennock, 'and with all *your* experience! I certainly think *you* could be firmer with them, but let's allow Emma to vent *her* issues first, shall we? I'm sure she does not need your help, or anyone's in articulating her feelings.

'One of the problems with a school, you know, and indeed the country, is too many chiefs, not enough Indians, if we dare say that these days. I'm not saying you're like that, but we need people who are prepared to get on with a job, take responsibility, not grind issues- people who work hard when challenged. Did you expect an easier ride? Teaching is no pushover, no refuge for people who have, shall we say, perhaps not succeeded in some other career....

'You look upset. Please be aware, I'm afraid I have no tissues if you start crying. Young Dominic and I wouldn't want that.'

*

'I've never been spoken to like that, even by some of the s-ts I came across in marketing,' cried Emma, incandescent afterwards. 'I'm not putting up with it. We're in the twenty-first century. Playing silly power games with his put-downs. He's not going to get away with it, I shall make an official complaint.'

Dom shook his head.

'I don't understand him. He has a point about our responsibility, but why does he have to be like that? What's he so defensive for? He's supposed to be helping us. It gets nobody anywhere.'

'Oh, there's no reason,' cried Emma. 'He's just a sexist bastard who gets satisfaction from trying to intimidate others: it's misogyny, outrageous. I've handled far more difficult people, worked in environments where deals have been lost and made that make this place look nothing. Making references to what I wear!'

He wondered if it would console Emma if he told her now about his adventures earlier in the term, his suspicions about Hennock, but he came back to the fact that without concrete evidence, it counted little. And Emma was even less likely to be discreet about things after this.

As they parted to go and teach once more, Emma repeated threats about going to her union, seeing Waseley and Alison, but then she added:

'What really hurts is that he has a kind of insight in his nasty little games. Is my heart in it? And can I cope? I'm exhausted all the time: he knows, knows what goes on, we all know that about him. He's learnt how to hurt, just where

-230-

to hit, enjoys it; but, he's not going to hold that kind of power over me. I'd rather leave.'

Dom knew that effectively they could pass or fail their probationary year at Hillview if Hennock turned against them; but the bullying was of an insinuating kind, hard to call out directly. At least his treatment of Emma made Dom feel that his enmity towards the man was no longer just a question of his own hurt feelings.

Dom could not let this stand. As their official mentor he would speak to Mr Royal about it all, whatever the vagaries of his responses.

*

'Ah, the noble knight errant rides to the rescue of his damsel in distress!'

Eventually Charles took it seriously.

'She mustn't take it so much to heart: it's his way, authority's way when challenged. Open challenges are never a good idea, especially when you start. I should know. I'll speak to her. I might even tell her how nobly you spoke up for her, although I suspect she may not like that. There's always someone like that where you work.'

In the meeting, Dr Hennock had repeatedly quoted a whole raft of good results all their pupils were achieving as an example of how much potential their classes had. Brightish pupils -so- what was their problem? They would get results, unless Dom and Emma let them down.

Mr Royal nodded as Dom told him all this.

'You mustn't take any of that too seriously either. I've had this all out with him time and time again. Results are sometimes inflated these days. We're all getting better at playing the exam games – the clearer you are about what you are trying to give marks for the easier it is to do it, except of course in my case according to our dear Deputy. And don't forget- all must do well!

'Everybody seems to win if people do well. The government is happy; pupils, parents, pleased; teachers look good. Until of course the wheels come off and the country wakes up to the fact that it has a workforce made up of tiddlypoms some of whom are lazy, illiterate, ill-disciplined, or just failed- not educated to what they could be. Cynical people would say,' he continued without any trace of irony at all, 'some are happy with an education system that works for some and leaves the rest dancing to the mindless beat of an empty culture whilst they reshape what's left to their own advantage.

'But I'll speak to Emma. It would be awful if she walked, wouldn't it? Especially for you, – all those extra lessons to cover,' chuckled Mr Royal, in his way.

What on earth was Dom to do with all that?

*

Emma caught Dom later.

Hennock had got in first contacting Alison; she had emailed Emma, all concern. A seemingly sympathetic report that she had received from Dr Hennock had come in saying Emma was not coping, out of her depth, ill with the stress of her own incapacities.

'He twisted everything. It's like one of the kids! The union rep wasn't much better, seemed I have to have more evidence. Everything I said amounts to nothing much in her view. She was on and on about procedures, documentation, not doing anything about it unless a pattern emerges. A pattern! What's she want the Bayeux Tapestry, with me with an arrow in the eye? I shall see the Head, even if he doesn't do anything.'

She looked at him for a moment, then carried on.

'Mike wasn't much help. Saying I'm opinionated, need to watch what I say whilst starting. I *shalln't* stay you know. I'm not like you. I won't put up with crap.'

-232-

'What do you mean? You can't let someone drive you away.'

'No, perhaps he's right: I'm not cut out for it, simply can't cope,' cried Emma.

'Don't keep saying that,' said Dom, 'I've told you –I, we need you here!'

'No,' she said. 'No, first rule of business, Dom, only invest your capital in a going concern. If they don't value me, I shalln't invest; and by the way, I can fight my own battles, thank you. There's no need to go to Royal pleading my cause. I'm not some weak and emotional woman from some novel.'

'I don't like bullying: it's nothing to do with your sex, or mine,' he had replied, not quite truthfully.

She had gone her own way after that.

Dom was left to chew on the complexities of school politics. Not much more than a little heap of beans, when you remembered the big wide world, all its heart aches.The trouble was, your world was the big wide world.

Working with 'grown-up' people was even more perplexing than teaching. And there you were ending up with just a different jumble of littleness again.

CHAPTER TWENTY-TWO

OBJECT JANE

'Sir, so you think the future will be worse for us?' Jane was asking in a concerned voice.

That class again. But Dom had been doing work with them on imagining the future, good and bad; and it was going well today, although you could never tell when they might turn.

'No. I don't know, but don't see why it should: things are what you make them. It depends on lots we can't ever control or foresee, but also lots we can. Look at tech- a few generations ago all this was fantasy.'

'Sir, do you think our generation are snowflakes, can't cope? Mr Walker keeps saying it: the most spoilt young people there have ever been. He says we'll never be able to deal with the future!' said Tim.

'I seem to remember one of my teachers saying that to us,' Dom replied, smiling.

'Sir, it's *so unfair* for our generation. Everyone's down on us. Our parents and teachers like you have literally taken everything, stuffed up the climate, poisoned nature. What's left for us?'

'Yeh, Sir: it's your fault,' came an accusing chorus of voices, glad to be able to revert to a more binary style.

Dom took a deep breath.

'Actually we forget how lucky we are today in this country. So many generations came and went unable to even read and write.'

'How did they survive, not being able to read *Pride and Prejudice*?' came a sarcastic voice.

Everyone including Dom laughed then.

'Just think. For most of human history, most people had to scratch a living, grow their own food and crops, or hunt until they got too weak and ill. Then I suppose some of them were whacked on the head at the back of a cave when they become a problem for the rest.'

The class looked vaguely interested at that, but some weren't convinced that things had ever been that different. They had it pretty rough: it always had been.

Perhaps they were right in some ways, thought Dom: human beings did all sorts of amazing stuff, but quite a few never got being kind and fair. Oh dear, was he becoming another cynic?

'Life expectancy for most was something like thirty, *if* you survived childhood – so don't rubbish schooling; it's one of the marks of civilisation.'

'We ain't got far then,' came a dissenting voice.

Dom laughed again.

No one was complaining. They seemed interested, had something to say, as they peered into the uncertainties and anxieties of the seeds of time. Where was that quotation from: yes, the Scottish play. Perhaps that was what it was all about, anxiety. Funny how you learnt when you taught.

But things were flowing thank goodness.

'Look, the future's our responsibility, neither naturally good or bad but what we make it. I said that, and I don't believe in the idea of us all being captives of history. I'm an English teacher. Imagine something better – it could happen!'

'Is that the end of the lesson?'

Dom was relaxed to it now.

'Sir's in a better mood today,' came from a pupil. Several laughed and commented, not all wisely; but most of their heads went down to the task he had given them.

Dom himself could believe in progress just then.

Something sang quietly inside him as they simply got on.

*

At the end of the lesson, Jane lingered.

'Oh, sorry, Sir, I'm interrupting your break,' she began, clearly meaning to stay.

'That's all right, Jane, I wasn't going to break, just mark some essays,' Dom smiled, wondering where this was going.

'Mmm,' said Jane, in the way she had. 'I don't want to disturb you.'

He really wanted to catch up with his colleagues, especially Emma, see how she was today, if she had recovered from Hennock, gone to the Head.

'That's all right, it's just some essays.'

'Are they ours, have you marked mine yet?' she said, tense.

'It's- fine; you just need to go into more detail.'

'Mmm,' said Jane, unconvinced. 'You always say that. Can I see?'

'When I give them all back,' said Dom, making his way apparently absentmindedly to the door ensuring it was wide open. He remembered a string of girls who kept pestering him on teaching practice about boyfriend problems, until his mentors had found out.

'How can I improve?' said Jane, agitated.

Dom detailed patiently for the nth time exactly what Jane needed to do, but her mind was not on explanations, only the grade. He was not going to give it her: she would be an open favourite then. No one missed that sort of thing in school, except sometimes the teacher.

'Do you think I can get a top mark, Sir?'

'Well, if you work hard, do your best, it's not impossible,' he said tactfully.

'Teachers never give you straight answers. I don't think I will. My parents want me to – that's why they sent me here, but I'm not clever, not like you.'

'I'm not clever, I just worked hard at school, eventually,' said Dom.

'Oh Sir, how can you say that! I bet you came top at everything. What were you like at school?'

He wasn't beyond flattery; no one ever was. He changed the subject. Jane lost interest, looking worried again.

'Sir, what did you mean about captives of history. None of us understand some of the stuff you say?'

'I don't either, most of the time,' said Dom trying to lighten things.

But Jane wanted him serious.

'It's just, well, I think we can make our own history, you know, if we try.'

'Really? You see you say clever things like that. Did you know what you wanted to do when you were at school?'

'Not really, except I liked English.'

'I like it now,' said Jane, 'but it's hard. It's so unfair, some of the boys do no work then they get good marks. I wish I was intelligent like them.'

'You are intelligent'.

'No, I'm not. They do nothing, get away with it. I work and work, do all the things you're supposed to and don't get anywhere.

'No good at sport either. Mmm. I'm not popular or pretty,' Jane was going on. 'I wish I was good at something, but I'm not. I'm going to turn out to be another Hillview girl, go to a second-rate college if I get in at all, drop out, marry someone boring, do some rubbish job. And then get old.'

Dom wondered quite where to start.

'Don't be silly. You've got lots of talents. Everyone's good at something, everyone's unique, important,' he said. 'You don't have to be really good at anything to matter, that's not the point.'

'You don't think that when you're directing a play, marking an essay, you're looking for the good ones. They get the attention. Teachers like ones who do well.'

'Being good at something is not as important as, well, as what you are, what kind of person you are.'

Jane pondered for a moment.

'That's what they teach you to tell us,' she said. 'It's not really true, is it? Most of the girls in our year will end up just the same. Rubbish job. Let down by some boy or other, taken for a ride – then dumped.'

'That's not true; things don't have to be that way. Come on, what's the matter really, – what's eating you? If it's something personal, you talk to your tutor, or Mrs Tenace,' said Dom.

'Nothing, Sir. Teachers always think it's our social life if we've got an issue. It's not just that but, well, everything at times- all the stuff we get drummed into us here every day: doing well, doing this and that, all the stress, pressure. Where does it get us in the end? Especially if you're a girl. What's our future going to be?'

'Oh, come on. People don't think like that today. You all have much better chances here than most of the people who have ever lived, and lots who are alive today.'

He wondered if he sounded like a politician to her, peddling some vague hope, evading questions that needed a direct answer, even caught up himself in some adult betrayal that told children fairy stories, then left them to find out for themselves.

'Look at what we were saying – what people went through in the past, or go through today in most of our world. I don't think I would have lasted long!' he continued, trying again to lighten things.

'Do you think we have better chances? Do we really – isn't it literally just some machine that wants to turn us into some Hillview product – so that Mr Waseley can say what wonderful pupils we produce, what great results, before we head off for some boring life. It's fake, Sir.'

Dom could hear her.

'Well, doing well, competing are important, said Dom, trying to sound constructive. 'If we don't do well then... someone else will ... and it's our responsibility to make the most of ourselves. If we don't then, we'll all be speaking Chinese one day!' he ended lamely, trying to be funny.

'You can't say that, Sir! You're always on about the Chinese!'

'Why not? I just did. It's not racist: life's a competition,' said Dom, wondering what he was on about, even if he had overstepped the mark.

Jane looked sad, however.

'And a moment ago you said we were valuable for what we were, now you say we have to compete to count.'

She had him. Here was a kind of innocence you could betray with either truth or lies.

'I know what you mean,' he continued quickly, 'but you don't have to become the same as everyone else. There's only one of each of us – or ever will be,' he said, wincing at his own words, but hoping she would hear something sincere.

She paused, looking at him. Suddenly she seemed much older he thought, as if she were looking down on him from somewhere beyond.

'You are funny, Sir. You say all this stuff. None of us listened much when you first arrived. You sort of seem to mean it so we do- a bit now! But it's not answering the question is it, or what's going to happen: to me, all of us!'

Jane paused, then crossed to the window. She looked out on a darkening campus, more rain clouds sweeping up from the south west.

'I'd love to be popular like some of the girls here. But I've never fitted in at school. Tears from the start with me, hasn't it, Sir?' she said, looking at him, directly, then away. 'There's always an in crowd at all the ones I have been to- all the cool, good-looking people together. Then there's the clever ones, and the IT nerds; but the rest, like me, just never fit, never quite get it. I sometimes wish I was like Rachel, if she wasn't such a twat – don't laugh, Sir, and could be first with all the boys, or clever, like Tim, always top, or good at sports like Andy – who just gets away with anything because he's so talented, good looking. Most of the teachers are frightened of him. You stood up to him, Sir. Mr Royal does, but no one else.'

She turned away from the window and stared at Dom.

'You can't imagine what it's like to be a girl these days in a school like this. Pretending otherwise, well, it's wrong, it's just not true,' she said simply.

Dom wondered what he should say now.

'Perhaps you have other qualities that are more important, thinking about things, being aware, understanding for a start, and you seem to me-,' he hesitated – compliments were rarely forgotten, you never knew quite where they could end- 'you seem a kind person, sensitive to others, as far as I know.'

'And where does that get you? It's literally Lizzie Bennett. Darcy would never have been like interested if she hadn't been really fit. It's nothing to do with respect in the end. All these books, Sir, claiming one thing, not being honest. Dr Hennock told us in geog that books are written by failures or dreamers.'

'Well, I wouldn't agree with him there! They're written by people who want to understand and be understood. That matters.'

'Do you like Dr Hennock?' said Jane suddenly looking at Dom.

'You know you shouldn't ask questions like that.'

Jane laughed.

'You're so shy about some things, Sir. You hold back. The other teachers say they hate him – because he's such a shit.'

'Jane!'

'Everyone knows it, but they all pretend he isn't. You see what I mean, Sir. I suppose he gets things done but people only respect him because they are frightened of him, like Andy. That's how things work in the world isn't it? See, that's what books get wrong too, imagining anything better's just a dream.'

'It's never wrong to imagine something better, even if it isn't the way things work,' said Dom.

But he knew his words were nowhere near as good as hers.

He could see the clock ticking away in the corner of his eye. Emma would have left the Staff Room, off by now ready for the next lesson.

'*Did* you like school?'

'Not much most of the time, but I enjoyed some of the lessons.'

'Your lessons are all right, but most of them are so boring, and there's so much work.'

'Do you really think the pupils here work hard?'

'No. But I do; but it doesn't get me anywhere.'

'I just told you, you're sensitive, thoughtful – that's worth the world. Turn it around so you are sensitive to others. I'll let you into a secret. Someone once told me that, one day when I was feeling sorry for myself: use it to understand, help others in turn.'

'That's not what boys go for, Sir'.

Boyfriend problems? But it wasn't his business – nor was demeaning her with such a conclusion.

Jane turned away again, repeating herself.

'Being a teenage girl at school! People don't understand. The boys are so rough, some of them so strong. It's intimidating, some of them fancy themselves so much, don't care about anyone else, respect anything, not staff or parents, certainly not us.'

Dom thought of Dr Hennock at work on Emma.

'Things change when you leave school: other things count more.'

'Do they? Do they really?' she said.

'People grow up. Respect other things.'

She looked hard at him.

Words.

'You're different, Sir. But only because you're new. You wait,' she said, and then, 'Do you believe in God, Sir?'

God now! But he would never change, be like the older teachers.

'I don't know. I'd like to.'

Jane turned away.

'If you're yourself, here, or any school I've been in, everyone just thinks you're weird. No one wants that. Look at that boy who ran away.'

Jane looked out of the window again.

Dom suddenly remembered his mum telling him a story of how, when she was a little girl, she had lain on her back on a sunny day looking up at the sky, clouds streaming by, wondering, excitedly, what wonderful things would befall, who she would become, what marvellous future beckoned.

Jane continued to stare out of the window.

'I better go now. I've got Hennock next. You've literally no idea how boring it is. We have to sit there, anyone steps out of line – he shouts. No one dares ask a question. He never listens. Hours of copying down stuff from a textbook, slides about places you've never been to, things you've never seen. I wish we had English next.

'Everyone pretends most of the time, puts on an act. I bet it's the same when you grow up.'

There was a pause, then Dom said, quietly:

'Not everyone, not all the time. Growing up isn't easy. I said that to you once before. Give it time.'

The bell was ringing.

Jane summoned a smile, apologising for wasting his time, and the world's, for being just a silly girl.

Then, she was gone.

*

Dom tried to get back to the business of marking- making sure all the correct things were there, but Jane had unsettled him.

Some of the papers were studded with little insightful gems of understanding, but most were dogged, laboured rather than inspired, some, well, pretty dire.

What was *he* doing, to change that?

He remembered a teacher at school, in a foul mood, telling his class once that none of them would ever be rich or famous, do well. They'd dismissed it: bitter old fool.

Mediocre. He looked at the pile of essays. He thought about Jane, then that vacant boy in Emma's lesson, the boy who had run off, others known, others imagined.

It was easy to become cynical. You weren't really what the world was all about. People were only the product of the structures that created them, objectified victims of the rich and powerful.

Object Jane.

But he must refuse all this, refuse it with passion and spirit. They'd told him at university that there was no such thing as the soul, and they should know; but he wanted to believe it in some fashion. If given a chance, encouragement, someone's belief, trust, people could grow into something better, overcome unfairness, break the chains of nature, nurture. That was what education was about.

Mediocre: no, nobody, all least not in potential, he would never accept that.

But still Jane's words would not quite go away.

CHAPTER TWENTY-THREE

SUNDAY AFTERNOON

It was Sunday afternoon, just before half-term. Dom was caught up, both with a duty and a play rehearsal. He had been left in charge of some pupils in the boarding house, a stint that fell to only a few staff all of whom disliked it, because it was dull that day of the week. He believed he was being clever, saving time, doing both things at once.

Mr Walker and Mr Royal had warned him that pupils and staff got fractious at this point in term, but as he paced repeatedly around the boarding house he found it all unusually quiet. Most of the pupils, the rest of the staff, had disappeared to their families. Emma was away catching up with a girl friend, recovering from her trials at Hillview she said. Mike was playing in some local hockey team. Paul had escaped to see a university chum. He was pretty much alone.

After a bright morning, a gusty wind and rain set in. Campus had begun to look messy, bleak, with new bare spaces opened to view, drifts of leaves scattered about, playing fields and tracks turned to mud: everywhere the sad litter of autumn. Curtains flapped wildly at dormitory windows left thoughtlessly open. Little swirls of wind and leaves tracked after pupils who retreated indoors, piling up work for an irate Terry come Monday. Those not out on expeditions, or away, did bits of leftover homework without much enthusiasm, flicked more eagerly through the latest social media novelties, watched films they had seen before. Only the computer geeks and pool players remained implacably content as the gloom of a wet Sunday worked its emptiness into the corners of the college. Even Dom found it hard himself to summon up enthusiasm for his play: he had had a long and tiring week, wanted to be somewhere else.

He arrived at his rehearsal to find more students had dropped out of coming – without telling him. Still, some of his keen stars like Lucy and Robert were there, and characters like Jane and Tim would always show, perhaps glad to have something to do at this time of year. But most of the cast's attention focused only on that which was imminent. Didn't sir have a life?

Rehearsal was like wading through mud. He was more tired than he realised, more irritable than he recognised. Couldn't they put more in? Did he have to tell them everything, again? His own lack was quickly felt. Things spiralled down and down. But he kept at it, only dogged,mediocre himself today.

Rachel, unusually, was present, and so surprisingly was Andy. There were rumours they were going out, and unbelievable as this seemed to Dom, they were clearly enjoying each others' company.

Soon open moaning broke out. The rehearsal was stuck at a scene where there was only one member of the cast actually there.

'Sir, it's Sunday! Just cos some of the boarders are around. It's our weekend!'

'Do we have to rehearse with so many people missing. It's pointless.'

'Sir, why don't you make those who aren't here give up their free time- it's not fair.'

'Why don't you cancel? Do it next term?'

Dom wondered if Spielberg ever had to deal with this kind of thing when he was filming his latest blockbuster.

Sorry Mr Spielberg, our Ted's on a sleepover. Can't get hold of him, and Catherine's still wasted from Callum's party.

He set things going again, but Sunday listlessness had them all completely in its grip. Things stumbled on, empty of spirit. Now the lack of effort felt provoking: why turn up, get involved at all, if you weren't interested, going to try. He wasn't doing it for himself.

He began to notice how Rachel and Andy's good humour extended only to themselves. They persisted in talking loudly all the time, distracting others, then being awkward, or just vacant– when asked to do something. Soon they were laughing quite openly at what passed that day for everyone else's best efforts.

About half an hour into the rehearsal, it seemed much longer, he realised the pair had slipped away just when they were needed.

Dom sent others out to find them. They, also, did not return, causing the rehearsal to limp even more haltingly along, every dragging moment a reproof. Finally, giving the rest a break, he went out in search of them himself, openly angry.

Eventually, he located them. They were together in a corridor near where the fire had been, somewhere technically out of bounds, but he wasn't going into that. There was an atmosphere: Rachel in tears, Andy sitting moodily apart on a staircase.

Dom felt a momentary sorrow for them: the frustrations of adolescence, the endless crises over being liked, not being liked, not liking yourself. He thought of Jane, what she had told him; but things needed to get done. A hard professional voice spoke: they had signed up to do this; they had a world of time to sort their feelings. He remembered Jane's other words – why should people like this get all the attention?

Just about mastering his irritation, he asked Rachel if he could help. Tears welled. He went, got one of her friends, told her to look after her, see if she could sort it, then come and find him later. Rachel went off with her resentfully, black glances thrown at Andy and Dom. He even tried to be kind to Andy, who was glowering away, strung taut with some frustration. But Andy was not going to be sensible. Eventually, Dom persuaded him back into the rehearsal where he sprawled at the back, monosyllabic, texting sporadically, silently intimidating, deliberately apathetic, taking revenge for his knotted feelings on the rest of the cast, jeering mistakes whenever he bothered to look.

When eventually asked to step up for one of his scenes, Andy could seemingly remember nothing at all of what he had done. Dom was back at the beginning with him, as if all that work had never been; but still he kept on. As soon as Dom's attention went to someone else, however, Andy would wander off, dismissing the scene from his attention, start talking to someone else, about something else, the play of no importance.

This happened over and over; over and over.

Finally, even Dom had had enough. He spoke calmly enough, he thought.

'Look, I know this is difficult, people missing, but will you please try to cooperate. I'm not here for my own amusement.'

Andy laughed openly, loudly.

'*Amusement!* You joking, Sir! We done all this before. Why we keep having to repeat everything? It does everyone's head in. It's so boring. Time for a break.'

He walked off stage abandoning those he was acting

with, and went and sat down with one of his mates, back turned on everyone else.

It was too much for Dom, just then, that afternoon, with all the heaped up tiredness of weeks of work, trying to be patient.

'That's it!' cried Dom. 'Go on, off you go! You clearly don't want to be here. You don't do anything I ask, can't be bothered to remember anything we've done together, then moan about repeating things. You've got your phone out, that's rude. You're wasting my time, others' efforts, your own Sunday. I'm not putting up with this any longer. Go and sort yourself out! Don't return until you can learn to do what you are told and not muck about!'

For the first time that afternoon, there was drama.

It seemed to Dom that they had all been waiting for this, even him. It had been building, coiling like a spring all afternoon, always going to happen. For a split second, he felt detached, as if looking down on some scene, an audience himself, with a choice to stay or leave; then he was lost in it, no way out.

'Are you tellin' me to piss off after all I've done?' returned Andy slowly turning and standing up.

Dom gritted his teeth, but his blood was up.

'Yes. Go off, cool down, come back when you're ready to do some serious work: acting takes concentration, effort. All you're doing at the moment is disrupting everyone else.'

'You pickin' on me again? You always pick on me. What've I done? Everyone else thinks it's crap. You don' have a go at them, just at me.'

'You do, Sir,' chimed in one of his companions seeing an opportunity.

'Sir, this is not a good time for this,' muttered Tim.

'Can we just get on?' came from someone who wanted to get in a game of football before the end of the day.

'I'm not arguing,' continued Dom. 'I'm trying to help you. Off you go! Come back when you feel you can make a sensible contribution!'

'*Sensible?!* I'm givin' up my afternoon for *this*.'

Dom said nothing, just shook his head.

For a moment or two the two men stared at each other.

Then Andy turned away.

'Ah, fuck it,' he muttered. 'I don't want to be here anyway taking part in this load of shit. There's nothing I'm ever goin' to get from this- or you.'

He walked, everyone watching.

Dom made no effort to stop him this time. But deep down, what twisted away inside was a sense he could not win. He had to stand, take it, as he'd already taken so much.

He took a deep breath. There was Jane looking at him, others too.

He kept something together, just.

'Look, I'm sorry if I am angry, but you must see how trying it is. He has no right to speak to me like that,' Dom began.

No, this was not right, it sounded like self-pity, some admission of his being in the wrong.

There was no response from the cast. It was not their fight.

'Are you goin' to let him get away with that?'

'What you gonna do to him, Sir? Why don't you take him outside, sort him, Sir?'' said the twins, excited by it all.

There was uneasy laughter.

'Sir, I think this rehearsal was a mistake.'

Dom took another deep breath.

'Now, come on, the rest of you. We've not got long to go before the end of the rehearsal, let's make the best of it, not the worst.'

He continued: trying to direct, trying to look, sound,

unconcerned; making as if it was nothing really, did not matter, to him.

*

Half an hour later, the session was over. The episode had had a sobering effect on the remainder. They made progress; at least those who were still there.

Had he?

Dom knew he must still find, tackle Andy. That business could not be left unfinished. This could not be left to stand.

It was half past four. Dusk was gathering outside.

The cast disappeared with remarkable speed, although Jane and Tim had lingered at the end as if they had wanted to say something, but didn't. He had not wanted them to.

*

The empty corridors seemed particularly bleak and institutional as he paced around looking for Andy. He tracked about, picking up bits of discarded paper, closing doors that had been left wedged open with fire extinguishers, despite all Terry's injunctions, gathering stuff strewn on floors. The place seemed deserted. He felt as lonely as Robinson Crusoe on his island.

Eventually he found some boarders watching television in their common room. They were pleased to see him, bored themselves. They had heard.

'Looking for Andy, Sir?'

'Are you going to sort him out? Time someone did!'

'*Him!*'

'He and Rachel had a row, Sir; he's gone to fix her.'

But no one had seen him recently, their efforts to text drew blank. Dom knew there would be no formal roll call until just before teatime and the house parents checked.

Where was the boy? He couldn't give up, let it be, now.

Eventually his tour took him up outside Andy's study bedroom. He knocked, but did not really expect an answer. There was no reply; indeed there seemed to be no one in any of the studies or study area.

Dom paused for a moment, then opened the door.

He peered around the dim study: a duvet lay rumpled on the bed; posters of football heroes and almost naked celebrities adorned the walls; the desk lay littered with papers and books, a couple of lines of an essay had even been begun, actually handwritten, but that was all.

On the wall were many prints of pictures of Andy in teams, Andy with friends, a rather uncool one of Andy and – presumably his mum, dad, or stepdad, perhaps before the divorce, all that awful stuff Alison had hinted at.

Dom was about to leave when he noticed another smell mixing in with the all-pervasive reek of antiperspirant, gel, burnt toast and the sharp stink of trainers that seemed to be everywhere.

The odour was one long buried in his memory, but not forgotten.

Images flooded back into his mind then of university parties and even school friends who had smoked it. He'd been offered some at a party; they had all been taking it; everyone did these days they said. He could remember the dim-lit heady atmosphere in the room where they had been, the giggling, gloating faces, watching him, daring him, laughing at his little innocence, all that roaring temptation to yield.

Surely the boy had not been stupid enough to- inside, in his own room.

For a moment or two, he found himself wishing he had not gone into the study at all, imagining what he now imagined. He wished all this could just go away. You were trained to understand, anticipate such things. But, in all the personality of someone's room, it was different.

He looked at the photo of Andy, his family again, a much younger Andy, boyish, with a little dog at his feet, a dad's hand on his shoulder. He remembered the picture of Hennock, his family in the man's office, picking up the snap of his own family after his night adventures, that picture of all the staff and pupils in the school yellowed and old.

He thought again of that room at university, music playing, everyone laughing, eyes all upon him, watching, always watching.

Then he turned, left the room.

He did not look back.

CHAPTER TWENTY-FOUR

EVERY MOTHER'S SON

Twenty-four hours later, Dom sat in Hennock's office with the Doctor himself, Mr Jolson, for once not in a tracksuit, and Andy's mother, Mrs Thorpe. Mr Waseley and Alison were on conference, when they were most needed.

Dr Hennock was presiding.

It had been a torrid time. Investigations and interviews and accounts from various sides had been compiled, cross-checked, added up, but a human drama of denial, tears, had followed with its bitter recriminations; the worst thing Dom had had to live through since he started.

Fortunately for Dom, the affair had largely been taken out of his hands once its importance had been recognised, but an unpleasant, seductive fever of interest had infected first his colleagues, then spread to the pupils. Exactly who and how many was still being investigated. Feelings were running high on all sides. Rumours of expulsion were in the air. Even the police were believed to have been contacted.

Once Dom's part had been revealed a handful of the pupils had been hostile in a way he had not seen before. That, too, had taken him aback.

A girl had spoken out in a hushed lesson.

'You're pleased this has happened, aren't you?'

Dom could not forget the look in her eyes.

It all drew hard lines between pupils and staff, tore at a sense of trust and relationship. And there, again, were feelings of complicity, of failure. Everyone was diminished.

Dom was sitting opposite the furious, bitter and humiliated mother of it all. She would not look him in the eye. The stepfather was absent, abroad on business, but he'd been on the phone, outraged, implacable, blaming the school as Mrs Thorpe was now.

'Why are they left with so little to do on Sundays? This would never have happened if he was kept busy. My Andy's not that sort of boy.'

'There is a proper programme of activities for those who are here at the weekend. I understand Andy had just been at a rehearsal in fact. However, this is not the key issue. Andy, sadly, has broken one of the key school rules. It's an issue of trust,' responded Mr Jolson.

'Mrs Tray said the rehearsal was an absolute shambles – half of them missing, teacher shouting all the time, when they're giving their free time for the school. Andy was upset – he's a sensitive boy.'

Dr Hennock moved.

'I understand there were minor issues concerning the running and conduct of the rehearsal which is admittedly being organised by a junior member of staff, but, if I may say so, I do think Mr Jolson right in insisting that the real issue here is trust- the simple fact of possession and consumption of an illegal substance in school.'

'And what were teachers doing snooping in his room? What right had he to go in? Don't they have rights of privacy in this school? Who's supposed to be safeguarding my Andy? He's always being picked on. He deliberately went out of his way to try to get him, catch him out-he doesn't like him, can't control them,' she pursued, still blanking Dom.

'The fact remains, Mrs Thorpe-,' began Mr Jolson.

'How do you know it was him,' she continued, looking for the first time at Dom.

'I'm sorry Mrs Thorpe but I had just gone to find Andy. He had been rude to me in a rehearsal. I wanted to sort things out,' replied Dom.

He had been told to keep quiet, but he could not hear any more.

'I don't want us to get bogged down in the way he spoke,' said Hennock quickly, 'it's the boy's own welfare we are concerned about, as well as fire risk. You may have heard about our little recent fire, fortunately no harm done. We're not bothered about Mr Greaves's rehearsal.'

'My Andy says that fire was lack of proper staff control too. I've told you: he will have been led on, provoked. You've made him like this,' cried Mrs Thorpe. 'The school is supposed to be a caring place. You don't provide enough for them to do, they go along to something, give up free time, none of them enjoying it. He's trying so hard: he was upset. And after all he's been through. Don't the staff know what he's had to deal with? Don't you communicate with them?'

'He was rude, and moody in the rehearsal, behaving as if he had been smoking it before,' said Dom.

Hennock tutted, frowning at him.

'You've no evidence. That's a terrible thing to say. He wasn't there. Where's the proof? His girlfriend says you don't know what you're doing. You said that Dr Hennock, when we talked last time. He's been humiliated, led on, intimidated into all this. It's not his fault!'

'We have statements from some of his friends, I'm afraid,' said Mr Jolson.

'I know my Andy, he's a good lad, a good lad at heart. We all know he's a rough diamond. He's been allowed to get into bad company here. You've let him down. You all pick on him, like Mr Greaves – because he speaks his mind, says what everyone's thinking. You're just supporting each other, because you know you're wrong. There's bad lots in his year; there's bound to be more of them involved, but you blame him. He never does anything at home. Who's introduced it? Who's supplying it? What's going on in this school?'

'Look, we can't establish the exact source, but sadly these days-' began Mr Jolson.

'Why not? You're hard enough on Andy, and you keep brushing over all this trouble in the rehearsal.'

'I assure you,' intervened Dr Hennock smiling, 'we shall be doing all we can to ensure Mr Greaves learns *his* lessons from this experience too.'

Even Mr Jolson looked surprised.

Dom had had enough.

'Look, I'm sorry that this has happened, but your son swore at me, not for the first time – then stormed off. I was giving up my time to rehearse a play for the pupils. I was on duty and trying to find Andy after he had behaved badly, upset a school event. I went into his room-'

'You went in to see if you could get something on him.'

'Now, now. Please, Mrs Thorpe! I can see we're all getting very emotional over this. I'm going to ask Mr Greaves to leave the room for a while. Mr Greaves, wait outside. No, the main issues here is the boy's possession-'

Dom, quietly furious, was nonetheless relieved to escape. As he moved to leave Mrs Thorpe resumed.

'You know there's a problem at this school. Nothing's ever done about it- just like the time when-'

As he closed the door, she was on the edge of tears.

Alone outside Hennock's office Dom crossed to a window, looked out.

The weather had turned again. A mellow autumn day and misty glow bathed the landscape. Two or three pupils were happily kicking a ball around in one of the courtyards, showing off as if they were pros. Somewhere Mr Tring was rehearsing a choir; voices rising and falling in arcs of glorious musical colour. Here and there pupils made their way to and from lessons, calmly but with a sense of purpose. Beyond the immediate prospect, stretched the stray towards the Hill, its view of the sea.

Dom's gaze diminished, came back to the present.

Eventually, the door opened. Mr Jolson came out, looking cool, unperturbed. Did nothing ever rattle him?

Mr Jolson closed the door, crossed to Dom shaking his head.

'You all right? You look a bit pale. All in a day's business. We can run along in a minute or two the boss says. Glad I don't have to deal directly with this sort of thing when it's serious. He's an idiot, but poor mixed-up lad. We'll miss him from the team if they kick him out... See Spurs?'

A few minutes later Dr Hennock came out with Mrs Thorpe. She walked past them, neither acknowledging them, nor seeming to see them at all, head held high, an unforgettable look on her face.

Hennock gestured for them to return to his room, sit down.

'Challenging, I'm afraid. She has us on a few points. And there remains the issue of where it's come from.'

'Rumours have it he supplies it,' said Mr Jolson.

'But we need proof; it would all be easier if he had admitted things himself, but we seem to have antagonised him.'

Dr Hennock looked at Dom.

'This will all have to go to the Head, when he returns. Let's hope he can make a decision… swiftly. In the meantime, the contents of the meeting must remain confidential. I don't want increased staff speculation. Normally, he would be straight out, but, given the circumstances, his background, all you and I know, Mr Jolson, it may not be straightforward.'

'And what about his behaviour in the rehearsal?'

'Is that your only concern in the midst of all this? Let's not be vindictive,' cried Dr Hennock. 'Where's your sense of compassion? There's the boy's welfare, wellbeing.'

'But isn't this serious stuff?'

'Of course, but if schools were to expel everyone they suspected who dabbled in drugs, there wouldn't be many pupils left. Are you telling me you've never come across this stuff at university, or school yourself?'

'I don't see what that has to do with the matter, and, as a matter of fact-' but Hennock was not listening.

'If he'd confessed himself-. The issue of your confusing the lad, the lack of evidence weigh, as does his being provoked, you going into his room. Rachel has spoken personally to me of how upset he was.'

'Provoked? But-'

'And there I think we need to leave it, certainly as far as you are concerned – *for all our sakes*. Now, as you may imagine, I have important calls to make: emails, letters to write,' he sighed deeply. 'And I need to talk to Mr Jolson. *You've* at least got away lightly and should be thankful that I – and Mr Jolson- have been here to support you.'

*

Although he had been told not to, Dom spoke later to staff. Everyone knew. He could see no harm in anything he said; he needed to work out his own sense of what had happened.

At first, Dom received praise for raising an alert. Many claimed something had been going on for a long time, blind eyes been turned; and Andy definitely had had something like this coming to him. But, curiously, then, Dom found the mood of the staff shifted. No one doubted Andy had probably done wrong, but perhaps he had been unlucky. He was not alone. There were others, rumours of who supplied, those who got away, had never been caught, even suspected. The whole thing was messy, led all over the place. Then how would it end for the boy became, how would it end for the school.

Of his three friends, Paul seemed to sit on the fence when it came to what should follow. He was happy to talk of firmness, but seemed to haver for some reason when it came to action. Mike, perhaps wary of Emma, merely said he was a prat. Only Emma was outraged that the boy had not already been sent packing instantly, that there could be the slightest equivocation.

'What do you have to do to get kicked out of this place? Shanghai a few staff and secretly sell off the school's assets?' she had said, beyond exasperation.

To Dom, then, after so much high emotion and drama, everything seemed to disappear into sand. Perhaps Mr Jolson was right not to get, or at least, feel too involved. The more he thought about things himself, the less sure he became of what positive outcomes action for justice might bring.

He remembered the sorry picture of them all sitting around in Hennock's room, Mrs Thorpe's face most all. But the tableau of their meeting in the office had another resonance. On the desk, a shining, all too familiar folder, had lain throughout the meeting. At first, he had not noticed it, but then he recognised it with a double shock in the charged atmosphere of the day. He knew, with deep certainty, that it was the one he had seen before, looked through so avidly. Its stacked secrets were an awkward reminder of a potentially wider world of secrets, deception, different kinds of betrayal. Dom's righteous anger at Andy's crimes began to mingle with a widening and confusing sense of his own responsibilities.

The image of the folder on the table was eloquent, and now rested with him almost as much as all they had just been through.

CHAPTER TWENTY-FIVE

ESCAPE TO THE CLOUD

It was the day after.

Eight weeks in: Dom needed to get out. He was tired, fed up with a landscape of only rows and rows of desks and chairs, whiteboards, metal screens, devices, dog eared exercise books, hard artificial strip lights bearing down, bells always summoning. When things were difficult, it seemed as if they rang only to draw you on to the next thing that was never an end in itself, but only a provisional present contracting into an endlessly elusive future when things might come right.

One day!

It had all got under his skin. The Andy business summed up the darker side of school, and he felt snared in it today. He must clear his head: this tangling with so much, so many new things, difficult things. He needed to recover his soul, renew some faith in what he was doing, could do; to get away, get out from under an almost stifling sense of institution that just now lay on him like a dead hand.

*

A free period! A billion things to do! But he slipped away, determined on escape. You were supposed to let them know during working hours, in case of emergency. Damn that.

As he was leaving his classroom, he could see emails still pinging into his box, stacking up. Near the Staff Room there was a child he knew was waiting to see him. But he ignored all.

Outside he passed James, loitering outside one of the teaching blocks, phone in one hand, yet again a plastic carton of coffee from some local outlet in the other (how on earth?). He waved cheerily at Dom, continued texting, acting as if he had no lessons to go to at all, no worries, all the time in the world.

The ways of school.

*

It was one of those perfect late October days: warm, still, and mellow, golden-hazed and long-shadowed, suffused with a country autumn quietness – like that day in Emma's lesson. Inside Hillview, the daily round would be continuing whatever. Outside, everything seemed gentler, self-ordering in some wiser way: nature listening with infinite patience to its own becoming.

He walked briskly across the stray, skirted the river, crossed the little dyke that marked the end of the sports' fields proper, began to climb the Cloud, all the better for every onward step, school falling away.

Unnoticed, a rare adder, disturbed by his footfall, flicked its escape into dense wet undergrowth where it had been basking on a bank of cropped grass.

He went quickly up the hillside. The grass lay still long and thickly green, not yet spent and blanched, dotted with patches of late wild flowers, alive with humming insects, gnats caught in the sun's rays, tumbling, dancing in the warmth.

As he climbed, the trees gave way to close sheep cropped turf with stones, limey slates protruding here and there along a well worn pathway. Even at the top, although the airs of the world were stirring on the crest of the hill, there was scarcely any breeze, and, far off, Dom could see the sea, blue and inviting, transfigured by afternoon sun.

All the difficult things in the last weeks that had heaped up, got all out of proportion in the tides of their arrival, fell back. All this was there, still: glorious, quite indifferent to, beyond, his little dramas.

He sat down careless of the damp ground, looked back towards the campus, bathed in the same hazy warm yellow light of yesterday as he had seen it from outside Hennock's room.

Soon, he felt only embarrassment at what seemed now much overreaction. His restless mind stopped replaying frustrating scenes, stretched itself out as warm and content and as lazy as the day itself. Cradled in its low hills, the school became once more for him a picture arrested in a time long ago, a dreamy, golden, balmy Camelot of a world, blessed by gentle blue, soft air.

He lay back on the warm grass, arms spread out at his sides in a cross shape, giving himself up entirely for a few moments to the wholesomeness of the sun, the richness of the earth, forgetting those disagreeable, brash, noisy episodes of the past months that could so easily define, limit everything if you let them play too loud.

Instead, he thought of good days: the unexpected camaraderie with some of the children; the unpredictable but heart warming feel of flow in lessons that could take you by surprise; the warm affection and kindness and moments of life opening trust that would randomly shine into the most tedious or difficult of times.

Up here, life was blessed; things could be what they promised: the only obstacle came if you lost sight of possibilities. And compared to so many now, and always, he had little reason to complain, enough in his work and life for answer.

*

After a while, he sat up opening his eyes.

The sun had gone behind a cloud. It felt chilly. The distant sea had become a shining bar of metal, and grey clouds were approaching, although right in the distance, there was still light on water. In one direction, on the other side of the hill from school, the furthest suburbs of Wellsway lapped up messily against the lower slopes of The Cloud; gentle grass fields and meadows and dark green giving way abruptly to hard lines of modern brick, and the blank windows of rows of identical houses, built too close to one another, their bare young gardens soulless, no trees.

Was the land beside, he wondered, the part of the school estate where further development had been proposed? How far up would they build? He remembered the emails and letters he had seen in Dr Hennock's file.

He stood up, brushing himself down.

There was a couple hand in hand, and their dog, coming up the hill from the Wellsway direction. They were just passing into the scrubby trees and bushes that formed part of the slope there, the dog scampering from side to side in delighted freedom. They called; it answered.

It was half-term the day after tomorrow.

He had exciting plans – first home, then to visit friends in London, a wider world indeed: time for something more.

Getting by *had* blunted his sense of purpose. The future had become the shape of his own frustrations. And it had started to control his sense of others he was sure; but they and theirs were not him, his to control. He was not being true to the life in him or that that beckoned – when he was like that; nor did it allow him to be true to them. How selfish, how foolish.

He picked himself up.

Sometimes you needed nature like this. It took you out of yourself, so you could go back in, better, remembering important things.

*

He turned, went down the hill, eager now to get back.

CHAPTER TWENTY SIX

HALF TERM ASSESSMENT

Dom remembered he owed the world he inhabited more than his own happy passage. Things had to be said and done, and now, or the something more, that was his kind of mission, would be lost to something less.

Whether or not he had that clearly worked out yet, or even a right to say it, he could not be absolutely sure. But he needed to speak out, to someone. After all, he had been here nearly half a term; ought to know what he was talking about.

He was going to go to the top. Yes, part of him, perhaps arrogantly, wished he were a Mike, or a Mr Jolson, could just leave things be. But if today's dance were all the horizon it was not enough.

And there was something else that would not let him rest: Emma. He didn't really understand quite why, or how. There was no sign at all on her side that she cared much about him, or more than any of her other friends. She had Mike. She could be headstrong, opinionated, hard. She was talking of leaving- already. And she certainly had this whole work thing wrong, didn't she?

But there was something more there too, something else that would not leave him alone. He wondered if it was part imagination. He was vaguely aware that he didn't always see clearly what was right in front of him. Friends always told him he lived a bit of dream; but what did they know? All he knew was that he looked up to her, and even more often at her, for reasons beyond reason: ones that wanted clarifying, along with other silly confusions.

All these niggles needed sorting. Then he could get back to his true mission. When Emma had something on her mind she said it. She was fearless, together, forthright, clear in the confusing, muddy waters of a new job, of teaching, of Hillview.

He must be too.

*

As usual he had to wait simply ages for Waseley.

He sat outside his office, brimming with his experiences, his ideas, conclusions, yet feeling as if he were back on interview. Dr Hennock emerged at one point, stared through Dom, said nothing. Alison came and went, smiling but preoccupied. A secretary chatted politely to him, taking off her glasses, asking him what he was up to at half-term, rolling her eyes that Waseley was, as ever, so behind.

Finally, he'd nearly given up and gone away, he was ushered in.

Mr Waseley was on the phone, typing at a screen with the other hand. His shock of black hair was nearly standing on end today. He smiled broadly at Dom, trying to remember his name, gesturing with his habitual expansive enthusiasm.

He rolled his eyes for Dom as some phone conversation laboured on.

'No, no, we are dealing with the matter very firmly, very firmly indeed. We always do.... *Independence?* Well, we think we know what we're doing, where the train will go *if we get on.* No, no, I really do *not* have time before half term. An appointment in person- splendid idea! Goodbye!'

'So annoying when people don't listen!' he laughed, putting the phone down on a still babbling voice. 'Sometimes wish we could send parents back to school.

'Now, what can I do for you today, young man? What has most enthralled you this term? Still keeping those Wellsway gals entertained? ~~Looking~~ forward to a holiday I bet. Often think staff need it more than students. How's *Coriolanus*? I hear great things. Darren is *so* proud, you know.'

Dom had thought carefully what he was going to say this time. He began, perhaps none too wisely, on a rather lengthy list of trenchant concerns, seasoned with high-minded ambitions of course, determined to spell things out, as he saw them, after all his experience.

It was a little broad brush, he felt, but his concerns were simple.

Education-its real point, purpose! This school, where it was going, and if it was going anywhere? Independence, was this the right, fair thing? What was that all about: principle or money? The values that mattered in education. Oh, yes, he had been bogged down a bit by a few local difficulties at first of course, but the big picture! Dreams! And, er, practicalities! Trivia! They did seem to keep getting in the way.

O, yes, then personalities, the pupils, the staff! It all seemed to be about people! They could be difficult, they sort of got in the way, sometimes. Now, education was about changing the world. But how did you do that, particularly on a difficult day with a difficult class, with difficult pupils, difficult people. And, generally, how did you make everything perfect- and quickly of course! He'd only half a term to go before finishing his first whole term and –well, not all was quite perfection, just yet.'

Unsurprisingly, Waseley made no attempt to interrupt or draw him on but sat nodding. At first. As Dom went on, and on, he began to tidy his desk, then shuffle away in his seat as if performing some extraordinary exercise with each buttock in turn. At one point he picked up a photograph of his wife on the desk, pulling a rather strange face at the image.

Was she really completely loopy, being watched by the CIA, Dom wondered, slightly losing the thread of his threads.

He petered, at last, to a halt. Waseley was yawning openly, tousling his hair, then put his hands behind his head. When Dom stopped, he suddenly lurched forward and let out a huge sigh.

'Well done! Well done, Paul! That's a right bucketful, a right bucketful of... *concerns*!'

'It's Dom actually.'

'Problems with him too?' Waseley shook his head.

'Now listen, Paul. It seems to me you have had an *entirely typical* first few weeks. Well done getting your head around all that. But it's time for holidays, not worrying about all this. Isn't there some young lady, partner or other you could be off with, out of here, enjoying yourself. Forget the crap, endless *considerations*. You're only young once you know. Wish I was still your age! So does the wife!'

He roared with laughter.

'But I want to do the right thing, the big thing, the school to get better.'

It sounded as if it had some kind of disease.

Mr Waseley regarded him for a moment, seemingly surprised that any more than broad assurance might be necessary.

'Nothing like experience, or indeed *inexperience!* That's what you're on about, isn't it? You'll get used to it, find your feet, learn that lots of things are always like this. Didn't I say all this before? Hasn't Old, er, Tiddly, Charles, been doing his stuff with you? Boosting you up? I thought you'd be enjoying the job, glad to have one. Hard times out there, you know! Independence! That bothering you? To tell you the truth, Paul- and don't let Dr Hennock hear this for goodness sake- I'm still making up my mind! I can see merits on both sides!

'Look at me. I'm much more concerned today in getting Mrs Waseley 2.0 off on holiday, or there really will be hell to pay! What's the problem? It's not Dr Hennock's little put downs is it? He does that to me sometimes. That boy Andrew's little wobbles? All this kind of stuff happens in all schools everywhere these days, believe me! And don't we all get things out of proportion this time o' term? Living in a small world, eh?! I had Darren in here the other day on and on about Emma's tight trousers or something. Can't say I object. None of us, staff, pupils are perfect! You know, he thinks lots of teachers are lazy, out of their depth, can't cope. And by God some of them are, and can't!

Waseley was laughing again, shuffling his hair.

'Not you, of course! That's not what you're saying, is it? How *is* Charles by the way? You do keep distracting me from what I'm trying to say. Now, *he's* helpful?'

'He's a great teacher,' said Dom loyally, wondering if this was a trap.

'Course he is!' cried Waseley. 'Man of the old school- an absolute star for us here over the years. Well, that sounds positive enough: no problems with support. Any other concerns I can set your mind at rest over?'

'It's Emma too, really,' Dom continued, trying to salvage something. 'She works so hard... she finds some of the things that happen, the ways things are done here- I do too-confusing.'

'Mmm. Confusing. Are you depressed? Thought of getting a pet? Mrs Waseley 2.0 wants a dog, you know. Always gets her way. Would you like to come and take it out for a walk for us if we do- when she gets bored with it? Take your mind off all this clutter!'

'Sometimes,' Dom resumed, determined to get a response to one of his themes, 'things go wrong with pupils and I, well Emma and I, we feel we sometimes need a bit more hands on support, direction.'

'*That's* what's bothering you. Oh, we all feel that when we start. I used to be all over the place myself! Felt like giving some of them a whack; still do some days! And that's just the staff,' he chortled. 'Andy? Nice lad, Andy, Very talented. Will play rugby professionally one day. Thinks a lot of you.

'Everything's a crisis when you start: like being in love for the first time. You youngsters, bees in your bonnets, wanting instant solutions. I was talking to Dom yesterday, full of ideas for changing the place. I admire that, all that idealism farrago, but in practice, life isn't like that. It's all compromise. You'll see. You'll learn. Don't let a few pull you down, start getting depressed, good Lord, depressed at your age- depression! Tragedy is for the over thirty-fives like me!!'

Mr Waseley laughed. Dom was about to come back but he started off again.

'When I was your age, we had none of the support mechanisms you have today, all the guidance on how to do everything from taking them for a pee, which loo they should piss in, to massaging a moody parent. Everybody mucking in with everything, none of this carping, job demarcation that seems to have come into the profession. How many weeks holiday do teachers have, twelve, sixteen, more? Then there's exam leave, all these training days. Half the profession is on its backside most of the year. Said that to your friend Emma. And think of the privilege of it all, getting to know wonderful children, doing the best job in the world!'

'It's not the workload, the pupils, it's, well, what are we really here for – what are we doing: where are we, the school, going with it all?'

'My goodness, you do need a holiday, don't you! We all feel sorry for ourselves from time to time, don't we, when we get tired. No harm in that, as long as it doesn't become a habit.... Between you and me, we don't want another Mr Walker do we? Brilliant man, but, oh dear!'

Dom had one last go.

'I can see you think all I'm saying is only that it's new to me, and it's been hard and it's just all this stuff going on but- I think it's more than that. Dr Hennock, he's intending to change the school, completely you see, and who knows how, and is it right? He's got plans, secret plans, and I'm sure he's going to take control over the school, and, well... He's after your job!'

It was a melodramatic, ridiculous and at the same time lame ending, and sounded so, even to Dom. But he had to say something, push at one statue just then, even if he was tilting at windmills.

'Plans! *Secret plans!*' The Headmaster laughed and then pretended to be shocked for a moment.

'Ah, I see. A takeover! A coup! My job! Good God, well I never! What a terrifying prospect! How shall I face Mrs Waseley? It *is* kind of you to warn me. I had no idea, no idea at all. Well, I've heard some things in this office in my time, but Paul, *Paul!*

'Of course he wants change, to be head one day. And so do you: that's what you were on about wasn't it. Why on earth should that bother you? Now seriously, Paul, it all sounds like silly Staff Room politics to me. Who's put you up to this? Not Walker is it, filling your head with nonsense? Ah! I see. Pity you didn't say at the start. Now I understand! All those *concerns*! Too much staff tittle-tattle. You shouldn't let some of the older staff get to you. You just come in here and tell me if colleagues come out with this kind of nonsense in future, and I'll set you – and them – straight. Now, is that the time? Good heavens, your chattering away has made me quite lose track. I have parents to see, I'm afraid. I'm sure you'll get on top of these little problems, especially now you've spoken to me. Keep up the good work. We'll meet again soon. Remember, I'm always here to listen.'

As he left the room Dom swore to himself.

Why on earth had he suddenly said all that stuff about Hennock wanting Waseley's job – and to his face? He still hadn't a scrap of evidence. And made all his high hopes and earnest concerns sound vague or silly. He had even made it look as if he were being used by other staff to stir. It was almost as cringe worthy as his verbal assault on those girls at the start of term. Hadn't he learnt?

Fool; arrogant fool too.

But he'd tried.

Forget it, leave it, for now. He would go on speaking up in future, even if it was all a muddle, even if no one listened properly, even if it was a shambles and he came over as totally naive and a self righteous little prig. Yes, maybe he was hoping for a bit much; maybe half a term was a bit short a time to set his world to rights. But he wasn't going to give up on something more even if, just now, after all that, he felt embarrassed, stupid, and once again high feelings had blown themselves out in a silly squall.

Leave it.

It was half term-his holidays: he deserved that!

*

Alison caught up with him later. She had spoken to the Head: Dom was apparently bothered, upset, not coping with this and that. Could she help? He explained what he had tried to say, some of it anyway, reluctantly now.

She smiled at him, rather cryptically.

'What's your worst fault?' she had said.

'Where do I start?' said Dom, feeling deflated. Then, as it was his day of trying to be honest, he carried on.

'Thinking too much, too seriously?' he added, managing a smile.

'And I wonder if your parents and teachers didn't tear their hair at that, wish and wish you would change – and did you?'

Alison smiled back as Dom shook his head.

'As for Andy, if that's bothering you, he really does have a dreadful background, whatever he has done. I can't say much, but abuse you can be sure.

'Did the Head offer you more money, or suggest the plans for the school would help improve your salary?' she had said rather oddly at one point.

Dom was puzzled, wanting to laugh. Hadn't she been listening either?

'No, no. Not at all!'

Alison shook her head.

'Please don't ask why, but don't mention I said that to anyone,' was all she would add.

'But you did right to speak your mind, to him. Things *are* in turmoil. But, yes, it's bound to be some inexperience in your case. I admit we all get institutionalised, used to things, stop thinking when we've been here a while: *we* need to remember that. But it's best to take your time when you start: remember we have been at it for a good while. If any of it were straightforward…

'If you want some practical advice, pick your confrontations, your battles carefully. Someday, there may be a real need to fight.'

She sounded mysterious then.

Dom wondered what she meant now.

*

The rest of the last day seemed to creep along. Everyone was just waiting for an ending.

When he had put the embarrassment of the meeting aside, Dom could get properly excited himself that it was a holiday. Now, it really was his time. Rather daringly, he thought, he had offered to run Emma to the station. Her car, which she drove like a tank to the immediate peril of all before her, and the constant detriment of its engine, had broken down. Mike had gone on The Katie Trippett School Outing to France. Dom was glad he was off the scene; it was no use being quiet in a noisy world even if he'd just made a fool of himself with his boss.

Before he could leave his room to go and find her, however, Mr Royal arrived all of a fury in his classroom.

'I've just done ten rounds with Hennock,' he began, scarcely waiting for Dom's class to finish leaving. 'He says I'm not giving you – and Emma any help or support. You've been complaining to the Head about me.'

It took a good ten minutes of explaining and calming from Dom telling him he had said no such thing: and look it was his first term – things weren't easy.

God, what an arrogant whinger everyone must think me he thought.

Eventually, something of Mr Royal's flippant self returned.

'I see! Been getting at your girlfriend has he? *Tiddlypom!* She'll be toddling off altogether if we're not careful.'

Royal regarded Dom for a moment or two as if debating something.

'But as for Hennock! O, he's a bully of course, a bully of the worst sort; we all know that: but you mustn't let him rile you.'

'But I think- it's not just- I think Dr Hennock's up to something serious,' said Dom, feeling the ground carefully.

'What do you mean?' said Royal, his interest caught for a moment.

Dom backed away from saying much more than a sense of how ambitious the man was to change the school his way. One implication of paranoia, or some such a day was quite enough. He excused himself – he was tired, confused, a bit overwrought: the Andy palaver, all things. Mr Royal seemed quite content to leave it then, and actually thanked him for his efforts, before wishing him a jolly holiday. And then he was off to do whatever Mr Royals did out of school.

Dom wondered quite how his seeming complacency squared with Charles's own chastisement at Hennock's hands, or Mr Royal's first furious reaction to the plans to change the school. But before he could think far, far too much about everything again, he recalled it was the end of term, that all these people and issues belonged firmly in school, and that he was going to leave all that behind –for now.

Moreover, Emma would be waiting.

*

When he finally caught up with her she too had been briefed about his conversation with Waseley: provocatively. So their drive, which Dom had looked forward to, got off to an awkward start. They went along the busy Friday roads and the hazy light of an October afternoon in an atmosphere, at first, of strain.

'I've told you before.I fight my own battles. I have more experience of the real world than you, or most of this lot. I didn't ask you to go and speak to him about me. I am coping just fine.'

'I was only trying to help. It was supposed to be a chat with the head about my first weeks, some concerns about the school, education.'

'Dom! You are so serious at times, intense, pompous. They'll just think who the hell does he think he is. And get a life. It's holidays!'

'I've said I'm sorry! But Hennock should not have spoken to you in that way, especially in front of somebody else. And the meeting was not just about that.'

She seemed to want him to suffer her feelings and carried on for quite a while, in the way she had, of always seeming to want to vanquish any interlocutor rather than simply assert a view; but he let her have her head, then brought her back to Hennock, his real reasons for seeing the Head, even trying to warn him. He opened to her more of his suspicions than he had done to anyone else, if not imparting quite all he knew or suspected, or how he had come by his information.

She laughed it away.

'Detective Inspector Greaves now?' she said laughing. 'You have been busy thinking all this up!

'Oh, it's all this independence dream and some silly staff review. Even a place like this must have some kind of forward-planning. Darren's just ambitious, up himself. I can't imagine Hillview changing much in the current climate unfortunately, even after all that stuff in the staff meeting. I was in business, remember. There's no money in any risky schemes like going independent right now, I can tell you,' she paused. 'There's no conspiracy. Things are never like that. You do imagine!'

'Thanks!' said Dom.

At least she had calmed down.

Privately he resolved that one day he would have some proof for her and for the Headmaster, and even Mr Royal that he was, in some way, right about things going on, and about important things getting lost.

But then Emma became wistful.

'But the way things are managed, what has gone on! This place – intrigue, wishy-washy authority, people dodging responsibility, egos clashing, bullying, money worries. I thought I'd left all that behind. Not what education is about it, is it? I *shall* leave. I'll go in the end. Don't be surprised.'

Dom wondered. People said these things. He remembered a teacher at school confiding in them once that he hated his job, was counting down the days until he retired. Some of his mates had left their jobs because they were bored, some at college had even been on the cusp of leaving university, a money racket they said.

Emma would not leave, not when it came to it.

She and he and Hillview were all in it together, for the future.

*

They were early for the London train, despite traffic. Her mood continued to mend. They sat and chatted in the shabby buffet bar, all comical broken plastic seats and steaming tea or foamy coffee that tasted of washing up liquid; but neither of them really noticed, caught up in the fervour of plans. She was off to France on a long arranged trip with girlfriends. It was soon all Paris, her journey and then where they would each like to go, given opportunity, in the big wide world, that lay all before them now they were free.

Dom was surprised Emma had, like him, still so much to see.

There were, of course, one or two pupils from the school at the station, waiting for trains. This had to include James, of course, complete with yet another hair colour and style, and latest partner joined at the hip. The boy greeted them as if they were old friends, looking them up and down with a twinkle in his eye.

But Emma and Dom felt their teacher selves slipping away: somebody else could take responsibility for the pupil sporting an outrageously short skirt, and incredibly thick makeup, or the teenage boy over there- was he theirs?- who was in the process of being swallowed by his phone. This was their hour.

They moved onto the platform. Dom had had to jump the barrier that Wellsway still had for tickets. He had things to say to her, if he could find the words, but he felt awkward suddenly, now the moment had come.

A silence seemed to settle on them. They stared at the train tracks that led off into the distance both ways, blindingly bright in the October sun. Despite the sunshine, the wind was cold. An empty crisp packet skittered up and down the platform. Soon the sun went in. Afternoon began to fade, but still no train came. Departure times were adjusted without explanation; eventually the train was nearly an hour overdue. Other trains came and went, picking up passengers, taking the pupils away.

'You don't need to wait, look after me, you know,' she said eventually, with that familiar laugh as she looked him up and down. Dom felt how he had in her lesson, a schoolboy with some hopeless, impossible crush on miss.

He could feel the blood coming to his face.

'I'll stay.'

How romantic he was being.

His heart was racing.

Then, without warning, the train was finally arriving, suddenly having made up time.

There!

Everything was changing. Everywhere a flurry of activity. People moving, gathering cases, parcels, stowing phones temporarily- except for one tall, fat man noisily still doing a deal publicly, as if for display.

Much to his own astonishment, Dom suddenly put an arm around Emma, kissed her once, and then again, on the lips. She seemed surprised, grateful. She kissed him back, warm, intimate, momentarily another person, his Emma, generous, firm in response. He was excited, uplifted: everything else confused. Unknown people were bursting from crowded carriages in their own little hurry. Another world had arrived. Everyone was lining up to get on, getting on already, intent on separation, departure.

For a moment, only Emma and Dom seemed unsure, lingering together, apart from everything else.

Then he must gallantly wrestle Emma's cases on to the train, its engines screaming a readiness to depart, already late, almost too late for some; and still so much was left hanging, unsaid, undiscovered: things that might have felt long familiar, things that were unknown.

He struggled along the carriage, putting one of her cases on a rack, and then with another, trying to get it past the fat man, still dealing for the world. Emma might need her case near her on the journey, but the man would not shift. In the end Dom barged past, ripping his coat pocket, tearing some skin from the back of his hand.

'S-t!' he cursed, sucking his hand, swearing loudly to the general consternation of those in the carriage not fighting for their own seat.

'I've told you, you don't have to help, you know; you'll get trapped!' Emma said, laughing, concerned, then recovering something of her poise, looking exactly how she had when he first really noticed her.

'Are you all right?' she said laughing still and then even more as he was bumped and shoved as more people strove to get past, fighting their way to the imaginary nirvana of a free seat. Someone pushed past so hard that Dom was almost thrown into Emma's lap. At last he could see the funny side of it. They were laughing together now; but the train gave a lurch.

Departure was imminent. He must get off.

'I suppose you'll forget all about Hillview now?'

'I hope so,' sighed Emma. 'Thanks for coming,' she said warmly, looking at him intently again, serious.

The train lurched once more. Whistles were blowing.

Dom had to kiss her goodbye – or he really would be carried away.

'Text me!' he implored, parting, looking back.

She was smiling. But there really was no time.

Out he had to get, pushing, shoving in his turn.

Doors were slamming; the scream and squeal came from the engine again; things were beginning to move. Then the machine, roaring its farewell, quickly gathered pace.

He waved. Emma waved back and, too soon, all the lighted warm carriages and all those distinct and separate lives blurred into one and there was the end of a train disappearing into a tunnel, and she was gone and it was over before anything had really begun.

Dom stood alone on the platform in the cold wind as colour drained from the scene and twilight sprang up.

Back at school, as he walked to his study, the empty corridors seemed hollow without pupils. Terry had already locked up. A creeping cold told you the heating was off. The place was a virtually empty ship: odd words on whiteboards; here and there a forgotten exercise book; inevitable bits and pieces of uniform, curiously poignant.

Memories crowded in on him of so much that had happened, but it seemed unreal. Only unlit scenery remained, cold and hard and starkly fake without its cast, a bleak monochrome light shining unsparingly on a once captivating stage tableau.

Unable to settle to anything, he went for a quick drink with Paul, but both were spent. Now school was out, their common themes of conversation could not command any life.

He turned in early, slept like a dead thing.

CHAPTER TWENTY-SEVEN

RESET, RETURN

The first thing Dom learnt on his return to Hillview was that Emma had dumped Mike. He found out by text. So, apparently, had Mike. The second thing he discovered was that Dr Hennock was planning to get Royal sacked.

He'd had a great break. Going home first to see parents had had a restorative effect: it was heart warming to be amongst family again on whose genuine care and real interest he could depend. But it had been hard to explain Hillview. His father shook his head when he heard some of Dom's tales but his advice was unfailing. You worked hard for the greater good, wherever you were, whatever you did; you respected authority because it was authority; you gritted your teeth, braced up to challenges when things got tough. Systems did not matter, people did. His mother lived the ups and downs through with him, taking it all in, to heart. She wondered how he was making his way in the world: he would never be old enough not to be her child.

But they were off to New Zealand soon for the trip of a lifetime, and his brother Jack was home too full of his plans, his first weeks at university. Hillview quickly fell into the background, although Jack would tease him about Emma. They could all tell, more clearly than he, what she meant.

*

Then he had caught up with friends in London, leaving his car back at Hillview and following Emma, catching the train up to the city.

Just before he met them, Dom had bumped into a pupil by a big cinema; she had seemed shocked to see him outside a classroom.

'What are you doing here?' was her abrupt challenge – staring hard at him as if he did not belong. Between worlds again thought Dom.

London seemed overwhelming after Hillview, rammed and noisy. A frosty October dusk had settled even on the city. The noise of skittering dry leaves and pigeon calls mixed with the cold haze of a red twilight. He hurried along, one of thousands of people rushing who knows where and why.

He and his friends had met in a small bistro. Before he descended the steps to the restaurant Dom glanced up at a glowing, orange sky, a crisscross of vapour trails and winking red lights. Even the sky was capitalized.

Downstairs in several buzzing, cavern like rooms, the old friends gathered, their meetings reflected in many mirrors adorning the walls so that there seemed to be several of each of them.

There was John, his best mate from university, now in publishing, the most intelligent of them all, when he bothered, always with a girl, or two, in tow. Dom secretly wished he were like him, assured, self contained. He had a pragmatic streak that Dom admired, but he was always somewhere just beyond you. He was with Laura at the moment. A mutual friend, Joe, who was doing a higher degree was also there. Joe had views, a difficult background he wore openly. Joe and John were chalk and cheese, quarrelled all the time, but firm friends, needing each other to spar off. A girl called Lucy was there also, a fellow English student, who read for romance. She had always liked Dom. Friends always put them together. They had had a fling of sorts once, so there was always a kind of awkwardness when they met. She was working, not getting very far. When Dom saw her, he thought only of Emma.

Lastly there had been Mark, working in the city now. It showed, not just in a sharp new haircut, tan and trim physique. He seemed to have altered the most. Now there was something hard, simply transactional in the way he looked at people and the world. He soon became impatient with them all.

Initial awkwardness had given way to familiar themes, old threads. Joe went to town on Dom, what he should really be teaching them, the failings of the system, education, Dom's responsibility for it all. Lucy and Laura had winkled some information about Emma. He did not have much to tell. They groaned, teased him mercilessly.

Things had seemed the same between them all, and yet not the same. Work, getting on, had taken them, one way or another, except Joe.

Dom and Joe had then stayed at John's flat for the night. Laura was off on interview next day, a post at John's publishers. Everything always seemed to fall into place for him.

*

They had walked back to John's flat, slightly the worse for wear, Joe enjoying denouncing all he saw of glitzy greedy capitalism, its flamboyant consumers, its sleazy corrupt underworld of backstreets keeping the whole rotten sham afloat.

Dom dwelt again on how many people there were in the world; what a bustle and battle of humanity there was everywhere, intent on their own. The city had its own ego, more than indifferent to little concerns. How different from Hillview, its dreams of civilising possibility. The city was beyond any of that: a sprawling giant tearing wilfully away at all fetters. For some reason London made him think of war; yet it was real, exciting, sexy in some strange, seductive way: a heady mix of freedom and anarchy.

They emerged from some dark alley onto a plush mall, lined with expensive shops and restaurants, a showcase of luxury, splendour, glamour. It looked like a film set, connoisseurs inside performing for each other, for those outside as well. An argument began between Joe and Dom, about country, city, school: things true and fake, how all was, should be.

'Pair of dreamers you two!' was John's only comment.

Back at John's they had continued to set the world to right late into the night.

'You've sold out to the system!' Joe repeated to Dom. 'Look how greedy, screwed up Mark has become. Now he makes money out of money as if by magic; but there's no magic, just ordinary people being screwed. And that's all education is for most of the masses, a con. You don't teach the right things, make things fairer, just get kids to conform one way or another to what the system wants.'

'I've got principles, thank you,' slurred Dom.

'The future has to be better, fairer,' Joe insisted. 'There are better ways of living, it starts with education.'

'Christ, Joe, you benefit from the system. Where's the money come from for you and all your mindbenders at uni? What's any country's wealth built on for God's sake? What have you produced in your ivory towers that makes life better for working people?' cried John.

'Ideas,' responded Joe, 'ideas turn the world, not money. Dom – back me up: it's education, learning to think that matters, not feeding stuff the system wants back to kids. And decent education should be everyone's right, not just privileged white males who want their stake reinforced specially if your place goes independent.'

'You're a privileged white male,' said John.

'That's just clever shit. You can't get away from class issues by smearing me. Bet Dom's school's money comes originally from slavery if it was independent once, that part of the world. How's that fair?'

'What you on about now – we're all made up of our past. Most of our ancestors have been slaves one way or another,' said John. 'And you aren't some pure clean dick, no one is.'

'Bet you don't get many working class kids like me, or pupils of colour specially if you turn into a total nob-hole,' cried Joe.

John had plenty to say to that.

Dom, rather confused by drink, tried to explain how responsibilities for things turned in a real classroom. Getting them to listen to anything at all was sometimes the biggest dream you could reach for, rather leaving world revolution in the wings. But Joe was not listening either.

'What *are* we teaching them? What real choices are we offering? F-k all I bet. Education at the moment just defends an elite's truths, the privileges of a certain kind of academic knowledge, exclusivity, or provides slaves for industry or technology, or gives up altogether.'

Joe went on at length.

John, seeing his friend rather downcast, rallied to Dom's defence, but out of irritation rather than deep disagreement with Joe.

'You hate everything that already is bad and good, that's your trouble. Be practical. Your arguments depend on polarising everyone and everything, so you can indulge indignation as if you're above it all- us and them. Life's all compromise; dealing with what is, individuals.'

'You two are ready for a museum, bourgeois individualists. You'll be the wrong side of the barricades when the revolution comes. Individual kindness, serving the few, saving some from a basically crap system- it's just papering over shit. Look at our country! It's all finished here, broken – our ridiculous, biased, busted education system tries to shore it all up – shoving everyone into the conformity of school. Most ordinary people end up with crap lives because no one has any real aspiration for them to be any better, do anything more with their existence than scratch a living to survive. And it feeds them false dreams- those of the few that do escape the mindless grind.'

'And you can't hide from individual responsibility by exploiting a sense of the people's endless entitlement to some vague promised utopia.'

'At least I care. You haven't a f-ing clue what life is like for most people.'

Good job they were friends. It always got personal, thought Dom.

Joe lay back, slurping from a can, secretly sure of his own rightness.

'The state isn't God; can't be, shouldn't be,' Dom said at last, thinking obscurely of what Alison had said at school.

'But business is, right – or the Market or *the way things are.* F-k! Is that what you teach your kids? No wonder it all keeps repeating,' slurred Joe.

'For a lot of people God is just their ego,' John said delphically.

The argument had lost focus a little.

Joe had closed his eyes, appeared to have passed out.

John put an arm around Joe, half protective, half mocking.

'He'll never grow up,' he said. 'You talk about littleness, people stuck in the playground. He'll always be a child: heart in the right place, head in the land of dreams- looking for a lost Magic Daddy, someone who puts it all right. Or someone to blame. He's a narcissist – a kid stropping off on his own because he can't get others round to his way. You don't fix things by blaming everyone else.'

John shook his head.

'You're lucky, Dom. Don't let Joe knock it. Even if things aren't what they could be. You're doing something good, practical, helping others, whatever shit world we live in half the time. But – please, teach them to think their own thoughts or they'll end up like him- the victim of someone else's never-never land political theories. And stop taking it all so seriously. Life's a game, mate: no good if you don't play.'

'Life's not a game for the poor,' protested Joe stirring from his torpor. 'I think I'm dying,' he groaned.

'Well hurry up: put us all out of our misery!' cried John.

'Look,' he continued to Dom, 'live a bit. People can't do serious for long. Hook up with this Emma. Living isn't just work. Think how hard you graft for the pittance you earn. And if you want to keep your dreams, write a book. That's the best place for them. Writers make shed loads out of that, one way or another. But meantime get real about real things: now is all there is. Who said that shit. Pass me a can.'

*

A terrorist alert had cut into Dom's plans for his last day, but nothing, thankfully, came of it save a lot of inconvenience. He took an earlier train back to the West. It was a dark Saturday evening when he got back to Hillview, a day before he had planned. As he had bumped along on the top of the cold, empty bus that ran out Hillview way every two hours, its bright lights shining out into dark shapes and shadows, he had received the text from Paul telling him about Emma and Mike. Mike was devastated. Dom tried texting Emma. They had exchanged messages a lot at the start of the break, then he had heard nothing.

He alighted at the stop nearest the school. After the restlessness of London, the roar of the train, and the rattle of the bus, trudging off into the sudden quiet seemed almost eerie. It was much colder than the city. Grass and mud were freezing. His breath steamed out in front of him as he crossed the empty campus. He felt lonely then, wondering if, once you left home, you ever quite settled, or if this would one day feel like coming home, his new friends like his old ones.

Busy with thoughts, all the things and people that he had almost forgotten over the break came back to life for him, and, feeling a little as he had felt when he first began, he climbed the now familiar steps to his flat.

But he felt refreshed, reset, reminded of what and why he was doing things. And maybe things could develop with Emma as John had said; he could not deny his feelings, his hopes, even if he must be sorry for Mike.

Perhaps he would write some tale. But he had begun to wonder, just a little, if stories in books and films – even the best, ever told it right: especially things like romance. Perhaps people never really told the whole truth. Perhaps you never quite could.

And what sort of story was he himself making so far, how it would end? He knew as little about that as anyone. People who heard it would probably give up in frustration with him, or, more likely, dismiss it all as boring because it was not them: he would have. What egos we all were in the end. John had said something about that. God being their ego, or their ego being God- some such.

But for now, well, it was almost scary being in the building alone. He remembered James's tale of ghosts in the building. Mr Walker had told him some high tale too of how a butler had fallen to his death down these very stairs – when the school used to be a house, centuries ago. He doubted the truth of it, did not usually believe that sort of nonsense, but the steps were steep, the drop considerable, and, in the dark, if you started to imagine, all sorts of things-

Suddenly, he stopped.

Had he heard footfall somewhere? For a moment or two he fancied someone was following him.

He peered anxiously back into the shadows on the stairs below. He had locked the outside door firmly, bolted it. Terry had berated him about that.

Pikies had broke in during the holidays. Some soddin' teacher busy tellin' others where to go couldn' be arsed to lock up proper and tight, like as he'd shown 'em a thousand times.

Suppose someone had slipped in, just behind him, whilst he dithered in thought, and was lurking down there, waiting to creep up the stairs just when he believed he had reached the sanctuary of his flat.

No one would know what had happened when they found him on Monday morning.

Pull yourself together. Stop, listen carefully, in case there is a real intruder.

Silence and darkness settled about him. Somewhere he could hear that drip, drip of a tap, a trickle of water running. Stone and wood creaked as they relaxed, but otherwise a dark, empty void surrounded. All he could hear was his own breathing, and coming out of the dark, the slow seconds of an electric clock flicking by, time passing into eternity.

Then, from his landing, a little higher up, he suddenly heard a door open.

Voices.

Light blazed on the staircase.

There was Dr Hennock, another man, coming down the stairs towards him, straight for him, jangling keys like ghostly gaolers. They were talking away quietly, but steadily approaching, unseeing as yet, unaware of an enemy hiding in the dark.

CHAPTER TWENTY-EIGHT

EVENTS

As quick as a flash, Dom darted behind the door on the landing below that led to dormitories.

As they approached, their words became clear.

'As I was saying, once Royal is out, it should be easier to shift opinion amongst senior staff, get them on board, or at least not resisting. They still listen to him, he has sway. Walker is dismissed as some old cynic. The rest don't matter. Then we tackle Waseley. And I don't think there'll be much objection to that, and once they see what this can put on the table- for them, for the school.'

They seemed to stop on the little landing just the other side of the door.

Dom froze there, heart pounding in his ears, hardly daring to take a breath, straining to catch every word.

'It's not going to be easy.' It was the governor again.

On the other side of the door a light clicked off. The men must be standing there in complete darkness as he had just a few moments before.

'There's a paper trail on Royal. I insisted on everything being logged. Waseley knows, has put him on a last warning several times, but he'll never do anything: he daren't. All we have to do is to pile on pressure. He wants to retire: the drinking's a symptom. It's only a matter of time. He's had his chances. Now, if we had an inspection or something;–one's long overdue, someone outside -. He's too well liked here. That's the problem.'

'Harsh – after all his years here.'

'I'm afraid I've no sympathy, or for the Head.'

'You're a hard man, Darren.'

'It's a hard world, and it's going to be a rough six weeks or so, but there is no alternative. Do you want to have a look at the dormitories along here. There's no one around, no one back as I told you, see how they fit in the plans, what we could use, sell. There's a market for this old stuff – a bit of olde England. Independent schools have kudos abroad, like old buildings. Could be a summer school, residential, guesthouse in the summer. The Americans, Japs – Chinese'll go for anything like this – or offices. Even Russians: they've got money. Not all of the site needs to be educational business. We could make a theme park! Retro teachers included!'

Both men laughed.

The door was beginning to open. Dom's heart was in his mouth.

'No, not just now, Darren. I need to get back. The old girl is beginning to suspect I'm having an affair, all these secret assignations. I promised I'd take her to that new Chinese restaurant in Wellsway tonight, been there?'

'Not my scene; the Chinese are okay when you need money. Linda and I prefer simpler fare. Be careful down these stairs. I'd risk the light again, but Terry's back, pissed, in his cottage. I don't want him to know we've been here again. He's not stupid.'

The door in front of Dom swung completely shut again; a little gust of air beat on him. Finally, he breathed a sigh of relief as he heard the clomp of the men's shoes on the stone steps. They were talking restaurants as their voices receded.

Dom waited until all was completely silent again, cautiously pushed open the swing door, peered down into the dark, then up to the landing above to ensure there were no more visitors or conspirators anywhere. Then, he mounted the steps to his room, two at a time, at lightning speed despite his heavy rucksack, slipped into his room, locked the door.

He left the light off for some time, throwing his stuff down on the floor, crossing to the window to peer out. There was nothing to be seen – no lights anywhere, not even a moon shining, simply an empty campus, all in murky shadows, glints of frost spreading everywhere, quietly, mysteriously in the dark.

He lay down on the bed, turning over and over in his head the conversation he had just heard, with his own imaginings, completely taken over once more by the little world of Hillview.

*

By Monday morning, and the return of everyone to school, Dom had resolved he would warn Mr Royal directly, speak to Alison as well. No one could accuse him of being where he should not, that Saturday night, or of spying, looking at confidential information in this case.

He'd made a mess of things before the break, when he'd spoken up, vowed to keep quiet for a while at least. But he'd been shocked by the ruthless of what he had just heard.

And what other schemes lay as yet undisclosed?

Whether or not he would be believed, taken seriously, was of course another matter, but he must call all this underhand stuff out – and clearly this time. For a Dr Hennock to be conniving against a Mr Royal seemed a treason to all a school was about: a school was its teachers, its pupil, first and last.

Royal had been there all his own life, and more. What must you feel after thirty years of all that?

Royal's drinking was an issue, his unpredictability a pain, but these were not that important. Most people had some problem or other. The real evils in people were ones that did for others, not themselves, Dom decided. Bullying should be top of the list. And here it was alive and kicking, literally kicking out, in a school.

It needed stopping. It would be.

*

The news that broke at break that first morning back, however, swept all else aside.

Dom had had a good first two lessons. The break had worked some magic. He noticed staff's and pupils' softer, fresher faces. Perhaps there was just too much school sometimes.

But Mr Waseley's announcement that morning, had wiped smiles from everyone's faces.

There was to be a snap inspection of the school.

Tomorrow.

Under yet more changes, the latest rules, the school was to be done – and thoroughly done this time, starting the very next day. Whether or not anyone in the management had heard definitely before that this was to happen imminently, no one knew. Hennock, Dom remembered, had mentioned it, but nothing definite.

At least they'd had a holiday first.

Soon 'inspection' was on everyone's lips, a worm in everyone's mind. Tension was palpable in the air. Those clear, eager early morning faces, began to wear a different look.

From now on, pronounced Mr Walker, although everyone believed they worked hard and achieved so much, it would all be about how everyone must do *ever more, ever better*. The only one who seemed pleased was Dr Hennock; the only one who did not seem to care, for reasons unknown, was Mr Royal.

'It's all an opportunity for management, the Hennocks of the world to put us onto the back foot,' Mr Walker opined to all who would listen. 'When I first started teaching, I wouldn't let inspectors through my classroom door,' he claimed. 'I've been teaching thirty-plus years – man and boy. What can they possibly tell me that I don't already know?

'The whole thing will be a complete anticlimax, you wait and see. Just like a General Election: change that ends up the same old same old. They'll appear on the scene, all smiles: they're here to support and encourage. Then, knives out, they'll find something to cut into based on absurd comparisons with places that seem the same but aren't. It will tell us nothing we did not know before, all which they could have found in five minutes had they bothered to consult staff. Oh, it'll leave the leadership with more ammo, all of us more paper work, more boxes to tick so that when they come back in a couple of months' time they and the school leadership can smugly congratulate themselves on how good a job they all did, and how everything and everyone in every way is now getting better and better.

'Meanwhile the school will carry on much as before, while the latest trends, failing procedures and bureaucracy lock their crushing stranglehold ever tighter on what remains of goodness and trust.'

'Oh. Right!' Dom had said, with just a touch of irony now that he was into the second half of his first term.

Alison, however, had overheard his tirade, and, for the first time Dom had seen, became quite angry with Mr Walker. Everyone needed an inspection from time to time or they became a law only to themselve. How arrogant can people be?

Mr Royal had his views as well.

'Bureaucrats! They're mostly interested in is systems, pathways, plans, and results: things you can measure, not the rather inconvenient truth of the people who make things good or bad. Education works best on personality, qualities like trust, leadership, inspiration. You can't precisely measure the things that make a good school or a good teacher. Except hard work, endless patience and putting in the time which no one ever really sees, and certainly does not want to pay for. But seen it all before. It doesn't bother me!'

Dom wondered if some of Mr Royal's apparent unconcern was bravado. Warning him, however, of what he had heard Dr Hennock say, was now all the more imperative. In his heart he sympathised with Charles, admiring Mr Royal for beating against a system, any system really, as Joe had sort of reminded him. Almost everyone else, like Paul, seemed to display only an eager servility before the impending examination, too ready to bend their knees, not ask the important big questions of what the real issues should be.

But Dom's head, nevertheless, told him he had much to learn, much to prove, and counselled caution to him. He wanted to know if he were doing the right thing by the current lights, especially after some of the drops of his first term. Yes, he secretly fancied he knew better already; but he had some sense.

Meanwhile, his thoughts kept coming back to how was he to tell his mentor, in the current febrile circumstances, what he had heard?

But say something, once more, he simply must.

CHAPTER TWENTY-NINE

SNAP INSPECTION

Later the very same day, Dom plucked up courage.

He kept the source, and details, rather vague. When it came to it, he felt mean telling tales out of school again; but he did it, did his best, first with Charles, then with Alison.

They certainly both reacted. Royal was furious. He had nothing to fear, was cross with Dom for speaking out of turn, relaying gossip about senior members of staff that he had no business to believe or credit. Of course the Doctor and he did not get on – that was an open secret. He did not need warnings, from a junior member of staff, nor help in looking after himself, thank you.

Alison seemed to think Dom must have misunderstood something, then told him he was being very naive. It must be nonsense, a misunderstanding. Hadn't she warned him about something like this before? Of course the two men were chalk and cheese, old and new school; but this kind of clash was more cause for shoulder shrugging than serious reflection. He had to learn to ignore what staff said about each other. Gossip, rumours, there would always be: it was better to rise above, or keep out of it.

'Don't get pulled into staff politics: it's mostly silly pettiness,' she said.

So Dom was left, once more, feeling foolish, thinking ironically of his professed disdain for littleness. Was he once again nothing more than a pert upstart who thought he knew it all, believed he was being noble, but actually just another gossip – Katie Trippett Mark Two. Waseley had implied as much in their last meeting.

And so much for his generation's willingness to call things out.

It did not help that everyone was in a whirl now about the inspection. There was enough stress and gossip brimming to float a flotilla.

Alison, however, whatever her public thoughts, Dom later found out, did speak in a general way to both Dr Hennock and Royal. She asked them to bury any hatchets in the interest of the school, be good examples to the rest of staff, particularly young ones. Paul, as usual, got wind of this little storm, and told Dom that both men resented her for it. Hennock wanted to pursue Alison's reasons for coming to speak to him with a full investigation into what had provoked her intervention. Mr Royal spoke angrily to Dr Hennock about rumours, how unprofessional this was; but he would not substantiate his comments, name a source. Hennock was too busy with the inspection to follow things up, so Dom did not come under close scrutiny; but Hennock did not forget the episode, nursing suspicions. Dom was on his radar anyway. As for Royal himself-.

Ironically, for all Dom's efforts, Mr Royal seemed to get worse at acting in his maverick ways, rather than better, as the hours ticked by to the arrival of the inspection team.

'Ah, ha, ha! Is there something going on?' he would say, sitting in his favourite seat in the Staff Room, apparently with nothing to do as all the world rushed by, faces knotted with stress, daggers drawn for anyone who did not share, understand their particular crushing burden of pre inspection trauma.

'Now, my dear, you do seem to be in a little hurry all of your own,' he said to Katie later the same day. 'You look unwell. Nothing bothering you? I find an afternoon nap these days most beneficial. Tried a lie down?'

'She's nearly there already,' whispered Mr Walker audibly.

Katie reported direct to Dr Hennock.

Mr Royal and Mr Walker continued to feed off each other, like a malicious comedy double act of some past century, quite unreconstructed in its attitudes. Dom was divided between respect for the kind of real intelligence that will always demur, incipient doubts about the integrity of his mentor's professionalism, and feeling bruised for trying to help at all.

Soon, however, it was as if Mr Royal was deliberately being provocative, working up some awful crisis with Dr Hennock, playing into the catastrophe that Dom had heard the Deputy Head wish for only days ago. In the little time he had to think about anyone else, he wondered where it was leading. He tried, at least, to make Mr Royal see that an inspection felt important for him as a first-timer.

'It shouldn't be causing this much stress if people know what they are doing,' responded Charles, not terribly helpfully. 'I for one am not going to be bullied by anyone. Who do they think we are?'

*

The biggest immediate problem for them all, including Dom, was that no one seemed quite sure what to expect. Things had changed so much since the last inspection, even though the ink on that was scarcely dry.

Once more, Dom wanted the practical guidance only experience could provide, but no one could help much, except Alison, who took it on herself to give some supportive words to the newbies. Hennock, was too busy with his paper work; the rest of the staff in their own lather.

Meanwhile, the Deputy Head took a particular delight in hounding Terry who was always – deliberately-slow to respond to staff under stress. Terry took revenge simply by plotting the removal of two chairs the next morning from every classroom so everyone's seating plans would be in a mess from Day One of the Great Event. They all sat around on their arses too much anyway, pupils and staff.

Just at the same time, to crank everyone's nerves up another notch, Mrs Dot volunteered to help with the invigilation of some important public exams on the menu at that time. She got the job before anyone realised, and screwed the whole procedure up so completely as to annoy every single member of staff, pupil and parent involved. Many were given wrong examination papers, or incomplete ones seconds before kick off. Those sitting papers electronically found parts of finished answers mysteriously vanishing, parts of last year's questions incorrectly downloaded. The resulting pantomime, including the breakdown of all campus photocopiers one after the other as the overload spread, finally shredded what was left of staff nerves. The exams officer threatened resignation if Mrs Dot ever darkened her door again and regaled anyone who had time to listen with stories of her traumatic *Two Days in November* for years afterward.

*

Meanwhile, where was Waseley in all the mayhem? How had he escaped the maelstrom?

No one seemed to know where the Head had gone after his initial announcement, that is until it became generally known that Mrs Waseley 2.0, with an emphasis on the 0 all the staff chorused, had needed running to Heathrow. She was off to the States. Only he could oblige. Indeed he had hoped to go with her on some lecture tour to promote a forthcoming book. But he knew when his staff needed him, would be back, early-ish tomorrow, or the day after.

'Off flogging books at a time like this!' one member of staff declared, incandescent.

'She's toddling off to tackle her CIA operatives face to face,' cried Mr Royal with a laugh.

'To see a shrink. That whole family should be in therapy,' Mr Walker averred – correctly it transpired.

The staff could not forgive.

*

Although most of the planning and documentation was supposed to be already live, Dom and his colleagues were nearly carried away in an electronic and paper typhoon emanating from Dr Hennock. Inboxes were flooded, staff strangled up in documenting everything they had ever taught, done or said, and quite a few they had not. Then they must reorganise and tidy rooms, as well as track down work to be reviewed by an inspection team ravenous for evidence of good, and especially bad practice. (The bad was particularly prized by inspection teams Mr Walker claimed). Books could not easily be found as students were just back and seemed to have lost everything. One member of staff was even seen late into the night apparently forging his own pupils' work for proud exhibition the next day.

Everyone, or almost everyone, was making new displays and, in Mr Tring's case, moving things in the music rooms that had not been touched since the last inspection. Terry was summoned to dispatch mice who had colonised several of his store cupboards and eaten through a few dozen scores, and some pupil compositions. Meanwhile, liberated from invigilation, Mrs Dot was helping everywhere, until staff went in petition to Alison to get her sent home, or some secure dungeon, before she started world war three.

Demands for updates on schemes of work, although these had only recently been done Dom was told, appeared for subject leaders to slave at well into the small hours; a new lesson observation form which no one could understand did the rounds. Mr Royal ostentatiously tore it up and put it in the bin in the Staff Room (Katie reporting). A new version was then produced which was even more complicated than the first. Bins filled again with discarded attempts at writing plans for lessons that most could teach perfectly competently with no plan at all.

Terry now had to attend to all this overflowing waste, as well as broken photocopiers, speed up general repairs, flick a lick of paint on any really disgraceful damp and leaking areas, patch and mend on a vast scale, all in a tearing hurry. When the boys' toilets overflowed, his main boiler went on the blink, and an ancient display that was taken down from time immemorial revealed a particularly vicious case of an exotic fungus, he blew. His raised voice and free use of expletives caused a much needed laugh in the lessons that adjoined the earthquake. Merriment was brief, however, as his histrionics almost exactly coincided with all the computers systematically closing down completely for the day – something to do with putting the clocks back an hour, basic information that always took the sophistications of IT by surprise.

A deputation broke in on management's final meeting before the inspection (those not at the airport), threatening strike action unless something was done to stem the chaos-and done now.

For once, the staff had to be attended to. Briefly, all too briefly, they had the upper hand.

During all this, Dom was alternately amused, incredulous, bewildered, anxious, and finally just overwhelmed. Mr Royal took off home with one of his migraines, leaving him to sort out quite a lot of the paper work. In the end he was up with others in the department until midnight, creating, copying, patching up as best he could what he thought he was supposed to be doing, and wondering where in all this bureaucracy, trust and common sense had gone.

*

All the day long Dom had desperately wanted to talk to Emma, spend time with her, even a few moments. She had only got back late last night; but he had scarcely seen her since Waseley's announcement. He genuinely felt for Mike, and he was neither vain nor foolish enough to credit himself with much to do with their break up. Despite what he had done, he must remain a supportive friend; but his feelings and his understanding were not entirely his own to command where Emma was concerned. A few texts flew around, but everyone had their heads down.

As that day wore on, nonetheless, some of what had happened had become clearer. Meeting old friends on holiday had crystallised feelings about where Emma felt she was in life, socially and professionally. Things had not been working for some time between Mike and her. She wanted clarity, resolution, one way or another. She had told Mike straight. She wanted space, time, not just from him, but to think about her future. It had needed a text exchange, unfortunately, to convince him she meant what she said. That cut him deeply in ways she had never meant. Time and distance made things worse.

When Dom had tried to talk to him, Mike was distant, Dom conflicted. He must wonder at the brevity of the affair. It did not accord with his ideas, professed at least, of love and romance.

As for Emma and him, when he had first seen her on her return she had looked really pleased, smiling, warm. Then she too closed up.

'I don't want to talk about it,' Emma declared, and walked off once she had done her bit for the department.

Since then, it seemed almost as if she was avoiding him. He did see her briefly late in the afternoon. The newbies had been summoned to see Dr Hennock. Dom hoped the Doctor might finally give them some last minute tips. But the man was only interested in getting his own administrative procedures right, and once more had no use for, or understanding of, the emotions of any staff first experience. Emma seemed somewhere else. Dom must conclude the station episode meant nothing. At least, he told himself, he could feel a bit better about Mike.

Hennock had issued all the staff big new shining badges for the inspection, user friendly he said. So they were all labelled, claimed Mr Walker, as if about to take part in a banal reality television show, or access a ward for the severely deranged. There was a spirited exchange in the meeting between Dr Hennock and Emma on the subject. She protested loudly at having to wear one that was designated *Mrs* Oakley, something that stung, particularly in the current heady circumstances.

'It's not only discriminatory and illegal, but it's just wrong: typical of this place,' she declared.

'I'm sure you can manage. You don't have to wear them at home or on social occasions yet,' Dr Hennock insisted smoothly.

Even Emma was lost for words.

'I hope they don't come into my worst class,' said Dom as they walked back to the Staff Room, alone with her for a few seconds.

'I hope they don't come into any of mine,' she replied. She took her badge off, chucking it publicly in a bin.

'But how splendid you all look in your new labels. There I was never quite sure of your names, before!' cried Mr Walker when he saw them. 'Who on earth are you?' he addressed Emma. 'Will the inspectors be wearing badges too, or do we need to get them to stand up and give name, rank and number? Show them the door if they get frisky,' he continued to Emma, smirking.

She was not amused.

He was not wearing a badge. Neither was Mr Royal the next day when he eventually returned; but everyone could smell his after shave.

*

Inspection, inspection, inspection. It seemed to Dom as if nothing else had ever mattered to anyone, even himself. They were all submerged in a parallel world where the transient significance of a passing reflection loomed larger than any reality. But he had no time to think it all out. Dr Hennock, then Alison were demanding yet more documentation from him, even him, the lowly newbie, first on the play and rehearsals, then on his induction. He must feed the hungry maw its endless cravings. And could he tell the truth?

This was his one horizon today, that and wailings and lamentations over jammed photocopiers, wayward IT, and the omnipresent scratch of egos, one against another, under too much pressure.

Bureaucracy, as usual, had much to answer for, and, seemingly, no one human to answer to. It took off on a flight all its own, growing and growing into a giant mushroom cloud of business whose shadows fell on all in Hillview, appeared in everyone's dreams, great and small, that day and especially that night.

CHAPTER THIRTY

INSPECTION IN ACTION

The next day arrived all too soon. So did the inspectors, or at least two of them, the advance guard of an invading army scouting out the land they were to take. They had already been meeting with the school's leadership team, 'Firefight Command' Mr Royal christened them, whilst the rest of the staff were still rising, even earlier than usual, from the turmoil of their sheets. Mr Walker stationed himself like an old crow near the entrance to the Staff Room greeting all as they came with any dark scraps of information he could glean or embellish.

For Dom, not being the subject of a direct visitation on the first day, it all seemed initially rather chaotic and, even, he had to admit, comical, when he wasn't fretting about might-bes, what would happen to him. He wondered if these rather grand 'adult' things like inspections, commissions, reports might not be another one of those things that was rather less in practice than they sounded in theory.

The day began smoothly enough. Initial disappointment at the thought of only a small team arriving, despite all that preparation (perhaps the school was only being lightly tossed and gored) was soon pushed aside when gossip got a grip. Anxiety took wing once more: there were actually another twenty inspectors on their way, perhaps twenty five;

they were coming into everyone's lessons, several times; the advance guard had already watched x's lessons and trashed it; now they were after everyone's blood. Less scrupulous members of staff sent inventive texts to each other: Waseley was not really on his way back from the airport but in hospital heavily sedated following a complete breakdown; his wife had run completely mad, leaving the country for good, taking with her the school's few portable treasures; meantime, the school was to be closed down by the end of the year, the site converted into a maximum security psychiatric institution.

'No change there then!' cried Mr Walker.

The open rumours were ridiculed by Alison. She did her best to calm waters. But others sprang, quickly gaining the currency of the only news in town. Soon it was being chillingly asserted that one of the inspectors was an agent of Dr Hennock, a friend indeed, if he had such things. This was against the rules, but Hennock had contrived it: they were now all doomed.

The children, initially only vaguely aware that anything was up, eventually joined in the rumour mill, adding flourishes of their own. When a further female inspector appeared on site, one of them claimed to have found a salacious past online that matched her profile. She was, apparently, the author of several erotic novels. Spicy clips of her in a previous, very different form of working employment, were said to be being widely circulated. There were even rumours of her becoming a pin-up amongst the lower years, but no one could ever prove this, although Terry was ordered to tear down anything put up by a pupil for the duration. He actually ripped down quite a lot of vibrant photographs that had been proudly put on display by the art department, glad of a destructive outlet for his frustrations.

When the story was proven to be largely if not wholly false, another rumour ran that she had once been a white witch, and had cast some terrible spell on a school she had recently visited resulting in the demise of a good number of staff. Emma and Katie were too busy to challenge that one; but the rest of the staff were confirmed in their darker prejudices: inspectors were sharks following the faintest blood leak with utter ruthlessness, determined to devour anything that had the temerity still to be moving by the end of the week.

Mr Walker and Mr Royal sat on commenting loudly that the inspectorate involved, Offcrap or whatever it was (Hillview being a unique place was being done in a unique way), needed to keep a stronger lock on its laboratory doors to prevent its creations escaping.

*

Observations!

Staff steeled themselves to all the 'tease and doubt' of who would be mugged next, how judgements would fall. What was trending educationally or at least correct for this inspection round? Talk all the time? Never say a word? In the event, some managed sparkling performances. But a few taught nowhere near as well as usual because of added stress, a feeling that every box needed to be ticked then and there in that and every lesson, or some axe would come down on an otherwise successful career – a damning word or two, a life's epitaph.

Hours passed in fevers of activity, apprehension. More definitive and specific reports began to come in from front line skirmishes. There was a general consensus on two things; first, that they were being given a thorough and ruthless interrogation. Mr Waseley, who had condescended to arrive back halfway through the afternoon, spent his time trying to jolly his troops with various blandishments against such a notion until an incandescent Hennock caught up with him, pinning him down for an hour and half's debrief on all the detailed issues, big and small that were already boiling.

Secondly, one of the inspectors really was poison (witch or not) a pert bossy dragon armed with stats, fixated with that dreadful ticking boxes mentality, and definitely out for error. There would be no quarter in her battle zone, no prisoners taken, unconditional surrender only. Mr Royal met her informally at one point. He declared he had never met anyone quite so lacking in imagination. There was an online scramble to find out where she was, track her, so colleagues could be tipped off as to her latest carpet bombing.

She had been shown round by James. It did not help that, surprise, surprise, he seemed to have had some knowledge of her daughter from a big party in London last summer. This stiffened her resolution to resist not only his charms, but those of the school, and the whole generation, he must embody. Even Dr Hennock was worsted by her. The whole team had by now arrived, and wanting to get their teeth into something, there had been a clash over the statistics he had presented. She had led the charge, even, rumour had it, asserting that some of the figures she had looked like a doctored work of fiction. Her treatment on the subject of value added, in particular, had been forensic, ruthless, and Dr Hennock, who usually seemed to have a ready answer to the slightest critcism, was left temporarily blinded by too much of his own science.

She had moved on swiftly, was now demolishing the school's financial operations – trashing her way through the accounts, budgets, devouring future planning. She must be everywhere, it appeared, even in areas where she had no remit Dr Hennock declared, lifting every stone, straining every sinew, squashing all hope.

Then Mrs Tray broke into the school. She had come in for some reason, determined to say her piece, or several pieces. Unable to find Waseley, she bent the ear of one of the rather more gentle inspectors she and her husband managed to trap in a pincer movement, for over half an hour.

No one was sure how Mrs Tray had got in, but the infamous female inspector, now known, unoriginally, as Attila the Hen had then been drawn in to the punchy exchanges, which seemed to centre, surprisingly, on the inadequacy of the school's recognition of Mrs Tray's daughter's genius. Carnage ensued when Mr and Mrs Tray started to argue with the inspection team in turn for not listening properly, demanding to be put in contact with the inspectorate's higher command. The mild inspector had apparently at this point retired to his hotel needing some time in a darkened room, but Mrs Tray and Attila had continued to lob grenades at each other for another half an hour, until even Mrs Tray had had to withdraw, although not before brandishing the threat of a charge of being bullied. And she had her evidence – she had recorded the conversations on her phone.

By now, no one, including the Trays really knew what all the fuss and drama was actually about at root, but the affair had continued to escalate on some stress induced dynamic of its own. It looked like pistols at dawn tomorrow in an urgently called meeting with Waseley.

Then came news that Rachel Tray had herself knocked the gentle male inspector over. She had been charging out of a lesson just as he had plucked up courage to return to the fray. As he had picked himself up, dusted himself down, he had apparently asked Rachel, as a joke, if she were a member of the girls' rugby team. She looked momentarily puzzled, then pushed past, treading heavily on some of his precious papers, irony quite lost.

*

Meanwhile, Attila, resuming her scheduled duties, zealously and ruthlessly pursuing evidence from children in some meeting about IT Safeguarding Policy for Blended and Remote Learning and Teaching Strategies Paragraph 205, Section 41 B (2), had got herself stuck in one of the shabbier rooms near the site of the recent fire. The handle on the door had come off at the end of her meeting, and she had been forced to talk for twenty unplanned extra minutes to a few of the school's characters, including the twins and one Andy.

By the time Terry responded to the call to come and rescue them there was near hysteria in the room. Everyone was late for something. Dr Hennock's inspection stipulation that lateness of any kind would be severely punished, had incited something like revolutionary spirit with Andy leading an attempt to demolish the door with an improvised ram made up of a new teaching desk deployed by him and the twins. When it would not budge he set about the lock with the remains of a fire extinguisher. Meanwhile, one of the girls and two of the boys trapped in there were having panic attacks occasioned by close confinement, and a growing certainty that they would all have to spend the night together with this creature from another world.

Terry's grasp of the situation and his subsequent action took place in a very leisurely manner. He was resolutely in first gear for the duration, having decided that this was another way of getting his revenge on stupid teachers and heartless management. He was unaware that there was an inspector inside, thinking it was only kids 'pissin' about as usual' and discharged himself of many familiar, and some newly minted expletives whilst tackling the lock, though still taking his time in his best West Country way. He entered casually, quite unaware of the great woman's presence, surveyed the scene, and launched into a lecture to all inside on the enduring need for basic civilities in life, treating people who did all the real work with some f-in respect, for a start.

'What the f- did they think they were playing at?'

He for one was fed up with clearing up after immature kids in this shithole.

'An' didn't they know there was a 'section'– that there was poncy spectors about, including one bitchy cow who would skin them alive if she knew what was goin' on.'

Attila emerged from the shadows livid, declaring that members of the group were amongst the most unresponsive youngsters' she had ever come across anywhere, and did he realise who she was. He gave her an unsolicited lecture on the inadequacy of his budget, the savagery of the hours he worked, the failings of the management, and the world in general, topped off with instruction on proper respect for other people's 'f–in' property even if it was all shite.

The staff all agreed that they would have played real money to have seen this encounter. One or two even went so far as to intimate it had shifted their relationship towards the idea of a benign creator.

*

Dom continued to hear all this from various sources, in various stages of elaboration and exaggeration, with a mixture of nervous laughter, and genuine bewilderment. A simple instinct to keep going and get through took over. Then, as still no one came near, and time passed, it all seemed a phoney war. His preparation was wildly overdone- several weeks' worth of teaching for the tired and not always enraptured children caught on the day's wild carousel.

But the young had their impressions too.

Did Sir know that Dr Hennock, no less, had once had an affair with the evil inspector? It was horrible, disgusting, much worse than anything that could ever be seen on social media, or the darkest of the dark web, and, also, Sir, did he know that Andy had just locked her in one of the classrooms, deliberately covering her from head to toe with foam from a fire extinguisher before smashing the place up with a desk? And Sir, *Sir!* Rachel's mum and this inspector, they were going to have a fight after school that evening. Everyone was going along to watch. Places could be reserved. Those who missed it, well, one of the Year Nine pupils was filming it so it could go viral.

Would Sir be placing a bet?

Could he lend a fiver?

*

Teaching, Dom tried hard outwardly to retain a professional demeanour, faith in the process, but if it tasked his idealism, it was at least not too serious – as long as it was not you directly involved. Bless the kids for keeping a sense of humour, he thought. But how many days would this go on for? How many days was it to the end of the week, the end of term – retirement, if it was going to be like this?

Indeed, Mr Walker was not alone in calculating just then.

But the next day, it was Dom's turn.

He was up.

CHAPTER THIRTY-ONE

IN THEORY AND IN PRACTICE

Dom had got through his first lessons next morning, with still no sign of a visitation.

Then, it began.

'Sir,' the class in his next lesson shouted out as he arrived, late, still getting used to having to rove around from room to room, terrified he had forgotten something.

'Look out – there's one of them on the way!'

'Is it the witch?' cried one.

'Is she the one Hennock banged?' another cried excitedly.

All turned to stare boldly at the door despite Dom's frantic attempts to shush them. A spear of remorse passed through him then for daring to find any of it funny yesterday. Here was a revenge.

A burly, red-faced fellow, who looked to be more at home on the games field than in the classroom, walked in. He looked tired, seemed wary. He grunted, smiled at Dom, went and sat down at the back of the room where he shuffled his papers, looking a bit perplexed, not terribly happy. The class had followed his every step, but unable to detect any striking abnormalities or supernatural aura on a first viewing, certainly nothing salacious on the surface, turned away disappointed.

Here we go, thought Dom. At least it isn't Attila. He felt how he did back on that first day, confidence stripped, nerves for all to see.

He started. Bless them, the pupils, seemed to be listening, did what he asked, even began writing something at one point, a thing not always known. After a few minutes, he almost forgot the man was there, even had time to steal a proper look at him, wonder who he was, how he felt, if it was easy being an inspector. Maybe even he was nervous, ill at ease. But whatever, Dom hoped he understood what it was like, standing there, still learning, still so new, in charge of all those kids, on your own, never quite knowing what was coming; juggling expectations, good and bad, a chance to change them forever, a second away from some car crash.

The inspector continued to avoid eye contact with anyone, pupils or teacher. Perhaps this was his professional mask – like a judge handing out a death sentence, quite impersonal, the blind operative of objective order. Or maybe he was just bored. The man's face was set tight, brow deeply furrowed. He had so many heaps of papers and forms. He kept sighing. Maybe it was all his weighty responsibilities: how lofty and serious and difficult it all must be, to know what was right, thought Dom, suddenly in awe, not so much of the man but of this wise aspiration, born only by those who must have proved themselves beyond criticism, whose judgement could only be infallible.

But he noticed the man had a stain on his tie, was wearing odd socks. Maybe he had no Mrs Tombs to sort him, and, yes, he did look really whacked, sleep in his eyes. He kept changing spectacles as if he could not see the papers in front of him, or the class, clearly. Perhaps this was no razor-sharp goddess of judgement wielding the staff of harsh justice in the name of an inalienable and impossible integrity of practice, production and assessment. Maybe some of these inspectors had human characteristics.

And Dom so wanted to impress, whatever yesterday's comedy.

The lesson continued – better than smoothly, well really. Dom could have waltzed off, then, down the corridor. Job done: sucks to Hennock, anyone else who put him down.

Then Dom divided the class into groups for activities all in the 'best modern manner'. The inspector suddenly stood up, started walking around asking individuals if they had understood what was going on, the tasks they had been allocated. Perhaps he was just stretching his legs. The pupils would look him up and down when addressed, staring back at him mostly with total nonchalance, one or two cowering slightly as if he were some alien being who might suddenly sprout some child devouring appendage that would dismember, then glut. Dom pretended to be busy with others, his ears straining for intelligence of what the man was up to, nerves taut again.

'Do you understand what you've been asked to do?' he said to a boy called Sam, one of Dom's more sensitive, gentle and slightly vacant pupils. Sam looked back at him, staring with angelic blankness, quite uncomprehending.

'Have you understood the lesson, so far?' pursued the inspector deep in the groove of his training.

Sam's mouth dropped open. He looked the man up and down as if being spoken to in Mandarin. A beatific smile appeared on his face; but not a word came out.

The inspector tried again.

'What instructions have you been given? What is the point of what you are doing? Do you understand?'

Help, thought Dom.

'Shakespeare,' said Sam, feeling that this might be a worthwhile, impressive thing to say, hoping this strange intruder might move on, leave him alone. But the inspector had a brief to tick.

'What's the objective of the lesson?' the man tried again.

'Homework,' replied Sam.

The inspector hoping that this was some kind of breakthrough nodded knowingly.

'Ah, too much?' he said with a cunning smile. 'You get too much homework?'

'Fourteen,' replied Sam.

He then started telling the inspector about his pet cow, Debbie, how he had to milk her for his dad when he got home from school; it had gone into labour this one time – the calf had got stuck half in and half out. Sam had helped the vet and was proud of it. He'd even offered to put his hand in, right up her cow shaft, he told him enthusiastically.

On the subject of his cow, Sam could be very eloquent.

The inspector was bemused. One of the other members of the group turned to the inspector and smiled. He had heard rumours at break.

'Borin' isn't he? He's always on about his cow. Sir, what's a white witch?'

The man seemed lost for words for a few moments.

The inspector returned to his desk rather confused, and looked at his notes in a desperate search for guidance – training hadn't quite covered this. Unseen by him as he studied his manual, one of the kids beside him, rather belatedly realising he had no paper for his task, suddenly took a piece off the inspector's desk, thinking it was spare, began writing on it, completing Dom's task.

Moments later, the inspector decided it was his duty to patrol again feeling his first sortie had not really secured the balanced, objective and empirical evidence he'd been told he needed for his report. As he began moving around, the boy who had taken the paper off his desk put his hand up addressing Mr Greaves, loudly and indignantly.

'Sir, someone has already written on this, can't we afford decent clean paper?'

Before Dom could reply the boy started reading in a wooden voice.

'*English. Interesting start, variety of activities and pace. Some pupils left behind. Sets too much homework question mark.* It's awful handwriting, Sir, like yours – it goes on: *needs to work on basic conprehension skills. What's conprehension, Sir?* Then it says *boy expletes.* Is that posh for f-t, Sir?'

But before Dom could respond, another boy who was allowed to use his device all the time because he could not write or read much, cried out, half horror, half fascination, holding up his screen for all to see.

'Sir, this pop up! I didn' do nothin' honest! I was only lookin' up what cowshaft meant.'

Even the more hardened members of the class, alongside the most outraged and disgusted, must volubly share their reactions to that whilst Sam sat back, proud for of his contribution to class that day.

A rather red-faced Dom could only deal with it all in his best professional way.

There was a sigh of relief from the class when the inspector left shortly after that.

The class instantly lost interest in doing any work, teasing Dom about his prospects. Vaguely aware that he had been a focus of real interest at one point, Sam put his hand up.

'Don' worry, Sir, he loved my talk about Debbie's shitter!'

*

That was almost the last Dom saw of the inspectors in the flesh, although one popped into a rehearsal later that day and seemed to be enjoying it; but he did not stop long. Two of the actors were reading in parts for people who had been stolen by Dr Hennock under the pretext of some special inspection duty or other. The impression gained could have been better.

Dom thought of all the good moments in rehearsals when something magical had seemed to stir amongst the cast, and rather ruefully of the ephemeral qualities of drama. Now and again, a moment could become a window into eternity when things flowed; but how could you ever capture that on demand, have it on tap? Hennock had emailed the staff over and over that the inspectors would judge on what they actually saw. How odd, fleeting, unsatisfactory their glimpse must sometimes be.

That, and a story and a picture about a cow's back end.

Alison saw him later looking rather down.

'Don't worry,' she said. 'Whatever they've seen, if they're any good at their job, they know it's only a snapshot. If they're not realists and human beings they have no place in a classroom.'

Some snapshot, he thought remembering the pop up. He hoped she was right. He wished it had all been marvellous, every second: and that could be known, objectively on all sides, for always: vanity, of course. But you had to begin somewhere. If these people were human as Alison claimed, the lady inspector apart, they must know something of that.

*

The four new colleagues chanced to meet later in the Staff Room. No one had time (or thought it discreet) to retreat to the pub whilst the inspection continued. Attila might be lying in ambush out on the road, in the woods, spying with a telescope on the Cloud, or hovering on a broomstick over local hostelries, picking out the debauched.

Although there was inevitable awkwardness now between Emma and Mike, they were still young colleagues together, wanting to swap stories, exchange experiences, find common ground in the current storm.

Paul was full of the fact that one of his lessons had been observed and the inspector had commented on its excellence at the end. Hennock had found out (with Paul's help): it was to be used as evidence of outstanding practice. Paul could hardly contain himself -he had conducted it all in the key language, all the pupils contributing with little prompting. He'd also spoken to Attila about his plans for his ideal school. She had praised his enthusiasm, Hennock told him.

Dom was more reassured by Emma's experience. She was angrily indignant that the same lady inspector, she refused the nickname, had only been in her room for minutes. The class had been doing some acting, mangling it again. The lady had cast a cold eye on pupils and staff, written copious notes, taken one or two aside to interrogate, then left without a word, or even a ghost of a smile.

'How can she assess anything from that? This whole inspection business is a farce here. I was commended on my last placement.'

Mike had had a good lesson, but Paul wanted to hog the limelight.

'It's a given they always like active lessons like games,' he told Mike.

Alison bustled through at that moment, looking for the Doctor.

'Cheer up, you four. They're all right, even Attila. Yes, I've heard the name. Hope she hasn't. She's just doing her job. Most think more of the school than we give ourselves credit for, and the pupils and teachers. And they aren't here to trip us up. You always get one or two who have something to prove. You lot have nothing to worry about,' but before they could pursue that she was gone.

Seconds later, Dr Hennock stuck his head round the door looking for Alison.

'Everyone finished for the day? Taking it easy? Not complacent, I hope? There's still tomorrow. Remember, they can observe lessons twice if they have serious concerns. Professional demeanour is important at all times, not just when we're being formally observed. Anyone know where Alison might be, or are you all too busy? Badge, please Emma!' he said, departing with a smile.

Even Mike was rattled.

'What is it with that guy?'

Emma looked as if she were about to follow, give him a piece of her mind.

'You know, the pupils think Attila and he are old friends, had a fling once upon a time. Frankenstein and his Bride,' commented Paul trying to recover their mood.

But their moment had gone.

They made as if to leave. Other lessons were calling, even before much of a breath could be taken. Their moments in the spotlight- or headlights- was history.

When the others had left, Dom and Emma lingered.

'All right?' began Dom, unsure where to start after his recent rebuff.

She shook her head.

'If I can help in any way.'

He wanted to say he was always here for her; but it sounded cheesy.

'Maybe we could- let's have a drink, go to the pub, when all this is finished?'

'Leave it, Dom. Please, just leave it.'

Dom was determined not to, but Dr Hennock and Alison came back in at that moment.

'I'll text later,' he said, trying to sound matter of fact.

Hennock looked at the two of them and then seemed to dismiss them from his thoughts, moving off with Alison into a corner of the room, where they talked earnestly, confidentially about something.

Dom smiled warmly at Emma, but she was preoccupied. He had to go.

Emma remained, looking sad. She glanced at Hennock and Alison in the corner, then looked away, sighing. She turned to stare out of the wide Staff Room window, her eyes fixed on some far horizon of her own.

*

The following day, there was more a feeling of simple acceptance than anything else; they'd done their bit, their personal best, if it were not good enough it was too late.

Whilst the inspection team might reach for its thoughtful conclusions, the staff must wait – as usual for theirs. Some hoped, naively perhaps, for some blessing from above: *the school was a successful, unique and precious institution. Pupils and staff were happy and fulfilled.* Most expected rather less. Sam might have put all the palaver and expectations, good and bad, more simply and eloquently. Mr Walker confidently predicted a disastrous report – but he was going to retire.

Waseley, Hennock and Alison had a meeting after school with some governors to hear the first conclusions. Everybody who still cared held their breath.

Things had one final sting in the tail on the last full day, however affecting poor Mr Royal in just the way Dom had feared.

Dr Hennock had stubbornly insisted on continuing with his own programmes of mutual observation during the inspection. Even Alison could not deter him: good practice in action he insisted.

Dom suspected otherwise.

Dr Hennock himself had demanded to go into one of Royal's lessons. Charles had gone to Waseley about it, saying it was too much during an inspection, almost bullying, and reminding everyone of his thirty years of doing; but Waseley had backed Hennock, perhaps to placate the man who was running the inspection, doing the heavy lifting.

There had been a row and then another one after Royal had ended up being observed with a member of the inspection team in his room alongside Hennock- something quite beyond the pale, totally unprofessional all agreed.

Dom heard it all later, this time from Charles himself.

'Do you know, they sat there side by side like Star Chamber members, actually conferring at one point: talk about unprofessional behaviour. I shall speak to my union. I have complained to Waseley again, but he won't do anything. Yes, I got a bit sidetracked. But the kids did so well! And did any of the grownups in the room say anything at all at the end? That man!'

Paul gave a different account.

'It was a trap. Hennock wanted someone else to witness what he calls Royal's Ramblings –lack of planning, hinting about his drinking. From what I hear, he got his evidence.'

Dom imagined the lesson. Surely they would have seen something of what he had himself, even if only some of it ticked today's right boxes? But no quality of mind or teaching and learning mattered if Mr Royal were under the influence. There had been something about it in his contract Dom remembered, drink, drugs, professional behaviour. It had rather startled him to see it there in black and white. There had been rumours of teachers like that when he was at school but it all seemed so remote, unreal then, funny even to think of teachers wasted.

*

In the way of Hillview, however, nothing to do with Mr Royal or the inspection as a whole seemed to rise to any immediate crisis or conclusion. Soon their own judgements carefully reached and wise recommendations drawn, despite the inevitable and sometimes comical misadventures, the inspectors were gone, even Attila, though rumour ran she had to be prised away.

'Left on her broomstick?' said Mr Walker, but no one thought it funny anymore.

There was to be a formal debrief tomorrow after school, but all everyone wanted today was to get away home.

How long was it till Christmas?

It was Terry who really had the last words as he went round locking up with a vengeance like some keeper of hell, turning the keys gleefully on the eternal captives, pronouncing to anyone who strayed within fire.

'Section? My arse! Nobody asked my f-in' opinion. A school, and a bunch o' jabberin' teachers? What do they expec', f-in' Camelot?'

CHAPTER THIRTY-TWO

WASH UP

Inspection might be over but more dramas were soon upon the staff. First of all, Mr Royal did not show the following week. No one knew where he was, why he was not at school. The leadership team would not be drawn.

It fell to Dom and Emma to cover his lessons, with no information on what to do with his charges. There was another full time member of staff, a Miss Tidy, and staff who taught English part-time, but the bulk of the examination teaching fell to Charles, Emma and Dom. Miss Tidy's name suited. She was a neat and effective operator, but happier with younger children, coloured pens and paper, and as little homework as possible. The extra fell, heavily, to those left. Dr Hennock was too busy to be helpful; Emma unleashed her indignation on Alison, but she was saying little except that it was difficult to get supply teachers, especially English teachers who were up to it. Dom wondered what she meant; but she seemed irritable, not her usual calm self.

Then came a meeting with provisional feedback from the inspection. The staff expected that, but not other developments.

As a reward, they had been promised a celebratory tea. Katie had objected as it clashed with an extra class, and one of her after school activities; but she was placated by insisting on a vegan tea for everyone else. The 'vegan scones' were concrete in texture and stemmed from Dotty's cookery classes before the fire it was alleged; only Mike was constitutionally strong enough to manage more than one.

There was a long wait before the Head appeared, wearing his habitual bonhomie.

'I shalln't keep you,' he said with no trace of irony. 'I simply want to share with you a brilliant outcome for the school, although everything depends of course on the final report.'

He went on to paint a broad picture of all the pleasant things that had, he said, been recorded about Hillview, and indicated, more perfunctorily, that there were indeed, of course, a few, very few, and only minor areas of the school and its life that might need to have some marginal acceleration in the pace of their improvement.

Dom could see Hennock nodding at this point as if only criticisms met approval.

The Headmaster wrapped up. Some of the staff tried to find out a bit more about exactly what the inspectors had recommended, but Waseley only did broad brush, and was as wily as a politician with difficult questions. Challenges came. How did all this relate to the recent controversial proposals to change the school's identity completely, what had they made of that, the possible independence of the school, how this all fitted together. What was really going on, please?

Waseley was all assurance: it was a great school, the best school to go to in the county, one of the best in the country indeed. Whatever happened none of *that* would ever change, only get better.

'Now, I suggest, as that seems to be all, we've all had a hard few days so let's all adjourn and enjoy some more of

Mrs Dot's delicious cakes and sumptuous tea!' Mrs Dot was all smiles in her corner, although she spoilt her moment by dropping a plate of scones, and apologising to anyone who came near her for a quarter of an hour on the theme. The scones bounced like dambuster bombs when dropped. Mike said they might be useful for cricket, but where was the cream.

But before they broke for tea Hennock had suddenly started speaking.

'If I may just add, Headmaster: what of course, the Headmaster has not said is that on the back of the inspection, agreement has been reached on the urgent necessity to proceed with planning our future, reorganisation of the school, possible independence– particularly its financial base, something that could be discussed only very informally with the inspectors behind the scenes. Further details of this will emerge over the next few weeks. The general consensus is that Hillview does need to secure its own identity, its future more clearly.'

What did that mean?

Dom, watching Mr Waseley closely, noticed a momentary flash of anger cross his face. For a second or two he seemed at a loss for words, as if he, too, were taken by surprise.

'Right! Thank you Dr Hennock and, er, he means of course only *planning*, and with, and not before full consultation, with all our constituent bodies, a vote, agreement from staff,' added Waseley quickly. He looked hard at Hennock.

Dr Hennock sat back avoiding the gaze of his boss. For a moment or two there was palpable awkwardness.

'Headmaster. I think you'll find the main thing is to let staff know that big changes, – reorganisations, are now urgently and actively being considered. They lie before us in the near future, not some never, never-'

Another crash from Mrs Dot – this time a bottle of water and a teapot– broke the tension. Some laughed, but staff were concerned, confused. It's possible that if Mr Royal had been there, or indeed Mr Tring, who was catching up training his musicians, one or the other would have led a more robust enquiry into what was up. But Waseley swept all aside.

'Thank you, Dr Hennock, but all this is of course for *future* consideration at a proper time and place. Now I ask staff to focus on our little celebration after all that. Relax in the knowledge that we have much to congratulate ourselves on!'

Before anyone else said anything else, he was up, leading them all quickly to the back of the room where Mrs Dot's pantomime continued. No one was deceived, however. Things that had seemed a distant prospect now loomed large. And there was obviously some kind of rift between Waseley and Hennock. The inspection was to be used in some way or other, by one side or another.

Whatever, the staff would have to work it all out, then live the practicalities. They might even have to learn to live in a very different world as an independent school, about which they could know very little until, and if, it happened. Over the hurdle of the inspection, many saw a whole tide of further anxieties surging towards them. Couldn't they please just get on with their jobs?

*

Paul, Mike and Dom met later, at last able to escape to the pub. Emma would not be joining them. She had work to catch up after being away, then the inspection. So she said. Dom felt her absence as acutely as anyone, including Mike.

They agreed on one thing: it had already been a long half term.

Paul was late but that gave Dom chance to speak first to Mike about Emma. He knew his own motives too well to think he was just being kind, but learnt little more. Mike did, however, confess to stronger feelings and more hurt than Dom had supposed: there had been more going on than he had known.

Guys were not much good at talking about feelings or relationships, thought Dom. People kept up a front, some image, especially men: there was always a degree of pretence, as he was pretending now.

Things had come out in pieces. Dom had to wonder how deep Emma's feelings had been. If Emma and Mike had begun because they were simply single, thrown together in a new world, it was clear feelings had developed strongly on Mike's side. Perhaps it had been mostly physical attraction. And a proper relationship had to be more than just enjoying yourself Dom told himself, in his way. But then he reflected that there were some things about others you never really knew – a dishonesty even to think you could imagine.

Their talk of starting their own school had not been fancy, however. But they had begun to quarrel, parted in misunderstanding when Mike had gone on his trip. After the text exchange, they had met up right at the end of the holidays. Emma had drawn her line then. She would always care for him, but it was over: it had been going nowhere. Mike could not accept an explanation that was no answer to his feelings. So there was impasse, resentment, bitterness.

'I thought I'd found someone different, special. She's weird – doesn't know what she wants. She says she wants us to be friends still. I need to be mature about it. *I* need to be mature!'

Dom realised he had always thought that he could easily place Mike, fancying his own feelings finer. He felt embarrassed. It made him pull at a disturbing thread of thought he had had before: namely, that everyone liked to believe themselves secretly superior to others, in some way or other.

And what did all this say about Emma herself?

But Dom's repeated 'I'm sorrys' did not bear too close an examination. Mike was quite unaware of any kind of duplicity in his friend, consoling himself by stoking up feelings against Emma. There had even been a bit of a storm on social media. The kids, some of the staff at school, had got wise to something, taking sides as they might. Bitterness intensified. It had been quite a drama, for as long as anything lasted in a virtual world.

Paul arrived then, hot with other news.

'Royal is signed off for the duration – supposedly sick,' he announced, but only when he had settled himself comfortably by the fire, made his audience wait whilst he downed a half, chomped his way through a first bag of crisps, would he give more.

He made a drinking gesture with his hand.

'We know what that means. He's been told to 'rest', sort himself out by Waseley, instigated by you know who. If he ever comes back, there's to be guarantees. If I were in charge-.'

Mike was in no mood to be anything other than dismissive.

'How's he got away with it for so long?'

Dom said little. What future lay ahead for someone whose whole world was school? After all that, to disappear under some cloud, a shadow of all he'd been. He thought of his grandfather, now dead, slowly crucified by dementia, a shell of a once great spirit, haunted by memories of things he no longer understood, his own ghost in a world peopled with figures he could not recognise, everything that makes life – except sleeping and eating taken. In his imagination, he followed Mr Royal home, all sad thoughts.

Paul talked on- more about his plans, school plans for reforming Hillview. Dom might ordinarily have been excited by prospects of change, stirred recently by Joe's criticisms, even if he hadn't agreed with them. But when he thought of some of the personalities caught up in it all, he felt only frustration. It all muddled up with feelings about Emma being free, mingled with confusions, doubts. And the fate of Mr Royal. A shiver went down Dom's spine. He remembered Alison's warning not to end up like Charles. Perhaps Emma was right to be shy of school, so much work. Could it suck you dry, empty you out, push you aside when you were no more use? Who would say thank you for that?

'You look so miserable. Cheer up! We're survived inspection, the school's still standing – for the time being anyway. Only your crap drama production, then a few weeks to go and it's Christmas!' Mike said. 'I'm the sad case.'

'The course of true love,' said Dom, giving his mate an affectionate hug.

Paul's ears had pricked up. He looked at Mike knowingly. Perhaps he had been all over social media, he must get his information from somewhere.

What a triangle they were, Dom smiled wryly. Was there ever completely true friendship or did it always mask secret tensions? It ought to be pure, like true love, self sacrificing, as the old books said.

But Paul had more.

'Things are going to get interesting. Royal out, the old guard put in their box. I hear the inspection was nowhere near as rosy as the Head made out. He's a casual liar that man. There's differences over what to do, Hennock, Waseley, we all saw that. Darren is trying to outflank the Head, push change.'

Paul sat back, tearing into another bag of bad crisps.

Dom's frustrations hardened into anger. Here it all was again. He felt a rush of contempt, the mean things people could do and become, like Katie Trippett: nip, nip, nip at each other – tearing into things, turning people into cartoon characters, carping caricatures.

'You enjoy all this don't you; like a pig in shit: school intrigue, politics, everything and everybody trivialised, less than they should be?' he blurted.

'Deep Dom's back!' Mike laughed.

Paul merely smiled, noisily finishing his bag, licking the salt from his fingers.

Dom looked around the pub. There was the landlord bantering crassly about something or other with the wags at the bar. One of them he remembered from before, his laughs coming frequently, unbearably harsh across the floor, like an excited donkey braying.

They sat in silence for a few minutes.

Eventually, under the pretext of ordering more drinks, Mike went across to the bar, started chatting up the barmaid. Paul began again. Dom listened, as so often before: who was to rise – who fall –what would change, what would be chucked, as Hennock gained sway.

Indeed: it had been a long half term.

CHAPTER THIRTY THREE

CULTURE WARS?

Post-inspection blues did not, however, last long. The inspection might be something of an anticlimax for someone looking for that key to all things – but whatever had come and gone, whatever things might be or were, Dom was young, was keeping his dreams of better, thank you.

The job.

That was always a rollercoaster evidently, but he was continuing to learn; and, well, life was never dull. Today, for example, was a particularly interesting challenge as Dr Hennock's long-planned Chinese student exchange visit had begun, hard on the heels of inspection.

Whatever the real motivation for the students' appearance in the school – rumour said it was recruitment for the future – it was genuinely exciting to have some of nearly forty pupils, from such a vibrant, different culture, with him that day. They sat there, mildly bemused at first, still jetlagged, culture bumped, understanding less than they seemed to, yet immaculately behaved.

An English person teaching English, British culture, in a small country school, eccentric in its make-up, under its own pressures of change, in a quaint, unbelievably cosy and pretty landscape, even on a dank November day, must inspire their interest, their envy.

It was an infinitely better world, Dom believed, for them, so different from the corporate China of his imagination, with its dystopian urban jungles – all modern high-rise towers, relentless productivity, crushing state technology, surveillance. He felt confident, even superior: quietly proud of his Englishness, sure of its generous humanity, whatever identity crisis the school itself might face. He was, after all, a free man in a free country, whatever the likes of Joe might say, representing a way of life that, for all its flaws, was a privilege.

His class, *that* class again, were finishing off the unit on the future that had provoked Jane's push back. They were talking freedom and control, nothing small or mean here.

This topic will make my guests think too, he told himself.

Tim was asking a question.

Thank goodness one or two were always ready to speak up, whatever the rest.

'Are *we* free, Sir?'

This turned into an argument, after resistance to think at all. But then Dom turned it, cautiously he hoped, on to education itself. It became a conversation about how choices and chances were limited in Hillview. *They definitely weren't free.* So the pupils told Dom. But he felt he could use that.

'Let's ask our Chinese friends. You live in a different world to ours. Do you have lots of rules and regulations you don't like, complain a lot?'

There was a pause. The Chinese teacher, who was minding his pupils, did not say anything for a moment.

Tim smiled at Mr Greaves: he'd got the point.

But Jane spoke up.

'That's not fair, Sir. We've been doing China in geog. Dr Hennock says they have given so many poor people a far better way of life in the last decades.'

In rather faltering and broken English the Chinese teacher took his cue.

'I think freedom, it depend on point of view. Is freedom to be poor and ignorant or unfair a freedom to respect?'

Some of Dom's pupils, those who were listening, smirked. The Chinese teacher had kicked Sir's ball back hard.

Dom could not resist, however, pushing on.

'That's a very fair point Mr Zhang'. He hoped he'd got the name right, however else he might sound. 'But many in our country see yours as one where there is a lot of state control – surveillance. Spying I suppose we would say, on people -to keep them in line in ways we would not accept.'

That'll make my lot think.

'But for most people, this not seen on daily lifes. If you mean we keep order, that different. But, and we think important, without authority, there no freedom for the people to do well, improve themself. Everyone lazy and poor,' the Chinese teacher replied.

The class, those who were with it, looked momentarily at two different worlds.

Dom had to admit it was quite a good reply.

One of the Chinese pupils said something which no one could understand.

'He says, anarchy not freedom,' the Chinese teacher nodded wisely.

Another spoke up -first in faltering English- then in Mandarin to the others.

'She say that we not see things that foreign media say about us in ordinary lifes and that state control is for our freedom.'

Dom nodded smiling, but his tactic was rather backfiring. When you thought of how things had been in politics recently in his own country, or goings on in the school! Perhaps the class could rally, realise their better luck, brimming good fortunes.

'D'you have to work so hard as we do at school?' cried another pupil.

It struck a chord with the natives.

There was a chorus of agreement: *it's so unfair*.

The Chinese pupils, however, seemed to be smiling. Eventually, their teacher spoke for them.

'They say they think your pupil very lucky here; but do they respect what they have? For Chinese, freedom is freedom to understand what they have recently, and not take for normal. Pardon, but they say Chinese hungry; are English hungry still?''

'They eat dog!' came a mutter followed by a few laughs.

Part of Dom wanted to laugh, but he hoped his guests had not heard. He felt like giving his class a few well-chosen words. Someone in another class had apparently banged on about how people ought to stay in their own country. But you weren't always free as a teacher.

'See, I told some of you lot that you don't work hard enough!' tried Dom.

It sort of worked. Something stirred. Grievances about school flowed, not all idle ones.

The Chinese students watched politely at first, but then made comments.

Dom thought how sensible they sounded, how mature. He was quite certain that they could be selfish and awkward, and little bs in their own way when the mood took them too, but they were intelligent, curious, hungry to know things; little apathy here. He remembered a Modern Language teacher they had had at school, when other languages were still vaguely popular. He had been so rude about Britain. Where were all the facilities, the music, the civility, the society and culture he had at home in Germany he had asked.

They had responded by giving him a Nazi nickname.

He looked around the room, the debate continuing, a sort of cultural exchange he hoped. His eye caught the word irony, its wise teacherly definition on the wall: *the reverse or opposite of what it appears to mean*, it read.

He was learning, as usual, something different from what he had set out to teach.

They eat dog.

Food for thought indeed.

*

Soon the Chinese guests had come and gone their way. Mr Walker and a number of staff pronounced the visit a waste of time, and complained to Hennock and the Head about the pressure of accommodating all this straight after an inspection. For once, Dom was on Darren's side.

When he spoke to the class they had visited next lesson, they, with one or two exceptions, were definitely very glad that they were not at school or had to work in China, thank you. It was much better being British, living in England. They would not swap.

They had to work too hard out there.

Dom played devil's advocate.

'Sir's on their side. You hate us now you've been here half a term like all the old teachers,' ventured one.

'No I don't, don't be silly. Actually I would much prefer to teach you lot: you're more open, more fun, even if you can be a pain. I'm just putting another point of view,' said Dom, not quite sure what he really felt.

'They *do* eat dog there, Sir,'

'So we heard last lesson.'

'Snake.'

'Teacher.'

'Sir, I think you're right. My dad says they're taking over the world – they work harder and are disciplined. Not like our crap country. There's too many of them. He says we'll all end up looking like them.'

Uproar.

Dom reflected: maybe he still had some way to go with this class.

*

Shortly after the visit, Dom tried to talk to Emma.

He had found her alone in the Staff Room. She never answered his texts, or calls. He had tried unsuccessfully several times to catch up with her. She was spending time with other members of staff now even with Katie with whom she seemed close.

He went and sat by her, making pleasantries. She scarcely seemed to notice.

She was marking at one of the big tables, every so often looking out of the windows across the school campus towards the Cloud, all veiled in the drizzle and mist of a cold November day that would never grow properly light. Every so often she would push back her hair, lift her eyes from her brisk tick and flick progress, see some world all her own.

This close to her, he could have reached out, put his arm around her.

Different from books.

'How's it going?' he asked a second time, heartily.

He hoped no one else would barge in.

'Trying to get these finished-before last lesson,' she said, not looking up.

'I had those Chinese in my lesson,' said Dom, after a pause. 'You know, they came across as more mature than some of ours.'

'Why shouldn't they? I hope you have not been infected by country school xenophobia. Good chance to challenge some of our kids' silly prejudices.'

'I was trying to get them to talk about their way of life how different it is from ours.'

'You would,' she said. 'You're always so intense. You realise the school is only interested in them because they hope to make money from them one day.'

Dom sighed.

'It's interesting culturally. Did they come to see you?'

'Me?! No!' said Emma continuing to mark.

'It was like these Chinese kids had a stronger sense of loyalty to their school – and country than we do. They care, whereas sometimes ours don't seem bothered, it doesn't matter to them, what we owe to what's around us. They take it for granted. I s'pose they're only kids.'

'We're all kids these days: you heard Charles. Identity begins and ends with what we want.'

'Oh!' replied Dom.

There was a pause.

'I'm sorry, I'm interrupting you.'

'Yes, you are.'

Dom sat back for a moment, putting his hands in his pockets, resting the back of his head on the top of the chair.

He looked around the room to see if they were still alone.

He sat forward, moving the chair closer, turning more towards her so she could not continue to ignore him.

She seemed to stiffen.

Dom ventured once more.

'Look, have I done something wrong? I'm sorry about you and Mike. Can't we still be... friends at least? I mean...If you want to talk about things or if I can help.'

'You, help? How can you help?'

'I just wondered if you were a bit lonely- if you wanted to talk.'

'Why should I want to talk to you about anything to do with that? Let's leave it, can we? I've got stuff to do in case you haven't noticed.'

'There's no need to take it out on me. I'm just trying to help,' said Dom.

'What, so you can go and gossip about me, talk to the kids about things, I suppose?'

'No, course not!' Dom cried. 'Who would say anything to the kids about anything?'

She looked at him, for the first time, shaking her head slightly.

'Someone has.'

'What do you mean?'

'Someone has been talking – making up things about me on social media. You know.'

'What about, you and-.You know how much rubbish there is. I don't do social media anyway. You know that: it's one of my things.'

Emma seemed to tut at that.

'So you said,' she continued, not looking at him now. 'Someone has been posting stuff about me – Mike: it's worse here than-' she put her pen away, looking out.

Then she began to gather her books.

'Anyway, it doesn't matter-as you say, so much crap. And I've told you I can't hack it here, so won't be around much longer having to deal with it, will I? '

She was sorting her books aggressively into piles.

'Look, I don't do social media. Honest. And I wouldn't-It's just first-term blues, the inspection, stuff. I'm sure there's all sorts about me. Don't read it, that's my advice.'

'There's plenty about you. And I definitely wouldn't read it if I were you. But everyone does, all the time, lives by it in this little puddle of a place. Except you, of course. You never do anything wrong. Not much fun when you're the target, is it?'

'It's not me. I've told you. Anyway, It's just stuff people make up.'

'How do you know if you never look?'

'Look, ignore it: unless someone's actually done something really unworthy, what's it got to do with anyone else?'

'God, you are naive, aren't you? And what do you mean by *unworthy?!* What do you know? What's Mike been saying?'

'Nothing! Well, nothing much.'

'You see!'

'Well, he is hurt, you know,' said Dom, stung into saying something.

'Ah, that just proves it all. *Thanks.* I'm not of course.'

'I only said Mike was hurt. I'm not laying blame.'

'How kind of you! But that's what you think, I know it. *Unworthy, blame* – your words!'

How had they got here. Dom was lost.

For a few seconds they sat there in silence.

Emma looked around then. She lowered her voice.

'Some people think they can say and do whatever they want to whoever they want. It's all a laugh in the end. Someone like me tries to make her own choices, and then she always has to endure some kind of public moral humiliation because I'm female!'

'*Emma!*'

He looked at Emma, her face sad but hard. She'd not spoken to him in this way before.

'Look, I know how in silly rumours and opinions, blame gets spread. They're nothing to do with me, honestly. I'm not that sort of- Mike isn't either. I never know what's going on around me anyway until it hits me between the eyes. Even then, everyone seems to be a couple of steps ahead.'

He was trying to be sympathetic even whilst he nursed his own little resentment that she should take it out on him. He sought around for something more robust to add.

'I always try to hold on to the idea – with real friends – you shouldn't ever use each other in anyway. You're not like that.'

'God, you are pompous, you know. Do you think you're better than the rest of us or something? What do you know about any of it -or anything? Nice little speech, but I bet you think all sorts of things,'

'Oh, *please!*' cried Dom.

He got up, moved away. There was a pause. Emma had taken her pen out, started marking once more. Dom looked at her. He couldn't not feel sorry.

'Let's not quarrel. Aren't things enough of a muddle. This is silly. I'm sorry. I'm...fond of you. I think you know that. I am trying to help...I'm here for you, that's all I'm trying to say.'

'You are, are you? Even though I am unworthy?'

Dom shook his head. He came and sat down by her again, facing her.

Gently, he laid his hand on her hand as her pen poised over all the mistakes in front of her. For a second he thought she would pull away angrily.

'Emma, there's only so much time...specially in this place. Please. I care- when you're upset – hurt. Whoever is at fault, this is all just going nowhere as it is now.'

She seemed to be about to speak when they both became aware Dr Hennock had quietly entered the room, was standing observing them. Dom wondered if he had been listening outside.

He was smiling his smile. Dom let go Emma's hand, sat back in his chair.

'Personal problems?' said Hennock, looking from one to the other, taking it all in.

CHAPTER THIRTY-FOUR

VIRUS

The interest an inspection, then the Chinese visit, had generated, was fast succeeded by a series of mini-crises that rocked the little world of Hillview.

First, in the wake of the departure of the oriental students, a new kind of flu struck, and either distracted or quite disabled most of the community for a couple of what would normally have been very busy weeks.

Everyone was affected in some way.

'So much for global Hillview!' cried Mr Walker, triumphantly claiming that the bug was the practical consequence of someone's greedy dreams – for Chinese pupils' cash.

For a few days, alarm ran high, but all too soon diminished as it was confirmed that the virus was, after all, nothing specially new, just another variant of an old foe. It was an education in itself- administering a dose of humility to all- if temporary. Meanwhile, Mr Walker developed a new version of an old theme: modern science and technology would never match nature.

Dom, as he had told James all those weeks ago, had never been to a school with boarders, worked anywhere that had some pupils who lived in, so he was surprised how quickly the bug overcame not just the residents but pierced the whole community, staff, support workers, admin staff, and most of all the children themselves who developed a particularly nasty symptom, throwing up without warning.

The twins hurtled around everywhere pretending to be ill, especially in rehearsals, making vomiting noises, until they went down with it. Even Mr Jolson got angry when they started a competition to see who could make their bile fly farthest. They continued to torment teachers for the rest of the term with the threat of projectile vomiting if things ever became dull. Terry banned assistance from his workforce out of concern for health and safety. He'd not forgotten being told off for messing up the chairs during inspection, and was threatening to strike, or leave. No one took him seriously, but it was an added palaver for staff. Miss Tidy was an early victim, leaving Emma and Dom even more stressed with their workload, struggling with cover teachers who themselves were even more in short supply, if not stricken. Dom remembered his first day at school, the girl in his first rehearsal. Omens?

The bug spread without fear or favour. Some pupils who caught it straight away were quite laid up; those who didn't lived in a state of apprehension where they fancied they were getting it; those who appeared completely untouched got irritated in turn when they found lessons and activities – even teachers wanting, and began to appreciate the merits of routine. Pupils went back, gingerly, in time, wax-faced, washed out and jelly legged into the hurly-burly of classes only to find staff missing in turn, or alien teachers in not very effective charge. They wondered why they had bothered to rise from sickbeds at all.

But no one died. This time.

Mr Walker relished telling of an epidemic some twenty years ago when there had been more boarders. No one had taken it seriously at first, realised quite what was to come.

One boy had actually died at school, in the night, alone in the school san. It was a terrible story. The boy had been found on the floor, trying to get help, even reach a phone to get his parents it was said, before his lonely battle had done for him. The tale lived hard in Dom's memory, like some Dickensian shadow of another age, outrageous in a modern world where progress promised everyone everything forever.

For a while, the school nurse, a Miss Joy Bistle, a cheerful kindly character, a good friend of Mrs Dot (Mrs Dot claimed), came into her own, running her own world within a world of the sick and ill. She usually spent most of her time listening to the anxieties of a generation warped by the expectations and depredations of social media, its bullying comparisons. She helped with the costumes for the play too, when not abetted by Mrs Dot, so Dom knew her a bit, liking what he found. She understood young staff.

She had redecorated the san, still called a sickbay then, with some of her own money, even had its name updated to the welfare centre, but the term sickbay lingered, horribly fitting for the latest health crisis.It had been a rather run down place, poorly equipped; but few had bothered until they were forced to use it: it was for other people's emergencies. It was at least bright and cheerful now, a bit of a refuge for pupils, even staff, in normal times, desperate for some non judgemental kindness. Dom would have been surprised had he known just who and how often some of his colleagues found their way up there, sometimes just for a lie down.

Now Miss Bistle was everywhere, deploying first cautionary advice, then prescriptions and doting care. Every so often she emerged from her war zone to report on the latest ebb and flow of the epidemic. Her word became law and held even more consequence than that of Waseley or even Hennock himself, who for once lost his supremacy at the crossroads of every decision.

The Headmaster was off ill with the curse of the bug for a good week. He went under the supervision of Mrs Waseley, recently returned from America with a mass of new-minted theories about mental and physical health, especially diet, which she was burning to impose on anyone she could capture. Subject to her ministrations, he eventually needed even longer than most to recover. Meanwhile, the good doctor was the only one who seemed untouched by any kind of infection, much to the dismay of rather more of his colleagues than even he might have guessed.

Whilst Miss Bistle was a kindly soul who put herself out for others, her deputy, Mrs Trotman was a woman of an older school, brusque with anyone who was not really ill, and contemptuous of malingerers. Anyone from the boarding house who felt rough was presented without ceremony with a green plastic bucket to throw up in. Woe betide anyone who vomited anywhere else. But beneath a fierce exterior she too had a kind heart and a deal of experience that probably did a lot more good than many worlds of kindness so easy to take advantage of.

She tut-tutted at staff who tried to keep working when ill, was quite rude when they resisted looking after themselves, feeling they were indispensable, had to keep going. Whilst Miss Bistle had a collection of interesting DVDs and games for pupils on the mend that played fast and loose with age restrictions, and spread the various infections even more, Mrs Trotman believed that silence and proper bed rest speeded recovery. Occasionally she would break off from her duties to bemoan a culture where everyone was ever fearful of missing out on anything that was going, everyone so obsessed with themselves. They lacked, for the most part, she declared, the inner resources to deal with the slightest boredom, the simple sense to stop when ill, the very idea that the world could do without them even for a little while.

When Waseley returned from his own sickbed, he was confronted by Hennock who believed, not without some evidence, that some of the staff and pupils were taking advantage of the situation pretending to be more ill or ill for longer than they really were. Mrs Trotman put them both in their place, telling them how serious it was. Waseley tried to impose a kind of lockdown on the boarding house where the infection seemed to linger, but no one took it seriously, believing themselves mystically entitled to magic immunity. Meanwhile, the bug went its own way, armed with an efficacy all its own, quite unaware of any responsibility to anything except its own survival, like an untaught child of zero imagination.

About a week in, the epidemic spiked, with about a quarter of the pupils and staff laid up in one way or another. The school limped on. Teaching carried on through blended learning, those staff who remained on their feet having to deal with a class in front of them and more pupils, supposedly, online at home, never completely sure who was there or not. They were not allowed to view their charges in situ at home for safeguarding reasons. So they were never entirely sure if they were there, or if they were talking to themselves- a situation sadly familiar to them in some cases even when the pupils were physically present. Some felt they would run mad trying to teach several audiences at once, especially when they could neither see nor hear them half the time. It was *virtual* in both senses of the word, unlike the sneezing and coughing pupils who remained in class, a new batch vociferously ill each day.

Dr Hennock insisted, Waseley promised: it would all be over soon enough. Christmas was on the way. And they would resume the vaccination programmes the school had recently abandoned to save money, next year or the year after.

Hennock saw there would be a price to pay for all this, lost productivity, lost time whilst the school's future was all in the balance; but most staff were too busy to look beyond the immediate horizon of whether or not they got it, and if they did, how quickly they got over it, or if it lingered on into painful weeks of being neither properly better, nor poorly enough to take the time for the secure recovery they needed.

*

For Dom, it was another vivid learning experience. An almost Dickensian workhouse scene of washed out faces, the smell of hot palliative lemon drinks, pupils trailing around in slippers and tattered robes became a familiar pattern in the house above which he lodged. It made a deep impression on him, like the fire, coming out of nowhere, challenging the routines, perhaps illusions, of safety, stability.

He spent a day feeling ill but kept going, largely out of pride, feeling he was letting everyone down if he too went off alongside Mr Royal, Miss Tidy. Illness was weakness: he was a hero. Then he began to feel really awful, fretting about not being able to work, rehearse, do anything much. He struggled on, shivering and shaking, light-headed, every one telling him he looked awful, making it worse.

Eventually, Mrs Trotman caught up with him, took one look, told him he was a prat, angrily sent him to bed – but she turned up later with a hot drink, and kinder words.

Dom wondered if he were dying. For a day he disappeared completely into his symptoms, time circling to the rhythms of his own illness, a cruel captor, playing cat and mouse with his moods, whilst he lay a prisoner of a throbbing head, fitfully sleeping, waking to soggy sheets, an illusion of relief that vanished as soon as he sat up or tried to move much.

He became a child again, consumed with his own vulnerability and weakness, remembering when he had been ill as a kid, off school, hearing the sounds of the well world hurtling along indifferently in another time that he could not keep pace with. He lay helpless, almost tearful with weakness, surrounded by all the litter of the invalid – sticky spent tissues, bitter hot drinks, uneaten food that had no taste, crumpled, uncomfortable sheets. All his life and plans dwindled to a dot, the tiny room of his sick bed, a little world of suffering all his own. His last conversation with Emma grew in his imagination until it was the end of the affair, all affairs; he would never find love, happiness, but die young and alone like that poor kid all those years ago.

Mrs Trotman looked in on him.

'Still feeling sorry for yourself? You'll feel better if you give yourself time to rest,' she told him.

He turned over when she had gone, wondering how long it took to die.

Time changed and became his own. He existed quite apart from the world outside. He could hear far off bells ring as a day went on without him. Remote voices and the distant, so distant but almost endless clomp of feet between lessons, the scrape of desks on floors came to him. It all seemed to be muffled, taking place somewhere else, behind a gauze, a world as insubstantial to him as if he were its last ghost. He imagined his bed, spinning slowly far out at sea, beyond the reach or touch of any human hand, lost in a silent dark battle of body and mind.

But then, after a couple of days, when he thought he might just live again, he came back from that strange country of the unwell, still weak, yes, frighteningly weak, wondering if he would ever be strong again, but back in time and space once more. Miss Bistle, this time, looked in, took his temperature, told him he was on the mend. He began to cheer up, fret about what had been lost.

Dr Hennock phoned; to know when he would be back. Mrs Tombs appeared suddenly in his room and teased him for not pinning some socks together, but then told him he looked better than he had for days. It was a nasty bug – he shouldn't work so hard: young staff always overdid it. He was a good lad, deserved better.

Dom felt curiously emotional at that. He hated to show vulnerability, be weak. Illness had stolen some of his pride. People in books were never ill, lost days like that, unless it was some romantic part of the plot; but then, as he felt more and himself, his sense of humour came back. He wondered if all that intimacy with staff and boarders' undergarments had bestowed on Mrs Tombs the immune system of a lion.

He was soon back at work, wobbly and weak, but anxious to get on, get things sorted. Adrenalin kicked in, and he felt better, but he was more tired each evening than before, and began to leave what he could, what he absolutely did not have to do, and not strive for everything to be the best.

In a few days indeed, he was almost himself again. He almost completely forgot his own frailties, how they had defined him. The well forgot the ill world. He did determine never, ever to get ill again, however, just as he had before to never grow old and grumpy like Mr Walker, or Mr Royal.

*

Poor Emma had had a much harder time of it, disappearing to her flat for over a week of lonely battle, hard for one who had rarely been alone in her life before. Colleagues were sympathetic, but they'd been through it: these youngsters had to learn to cope.

Resilience, these days!

Dom had kept in touch with her through it all, but it had been one-sided apart from her teasing him at first that he was indulging in man flu, until she succumbed herself.

Back at work first himself, he had wondered how she was. No one seemed to know much. He covered one or two of her lessons that he did not have to. The children seemed pleased to see him- perhaps because Mr Walker had been teaching them. He tried speaking to Katie about Emma, although it annoyed him that he had to go through some intermediary.

'She's had a bad dose, but we're getting there,' was all he got.

Dom could not forgive her.

When Emma did return, at the effective insistence of Dr Hennock who was good at making others feel guilty, she looked different, strained, withdrawn, not herself.

'Why not take some more time off and get yourself properly better?' he ventured one moment when they were alone.

Emma was adamant.

'I'm so behind,' she said. 'It's impossible to rest properly anyway. You still have to send in work. There's all the marking. The kids aren't getting taught or doing anything, especially online. Hennock was such a s-t to me on the phone about cover. I'm never ill. '

'You don't seem quite yourself. In fact, since the holidays-' Dom ventured.

Emma looked at him for a moment then away.

'Don't let's go over all that again,' she said, but then, more like her old self, 'but thanks for keeping in touch... I'm glad someone remembered me. I've certainly had time to think. In fact I've more or less decided. I am not going to stay; not long anyway. The kids are all right; but this place, it just gets worse. Katie says there are more problems with staffing, duties – even finance, because of the flu. I can't see things getting easier here, can you? And what is there here for me?'

As things began to get back to normal, Emma seemed to fall more and more away from everything, slipping ever deeper into her own world, down and done in by flu and the torrent of things that were always flooding in that had to get done, even if the world was ending.

He hoped for another chance, a chance at least where they could talk; but then with all the lost time, school was even more of a pressure cooker: like marriage with extremely young kids, a matter of sheer survival.

CHAPTER THIRTY-FIVE

SNOW DAY

A good deal of November had already gone before it was really noticed that the leaves had finally fallen, the nights reached deep into the days. They were far into a second half with so many outcomes uncertain. Plans for change continued to rumble around in the background like a distant winter thunderstorm that was going on somewhere else and threatened always to approach with stinging hail and snow, but never quite arrived. Time was flying by ever more quickly, Dom thought. How would he ever get his play done?

Then, just as things seemed to settle, as the last weeks of November arrived, the country was hit by an unseasonably early snowfall on the back of a week of unusually hard frosts. Hillview's relative elevation and isolation meant more drama. The snow threatened to cut the school off altogether from the outside- for almost a whole day.

*

The pupils greeted the fall with enthusiasm. Impromptu snowball fights took place with the connivance of some of the younger staff, especially Mike, but a boy's cut lip and girl protesting about her soaking skirt, plus a rumour that some of the older, less scrupulous boys, were putting stones in their snow balls for better flight soon drew a notice resisted by the all pleasing Mr Waseley, but commanded by Dr Hennock, outlawing further fights absolutely.

Hennock himself was soon everywhere hoping to catch someone violating a new rule; but the pupils anticipated his interventions. Andy organised an elaborate system of lookouts that foiled his plans until Rachel herself appeared at the Staff Room utterly drenched, shivering with cold and claiming a cut on her leg had been caused by one of the boys. She had in fact been enthusiastically indulging in pelting some of the younger kids, and slipped over running away when they got fed up and retaliated. Mrs Tray threatening to storm in to see the Head, however, brought the final red card to any snow merriment.

Nearly ten centimetres, *a foot* insisted Terry, fell and there was a palpable feeling of excitement and tension as the school became isolated, a Christmas card scene at least for those who only had to look. Staff grew increasingly concerned. The country in general wondered why it had not been accurately predicted. Lights flickered as the electricity supply came under the pressure of increased demand, tight supply, and ice and frozen snow snapped power lines as storms had done earlier in the term. Windfarms froze adding to problems instead of solving them. Hillview began to taste, in minor measure, some of the perils of the developing world.

Rumours swept around that everyone, those who had got in at the start of the day, was to be sent home. Then, that everyone would have to stay the night in makeshift accommodation, with little food, perhaps no heating.

Mr Walker went about gleefully predicting the end of the world through climate change once more, delighting yet again in the unpredictability of all things in this age of science. He was less happy when it appeared so bad that it looked as if he too might be stuck overnight.

For a while the school was actually plunged into semidarkness when the outside supply failed altogether. A mini-generator from the days when snow had been a more regular problem was deployed to see if it could at least provide some microwaved drinks and food, fend off starvation, but it only worked intermittently and added to Terry's burdens; never a good move. He let fly once more about the school's hopelessly neglected infrastructure.

Hillview, like the country, had not prepared.

Pupils moved about in a grey twilight, the air thick with fat flakes of snow falling, strangely monochrome under the leaden skies outside, punctuated here and there with phone torches sparkling like Christmas decorations, a month early. Gusty wind flung the flakes into smarting eyes as staff and pupils with numbed fingers crunched their ways across campus, slipping and sliding in a blinding winter world. Sprains and chills backed up in Welfare just as the tide had turned on the last of the flu.

Across campus, at first, teachers invented games and distractions and all was cosy conviviality against the world outside, but next, when Terry's boiler failed, and he finally abandoned his efforts to keep the main drive free, and they still had to get about to go to lessons as Hennock, safe inside, commanded, things looked less happy.

Waseley allowed them to wear outdoor things then, so they wandered around for the rest of the day wrapped in scarves and coats, fingers aching with cold, wet feet, shoes that pinched and chafed, slushy puddles everywhere adding to Terry's vexations.

The adventure had become a bore. Disruption extended more significantly still to the digital world. An outage! Even phones weren't working properly. Who had perpetrated this outrage? Soon everyone was looking around for someone to blame, and someone to make it all just go away instantly. By the afternoon, partial chaos reigned, characterised mostly by lack of any effective communication, mirroring a national picture.

No one knew any more what was really going on inside or out. Secretaries brought messages round to children huddling in classes for a while, but these were confused and contradictory and soon dried up altogether.

The umbilical cords of civilisation had snapped.

It all became the teachers' fault, then. The cry was: *they should all have been allowed to try to get away earlier – prevented from coming in at all.* Had no one seen a decent weather forecast? And what about Mr Jolson, the housemaster and Dr Hennock, another geography teacher? What was their department doing?

Mr Waseley head held high, proud with how his school was coping, and with his management of the situation, retreated to his bunker. At last he made a decision, too late as usual, staff said. School was finally suspended. All spare teachers and maintenance and even some admin staff – those of robust nervous constitutions were ordered out to tackle the main drive under Terry's idea of supervision:

'Stop rattlin' and grab a f-in spade!'

Other teachers were ordered to meet with forms or tutor groups and to try to supervise them whilst it was seen who might just still have a chance to get home, if they could clear the drive, and who would have to stay.

There was supposed to be an emergency snow plan, but this could only be retrieved when the IT system was restored; when it was, it was found to be both incomplete, and practically useless, although it had been commended in the inspection Dr Hennock quickly declared.

'What are we sending them to school for?' demanded Mrs Tray, when she found out formal lessons had stopped.

To keep busy, she began to organise an online petition, following disruption from first flu, now this. Meanwhile her husband was deputed to find out if he could hire a four-wheel drive or even a helicopter, and if this could land at the school so Rachel could be collected and would not miss a singing lesson in Wellsway.

*

Dom watched events with first genuine excitement, then mounting concern.

Campus had become for him another world under its blanket of snow. The place had transformed in his imagination into part some usually hidden, magical kingdom, part an otherworldly, primeval place. It was a return to some ancient ice age. He begged the snow not to stop falling, until he too began to register the practical realities of having to be responsible. Outside, it was actually mind-numbingly cold. He shivered from snow stuffed down his back during one of the early secret staff–pupil snow fights. Inside, it took him ages to find out what was going on when organisation went into freefall. Eventually he located his tutor group- or most of them. They too had lost their excitement, were grumbling away, anxious. None of them wanted to stay overnight thanks very much: unless of course they could have a party, *a pyjama party, Sir, a no rules sleepover, and then a duvet day to compensate.*

'Sir, one of the boarders is offering his bed online tonight for a charge, don't you think that's creepy?'

'Sir, are we ever going home?'

Dom reassured, but could not help wondering himself. He looked at his class. They were dishevelled, soaking wet and cold, a few vainly huddling by the dying heat of a radiator, the floor a sopping mess of slushy mud, their faces pinched, their mood scratchy, rebellious.

What would really happen if one day roads stayed blocked, snow lasted, a spring never came?

He won them round in the end with some gentle humour, kindness and, particularly, some sticky jam donuts he brought down from his flat. There was a sense then of being all in it together, an odd camaraderie as he and the pupils swapped stories of wild weather adventures, and tales of all sorts they eagerly shared, each listening avidly to the others. It gave them a sense of belonging, of being part of something, to tell their stories, in that place, that moment, that day.

*

By late afternoon, the fierce weather that had taken the whole nation by surprise, was turning, at least near Hillview. Snow became sleet, then rain. Power came back on. With the lights returned some sense of sanity and common sense. The school buses could get through, it was reported to wild cheers.

There were headaches ahead: who could get away now; who was still stuck; who was looking after those left behind and where they were to go; but most managed to leave, so rapid became the thaw. Alison's lists, made at the height of the emergency as to who was doing this and that, soon resembled complete fantasy. She spent hours on her mobile, now working, trying to find out where children had gone as distinct from what they had said they were doing. Even Dr Hennock relaxed a rule in a small way, reluctantly suspending homework, not that many intended doing any. They had had such a day. Some begged lifts to friends' homes rather than face the horror of a night at school. Terry went mad again, ordered to find spare beds and spaces for anyone who might yet have to stay.

By seven o'clock, deep into the dripping cold of an endless November night, things were almost normal, although oddly there was now a feeling of resentful anticlimax, of time simply wasted, lost forever. The crisis was over, the apocalypse apparently postponed. Why did things never develop into anything really exciting after all?

By the next day most of the snow had melted as quickly as it had come leaving a great thaw behind, streaks of muddied grey and white, wilted grass trodden under a hundred footprints. A good number of pupils took the day off to recover, feeling they were owed.

*

Dom could not help reflect once more on another rollercoaster. A constant state of permacrisis seemed to be the Hillview way: its frameworks, from its very constitution and its constituents to its basic footings, its systems and structures and hierarchies seemed to teeter perpetually on the edge of some imminent collapse, then, somehow, stabilise – but never permanently, only until the next drama.

Revolutionary Joe would have been amused at the way in which crises induced a sort of socialism of effort and direction, even if it only lasted for the duration of an emergency, dissipating as quickly as the snow in a thaw.

More lost time from the play too! He was finding that so much depended just on that, simply getting any time at all for what he had to do. As for what he wanted to do, himself, personally-!

Perhaps that was only another secret of adult life, undisclosed till you started it. Time speeded up. You were left wondering where on earth the past had gone. Was it possible that you could be tricked out of a sense of time altogether?

But there was that something else, that something positive he had felt on the snow day; a something more he had felt now and again in lessons, in rehearsals. Sharing experiences with the pupils, although trying in some particulars, brought him closer to them, had actual heart warming rewards even if these were non quantifiable, and certainly never appeared as results or virility symbols on a league table.

He shook his head to himself at it all, bewildered for the nth time that term. If the word teacher comprehended so much, what a crazy muddle of feelings the words school and education held in reality as well.

CHAPTER THIRTY-SIX

ANOTHER NIGHT ADVENTURE

A few days later, as Dom was heading back from a rehearsal late in the evening, not long now before the performance of his play, he came upon Dr Hennock and his governor friend, once again behaving mysteriously.

His thoughts and energies had managed to tear free from the interruptions of inspections, cultural exchanges, flu, snow, the vagaries of his friendships, even Emma – almost. He still wanted to make a real success of something, prove himself, before his first term were done, even if it were only a school play. Looked at one way, it was ridiculous- all that toil for a make-believe world; hardly an educational or cultural revolution. But it might be a better thing, he hoped, than a lot of the stuff in which he kept landing. It became, somewhere in his imagination, a shining foil, even a rebuke, to a chaotic real world, an art against all the trivia.

And part of him would be content if it just happened at all.

He had managed to get some of those who were involved to an extra rehearsal that evening. It had gone well, lifted him, although some still did not know their lines. When he had first begun rehearsing, it seemed another age, he had felt sorry for the cast, all they had to learn; he had hardly pushed them, not wanting to put them off. Now the simple pressure of a performance made him impatient. They had to get on with things, get it done.

He was also on duty late that evening. The multiple things you always had to do; he was resigned to this given now. Patrolling around, finishing off his evening tours, he reached the final post which entailed him shutting and securing the main door before Mr Jolson took over, for the remainder of that day, and night.

To his irritation, he found it not only unlocked but wide open, a litter of leaves and cold air blown in as usual, heating bills forgotten. He stepped outside to see if anyone was larking around in the porch area.

Although cold, it was good to get fresh air after an evening of walking what seemed miles around the boarding house, putting children to bed. He had got used to the banter, the chasing up of pupils not wearing this or that, usually slippers, their mostly gentle teasing, cheek. Some, he sensed, even had an odd interest in him now he had been there a while. They must believe him much older and wiser, more interesting, than he was. He was amused by what they occasionally let slip when they thought no one else would hear. But he remembered some of Mr Royal's words too: people who flattered to deceive.

The twins had been tiresome that evening – thinking they were funny as usual, too full of energy that had no outlet: they had continued rehearsing their parts, showing off in front of their friends, destroying any novelty in what they were to perform. He had to tell them to stop, shut up, in the end, much to the delight of their peers. Then he had had to cheer them out of their chagrin, believing Sir was genuinely cross with them. All too soon they were grinning widely again, and pretending to vomit uncontrollably. They were up to something he was sure. But it was Jolson's turn.

Tonight he was done, wanting no one's company but his own; you got so little time and space to yourself, you learnt to value it, jealously to defend it. But it was hard to settle after a rehearsal and a duty. He needed to unwind.

Outside, he was able to notice the world again, as he had done on his first day, eons ago; the sharp stars glinting so enchantingly in the waste of the dark autumn sky. He wondered if they would have more snow. He hoped not now, not till his play was done anyway.

Contracting world! School again!

Then, suddenly, he heard distant voices somewhere, where all should be quiet.

Looking around, he observed the distinctive shape of Dr Hennock and the governor friend coming out of one of the admin buildings. He was back at day one.

He decided he did not want to be seen so slipped behind one of the porch's grand pillars. They passed, oblivious of his presence. They were deep in earnest, quiet conversation, and moved off in the direction of the Cloud.

For a moment he wondered if they were after pupils, someone 'breaking bounds', slipping off for a smoke or worse. There had been rumours of siblings, friends bringing in drink even drugs in the night, pupils going out when they were supposed to be asleep. But perhaps the incident with Andy had had a sobering effect. Maybe it was those silly twins up to some daft prank – some rumour had reached management; but in this cold? Even they had subsided as bedtime approached, though they had kept giggling, looking at him, laughing as if they had some secret thought about him, some plan they almost dared share.

For a moment or two he hesitated, then, sleep far away, curiosity piqued as he thought of past encounters, feeling he needed exercise anyway, he nipped back inside, grabbed a coat left hung randomly on a peg, put it on. It was as tight as a straitjacket- appropriate, he thought, as he set off on another of his mad adventures.

He closed, locked the great door, following.

Why should he not be out walking? Here was challenge, excitement; the child still alive in him somewhere wanted action, relief, a daring to be young and freely foolish once more, like the sleeping boarders he had left behind.

Cautiously he followed, feet crunching on bits of frosted grass, the moon high above acting as light. He stayed well behind the conspirators, intent at first only on seeing where they were bound, but remembering all he had witnessed in the file, heard on the stairs, so much more he had come to imagine.

He reached the foot of the Hill and crossed the tinkling stream swollen with the thaw, curious wisps of mist floating above. He began to ascend the Cloud, still following their distant shapes, puzzled at what they could be about going up there. Although the hill was less than a thousand feet high there were increasing mounds of snow in the hollows as he went up. A wider mist was rising. Dom slowed, realising he could see little ahead or above but the grey line of the path, curiously phosphorescent in the dark.

Soon he could hardly see that. He slowed even more, thinking of his play, the *Dream*, the characters entering their magical wood; but this was no midsummer forest rich in mystery, heady and potent, brutal, even, with adventures. Instead, it was a dying place, chilling, dank; a world of swirling mists, muddy or frozen ground, rotten wood and endless dead, decaying leaves. If it had its magic, it really was of a different kind.

Somewhere he heard the crack and fall of a branch. It startled him, causing him to stop altogether. For a while he hesitated, wondering what would happen if he came on them in the dark -or they on him. His imagination playing, they became creatures of another order – crooked, evil beings of some nonhuman world, stripped of any redeeming pity or purpose, wild animals on some lonely hunt of their own, pursuing their own ends, divorced from any sense of community. He himself was become some ancient caveman, tracking an enemy, simply fearful in the dark. He fancied that human life had not changed much really– out here, alone, in the cold. If discovered, he would be prey. Life was a hunt, a brutal, absurd game of life and death, for all the illusions of time's progress.

He moved off again. On he went, and would go, even if now they were far away, far beyond him.

Leaving the trees on this side below him, his feet finding the limey stones, the half formed steps in the path, he continued cautiously up, almost to the top, remembering the way.

When, finally, he carefully breasted the lip of the summit, he slowed again, crouching, almost on all fours.

They had, it seemed, disappeared completely. There was no sign of anyone, anything at all.

He stopped, looked around, shaking with cold.

Stillness and emptiness lay all about. A deep sense of strangeness settled ever more on him.

Up here, high above the world, he was in the presence of feelings, in a state of being, that was different, apart, at the edge of everything ordinary. Below him, looking back, he thought he could see a few of the yellow lights of campus blurred in mist; looking down the far slope he could see the glow of Wellsway through threads of fog.

But he felt he was on an island, far out on some empty sea.

For a few moments, he almost forget his chase, wondering at the emptiness, the desolation of the night world, so close to his place of work and a busy town. How little darkness had ever really drawn back, for all the civilisation of a world.

Slowly, his thoughts came back to the present.

He could go home, carry on towards Wellsway, then circle round by the road, easier going in the dark. He bent down, cautiously drawing out his phone, using its light to see if he could read the recent tread of feet. There were many marks, no clear sign.

Give up – go on?

Slowly, he began to descend the far side of the hill towards Wellsway, feet slipping and sliding in muddy turf, sometimes sucked deep into churned mud. He stopped frequently, wiping the side of his shoes on patches of snow to stop himself slipping. As he made his way, the mist seemed to rise to meet him, as if he were disappearing into a cloud. Soon he was walking on in his still, silent world wet with water drops that made his hair lank, his skin tingle.

On the further slope, he remembered how scrubby patches of woodland climbed the hill, just like on the school side. Branches and bushes would suddenly loom upon him from the darkness like twisted living creatures, impeding his progress. After snagging his feet several times on tree roots, progress became even harder. The ground was less frozen too, for some reason. He was slithering in a way that made an alarming noise.

Had he lost them altogether?

Suddenly, he became aware of a light ahead.

It was them. He was sure of it.

He crept closer. A pool of torchlight in the dark. Voices. Their voices.

Slowly, he moved forward, inching along, keeping the far side of a small hedge of black thorns glistening wet in the dark between him and the steaming pool of light. He got closer and closer, crouching along like some animal, terrified of the crack of a twig under foot.

Soon he could see clearly, hear; they seemed to be looking at a map.

'Development...up to here. There'll be objections...I told you David thinks he can swing it for us, given the political climate,' Hennock was saying quietly.

'This far up?' said the governor. 'Nice view. Bit of an eyesore for everyone else. Might have one myself- got some cash, and need it to work for me. There *will* be objections.'

'We can ride that with money. But thought I better show you – warn you. This is where our contacts come in,' he folded the map.

'We can't leave this much longer. David?'

'Everyone has their price. His kids at the school, if changes go ahead. Bursaries- that kind of thing. Nothing in writing yet. His building contractors. He said he'd meet us at the bottom of the hill Wellsway side. There's a walkers' car park. It's nearly eleven. He'd better be there. I'm not walking back to school. Seen enough?'

The figures moved quickly off further down the hill, two shadows following a blue light, soon vanishing into complete blackness.

Dom stood for a while looking after them. About a quarter of a mile away he noticed a car's headlights sweeping along the road from Wellsway. It slowed, stopped. The lights were extinguished. That must be their rendezvous. No one else would be about at this time in this weather.

Dom's mind raced over all he had seen and heard before. He remembered letters he had found in the file from council officers, talk in the staff meeting about development and housing and selling land. But why secrecy again? It was

-372-

like a story in a book, an adventure, where you peeled back layers of normality, found another world altogether from the one you thought you lived.

He should follow them further, meet this character – David? But the chance of him finding out anything much through random eavesdropping was absurd as he had just proven.

He noticed that the car lights had come on again. It seemed to be turning, pulling away – perhaps back on to the main road.

Too late anyway?

And now it was only perishing cold, a good way back, all that scrubby woodland traverse before he got to the summit, a couple of miles then.

He turned to retrace his steps, switching on the torch, his mind tugging the threads of his speculations.

As he turned, he jumped out of his skin, crying out!

Behind him, in the shadows, for a split second, he saw the figure of a young man or boy, small and slight, about five foot tall, standing dead still there, a bit further up the path, almost close enough to reach out to.

He was staring back at him.

There was a piercing squawk, like the sound of a pheasant suddenly disturbed, but monstrously magnified in the blackness, wings beating their way wildly through the brush, the crashing as of something frantic driven away in a burst of terror, twigs cracking, branches snapping. In his panic, fear clawing at him, he took a couple of steps backwards, involuntarily dropping his phone, the light going out, a blind dark descending like a curtain.

And then there was only silence.

Out of nowhere, a little night breeze came and went, moving dark branches like sinister arms. They scattered water drops in a mysterious patter. He heard them tap and creak in some eerie, secret dance, before they subsided.

A listening silence came again.

The darkness looked back.

He stared harder, trying to convince himself he had only imagined, bring his mind back, under rational control. Never moving his eyes from the spot where the figure had seemed to be, slowly he bent down, feeling around on the ground for his phone, eyes glued, terrified to let go his look, in case whatever it was came at him, there and then, as he was, alone, in the emptiness, his mind not his own.

After a few moments, he felt the cold glass and metal of his phone, his hands muddy with slime from the floor of the wood. He wiped them on the coat he had stolen, felt around for the buttons, eyes still riveted ahead. He was shaking; he could hardly hold the thing, let alone work it.

Desperate for the merest flicker of light, the torch came on at last. The engulfing shadows sprang back. He directed its light the way he had come.

Nothing.

Just the wood, waiting, listening, dead still.

He played the light around, shadows and shapes darting about.

There behind him, lay the muddy trail of the path, the indentation of footsteps clear in patches of snow or mud.

Once more, a breeze came and went, stirring all the trees so that the tapping and the creaking started again, louder now.

The wind was rising. From somewhere far off came the bark of a vixen, answered it seemed by the shrill cry of some other night creature, unidentifiable.

But of the figure he swore had been there a few seconds before, there was neither sight nor sound.

CHAPTER THIRTY SEVEN

SINGLE PARENT

By the time he was back in his flat, he had rationalised most of what he had seen away – the imaginings of an overactive brain, a tired mind. He had made his way home through empty woods, crossed silent fields, the rhythm of exercise calming him a little, although he could not completely get away from a ridiculous idea he was being followed.

Perhaps he was going a bit potty like poor Mrs Dot or Mrs Waseley. The stresses of term had finally pushed him over some edge. Maybe he still had flu. Damn his ridiculous imagination!

He lay sleepless on his bed for hours, turning things over: that first night, the file and his night adventure, the overheard conversation on the stairs, tonight.

After a while, he remembered the keys – the keys to that corridor and those rooms, the ones he had been given at the start of term and which he had searched for once before. He determined to search again, get into the corridor; he was convinced more deep secrets lay down there, some solution to all the weird things going on. It was too late now: but tomorrow or the next day, he would see what more he could find out. He'd gone this far.

He woke later in the night, heart pounding.

For a second or two he wondered who was standing at the foot of his bed in the dark, watching him so silently, but this time it was definitely only imagination.

*

In the weak, washed-out daylight of the following morning, it all seemed prosaic, crazy, absurd, some trick of a mind overdrawn. There could not have been anyone there; if there had they would not have behaved in that way, run off that quickly. He *had* imagined it, he told himself over and over. A sudden thought occurred to him. One of the pupils had played a trick on him; but no, they weren't that daft, peculiar, not even kids like that Rymer boy. It was himself, some eccentric imaginings- get over it. And then the day beckoned with its routines and challenges, its reassuring normalities, and took him away, far away from it.

*

That day's tasks were particularly consuming. Even as the end of term came into sight, the pace of everything increased Dom found. He had little chance to think, no time for a search for any keys. That evening would be impossible, too. He had been recently invited by one of his pupil's parents, Tim's mother, for supper, much to his surprise, and a certain confusion as to how to respond. Perhaps it was a relief that he was going out. He wanted something just then.

Dr Hennock brought him down to earth. Dom felt he should tell him where he was going. It seemed so odd for a parent to ask a teacher round. Nothing like that had ever happened at his own school, or on teaching practice. The man had regarded him for a moment or two, then reminded him about the school's reputation, told him to make sure the occasion remained strictly professional. He handed him a form with benefits-in-kind written on it, asking him to ensure he declared exactly what he had to eat and drink, any gifts he was given: – safeguarding and tax purposes he smiled.

Dom did not know if he were more appalled or astonished.

His friends had been amused but it was not unheard of at the school. Paul warned him that Mrs Thomas could apparently talk for England. Mike, who was now openly chatting up one of the other games teachers called Vicky, and had recovered his spirits, joked that it was about time he got some action. Beware middle-aged females! Mrs Tim, as Dom named her, was a single parent, must be desperately lonely to ask someone like him round, he joked.

Emma had said little. She was still distant, not well, pleading fatigue to any kind of invitation at all. He'd not given up. They talked a bit these days, but only ever, it seemed, about work. When he tried to go beyond, things fell away; they shared trivia, gossip, nothing more.

*

Dom readied himself for an evening out, a thing almost unknown in the last few manic weeks. He wondered what strange events might befall next. Had he fallen down some rabbit hole in going into teaching, at least coming to live, work here?

*

Mrs Thomas's home was a small terraced one – social housing once upon a time. It was on one of the older estates of Wellsway, a rundown part of a very mixed town as Dom had discovered on his first day.

Mrs Thomas greeted him enthusiastically at the door.

'Tim's just finishing some work, his chores. I make my two pull their weight with home stuff. They grumble their friends don't, but that's no way to bring them up; he'll be down in a minute. So pleased you could come.'

She ushered him into a tiny sitting room, left him, disappearing up some narrow stairs.

After all the days in classrooms moving around in an institution, it was comforting to be in a home again, curiously poignant. It reminded him of his own. Mum and Dad were on the other side of the earth now, having the time of their life. He could have felt homesick, had he not been grown up.

On the mantelpiece he noticed a framed digital photo: Mrs Thomas's family in various groups at various ages, including a man who must have been Tim's father. He had died suddenly years ago: some coronary disorder. He looked like Tim. He had worked in industry, a manual job; brilliantly skilled, clever, proud. Last of a kind, imagined Dom, like poor Mr Royal in his way.

How hard it must have been, must still be for Tim: no dad, like thousands, millions really. Mrs Thomas struggling with two boys to bring up, juggling jobs, childcare, desperate for them to do well, make up for things. He imagined the woman, dedicating all her life, efforts and thoughts, on her children, living through them every minute of every day: nothing much left over in money, or time, or even love for herself. One day, they would grow up, leave. She would be alone with her memories; but she would show no self pity. No one would ever quite know what she had been through to bring them up, let them go.

Such love turned the world.

Tim arrived, suddenly shy out of context, but pleased to have Sir there. Mrs Thomas bustled in and out as they talked of the day and of the school, Tim's hopes for the future. He wanted to be a writer one day: he was an ambitious lad, was thinking of doing English for A-level, at university too if he did well enough in his exams.

'I do hope you will be teaching him in the Sixth Form,' said Mrs Thomas at one point.

Next year! It seemed an eternity away to Dom, but he was flattered.

'And Mr Royal, too.'

'*Mum!*' began Tim, looking embarrassed.

'When's he coming back?' she pursued. 'We hear rumours. I've thought of going to see Mr Waseley about it,' she pressed. 'He did wonders for Tim lower down in the school, inspired him.'

Tim looked uncomfortable again. Dom ducked that one.

*

The meal was taken in an old-fashioned kitchen that was even smaller than the sitting room. Dom thought of a museum he had once visited. Not the usual dry collection of objects out of context, but one that recreated whole rooms in different houses through the ages. This all belonged years ago; the cooker, sparkling clean with tiny burners and an overhead grill reminded him of one his gran used to have.

The meal was simple, no frills: a lasagne, then a rich and heavy pud, and too too much vinegary wine.

He told her he would not drink. She insisted.

'You need feeding up, you poor teachers. You had that nasty flu. My lads kept going. Good plain food I always give them. None of this processed muck,' she said, ladling more on his plate, topping up his glass.

He felt hot, emotional for some reason. He was certainly relaxed. Perhaps he was with friends. Maybe he should tell them of some of his adventures....

'We're so pleased you came to Hillview,' said Mrs Thomas when Tim was out of the room. 'He says you're inspiring. Of course, he loved Mr Royal's lessons best. He was upset when he wasn't going to have him again this year, especially after last year's teacher who just showed them online stuff. And Mr Royal's wonderful- when he's there. His dream is to have both of you teach him, maybe even try for Oxford though he's probably not the right sort for that place. His dad would have been proud; both of us left school as soon as we could. Ryan hated school, although he was clever. I just wanted a job, money and boyfriends. No one ever suggested anything better at the time, bothered with me. And my school, well, pretty hopeless really. Regret it now. Mind you, Tim'll have to pull his finger out, work hard, especially with his background, whatever they say. You two'd get him on.'

Dom felt embarrassed once more, wondering if he could live up to expectations. How different Mrs Thomas was from Mrs Tray, several other pushy parents he had come across, who just expected school to do everything for their child to the exclusion of anyone else, however they acted, as if understanding were endlessly on tap.

They talked of worlds beyond school. Mrs Thomas then embarrassed Tim with stories of when he was young.

Dom wondered if they would have had him there if dad had still been alive. One of the many roles of teacher, he was discovering, was to be a sort of parent, a father. Strange really, when so many people bashed anything that had the faintest sniff of patriarchy. He wanted to laugh – he had never, yet, considered himself as a father. He wondered if Emma saw herself, allowed herself to be seen as a mum.

'I hear there's talk, going independent, private. Never. That's not us,' she fished.

He sidestepped the question, claiming he was too new a member of staff to know much that went on. He wondered if Mrs Thomas saw through his answers.

Tim wouldn't be able to go there if they started charging; they struggled as it was.

He wished he could be open with her. Here she was showing kindness to him who had as yet surely little claim on it. Meanwhile the school was in turmoil, and there was Hennock and his secret schemes, all that going on.

How different people were, but how simple in the end were the things that mattered about them.

'The only one Tim doesn't really like there is Mr/Dr Hennock, although he says he's one the pupils have respect for. I bet he keeps you all in order,' she was saying, laughing, but shrewd, looking hard at him.

Dom wished again he could be indiscreet, tell her more.

'Tim says Dr Hennock has all sorts of plans for the place, even turning part of it into a tourist attraction. I used to work at the council offices – a friend of mine said the school was after planning permission – for housing as well as school stuff?'

Dom thought of last night. Surely more parents ought to be more involved in the life of a school; but that was probably too democratic for Hennock, too radical for those who held purse strings: what could they know about education or what it was for, how it touched their children.

'Do you like it? Must be hard in your first term.'

Dom made some vague comment about how much he had to learn, trying to smile it away.

'You look tired, pale. Nasty flu, wasn't it? They work you too hard, young staff, before they get jaded, wise up. You must be lonely there. We're all looking forward to the *Dream!*' she moved on, sensitive enough.

Dom smiled weakly. He wasn't used to most of his colleagues talking to him like this. If he were a dad for Tim in some way, perhaps Mrs Thomas was playing mum to him: embarrassing; but he came back to the kindness, as you always must.

At the end of the meal, Tim went off to collect his younger brother from his swimming club. He was left alone again with Mrs Thomas.

'He has tremendous admiration and respect for you. There's a few teachers there that really bring it alive for them, make it interesting,' Mrs Thomas repeated.

Dom did not know quite what to say, nor would he believe it.

'I want them to love it like I do,' he faltered, thinking how clumsy he sounded, pompous Emma would say.

He wondered if Mrs Thomas had heard all that went on in Tim's lessons.

'Tim thinks you have some girlfriend stashed away. Maybe you and that Miss Oakley can get together. What's she like? She's one of Tim's friend's form teacher; he likes her but says opinion's out on her as a teacher. She's strict: that's no bad thing up there. Poor Mr Royal, everyone's favourite. Don't end up like him: never been married. He had someone, lost her – no one's supposed to know, but I asked him. That's me! He needs someone to look after him – with his migraines, this that and the other. Too much time on his hands to think about himself.

'Did you always want to teach?' she asked.

She was giving him the third degree in her own way, but she was interested: a lot of people never were interested in anyone much beyond themselves. He felt once more an overwhelming desire to open up, tell her some of all the story of which he had been a part, and which was so much in his head and so unknown really to anyone else at all; but no, this was her moment, their moment, not his.

It was then, that he suddenly thought he would write it all down yes, put it on paper, one day. John had suggested that, although he had been drunk at the time. Was the idea some monstrous ego speaking, he wondered, as she talked on, asking and answering her own questions better than he ever could.

A story. If it were any good, it must tell more than just his own experiences if it were honest enough about what really went on, even if it was a small world. It would certainly be funny, but sad as well?

He would tell it. And his secret adventures. You could never quite do that in life because it was always slipping away with doing things. No one but you ever knew quite what you witnessed. If you learnt to listen to what other people had been through, you really learnt – like this family now, in front of him, being kind to him, when they deserved the kindness. Hadn't that been what he was trying to say in that rather grim, never to be forgotten first lesson with Tim?

But Mrs Thomas had yet to finish.

'He does so want to be a writer,' she was saying again, 'we all know it's a bit of a dream, but well, aren't most good things? I used to read a lot. I write a bit of poetry, since Ryan died;– but looking after the children, working all hours, it doesn't leave much over,' she looked at him for a moment.

She told him something of what it had all been like, asked him if he would look at some of her writing.

Dom could only listen. How hard ordinary life could be, he reflected again. This must pull him up when he started to fret about things not being right at school. Him and his dreams!

He got up to leave, excusing himself, wondering if this connection would ever go even further, or, like so many in life, would remain a thread thrown out but never taken up because of fate and chance and circumstance, a million distracting things.

'Don't let them work you too hard. There's more to life than work,' she returned to her theme.

Oh dear, he did feel a bit unsteady. Mrs Thomas had plied him with cans of beer after they'd eaten, all that wine with the meal, a drink before. He was definitely growing quite sentimental under the effect of it.

Tim's return, with a younger version of himself in tow, delayed his departure. His brother looked at him curiously for a couple of seconds, a teacher thing out of a classroom, but then was eager to tell everyone how well he was doing at his swimming, how he had thrashed Archett at crawl.

'Any food?' he demanded.

Mum went off to heat up the portion of lasagne she had hoped to save for her lunch. His brother talked without self consciousness of his exploits. Tim and, then Mrs Tim listened, dutiful, proud, part of his team. He reminded Dom of Mike.

At last, he made his excuses again. They saw him off.

He always remembered the tableau of them together in the rather dingy porch in that one time council terrace: three dealt a savage and irreversible blow by life, struggling now and always with that loss, but confident in their own way against the world in the trust and love that they so freely shared.

He could teach them nothing, only learn.

CHAPTER THIRTY-EIGHT

WHAT HE DIDN'T FIND, WHAT HE DID

It was late and silent when he got back. As he mounted the stairs, he felt dizzy. He must get a decent night's sleep soon he thought, or he would never cope with the days ahead. Usually so careful over such things, he wondered if he had been over the limit. He imagined the headline Probationary Teacher Sacked in First Term: Alcohol Abuse. Then he thought of Mr Royal. Was this how he had begun?

But he poured himself a whisky, enjoying something of his own self-pity, recalling the warmth of a home and family, being acknowledged as a person not just a teacher. Someone showing genuine gratitude, not resentment because you were dragging the unwilling to study. And to be away from a world that could be so broad in its demands, narrow in its confines.

He texted Emma, ever hopeful, asking her how her day had gone. He wished all would come well between them, that she would properly notice him one day. He'd give up a lot, everything to be close. He wondered if Mr and Mrs Thomas had been happy: something must have given them a foundation.

He turned his mind away, remembering yesterday's mad adventure, the antics of other staff almost eclipsed by his own imaginings. Just next door was the corridor, and maybe some answer to all the mysteries, a key to what on earth was going on in this weird, weird world. If he could recall-.

Dom tried to picture his first few days. He remembered getting keys, detaching some he did not need every day. He'd felt like a gaoler walking around with such a huge bundle. Terry had gone on and on about looking after them properly, not leaving them lying about, *Pikies getting hold of them, ransacking the place.*

After a while he gave up, his mind going back to the evening, Mrs Thomas and Tim and his brother, his swimming. What would they think of him, contemplating like one of his naughty pupils another night prank. And why was he doing all this -trying to prove something to himself, impress someone, Emma? Big deal! A kid showing off! Hey,look Emma, I'm better than Mike! I beat Archett today!

Swimming. *Swimming!*

It came back to him.

He remembered, at last, recalling putting the keys by his swimming shorts, stowing them in a case, the ones he had brought along hoping, rather vainly, that the school might have a pool somewhere, or he could slip off into Wellsway for a workout now and then. Ha ha!

Excited now, tomorrow's demands all forgotten, he reached under his bed, pulled out his games bag covered in dust, unearthed his shorts. There indeed were the keys too. He had forgotten how many there were, entrances to all the secrets of the school's deep state!

Then he pulled back.

He would only try the keys, see if he could get in, but he would be careful, slow down, take care. He did not wish to get trapped again. What he was doing must be in the greater interests of the school –Alison's words about what they all owed the place, all that moral stuff he was supposed to avow.

Slipping his soft trainers on, cautiously, he crossed his room, quietly opening the door. It was past twelve. Even Hennock must be asleep by now. Keys in his hands, watching himself in his mind's eye in a sort of slow motion, doing something he knew he probably shouldn't, but which had taken hold, he crept down the corridor. He fumbled from one key to another, testing the lock.

Finally, a key turned and the lock clicked.

'Yeh!' he cried out loud, forgetting for a second, in his fuddled state, confident against all caution.

The door swung into the blackness beyond, just as it had done last time.

Chuckling to himself with a kind of crazy glee, he passed into the corridor, moving swiftly down to the room he had been in before.

He paused at the door.

Of course, it was locked. Again he tried the keys. This time, the first one he found fitted, turned, snug and neat. Wasn't he doing well?

He was inside. Easy. Everything falling into place.

Dom swept the scene with his torch. Here lay the familiar old books and papers, the photograph, the dried-out mug still standing sentinel; there was the window he had escaped through, completely fastened he noticed. He crossed the room and looked on the teacher's desk, hoping of course. He carefully pulled open the drawers one after the other. It would be there. This was his evening – the end of all these ridiculous mysteries, existing on the margins, in the dark about everything.

But there was nothing inside, certainly no file anywhere to be seen.

It all stared emptily back at him. For all his stealth and secrecy, self congratulation, he had found *nothing*. Maybe it was all nothing, another silly fantasy built on some absurd fiction of self consequence.

God he must be pissed.

He turned, about to leave, sobered.

Then he looked at the cupboard at the back of the classroom. Still moving as quietly as he could, he crossed the room, tried the door. It was not even locked. He opened it, stepping inside some kind of walk-in store.

Again he shone his torch about. The cupboard was almost completely bare as well: one or two ancient texts; some old, old fashioned exercise books on dusty shelves. That was it.

In sudden frustration he kicked the door shut. The noise reverberated; but Dom was too angry, too drunk to care. He turned his back on it, slumped against it, allowing himself to slide slowly down so that he ended crouching on the floor, shoulders and head resting on the door, arms at his sides with the torch light spilling uselessly down onto the ground, darkness closing in all around.

For a few moments, he closed his eyes, resting there on his haunches, lost in the silence and emptiness all about him.

What had he found? What on earth was he doing?

Only another silly, empty anticlimax after all. None of the buried treasure or secret ways or hidden truths or simple answers of which stories told, and he told himself must be there.

After what seemed hours, but must have been only minutes, he came back.

Out of the corner of his eye he could see one of the piles of exercise books, a faded yellow colour. Idly, he picked one up.

It was an English workbook, even had handwriting in it, neat too. He flipped lazily through. It hadn't been marked much. Hennock had told him many times English teachers were always the worst at keeping up with their marking.

He picked up another. There was an essay, tale in this one. Something in it caught his attention. He read a page, alone there, lost to the world, his phone his only light.

It was a story set at Christmas.

I was a little girl of eight at the time. We were supposed to open our presents together but that morning for some reason Mum started arguing with my Dad again. Then my brother got involved. Soon they were all shouting and fighting. My mother threw something at Dad, started hitting him, over and over. Later, I remember my brother sweeping up broken glass. Dad said goodbye to me and kissed me, then went out. He seemed sad. My sister took me out for a walk. I remember how cold and grey it was outside, rain with sleet in it. I can't remember much about what happened then. But Dad never came back.

Dom turned back to the front cover to see whose name it was. His own parents quarrelled sometimes, but not like that. And they made up. The ink on the front had faded completely. No name at all.

He put the book slowly on the pile, feeling different. Standing up slowly, legs numb and tingling, he brushed himself down. He was stiff and cold, and worked his arms from side to side, stamping as lightly as he could around on the ground to try to warm up.

Using a few odd pieces of paper still on the shelves, yellowed and curled, brittle with age, he swept the dust he had disturbed around a bit, scuffing any foot prints, hoping no one could tell someone had been there.

Sweep the dust behind the door.

Puck's words from the play.

The play too!

He did his best to cover all his tracks, closing and firmly locking the doors, both on what he had not found, and what he had.

CHAPTER THIRTY-NINE

SUMMONED

When Dom awoke the following morning, his first thought was he must have been a lot more drunk than he realised. He wondered once more if he really were going a bit mad with it all – his imaginings, so much on his own, stir crazy with Hillview.

Dom checked his emails, as he always did, before he washed and dressed. There was something reassuringly normal in the action, routine.

There was one from the Headmaster!

It was summoning him to an important meeting, that morning, first thing, in his free period.

Dom's mind jumped instantly to guilty, anxious, possibilities: his night wanderings had been discovered; he was to be reprimanded for unprofessional behaviour; for following staff, trespassing, breaking and entering, spying even- a betrayal of trust no less, a second offence indeed! Dr Hennock had found out, was even now piecing the whole saga together, Waseley had been alerted, told what to do.

Reason mitigated alarm as he showered and dressed, but it welled up once more when he had breakfasted and sorted himself. He splashed cold water on his face just before he left his room.

The Dom in the mirror looked older, pale, drawn: no longer quite him. Mrs Thomas had been right. And he was tired: too much going on, far too much.

*

Waseley was behind his desk, signing letters in the flamboyant way he had. He looked up at Dom and sighed. Dom was shocked at his appearance. He looked older, strained. Part of his mop of hair was sticking straight up as if he had just got out of bed under the influence of electricity. It would have been funny any other time. *Bed-Head* the kids called him, when he looked like that. Dom noticed for the first time, his roots seemed to be greying.

Dom wondered if he were ill, or something serious had happened: perhaps it was his sacking.

He hovered, not having been asked to sit.

'Just phoned the police,' Waseley began, 'one of the less attractive parts of my job.'

It was him. He could bear it no longer.

'I'm sorry,' Dom blurted. 'It was all an impulse. I was a bit the worse for wear and, well, I did it for a reason. A good reason.'

Waseley, however, was not listening.

'What?' he said absently. 'For goodness sake, sit! That's what chairs are for! You look tired. I think you know what I want to talk to you about.'

Dom could only nod.

'It's a pity when things come to contacting the police, but you have to bring them in when it's serious. Bad publicity, of course: police cars hurtling up the drive. Plods today like a drama. Ever been in trouble with the Plods, Paul, before you came here?'

Waseley laughed at his own description for a moment, then a morose expression returned.

Dom swallowed.

'Is Dr Hennock coming too?'

'God no -we don't want him talking to the police! Haven't we got enough problems? He'd start telling them what to do as well as me!' Waseley laughed, then pulled a face. 'That's er – what I want to talk to you about as well. But these blasted night time dramas – damn nuisance. We had this last year, intruders all over the place, going where they're not allowed: some of them walked into one of my assemblies once. Now, your version of what happened last night. I want your take on it before I move. You live in. Your peppercorn rent comes with responsibilities you know!'

Dom did not know where to start, but Waseley was still talking.

'Terry swears someone must have heard. What were you up to? Where were you? He's hopping mad, swearing away as usual. I spoke to him. That business with the inspector: not made a scrap of difference. We're stuck with him, like this wretched flu: wife 2.0 has it now. Spent all that money on alternative therapies – made me hallucinate. Ever hallucinated, Paul? You still got it? You look fuddled: that's what's making you like this? How on earth they got a grand piano out at all is what beats me.'

'Piano?' said Dom, completely confused.

'I don't know why Tring put it there. He said it was effectively bust, incapable of being tuned properly,but wouldn't get rid of it. Musicians! Dreamers or perfectionists, you know. Never easy to deal with, never satisfied. Off in their own world half the time. Glad you're not a perfectionist: no time for them; always end up with breakdowns, going potty. You're not going potty? A grand piano wheeled out of one of the school common rooms, loaded onto a van, doors and locks broken, thirty boarders, house master and his wife –

you on the floor above – no one seems to have heard a blasted thing. You must know something, rumours – a prank, some jolly jape? Jolson knows nothing of course: sleeps deeply that man, all day sometimes, I think. Kids don't usually have the imagination to try things on this scale, but there are one or two of them. Those twins, for instance: ordered fifty pizzas to my house from some takeaway last year, and sent the wife the bill!'

With a remarkable speed of thought and, he hoped, no loss of composure, Dom was able to absorb what had apparently happened whilst he was engaged in his own activities, and confess – in this case his hearty and complete ignorance of the whole matter. Had he been less uptight himself, he might have grinned. Even by Hillview standards, the theft of a grand piano, large and unwieldy, and completely useless except for firewood, in the dead of night, with nearly forty sleeping watchers just above, was something else.

Waseley, however, could not believe he had heard nothing; but Dom's obvious earnestness convinced in the end. The Headmaster continued to look disgruntled. No doubt Terry was giving him, the staff and pupils a tough time: sod the piano, what about security in the place? Dom could imagine Terry's expletive-laden denunciations; but Dom had little time to savour more than a brief moment of relief at his escape.

'Now, er, there's another matter rather more serious to me.'

Waseley looked uncomfortable – rather as he had in the staff meeting when challenged by Hennock. What was coming now?

'This is, of course, totally confidential, *totally*. I want you to respect what I say, Paul. No gossiping: your eyes and ears only – all that. I know we trust each other. I... er... you came to me before the holiday with some story or other about Darr-, Dr Hennock, plans for the school, even my er job- silly staff politics of course, nothing in it! I am not worried at all, but I wonder if you could remind me of the details: just for the record, of course, in the light of one or two minor things that silly old inspection unearthed. I may not have been... completely on the case the first time....

'Man to man: I'm not entirely sure what's been going on, but tell me again, Dr Hennock, what were you really on about.'

*

Dom nearly missed his first lesson of the day, second period. Then much of it passed in a blur. He could only think about all he had so recently experienced; but the class, with its own mood and agendas, pulled him back.

In front of Waseley, Dom had repeated what he had said before, more coherently he believed. This time the Headmaster had listened.

So something *was* going on. He wasn't completely stuck down his own rabbit hole.

But all these silly secrets piling up.

Leaving the lesson, he bumped into Emma. She looked pale too he thought: November washout all round.

He wished, as he started talking to her, moved by how sad she looked, he could tell her about his recent adventures. Perhaps it would cheer her up, make her laugh at least: more tales from the funny farm. He needed someone to tell.

In front of him, now, Emma – struggling with a load of files as she came out of her classroom

'All right,' he said casually, a world of feeling hidden in two words.

For a moment, he thought that tears were about to well up, but she shook her head.

'It's all right,' she began.

'No, it's not. Let me help,' he said, reaching out to take some of her folders. She shied away.

'What's up? Come on.'

Again, Emma shook her head, moved away, but then some of her books slipped from her grip smacking the floor. Dom moved to pick things up.

'Best place for most of this crap,' cried Emma. Dom could not help laughing.

'That sounds like the old Emma,' he said.

She looked at him briefly, grateful, almost smiling. Then she turned away, upset once more, white, stressed as he had never seen her before.

'You okay? Look, let me take your next lesson for you, or something: you're obviously – you don't look... you're upset, about something.'

'I'm all right,' said Emma, firmly now. 'I'm just tired – too much to do. You know what it's like. I'll get through it, I suppose. I don't need your help.'

'I really don't mind covering your class. I've just done two rounds with the Head; it'll be light relief.'

For the first time she looked at him properly.

'No, no. It's kind of you: especially – you're so busy. I'll be all right,later.'

'I'm here, if you need me.'

He hoped that did not sound pompous.

'Can you keep a secret, dead secret,' she said then, looking round.

Dom wondered what was coming – but before he could say anything he knew.

'I have to tell someone. I've handed my notice in. I'm leaving at the end of term, this term. I told you I wouldn't stay,' she said with a touch of her old defiance.

'But why, and what-. You can't, surely, just go- like that. What about finishing your first year and-'

'I told you. I can't explain now- but I feel better for having done it.'

'But-'

'Look, I have another class coming. I'll explain…sometime later,' and she was off down the corridor, as her charges, noisily oblivious, flowed past, into the rooms, eager to get on with, get it over.

Dom went after her, shouting back at his class to settle, start their reading as they'd been told a thousand times. He would be back instantly.

At least she was talking to him, seemed warmer again.

But, she was leaving.

Emma was leaving.

CHAPTER FORTY

EMMA

Dom was waiting in The White Hart. Emma had agreed, eventually, to come for a drink. He'd even cut a rehearsal short though the play was next week.

He sat alone, in their usual place, by the fire. The pub was nearly empty. Outside it was a forlorn, cold, wet, gusty November evening. Christmas was still only a horizon. Lights were going up, but not on. Most stayed home out of the wet cold. The landlord was grumbling: *custom not like the old days; how would they make ends meet, survive in the New Year with everything a mess? He'd had enough.*

Dom, however, felt upbeat. His crazy adventures were not forgotten, but they were background. It was all the play, Emma.

Another rehearsal had gone well: something was stirring, as it had, off and on, from the start. One of the cast had even asked him for another session. Better late than never.

Emma arrived. She was still drawn. but she was Emma again as she walked in.

He bought her a drink, as usual.

They returned to the fire. The crowd of die hard regulars at the bar noted there were only two teachers that night. Perhaps the rest were doing something about those idle lippy teens at last.

For a time they chatted about their day: Dom's latest rehearsal, Emma's confrontation with some pupil– casual gossip about staff and pupils; Dotty's latest breakages; Katie's current bee in her bonnet; Dom's time at Tim's. It was easier that way.

Dom scarcely knew what he dared feel deep down. He thought of all the things he could say.

Nothing took wing immediately.

Then, Dom broached the subject.

'Look, this, you leaving. You're not serious? Are you sure you are doing the right thing? It's not because of Mike is it?'

Emma said nothing for a while, then began.

'No it's not Mike, not Mike at all. Men are vain!' sighed Emma. 'They think a girl does this or that because of them, not because of who she is, what she might want.'

Dom left that.

'But why leave now, ruin your chances for the future? Besides- you can't leave me, some supply teachers, to do all Mr Royal's teaching for the rest of time!'

Emma was silent for a few moments.

'I'm sorry. I was rude before- when I thought-. You're kind. But kindness is no good if it just covers problems. I said that to you at the start of term, before-'

'What? What do you mean?'

'Things were fun for a while: Mike, me. But it was never going to last. He'd have kicked me out if I hadn't kicked him out. And he's soon moved on, hasn't he? Leaving! It's not me being some emotional female- what Hennock thinks. There's been some massive arguments. Contractually they have me, but the school can't afford to take it further. They don't want hassle now. What's the point anyway if I've made up my mind. What appeared on social media, that hurt. I thought you – but that's our world isn't it, part of the deal for buying into the brave new world of tech.'

'See, you say things like that. The kids need to hear that sort of thing from someone like you. And why leave now? Why don't you finish your first year: then you could get back in.'

Emma laughed.

'Dom! You don't know me, do you?'

'You don't let me!' he replied after a moment or two.

There was a pause.

'It all sounds as if you've given up on things. Please, tell me. I don't want to make a fool of myself – upset you.'

'What's it they tell you about teaching, *make a difference, change lives, the future*... something like that. Sometimes you can: but look at the place, and the practical reality of it all. At least in business there was a kind of honesty. In education everything's disguised, but underneath it's the same money-centred, competitive world, except there's not enough to do the job properly. It should be more than that,' began Emma.

'You sound like me! We're alike really.'

'No, we're not,' replied Emma brusquely.

Dom would not agree with that; and she was wrong about the job, the place, too.

'Education, teaching, it's a good thing in itself. Most of the kids, lots of the staff are nice,' he said.

'*Nice!*' laughed Emma. 'There you go again! Oh the children are fine: they're children. And some of the staff— but the compromises, the evasions, even the point of what we do in school. And the failure! How can some of the kids relate to what we teach; and what use is a lot of it – in the world they're growing up in. And even the good stuff... I've worked, Dom. It's not school, not like school at all. We pretend that's different: life's about your dreams –as long as you can do the right things in the exams, of course, play the game. And don't tell them any ugly bits yet, give them other choices: it's too difficult, too expensive. No wonder they're bored rigid at times.'

Dom thought for a moment of Jane; but he wasn't having what Emma said about teaching.

'You don't believe all that. People like Charles – they aren't like – they're honest in their, well, passions. He makes more of being a teacher, what's he say, helping them understand, ask their own questions, find their own voice, make them respect others, be kind. So do lots of staff. You do. You try. I try. I try to make it about something more, something better.'

'And look what's happened to Charles, and now you!' she laughed for a moment.

'What's that supposed to mean? I wish you would stop patronising me.'

'Even though I am unworthy?'

'*Emma!*'

Dom paused, but she had touched several nerves.

'It seems to be my luck always to be misunderstood – or laughed at by you.'

'Had another bad rehearsal? Looking for sympathy? You should face some serious difficulties.'

Dom shrugged. It was true; but after all, what did she think she was like, or anyone?

'You are silly at times, you know, in what you say.'

'Silly and unworthy! Whatever will become of me? Not silly enough to stay.'

'Why go into teaching in the first place then? Education's not a game.'

'There you go again, on some high horse. You sound like my father,' she sighed.

But Dom was not going to give up.

'I understand. It's not easy: if you really think about what you're doing, why. Some days, it's impossible. We've all seen a bit since we started... But I don't like to see people upset, going wrong, and you're good, and you're throwing something good away. Things'll change here – are changing. There's a lot going on behind the scenes.'

She scoffed.

'This place won't change whatever they do. Same old same old,' she replied.

Dom looked down at the table. He picked up a beer mat and began to flick it up with his fingers, catch it in the other hand. Then he started to fold it up into neat segments before tearing segments off one at a time, making a pile.

Emma watched him, smiling.

Laughing at him he thought. He wanted to hate her, what she said about their job. He looked away. Emma's regard grew more serious as she followed his long sensitive fingers working away, studied his hands.

A log in the fire by their side settled suddenly with a little tumble, a crack and shower of sparks, followed by a brief burst of dancing flame. Then the little blaze died down. It seemed to grow quieter in the room.

Time drew out. Their little world.

'I wish you would understand,' he said at last, still not looking at her. He had wanted to say *listen*, tell her some of his experiences, impress her with what he knew, had seen, show her they together could set a world to rights. But he was nothing.

Emma spoke then.

'You are young you know.'

He looked up.

'Thanks!'

'Maybe this place will do you good, toughen you up a bit, make you grow up. You look tired. Your shirt's missing buttons, you need to look after yourself.'

'That's almost the first time you have said anything at all that suggests you actually notice me, you know.'

He stopped.

She was smiling- still laughing at him he thought.

He looked down.

'I am tired. And Mrs Tombs has done for half my shirt buttons on all my decent ones. She literally boils everyone's shirts, you know, as if we're all sweaty teens. Hundred per cent. Everything's shrunk to midget size! I feel as if I'm in a straitjacket when I put my shirts on. Just right in this place. And if she tells me to *pin my socks together* again.'

Emma laughed.

'But at least I'm staying, trying to make something of it.'

'Back to that again. So I can add coward to my list of failings? I actually think it takes bottle to walk away from things when they've gone wrong. That's the problem here-everywhere, Dom, the country. Things are a mess, and it all just goes on! Paul said you were writing a book. There, you can put me in it as the spoilt rich bitch who flounces off when things don't suit. That's the top and bottom of it all really. It's me, not teaching. But you'll never have the time to finish it if you stay. And they won't let you.'

'*What?* Paul's a motor mouth,' said Dom resentful. 'I haven't started it yet.'

'I'd get on with it if you're serious. So you want to be the great writer now. What next, the master director too or the new Mr Royal? That's how the book ends, I suppose?' she said.

Dom had thought of several different conclusions, but none of them looked like this.

'What will you do?' he said suddenly, feeling cold inside, wishing again he could really dislike her. 'Suppose they hold you to your contract, make you stay.'

'They won't. Hennock'll see to that. Other fish to fry. I may travel for a bit. Go and teach English abroad; find something better. I may do all sorts, who knows.'

'And you call me young!' replied Dom.

'Life is for living, Dom. Take what's there, as much as you can, whenever you can.'

'You don't mean that. You're not like that, I know you're trying to wind me up.'

'Am I? How do you know what I really mean, or want. Weren't you listening earlier. You're being you again. Life's a competition, and a game, Dom, not a moral crusade.'

'Does that apply to caring about people?'

There was a pause.

'Mike again? We all use other people for our own ends,' she said coldly.

'You don't mean that either. A moment ago you were saying you wanted something more. I don't think that's the way to find it at all, by pleasing ourselves.'

'Neither is blind service,' replied Emma. 'Look what it's done to Charles'.

'You are quick to disguise selfishness as something good.'

'And you diffidence as virtue.'

'Sometimes, for all your cleverness, I really think you just don't get important things.'

'Now who's being patronising?' she replied, trying to laugh.

There was silence once more.

Dom looked at Emma. Perhaps in all her cleverness she was right: he was as arrogant and pompous as she said, deluding himself that there was more to anything than there actually was. No one wanted earnestness: just fun, silly cool people, stuff the rest.

'I'm sorry,' she said suddenly, different again. 'It's me, not you. Ignore me, Dom. It's today, and – I say, it's me and

Hillview, not teaching. I'm not right for it. That's all my decision comes down to in the end. You're trying to help, I know. At least I can talk to you. Sorry, Dom. I've not felt myself since that flu, since half term.'

'Me too,' he sighed studying his drink. 'We always end up quarrelling!'

He paused, looking at her.

'But if you must go- I'll miss you. I wish you wouldn't, more than- that's all. But if you genuinely want to.'

Emma made no reply, but continued to regard him, puzzling herself over conflicting feelings that she had only begun to realise.

There seemed nothing more then they could say, only a thousand duties that awaited them both tomorrow.

They parted shortly after, going their own way, driving home alone in the dark waste of a cold night, each dissatisfied with the other, but mostly with themselves.

CHAPTER FORTY ONE

GIVE AND MOSTLY TAKES

School rolled on, but it helped Dom just then: you could lose yourself in it.

There were tests now to set and mark for the end of term: a huge task; results to enter on seemingly endless different spreadsheets; reports to write on everything and everybody – again. Dom wondered why so much had to be recorded. Perhaps report systems, like viruses, once born, kept mutating to survive, replicating endlessly. Pupils must mostly know their faults and flaws, surely. *Doing something about it* —that was the hard part, rather than trying to prevent an imaginary court verdict one day that: *no they'd never been told that, never in their lives by anyone, ever, honest!*

Away he typed finding elaborate, sometimes naive, but ever supportive variations on: *doing his best; not doing her best; works really hard; should work harder.* Blunter things he would not write, even if allowed. But he sometimes wondered if he were writing very long, elaborate excuses.

Perhaps they should teach everyone more responsibility: for themselves, for a start.

*

One bright spot was the return of Mr Royal who appeared one Monday morning, looking fresh, rested. No one explained how or why or on what terms he had come back. He didn't either.

But no one could smell after shave.

By all accounts, he was soon his brilliant, eccentric presence in the classroom once more, his supercritical, provocative persona in the Staff Room. He said nothing about all the marking and teaching he had missed that had fallen to Dom and Emma. He did take up his own sword against all the endless assessment though, pronouncing in his way.

'Ah, systems, not people. Bureaucracy is easier to manufacture than trust is to create, you see. And pathways, not your own footsteps are necessary in case the stupid trip. We all hide in systems now. *Tiddlypom!*

At least, Dom felt, he had his teeth into something that answered with his play. In fact, work was now almost all *the play*. True, part of him just wanted it done, and ended, so he could have something of a life back – but he remained intent on proving something – to all the world of course; but, more creditably, to himself and for his pupils.

Things continued well. Endless practices were giving the cast ever more confidence. Repetition really was key to learning. Likewise, the camaraderie of rehearsals helped; Dom had grown to feel it every day, remembering how they had all bonded because of the snow. It was more and more like working with friends rather than pupils. In his passion, the enthusiasm and enjoyment he shared so generously without quite knowing it, he lost of that sense of his own lack of experience, of being a stranger, an outsider. And did he make them work! He kept on and on, pushing them for more, something better, each time, never satisfied.

'Just one more time' became a joke amongst the cast. True, some found it engulfing, panicking over everything else they should be doing at school; but Sir was working hard *for them*. They saw that. They still needed to 'Hillview him' into being less of a Dom, more of a broken in, make do and mend kind of teacher; but a thousand practical frustrations that dogged every day could be forgotten in the collective effort that took them out of themselves.

Mr Tring remained a pain, turning up when it suited, a law unto himself; but he could see something happening, wanted to be part of it. Katie still raided rehearsals whenever she could for pupils to take to her extra lessons. She seemed to believe, as well, that she had watching a brief on it all, interfering when she could, criticising freely, especially Dom- to his face and behind his back. She always heard about anything that went wrong, relaying it with advantage to anyone who would listen, whilst consistently reporting to Hennock; but even she stopped, fascinated, one day by a rehearsal she happened to be passing. She had to think hard before she found fault that day.

*

Then, just when Dom had begun to feel that, out of all the chastening muddles of his first term, real and imagined, something was going right, only a few days before the performances, everything went firmly into rapid and determined reverse.

He was back at the beginning again. Chaos. Nothing big nor small was any good any more.

Everyone grew fractious, he most of all.

Lines and cues were all over the place. Moves perfected in long rehearsals were forgotten, lost forever in some cases; the comedy became laboured; the lovers hysterical, unconvincing; the fairies and all the spirit in the poetry, wooden, boring, unbelievable.

Bronte, Austen: now Shakespeare having a wobble.

Then the flu came back, spurred on by the Headmaster's wife who made a rare appearance in school to watch a rehearsal, laugh inappropriately and loudly, whilst sneezing and coughing over everyone.

A second wave began.

Dom was aghast when he realised that there were still some scenes that he had never rehearsed with all the actors there. They kept turning pages, but there was always more, yet the finite time of all the school's other business was always eroding what rehearsals they did have.

And everyone had their grievance.

Costumes started the rot. At the first dress, nothing seemed to fit. Miss Bistle, who had been a saint during the flu, had to confess the epidemic had forced upon her drastic short cuts. This was eagerly seized upon by anyone who did not like what had been worked up. Her good friend Mrs Dot drafted herself in to help once more, turning a number of problems into a complete crisis.

'I'm not going on like that Sir, I look like a tart,' declared Rachel, kicking things off.

'You do look a little overexposed,' commented Mrs Dot not very helpfully.

'See, Sir! and she's designed the costumes.'

'Sir Oberon's split his tights. We can see through, it's disgusting!'

'Sir, Miss Bistle's just grabbed whatever came her way – the whole thing looks shite. Can we postpone?'

'Sir, you've stuffed up. Everyone looks wrong. Everyone's unhappy with what they have to wear.'

'Sir, why is Mrs Dot crying. Is it cos Rachel swore at her?'

Miss Bistle continued, in her superhuman way, patiently taking notes, making adjustments, soothing egos, adjusting things. Mrs Dot continued too. Finally she was given a commission to sort the makeup box out – to get her out of the way. She quickly returned to the main fray to say that she had, in fact, dropped it down some stairs. Wonderful children were helping pick up the contents, although one or two had been a bit silly and made someone up,with a black face, upsetting some of the others. Yes, there had been a deputation to Alison about racism in the play, and then that silly man Terry had arrived on the scene, furious, and had had a real go at her. It had brought back all that nasty business about the fire, her poisoning last year.

Dom tried to persuade her to stay at home until she was completely well.

Even Tim and Jane were moaning, and his stars Lucy and Robin wondering if they could save their talent from slow demolition by resigning and finishing off the whole production. Andy, who had not forgotten who was responsible for his drugs bust and all that hung over him, returned to his default setting of disagreeable form, pronouncing loudly.

'Everyone keeps saying this is going to be crap.'

Dom wanted to rise to it, but didn't.

'It'll be fine, if everyone learns their lines, does what they've been told.'

'Good job you're not being inspected next week,' added Andy. 'We could ask that female inspector back!'

James and latest girlfriend looked in at one point and were more favourable, delighted to see so many of their school friends looking ridiculously uncool.

'Sir, this is going to be *epic*. They all look so different-weird. I wish I'd been in it now. I love fancy dress. It looks a real laugh.'

Dom was left to thank and console Miss Bistle as best he could, but she was case-hardened. She did, however, insist on the complete removal of Mrs Dot from her production domain.

Dom knew Miss Bistle would now go away, work silently, efficiently,put all right; and would do all this, expecting nothing back in the end, only delighting in the pleasure of others when it came good. On such rocks must all endeavours depend.

Pity, however, he couldn't arrange for the kidnap and deportation of Mrs Dot, stow her away somewhere for the duration. Reports were coming in that she had found her way to the lighting box and was loose up there. Dom wondered if he could plead a return of the flu, a breakdown, insanity or something – leave it all to someone else; but he knew, somewhere in himself, that his vanity at least, alongside everybody else's, was far too deeply engaged for that.

*

Later, after a full day at school, he made his way to one of his longer rehearsals, his mind spinning with all the multi dimensional detail of production and direction, rehearsing things he needed to tell cast and crew, clutching lists for this and that, excited, apprehensive, nerves strung.

To his surprise, waiting for him in the school hall, was Dr Hennock's friend, the governor. For a moment he had a sudden pang of anxiety as old terrors of discovery returned. Had he left some sign of his recent trespass or shadowing them in the dark?

But it turned out he had come along, after chatting to Mr Waseley, and his wife, to lend moral support, even though he too now had the flu he said, sneezing over Dom and his stars.

Things got going.

At first the pace was cracking, everyone started acting out of their skins. Dom could not believe what he was watching;

but the effort of remembering lines still not fully digested, the apprehension about lines not learnt, once they got deeper in, soon began to tell. Those who had not done their preparation were quickly floundering, standing and delivering as if they were at some ghastly public speaking recital for Very Young and Challenging Children, or just freezing altogether, dependent babies needing everything wiping.

In all the tension of trying to remember words, the actions went too. Sensing Sir was not very happy, they tried to cover. Sometimes, the cast would borrow one another's lines spreading confusion to those who thought they were secure on their cues. Another variation was addressing characters by their own characters' names – which created yet more muddle and achieved an alarmingly surreal *Alice in Wonderland* effect.

The play kept stuttering to a halt with members of the cast looking at each other in amusement, then bewilderment or anger as lines cascaded to the floor, or were transposed or just conjured up from random bits and pieces of other parts of the play, or anywhere else that came to mind, often in Hillview speak.

The pace died horribly and slowly with the concentration, like a vinyl record winding down on a turntable.

Three quarters of an hour in and they were wading through mud, moving through darkness. Only the twins, who seemed, despite all their rehearsing to lack any understanding at all of what they were doing or saying, strewing words and actions as randomly as a Mrs Dot on speed, were undismayed by disaster. They kept braying and laughing loudly at their own and anyone else's trashy performances, capering about in delight when things kept going wrong. They could not wait to retell and re-enact each catastrophe to anyone who chanced to look in.

Dom tried to keep calm. He really tried.

He knew they were making an effort. He could feel their tension. He even started off feeling sorry for them, but as the hours went by and progress was limping, then disabled, he could feel his own frustration clawing away in his stomach and chest, tension spreading into his neck and shoulders, twisting his face and expression, knotting hope into strangled despair.

Soon, he was snapping wildly at anyone who did or said anything right or wrong, his tattered emotions master. They were selfish creeping little animals, Nibelungs, out deliberately to betray him, revelling in meanness and littleness.

He knew, somewhere inside, he was contributing to the cast's crumbling confidence and abilities, but empathy was start of term stuff. All he saw was wasted effort, what could have been, sliding into yet more triviality and absurdity. Damn them he thought: DAMN THEM.

Meanwhile, the poor cast were standing numbly around on stage, tired, drained, confused, wincing at the bright lights – rabbits trapped in headlights, hoping only for an ending to a ghastly mess, their spirits mashed, Sir a raving tyrant at them like a demon if they moved a muscle.

They were doing their best. This was all so unfair.

Dom thought of *Wuthering Heights* all those weeks ago.

Eventually he gave up stopping them, trying to set things right.

They were sulking; so would he.

At first, the governor had laughed loudly at the jokes and even more loudly at a lot of lines that were not supposed to be funny. He fancied he knew his Shakespeare, wanted to show it. He found the mistakes highly amusing, kept glancing at Dom as if to ask why he was not enjoying this more.

Dom wanted him destroyed, preferably a slow and painful killing, but stone dead anyhow would do. His laugh reminded Dom of the man braying in the pub: inane, feral, destructive, tipping everything into a cultureless, mindless animal void.

Soon the governor had become bored, however, and he had spent the last half hour conspicuously busy on his phone, or blowing his nose with a loud farting sound, the only funny thing left on the planet.

Alone amongst the cast, Robert – and Lucy- kept their heads and concentration throughout the evenings travails; the less accomplished were adamant that it wasn't their fault: it could only be Sir's. Look at the mess he had made with the costumes. They had warned.

Meanwhile, disintegration carried on in magnificent detail.

At one point Bottom had to enter with a light and blow out a lamp, but he had not practised with the props before, and suddenly seemed overwhelmed, quite lost, vacant. Something, somewhere, had got stuck, gone wrong. He decided to improvise. Everyone else was.

'Anyone still out there?' he quipped to the audience.

There was loud laughter from the lighting box. The governor looked up from his phone and brayed.

No one near Dom dared to laugh.

Dom bit his tongue. He could taste blood.

'Bottom's dream- cut two hundred!' Robin quipped, attempting to blow out the candle in a moment of metaphoric intensity, but the glass casing was too resilient and would not let air in.

Undaunted he blew again, and again and again, harder each time.

Those watching had cottoned on.

Andy backstage said something obscene about blowing hard that was clearly audible throughout the hall, but before Dom could attack, there came a shout from on high.

'What the f- are you doing?' came from the lighting box. 'It's supposed to go dark.'

There was a sound of scuffling up there – more expletives. Mrs Dot's voice raised in feeble admonition.

She was on it-help!

There were thumps and bumps from upstairs, more swearing, then laughter and another eternal pause.

What on earth was going on now? Time had stopped altogether. Perhaps this was what death was like.

Finally the actor started blowing at the light again. He blew, and blew, his aerosol spray caught vividly in the lights so that the members of audience who were not laughing manically, made derisive noises expressing disgust.

'Oh *SHIT!* Sir, I can't blow it,' cried Bottom.

More crude chorusing from Andy. Bottom walked off stage completely, to junk the lantern and simultaneously upbraid the props man who could be heard loudly offstage disclaiming all responsibility. He had never seen it before, nor indeed knew anything about it, nor any of the props, which someone had just dropped in from somewhere, and no he'd never read the play. No one had told him he had to, or when they went on or off, or indeed what the hell was supposed to be going on at any point.

There was a tense backstage exchange including further colourful expletives.

The governor laughed again, but modulating it with a reproving stare towards Dom: youngsters; their language.

For quite a while the stage stretched out, all brightly lit for once, but completely empty, and totally devoid of interest.

The sound of the escalating row backstage reached round to the cast, most of whom had been underemployed for so long that they had now wandered to the front to watch, forming an impromptu audience, alongside others from the school who had heard there was much fun to be had, especially a teacher about to go nova.

Then the sound of someone crying helplessly and hopelessly backstage reached them doubling their amusement.

A voice came from the audience, cautiously hopeful.

'Is that the end, Sir?'

'*NO!*' Dom knew the sound had come from him, but did not recognise what had happened to his voice.

Eventually the props man himself appeared, walking into the floods, blinking and peering out into the dark trying to locate Sir.

'I can't see you, Sir. Sir, what shall we do? I don't know where I am any more-and it won't blow?'

'Take one of the glass panels out so he can blow it out.'

The boy wrestled with it for a moment or two

'Sir, it's stuck,' he said shaking it vigorously. Then the panel flipped out at last, smacking onto the stage, splitting noisily into shards.

The audience couldn't get enough of it.

'Problem solved!' quipped Robert.

'Do we put that in the script?' came from the lighting box, earnestly anxious to redeem itself now.

The curtain began closing for no apparent reason, slowly and inexorably, with a terrible finitude.

'Somebody clear that glass up before we have a real accident on stage. Back to the start of Act Four, and the rest of you get backstage. I don't want anyone watching this pile of -'

The twins appeared, rather bored from backstage, and keen to do something, began energetically sweeping the broken glass off stage into the case of the grand piano below, bowing as they retreated, grinning all over their faces, enjoying every second, but genuinely pleased to have helped Sir. He seemed a bit stressed today.

Mr Tring, who had forgotten the rehearsal altogether and only just arrived, became Vesuvius again.

A few minutes later when some semblance of calm had returned, the governor came over to Dom. He seemed quite oblivious to the fact that the play was still running, had not finished and Dom needed to watch.

He put an unwelcome hand on Dom's shoulder.

'Great fun, but I'd do something a bit easier next time. Terry was telling me about a panto – good idea. Some girl was suggesting *Fame*. Still, didn't realise all this Shakespeare malarkey could be such a jolly old laugh,' he said chuckling, then sneezed all over Dom.

'I do think it is good that you give all these less able a chance,' he carried on, still talking loudly over the dialogue that continued on stage. 'That's what education is all about. Gives them confidence to get up there, give it their all, even if it's bollocks. By the way, do we have many disabled children taking part? Good for our diversity profile.'

For a moment or two Dom did not know what to say, but Rachel was at his side again in her latest costume.

'Sorry Sir, I know you are stressed but I simply can't wear this either. It got caught on a tree backstage. Is it all right if I get something else from town during school tomorrow?'

'Who are you meant to be, Lady Muck? Mustn't frighten the horses, you know?' said the governor roaring with laughter at her.

Rachel gave him a glance that would have felled lesser men.

Before Dom could deal with any of this, he was surrounded by the lighting team, now liberated from Mrs Dot. They were covered in dust and some paint they had found to play with.

They did look rather sheepish.

'Sorry, Sir, my bad. We have lots of pages missing. Matt keeps playing with the controls.'

'Where is he. He's supposed to be in charge. We haven't finished yet!' cried Dom.

'Sir, Mrs Dot keeps telling us what to do and it's all wrong.'

'Sir, my costume. Can I take the morning off?' repeated Rachel.

'Sir, Miss Trippett is on the phone saying can you remind members of the cast she teaches that they still need to do their homework tonight for a test tomorrow.'

Then came a cry from upstairs.

'Sir, there's a fire in the lighting box!'

'Sir, Andy's hit his head backstage and is bleeding. He was showing off for the girls. He says he feels dizzy.

'Sir, Terry's going ape on stage because he had to come in as someone has jammed the curtain.'

'Sir, Mrs Dot's trying to suck the ice cream out of the smoke machine with a vacuum. She bought some to cheer everyone up but left the box on it- it's all melted and runny'.

'Sir, Dr Hennock's on the phone for you. He says there are lots of irate parents wondering when they can pick their kids up.'

'SIR! *the fire in the lighting box is getting worse!*'

Dom felt it would be simpler if they just shot him.

CHAPTER FORTY-TWO

DRESS REHEARSAL

There remained the dress rehearsal and performances to put it right.

Dom could not get out of it now. Nor to his credit would he, even if it was turning into *A November Nightmare*.

Mike asked him what it was all about. Dom found himself struggling.

'How the imagination can trick you, especially in love; but without it, nothing really is.'

'*What?* Poor kids.'

Even when he was not rehearsing Dom made long lists of things to do, although new challenges and tasks simply welled up once he thought he had made progress. He was only just on top of his teaching, taking everything one lesson at a time, a page ahead of those he taught. His flat became a tip, the rest of his life discarded.

Looking into the mirror at night he saw dark shadows under his eyes, noticed with a real shock, for the first time in his life, a grey hair amidst the black. He pulled it out, horrified, wondering if this was the beginning of the end. When he went to sleep at night, it was instantly day again as the sounds of his alarm and the waking world outside roused him from a rest that never was. If he dreamt, or had time to remember his dream, it was always the same: up was going the curtain, nothing ready.

Lessons passed in a blur of waiting for the next rehearsal when he would come alive again, suddenly finding energy beyond exhaustion. Doing the play felt like walking a tightrope, your eyes blindfolded, over and over.

But for all his fears and doubts, somewhere inside him hope was alive. He could still – just – glory in the possibility, that, perhaps, one day, for a moment or two, a magic casement really would be thrown open.

*

The day of the dress rehearsal.

Even the scenery was now on the way, although Terry had done his best to obstruct its creation, movement and storage because of his never ending 'ell and shaft me' considerations. Mr Tring's interest continued to increase. He was scurrying around at last, dreadfully late in the day, organising band and musicians. He would even be at the dress rehearsal, he announced; well, some of it.

Alison came to see Dom repeatedly mostly about parking and refreshments and at least half the cast who, in one way or another she was fussing over. But she had time for him as well. She knew her staff, her school, really cared.

Meanwhile, tickets were selling, an audience eager. There had been no proper play at the school for a few years. They wanted to see their kids, have a laugh, for good or bad. Then an unmarked Mrs Dot got involved in the rush with ticketing, messing that up too, causing unprecedented waves of angst among the admin staff, nearly scuttling the whole thing by mixing up the days parents had asked for and the always delicate issue of who sat where. The school switchboard was overwhelmed, inboxes overflowed. Mrs Dot, undaunted, continued to spew instructions, all wrong to anyone in admin who was still sane enough not to have put their head in a bucket, or taken early retirement.

Dr Hennock was furious. Unbeknownst to Dom, Emma, however, heard about the steamy situation, offered to take charge. She was glad to turn her hand to work she felt more her, swiftly sorting the situation, not before telling Mrs Dot what she thought of her organisational capacities. Alison had to patch Mrs Dot back together, but Hennock, relieved not to have to sort things himself for once, was quietly impressed, even if he could not bring himself to say so. His mind, never slow to think how people could be used, began to wonder if Emma, whose resignation was now common knowledge, could be retained in some way, both to shore up the department and to facilitate some of his many burgeoning plans. But that was for later.

*

Not all the cast would be there for the dress, it then transpired. Bewildered at first when he found out, Dom subsided into a kind of weary resignation, spirits torpedoed once more. He actively wondered if it were all some dark plot by Hennock to finish off school drama.

Next, although the scenery was now on stage, no, it was actually not quite finished, and Mr Knutt, chief woodman of Hillview Design Department, would be needing to make adjustments during the run through – and possibly performances. Did Dom know he was giving up his annual darts match for this, and his wife was no longer speaking to him because of all the time he had spent on it.

Abetted by Terry, he had lectured Dom about safety screws and supply lines, the rising cost of sustainable four-by-two in the current economic situation at every and any opportunity for the last few weeks. These concerns increased exponentially once the set was up and Mr Knutt saw that children were actually going to use his creations, touching, even sitting on things, something he affirmed over and over had never been in his brief, and now necessitated plenty of revisions and constant reinforcements in situ.

Despite precise instructions from Dom, the art teachers had painted the set their own way, with many flaming, vibrant scary reds – so that rather than a magical mystical wood, the trees for the play looked like something out of Dante's inferno, or a porn movie according to James.

It looked a bit like hell Dom thought.

Meanwhile, the costume drama sub plot moved on. Before anyone could stop her, Mrs Dot had taken many home and washed them. They returned, mostly bleached a colourless grey, so shrunken as to be only suitable for dwarvish folk. Quite a few items had to be completely replaced. Even Miss Bistle began to talk about this production being her last. Mrs Trotman waded in with firm words for the children and harsher ones for staff.

Dotty blamed her glasses.

Whenever he had a spare moment, and there seemed to be plenty of them, Terry looked in, passing comment.

'It looks shite. You look shite. I hope you's learnin' your lesson,' he observed to Dom. 'Never work with children or animals. That lot's both.'

*

Things at last rose to a general level of readiness. The dress was to begin.

Dom stood there waiting to address the cast with some rallying notes. A message arrived from the lighting box that all his detailed and complicated lighting instructions could not now be accessed. They had disappeared into part of the system only that boy Tom Rymer had ever understood. He had done something to the memory, it was claimed, before he left- a joke, a kind of delayed gradual erasing of information that had only just begun to show its true scope.

No one else could now undo what he had set going.

A general groan went up. A frantic search began to see if he could still be contacted as he, apparently, had a key password that would reverse IT dementia. More agonising minutes of delay passed with actors peeping around the curtain every thirty seconds or so to ask Dom if they had started yet. Dom wanted to swear and scream again; instead he tried to remember it was all only a play, and that he must consider how much they all had to learn and do, and that stuffing up was part of the learning process.

Then he thought of exquisite forms of torture he could put all these people through one day.

Rymer's contact was found. He sent his best wishes to all; wished he were still there; in fact – was not enjoying his new school; wanted to come back; and much, much else beside. But eventually, yes, he did have the password, he would let them have it, but he was at his dad's sister's home apparently having left his new school and being home tutored. He had his chores to do first, or he would be kicked out of there too-including a long walk for their little dog that his counsellor insisted on every day.

At that, he received so many, and such colourful, requests for the necessary information, being told that the whole production hung by a thread because of him, and Mr Greaves was literally on his deathbed, that he finally bestirred himself, answered with the solution; and, at last their came the word from on high that things were unlocked, memory found, restored, technodementia halted.

YES: they could begin.

Only then, one of Terry's main fuses blew. As the school boiler was not intimately involved on this occasion something under his jurisdiction had to make its point.

There was another ten minutes of delay punctuated by Terry's increasingly violent language up in the lighting box, his refrain of why the hell was Mrs Dot up there, and why the f- did they not just do a f-in' pantomime like any f-in' normal school as he had said all f-in'along.

Eventually, and finally, and when it seemed no greater torment could be devised for mortal being, nor had ever been visited on man in the whole history of everything ever, when Dom felt so strung up as to feel he would tear apart at any second or go up in flames – they could start.

He spoke.

'Now, come on, think of all the effort you've put in, think of how amazing you can be when you concentrate. Think of the wonderful thing you are trying to do- capture our humanity, celebrate our imagination. It's yours for the taking.

'No one minds a few slips if the intention is there and the effort is sustained and you KEEP IN ROLE but *you must concentrate* and *FOCUS*. There have been too many people talking, doing their own thing, not listening to instructions. *Even now as I am talking I can see people NOT listening,'* he paused. '*Andy is there any reason you should be talking to Rachel now?'*

Andy was about to speak, thought better of it.

'Remember all I've told you. Let's blow them away, not bore them senseless, reach for the dream, and- I would like my job next term as well....

'*First act: beginners please.'*

There was a cheer from those who understood what this instruction meant. That slowly dawned on the rest.

Then came the voices, first from the lighting box once more.

'Sir, the fire's come back.'

'Sir, Rachel says she's got a sore throat and will have to mime. Andy says he feels sick and dizzy again.'

'Sir, he needs to go to hospital.'

'Sir, I can't find my script.'

'Sir, are we starting?'

'Not if there are no lights,' Dom said and sped off to tender to the hapless and the wounded, only to be stopped by a parent.

'Mrs Clayme' she introduced herself, 'Robert's, Puck's mother! I know it's really rude of me to come in and I don't want to interfere at all, but I just want to tell you that I need to have Robert home – by four o'clock – he's got swimming.'

The woman in front of him, like the children in the last rehearsal suddenly became a mean little animal, transformed in his imagination into some grasping, inconsiderate reptilian creature, whose only function was to kill, then engorge itself on other life forms.

Fat thoughtless old bat, Dom thought; then, shocked at his feelings, pulled back.

'Look I'm sorry, but he's known about this rehearsal for weeks. I sent you details and we simply can't do without him today, it's our dress rehearsal. We haven't started yet!'

'Well, that's not very helpful. I thought you'd want to be helpful, all he's done for you! I'm sorry but I arranged with his tutor, Ms Trippett. She said it was all fine. Swimming's his life.'

'Look, what I suggest you do,' said Dom, 'have a chat with his tutor tomorrow. I'm sure there's been some misunderstanding, but I made it quite clear I needed them all, all through this rehearsal. I can't waste -'

'I can see you're stressed, but this is more important to Robert,' she pursued, not listening. 'He will lose his place in the team. Dr Hennock agrees.'

'Look Mrs Clayme, I completely understand your difficulties, but this is the first I've heard about it. Robert has mentioned nothing. I have spent weeks working on this, the first performance is tomorrow evening and we have run out of time. I can't work on the basis of every single individual's whims to do this or that or the other.'

'I'm not happy,' Mrs Clayme continued. 'We've made all sorts of sacrifices for him to be in the play. Robert says you've wasted lots of time in rehearsals shouting. The school's always been reasonable in the past. They should have someone properly in charge.'

Before he could reply, the curtains suddenly opened very swiftly, the technical crew having overcome some impairment with the mechanism, revealing the substantial backside of Mr Knutt happily sawing at one of the trees, Mrs Dot still trying to vacuum clean ice cream out of the smoke machine, and two members of the general public who had wandered onto the stage, quite lost.

There were gales of laughter from some of the cast who were sitting in the audience, waiting.

'Excuse me, what are you doing?' Dom asked the general public.

'Hello,' they said warmly, clearly hoping for a long and friendly chat. 'The doors were open at the back – we were having a look around. We're cycling the county, staying in the pub up the road. We thought we'd pop in, sit here, watch for a bit if that's okay. It looks a riot!'

'Shall I tell them to fuck off, Sir?' cried Andy.

*

It was a disastrous dress rehearsal.

Dom did not have the experience to know that that was often the norm, but even if he had it would still have hurt like hell.

The cast, keyed-up early on, had lost concentration with all the delays, and just wanted to get to the end of it. There was no audience – why bother? Mr Tring and the band were bored rigid, and made up for it by making critical and rude, sometimes lewd remarks every time anyone came on stage. The lighting crew seemed to be overtaken by collective deafness, so Dom had to roar for any response at all. When they did hear, they became paralysed when any instruction reached them. The excitement of the fire seemed to have scattered what wits they had.

During a dance to evoke the magical dream world, plaster came down from the ceiling. Terry was summoned but had left for home so the production had to continue whilst avoiding the space under the suspect part of the roof, making a nonsense of most of the moves, and the choreography.

After an hour, in which things had got even worse than the last rehearsal, everyone was just going through the motions. Mrs Dot was the only one who retained any enthusiasm for any of it, or life itself it seemed. She was everywhere, telling everyone how marvellous they were, including the school cat who, during a longer than usual pause when the stage was completely empty, came on to wash and groom itself, and its intimate parts, before departing in a leisurely manner with a look that could only be described as one of disdain.

They reached the last act at the end of a Sisyphean epic of effort. Mobile phones were ringing in the auditorium from parents irate because their children were late again, whilst Mr Jolson wandered in looking anxiously round for the boarders who were supposed to be at some callover; but still things dragged, making watching paint dry look positively festive, all compounded by the absence of Robert. He had long ago gone off for his swim leaving Dom to fill in his lines for him.

The lights had packed up altogether, so periods of semi darkness alternated with searing house strips, turned on to interrogate the performance's futility like some horrific Gestapo searchlight. A flat came crashing down out of the wings, narrowly missing Rachel.

'It's always me!' she declared, quite without irony.

In the last dance, relieved to have reached the end, the twins got so carried away they fell off the stage into the band, who finally managed a laugh. Musicians, apparently, were not cynical all the time.

They reached the curtain call; but it jammed, would neither open nor close.

Then on wandered solitary Mrs Dot, blinking out into the auditorium.

'Is Mr Greaves out there? There are a lot of parents back here waiting to take their children home some of them seem a bit agitated. Shall I give them my scones, ice cream-'

Whether or not it was deliberate, Dom never found out, but she happened to be standing over the trapdoor in the stage, and as she was elaborating the different complaints she had received she began a slow descent underground. Even Dom had to laugh as she kept on valiantly talking and apologising as first her body, then her still talking head disappeared. It was the only round of applause of the evening, perhaps the biggest she had ever got in her life.

*

'Right, on stage everyone!' Dom cried at the very end, just glad there was no more; and, of course, nothing happened.

'Sir, the lights are working!' came a voice.

A derisive cheer went up.

Dom shouted his instruction again and the curtain jerked suddenly into life, now closing completely.

He sat down for a moment and put his head in his hands wondering if he could still plead insanity.

Behind the curtain he could hear the stage filling with people, confused, spent, exhausted.

Finally, the curtain opened, floods came up blinding a cast who stood blinking, squinting into the light of their disaster. Eyes sought a director in the black oblivion of the auditorium.

Eventually utter silence fell.

One or two of the backstage crew wandered on looking pale as sheets. Stillness.

'Sir, Rachel's crying back stage,' began one of the twins. 'She says we should have done *Fame*.'

Dom stood up, very slowly, wondering if he had suddenly turned geriatric.

Here they were face to face. After all that.

As he was about to speak he became aware of Dr Hennock standing behind him in the dark, taking it all in, poised for his moment.

'I can see you have you hands full at the moment, but I need to talk to you about Mrs Clayme before you pack it in.'

Then he looked at the stage, back at Dom. His look said everything.

He walked off, disappearing into the shadows.

'Well,' Dom said at last, with a sigh that came from his soul. 'Tomorrow can only get better. I know you're tired. Well done for at least-. We got through it. Now, listen, and I mean *really listen* this time: you have to *listen now, or all is lost, forever.*'

*

When they'd gone – finally- they seemed to recover energy when it was finished, and it took him a while to chase them away despite fuming parents waiting, he was left on his own again.

He stood there for a few moments, trying to get his head around what he had done, not least to himself.

His phone pinged; an email from Paul.

News whilst you've been buried alive. Royal's retirement, sacking, to be announced imminently. Hennock and Waseley at odds. Waseley out too? Crisis over school's future coming to the boil. How's the world of the imagination, hell? Break a leg- or somebody.

The kids did not seem so bad then, when he read, took all that in.

He left, turning out the lights himself.

CHAPTER FORTY-THREE

INTERVAL

When Dom finally got away, he went up to his flat but could not rest.

His baby. His responsibility.

He could feel his heart still pumping hard, every nerve and muscle in his body firing. He texted his friends, Emma; there was no reply from her as usual, but he'd heard about her help.

Mike sent a message. *Do something fun next time.* There was an irritating one from Joe reminding him how privileged he was. John's said more simply, *Get a life!* But there was a message from his parents, having the time of their life on the other side of the world, far away. They wished him luck, thinking of him.

He pulled himself together. Come on. There's no moral injury not like with poor Mr Royal, the future of the school. It's vanity, your bruised ego.

He played with his phone for a bit, watching video clips selling him something false under the guise of something better. He turned on a tv he rarely watched, tried to get interested in a vapid football game, but the players all strung up because they were losing reminded him too much of himself. He surfed on: inane game shows, a sniff of riches and the illusion of success; an unbelievable romcom; rolling news channels, economic bust, global meltdown, political corruption, war, sickness, terrorism, starving millions – followed of course by sport and weather: all would be well tomorrow.

He landed on another channel: unbelievable photography of wildlife given a human voice over. The dumb face of a victim zebra, eyes staring agony and submission, still alive, locked in the jaws of the lion. It shocked, fascinated; for a moment.

He went outside to clear his head. A slab leaden November sky had given way to a thick, foggy darkness, a faint and feeble cold mizzle. Lights were still on here and there across the school campus, fuzzy in the mist, but Dom turned away towards the stray, walking quickly. Regardless of the damp, not really knowing where he was going or how far, he pressed on in the direction of the Cloud, expecting to see Dr Hennock appear out of the smoking gloom.

Eventually, he found himself at the foot of the hill, not sure how he had come there, or why.

He sat down on a fallen tree branch, in a little copse, despite the cold, the damp of the wood under him. After a few minutes, he felt curiously cocooned there, apathetic, indifferent even, though rain was coming on. He was a meaningless thing of nature now, not of man.

Somewhere in the distance a car splashed its greedy way along a road, its tyres tearing across tarmac. Across the fields a dog barked over and over again: fierce, frustrated, unanswered.

Dom could feel the rain seeping into his hair, the creeping damp into his clothes. His breath steamed in front of him, a haze around his head. He bent down and touched the earth, then, on impulse, stuck his fingers hard into it, digging a handful of dirt. Surprisingly, here, it seemed a sandy soil.

There were even small rounded, shiny pebbles. Perhaps once upon a time this had been the bed of some ancient sea.

He lifted a mess of soil and stones to his face, examining it closely, inspecting it with his phone. The smell of earth and stone reminded him of something. Then he was back in the garden of his infancy with his Dad, a kid once more: the smells of childhood that come so intimately when very young, never quite lost.

Dom let the soil and stones slip away through his fingers. He wiped his hands as best he could on some grass that still grew long in the shelter of the glade. Then, for a long time he just sat there.

It grew very late. The remaining few lights on campus went out; the rain became a mizzle once more and a chill breeze stirred now and then, rustling a thousand dead leaves. November darkness.

*

Thought came back slowly, sought its own sense.

Scenes of term, good and bad, came and went in his mind: his hesitation on the stairs at the start of term; terrors on the wall outside the night he had got locked in and seen the file; creeping around in the dark, finding nothing but that girl's essay about her mum and dad fighting. He thought of Hennock, and Waseley, of bad Andy, irritating Rachel, infuriating Mrs Tray, crazy Mrs Dot, that red-haired kid, pathetic Tom Rymer who'd nearly done for his play; following those two to their secret meeting on the hill, that moment in the dark when he thought he'd seen someone. Then, he was on top of the Cloud just before the holiday; at Tim's home; listening and learning from Jane, all his pupils really; his first trip, his first rehearsal, times with Emma, colleagues.

He might never understand all this completely, know what he had been taught, but rising from a sea of memory, somewhere, sometime, these things, moments would always come back, forever part of him. Even the play.

He could still sort it.

*

Suddenly his phone beeped loudly.

It was a text from Emma

Break a leg! Life's not a dress rehearsal!! Xx

He had his job to do, something to prove.

CHAPTER FORTY-FOUR

CURTAIN UP

Later the next day, a strained, pale looking Mr Royal found Dom.

'Heard you had a jolly dress, old tiddly pom,' he laughed.

Dom shook his head; he'd wanted to avoid colleagues. Despite yesterday, perhaps because of some sleep, Dom was feeling better. He'd given it his all; the kids had trusted. He would not let them down now.

'Don't let them get you down. In the end, you know, it's up to them, ' continued Mr Royal, more gently, to his surprise.

'I suppose so,' said Dom warily,' It doesn't feel like that. People keep saying not to take it seriously, it's only a play; but what's the point of anything if it's only rubbish.'

'You've done your best: that's all you ever can. Perhaps they'll surprise you.'

Dom was expecting something flippant, even cutting. Just then, Mr Royal's words meant more than he could say.

'You can always pull it you know!' cried Mr Walker who was hovering about as usual. 'I remember, just after I started teaching, the HM called in the drama teacher, a Mr Crackall was his name; good name for him. Remember him, Charles? Gave him a carpeting – his production was absolutely ghastly.

He left soon afterwards. He became a stand-up comedian, I gather. Can't think anyone laughed much though.'

'Does he know?' said Mr Walker, in a slightly lower tone addressing Royal.

'Ssh!' said Mr Royal. 'We don't want him jaded and old, like us. How's the cast? Chastened I hope – they'll be better now they've got it spectacularly wrong. That's how you learn.'

'It's just- I wish they'd bother a bit more sometimes, without me on their backs all the time,' said Dom.

The two weren't listening, however, and went off together into a corner. They began muttering about something. Dom the outsider still. He felt a surge of anger, but then Mr Walker left.

Mr Royal read the expression on Dom's face.

'Now, Dom, I've told you before. Don't take things – especially old men too seriously. I'll have a word with some of the cast if they aren't pulling their weight; known some of them since they were little. It makes a difference. And they won't let you down in the end as you won't them. No, it's not the kids in a school I worry about. They can grow up. It's some of the adults who bother me. Talking of which, I must go and see the Head.'

He patted Dom on the shoulder on his way out.

Dom felt mean. Thinking only of himself again. He could guess what was happening.

He wondered where, on the long road of his life, Mr Royal had lost his way, or been suborned. He vowed for the thousandth time he would never end like that.

*

Somehow he got through that day. He still had to teach. Dr Hennock insisted. Much to his surprise, it was Emma who helped most. She took one look at him, became almost motherly. She persuaded him to go back to his flat for a rest, although he could hardly settle. She covered for him, not telling Hennock.

Her text, her behaviour: something had changed. He did not have time to begin to understand, but he was grateful: Mr Royal, now Emma.

People could surprise.

*

Before he knew it, Dom was back with his cast. But today there were two hours to go, not enough seconds left to do all that needed to be done.

Yet now all fatigue was forgotten, all weariness and frustration set aside. The youngsters who had seemed dissipated in rehearsal yesterday, even worse in lessons today, were suddenly young again, their young director no longer world weary or in some soup of self-pity. It was mostly sheer bloody-minded determination on his part, but he felt curiously alive, in every part of his being, living large in every moment of what he was doing for, with, them. And the cast seemed to feel the same now; at two minutes to midnight. After weeks and weeks of both fun, and undreamed of toil, it was finally real. All at last coming together. Where a day ago there had seemed to be only confusion and incompetence, stupidity, and frustration, even resentment, there was today purpose, focus. They were indeed sobered by failure as Charles had predicted, prepared to defy, dare all.

Despite his appointment with the boss, Mr Royal, true to his word, had been down and spoken, as only his character could, to those who were still laggard, characters like Andy. They had listened, contrite.

In short, impossible as it had seemed a mere twenty-four hours before, it mattered. They tore themselves away from virtual or imaginary worlds, parochial concerns, the this and that and mostly nothingnesses and smallnesses of getting by.True, they did not want to let themselves down – especially in front of peers and parents – but they did not want to let Dom down either. It mattered to Sir: it mattered to them.

If Dom could have known that for sure, felt it completely, it would have helped. He realised more than anyone perhaps, how much luck would play in any outcome. That was the real drama, and thrill, and terror to those who had skin in the game. No one could ever tell with something live where it would land.

He told himself over and over: he'd given it his all and here, at the end of weeks and months of work, there must finally be a weaning indeed.

*

Soon, all too soon, an audience was flooding in.

Please get involved, enjoy, laugh in the right places Dom thought as he watched them spill into the hall, heart in his mouth. They looked so casual, relaxed, a leisurely shambles in their entrances.

Behind the scenes, it was different. Instructions were flying about, impromptu rehearsals taking place, props lost and found, costumes altered. Near hysteria reigned at one point as Rachel tore her latest. Emotions flared over this and that until all the cast, or nearly all, were consumed with a simple awesome fear of those first steps into the limelight where all the world watched to see if terror or bravery would win the day.

Just before it all began for real, Dom said his last words to the cast, to calm them down, focus them one last time, contain their surging spirits from taking off completely. Despite a show of confidence, he knew he was dead excited too, as nervous as them, desperate for it to go well. The cast saw that, but respecting him because they knew he cared, took it to heart.

He made them sit quietly, then, looking at their scripts, ready to go on, some even waiting on stage, just behind the curtain. Some paced nervously around, on tiptoe at Dom's insistence, others stood still, almost frozen, cold empty nobodies, in a limbo of ephemeral identities, trembling on the edge of an abyss, hardly daring to breathe, imagining the possibility and impossibility of it all.

Once the audience were more or less settled, and had been plied with alcohol and pressed to some of Mrs Dot's triple blasted and inedible nibbles – she had insisted- Dom, redundant at last, went quietly around to stand and watch at the back. He wished he were somewhere else; but knew he wouldn't miss it for the world. He ignored Mrs Tray who was out front making some fuss. Just then, he did not want to talk to anyone about anything, but to see what happened, watch his cast either take wing now or sputter into darkness. There he stood, in his own magic circle, heart racing, wondering, perhaps a little extravagantly as usual, if anyone had ever died directing something.

*

At last, at last!

The houselights dimmed. Smoothly this time. No fires. No dramatic plunge into stygian darkness.

His heart beat harder, blood surging through him, ringing in his ears....

Silence.

Even a woman whose laugh had been a searing pain to all around her, and reminded Dom of the braying donkey sound of the man in the pub, stopped screeching.

House lights down.

Couldn't stop it now even if he wanted.

The world a blank darkness.

Inception.

Heaven or Hell now.

Slowly, the curtain rose, the lights came gently up.

Let there be light.

A set disclosed, awaiting the poetry of human life.

But then no one entered.

Nothing happened.

Disaster, after all?

Dom felt his heart drop.

Then a cast sailed on, completely in role, as if this was the entirely natural thing to do, and they were somewhere else and something else; and conviction was upon them all, an audience enchanted in the darkness, and all took wing: imagination becoming real, creating something better, finally.

*

The verse speaking, the songs, the choreography, the slapstick and the pathos, the energy and the roll swept all up together in one cosmic whirligig of flow. Entrances and exits propelled along a defining purpose in some unified dimension of pure acted awareness.

Art from life. Life from art.

Even Rachel and Andy seemed to be part of it all, most of the time.

Even the lights worked, except for a couple of accidental blackouts and a very loud 'Shit' from the lighting box.

Even the twins only fell off the stage once. And they got the biggest laugh.

And the music, the musicians!

The cast danced their way through words and actions, perfectly in time with each other, a text becoming theirs, their time completely.

Dom stood at the back, relieved, humbled, confused.

He wondered where it had all come from, pinched himself when things went well, held his breath when – only occasionally now – things did not. Even he was carried along, caught in a torrent of emotions: awe, pride, a gripping tension that they would keep it up, disbelief that this dream was real. And relief.

He even started to laugh himself, towards the end.

As Puck, no departure now for a swim, finally drew down his imaginative curtain, the audience in the palm of his hand, hanging on every note, the 'dead words' Dom had for so long struggled to bring to life in the classroom finally lived.

There were a few seconds silence at the end.

For a moment, Dom wondered if he had got it wrong. Perhaps they had been bored rigid, the laughter forced, the attention a mirage. Then the audience erupted with what sounded something like approbation.

Tim and Jane tried to get Dom on stage but he was having none of it. They had done it in the end, and yes, he was a part of it, partly responsible; but it was their play, alive through them. Never mind where it had come from, who had begun it; they had made it their own – at bloody last!

It touched him more than almost anything he had ever experienced before.

*

Afterwards, everyone was happy.

'Sir's learnt how to smile again,' said one of the cast.

Dom went around dazed, but congratulating everyone, not too much; he wanted them to do it again and again, and better and better, in the following performances, prove it no illusion. He gave them notes. They listened now, understanding, confidence alive in success.

But was he pleased?

He said yes, quietly, carefully, reminding people gently of what more needed to be done still.

Inside he sang.

He went to the changing rooms, thinking of the difference a day might make.

On the mirror of the wall of one someone had written in lipstick, 'I love Greavsie'. Underneath someone had added: 'We all do'.

*

For the following few days, Dom was the happiest person in Hillview, if also the most exhausted, and definitely the most relieved.

All the frustrations of the past weeks were forgotten for now. He had made a mark, but more importantly, the kids had acted out of their skins. Best of all, they had become a team: a kind of secret connection had been forged that allowed all those who had taken part to feel something special. Their smiles, for him, meant even more.

Mr Royal said simply: 'Well done, old boy. That really *was* good.'

Then added more delphically: 'You see, tiddly pom, reality is at least half imagination, isn't it? '

Even the most hidebound of colleagues had to admit they had almost enjoyed some of it. Mr Walker could only find a few dozen criticisms to advance, including: actors were childish and narcissistic weren't they, and the whole thing proved, didn't it, just how silly and dangerous imaginary things must be.

Mike said it wasn't as boring as he thought it was going to be: he'd quite liked the funny bit at the end, but Shakespeare was overrated. Terry told Dom he had saved himself by the skin of his teeth from a carpeting, but continued to recommend pantomimes in future, if he must do anything with the little sods.

Mr Waseley rather cryptically thanked Dom in person for finishing his term on a high note. Dom wondered if he were going to be sacked or if the Head were leaving as rumoured. Just then he didn't care. The Head followed it up with an effusive email praising Mr Workman's fine production of *Coriolanus*, adding that even his wife had enjoyed seeing it in rehearsals, saying it had been a riot. A pupil had spoken to her about doing *Fame* – a wonderful idea: – she had always wanted to act herself. Did Dom think he could get her a part, one of the main characters, when they did it next term?

Mrs Tray told him she had quite enjoyed it, despite her seat, whatever that meant, but complained that Rachel's part should have been further developed, something she was going to take up with management, Shakespeare being unavailable for comment. But as any praise at all from her was almost unheard of, Dom was content to bank that one, especially if the *Fame* debate took off again.

Even Mr Tring, who'd seen it all before, was delighted, and talked excitedly, but quite insanely about staging a Mozart opera next, or possibly *Fidelio* with Rachel as lead, naturally.

Dr Hennock who, for once, could find little to criticise, took solace in saying nothing at all about the performance, except to threaten a post mortem over all the difficulties it had thrown up. He dwelt long on the disruption caused to learning, and the real business of school, the parental complaint of Mrs Clayme, and even longer on some minor problem with parking that Dom, no doubt, should have foreseen.

Dom did not realise, and he was too tired afterwards properly to register it, but he became a sort of hero to the cast. They adored him, it was said, at least for a day or two. He was told much of the credit was his. He could only think what a total disaster it had been only the day before.

Even parents such as Andy's mother, a different creature from his last encounter, came up to him, said it was wonderful, although she ruined it all by echoing the governor's comments saying it was good of him to put all those challenging pupils with such crippling difficulties up on stage without everyone laughing.

Hadn't Andy done well, too, despite the way staff treated him.

*

Dom's joy was sealed by Emma. She had helped even backstage in the end, despite her protestation early in the term she was too busy, and sensible, to have anything to do with it.

Whatever her future plans, her thoughts about the school, or him, she had come and stood by him when he watched the performances from the back, eager, it seemed, to share something of it. He could not chose but wonder again, but decided, uncharacteristically, to play it cool with her: or try to. He was too wiped to do anything else.

Perhaps he was learning.

She had said little at first as she watched, then: 'I'm jealous. I never believed you would pull it off. I could never do something like that.'

It sounded as if she meant it too.

At the end she had kissed him, warmly, on the mouth.

Here I am, then, he had said to himself on the final night, having seen it get even better as confidence, experience had grown, listening to applause: delight and bewilderment complete. Here I am – at the exact centre of things, all the pieces at last more than the sum of their parts, making sense, becoming something more.

But he wouldn't – ever again- take things, himself, so seriously, he vowed solemnly.

Later, he even began to think of doing another play, one day, long, long in the future, of course.

CHAPTER FORTY-FIVE

DREAM DONE

Dr Hennock struck his first blow the following Monday.

Mr Royal had gone off one lunchtime into Wellsway, come back worse for the wear, bumped into some younger pupils, naturally mucking about, pushing each other around. They had collided with him as he mounted the main stairs unsteadily. Royal had flipped, unusual for him, but the man had a lot on his mind, ripped into them, lambasting them for idiotic thoughtlessness, angrily pushing them aside.

It was a second's mistake, done in the heat of a moment, but the pupils, understandably upset, had gone to Alison who had spoken, reluctantly, to Hennock. Waseley had had to become involved, only a few days after issuing a final, final warning. Hennock's ascendancy, Royal's record, the inspection episode, and Waseley's current insecurity all pointed only one way.

Everyone agreed: children had to come first.

No one, except Hennock, and Katie, who was delighted that the zeal of her reporting finally bore fruit, wanted the disaster that was about to overwhelm someone who had given such long and distinguished service. But, with a puritan morality abroad in the wider world – at least for adults in some professions- enough was enough. Dom might have approved, in abstract, the principles and ideals at work in the case, had he not begun to realise how vulnerable human failings made teachers in particular.

It was Mike who told Dom the news this time.

'Here's your opportunity, Dom: get in before Emma changes her mind, Hennock keeps her on. You have his job. You did the play thing. The old man's had his chance.'

Dom had been too happy straight after the play to register much beyond relief. Then he felt as weak as a new-born kitten, barely getting through the days, dealing with all the flotsam and jetsam in its wake, trying to catch up on marking, completing more reports, picking up a million threads. But he knew big things were happening. When he found out about Charles he tried to phone, texted repeatedly, but there was no reply. The man was not only no longer in school, it was claimed he was now no longer welcome on site. Royal had gone to ground.

It shook Dom. He must see a bit of himself in his mentor, even if he did not want to. As the warm effects of his success with the play wore off he even dared wonder if Mr Royal's vocation for teaching, his subject had in some way contributed to his fall. Imagination was a potent drug. Its promise, like the lure of a line of distant hazy hills, a far glimpse of the sea, the sounds of certain kinds of music could inspire undreamed of riches in the mind. But might you easily spend a life living an imagination, never quite seeing what was really there, then fall into disappointment, find consolation as Charles had in some sorry fashion?

He did not begin to know the answer to that one.

An email went round from Waseley saying that Mr Royal was off sick for the rest of the term, had decided to take early retirement.

Everyone knew. Everyone knew who had given the final push too.

Mr Royal's extraction from the arena was only a beginning however of Hennock's march to power.

At lunchtime that day, the staff were all summoned to another special after school meeting. The full inspection report was in. Soon rumours were flying around that the meeting was to be about more than that, and that big changes at the school, so long in the air, staff votes on this and that long talked about, were finally to be realised.

Driven by harsh winds of economic change a day of reckoning was upon the school. A dreamily imagined future, and practical realities were colliding once more.

Time up.

*

Dom was lingering in the Staff Room that Monday during a free period just before last lesson of the day. He knew Emma was free. Since the play, she had continued to seem warmer towards him. He hoped things might return at least to what they had once been.

There was no one in the room. He settled half-heartedly to some more of his marking backlog, ticking and flicking, short changing his charges, himself, now he thought; but he'd done his bit for this term surely.

And it wasn't as interesting as doing a play.

Emma entered, making him jump and blush, his feelings as raw as his tiredness.

Then she sat down. By him.

They made small talk for a while, partly about the play, partly about rumours that were spinning.

Dom began about Charles. Emma was less sympathetic.

'He's a good teacher. I'll give you that. But where's all his wisdom got him? And he left us in the lurch. You can't behave like that, and anyway-' she seemed to hesitate for a moment, then continued, 'there must be something wrong.

Never married, no partner; never been anywhere else. Can't imagine him ever being young, can you?'

'But look what he's done.'

'Which is?'

'Well, all those years of inspiring pupils,' Dom countered.

'And the ones he left behind? The ones we all leave behind, even good teachers because the system rewards what suits it; and his sarcasm, his patronising ways, his sexism, childishness.'

'He doesn't mean it: it's his way to challenge, the tyranny of the majority, all that. Kids remember that sort of person: the unusual teachers. I do. I wouldn't be here if it weren't for-. He's a brilliant man- and no one's perfect.'

'Not even you,' said Emma, laughing.

Can't we be easy with each other, Dom thought.

'Poor Dom,' she carried on, 'always wanting to think, do, say the right thing. You shouldn't feel that sorry for Charles. You should be after his job. You've worked the hardest in the department this term. You're too bothered what people think; you'd be hopeless in business. No use: out you go.'

'It's a waste. I feel I should do something about it, like all the other crap that happens, except I don't. No one does. That's not me up myself. It's what you think, isn't it? But I'm staying on – not giving up, running away from it all.'

'Here we go again! Only because you daren't let go.'

'Because I believe I shouldn't give up on it, actually.'

'Sure you aren't flattering some idea you have of yourself. I'm not being unkind, Dom. You don't want to wake up one day – find you've become Charles, do you? I suppose you think because you did well with the play, that will change things. English literature saves Hillview, the world! Dom! Men always like to be praised.'

'I don't think anything like that!' replied Dom.

'You almost made me change my mind when I saw what the kids could do. But no, no! No, If I stayed, *I* would end up like Walker or Charles, or worse, Darren or Katie. Every day I stay I feel something inside me dies a bit. So much smothers the good. But you see only school. You believe it's all more than it ever is, or anywhere ever can be. I wish you would see things as they are. There are other worlds out there. Find yourself a nice young lady, get out of here.'

'I don't want a nice young lady,'

'Well, a guy then.'

'Oh, shut up! You're so cynical.'

'Only because you're so naive.'

'Most people here are trying to be good, do the right thing for the right reasons, staff and pupils, even Hennock in his own way,' Dom replied thinking they were trampling the same ground once more.

Emma stared at him for a moment, then shook her head.

'You credit people with more sense than they have, because you think about things so much. Most people aren't like that. Can't you see. Not even a term here with all this going on has set you right. Most people are caught up in themselves – out for themselves in the end. That includes Mike, me. Look at Paul too!'

'What about him?'

'He sucks up to Hennock, acts as informer, even on friends.'

She paused, then she looked around to see if anyone was listening.

'Remember that online crap I was upset over. It was Paul. I found out. He posted most of it: – stuff about me, Mike, you too, even us at the station. I thought it was Mike, revenge. I even suspected you – remember? At the time, I couldn't see who else would have spoken to Mike. I'm sorry, genuinely sorry, Dom. But you're too straight, I'll give you that. And, I've tried to make up a bit: you must've seen that. But you do have some fancy idea of yourself, even though you're not like Paul. Not yet. But stay here! ...Now, I sound like your form teacher or something,' she laughed.

'You sound like my Mother or Father! And you're wrong. People may be mean sometimes, but they're aren't just that, just out for themselves. And *I'm* sure of that. I can't believe Paul is some total sneak for Hennock.'

'Then you are a fool,' replied Emma. 'People are never what they seem.'

'I'm not a fool. I don't think badly of people all the time like you.'

'You mean you don't want to, but you think mean stuff. You just don't say it as much as most of us. That's just another act,' she returned.

Dom subsided. There was no arguing with her. But he would not accept what she said, for all the force of her experience, her character, his partiality.

'I wish we could talk without always arguing. You say stuff I don't understand half the time. I don't know what to think. I know people can be nasty, I'm not that simple. But one thing I do know: you're not like that even when you say such stuff.'

Emma did not reply for a moment, then she looked at him.

'I'm sorry. Perhaps I owe you more explanation – or is it excuses? But I think you have the wrong idea of me. And you are naive- and too kind. We girls like a challenge. And there was no need to buy flowers after the play. I don't deserve them; but they were lovely. It's flattering when someone thinks you are more than you are. There's nothing much about me really, no deep mystery, nothing different, special at all. I wish there was.'

'Oh, *Emma!*' Dom groaned.

'But don't worry, I think quite highly enough of myself, whatever I might say, believe me. We all do.'

'You're bloody impossible today, I know that,' cried Dom.

Then suddenly they both laughed.

'But, as I said before, at least I can talk to you. Perhaps we should go for that drink. We can't tonight – this wretched meeting, but we must celebrate: the end of the play, my freedom. I don't know whether to go. The future of the school! I told Darren I wasn't. He argued. He wants everyone there to show off his plans. On the other hand, perhaps I should. Maybe I'm not yet quite done with things here.'

She looked hard at him, smiling. But Dom was perplexed.

'You might stay, after all you've said!' he cried half indignant, half amused, and definitely too loudly.

She shushed him. Another member of staff was walking in. They must wait.

But Dom had plenty to think on both real and imaginary, whatever was happening, whatever this all was.

CHAPTER FORTY-SIX

STANDING UP

Dom's last lesson of the day dragged. It was hard to concentrate.

The pupils were restless, sensing both end of term, and a tired teacher. In the end he reverted to a game where they all had to construct and then retell individually the same story about where they had been, what they had done one day, as if claiming a group alibi.

No one seemed to have any paper,or suitable pens, of course. Electronic devices weren't an option. They told him he had their work books. When was he going to do any marking? Dom snapped at them in a way he wouldn't have done at the start of term, began a hunt in Hennock's room for paper at least. What a continuing nuisance it was having to teach in someone else's room, particularly his. He kept everything of any use under lock and key, complained if anything were moved a millimetre from its allocated position as if you were invading a foreign country or something.

''e keeps stuff in there. Forgot to lock it last lesson – was too busy goin' at someone at the end of the lesson,' said a pupil who was paying attention. The rest sorted themselves argumentatively into groups.

Dom gingerly opened the cupboard, finding several stacks of paper, all neatly labelled and sorted of course. He was about to turn away when he saw a group of files at the bottom of the cupboard, and then with a leap of the heart, surely *the file itself*. He pulled the door towards him, so he was partially concealed, and eased the file out, to confirm it was what he believed: yes, without looking, the thickness, colour, subdivisions.

'You'll be in trouble – goin' in there, pinching paper,' came another voice.

'Teachers get detentions for thievin'?' said someone else. Sniggers.

'Get on!' cried Dom this time, his mind racing through possibilities.

There was no chance with the class in the room, but at the end: the meeting did not begin for half an hour after school to let everyone get there. He could skim through it. Of course, he could snap the pages on his phone! Then he would have evidence, and Alison and Waseley, well they would have to deal openly with whatever was going on if it was all some private, devious scheme of Hennock's.

And Emma couldn't say he was just naive then.

'Sir, we're ready,' they pestered, far too quick to finish.

'You can't possibly be,' replied Dom, closing the cupboard door, turning back to the class.

They enjoyed it. It wasn't just relief from the pretence of work, but fun. Even Dom felt involved, though he could feel in the pit of his stomach a fist of anxiety now he had a plan, and kept glancing at the clock. The second hand seemed to have slowed almost to a stop. Never did the end of a lesson come so slowly. Then one group who had not had their turn perversely wanted a go, after school, in their own time, a thing unheard of ever before in the history of all teaching; but Dom promised he would not forget even if it had to be next term. They drifted off.

Seizing pieces of paper left over, he crossed to the cupboard and opened the door. There was the file of course, still waiting, its contents surely ready to explode on the school. Dom went to the classroom door, looked down the corridor.

No one.

Quickly, without shutting the door, he returned to the cupboard, drew out the folder. He started thumbing through.

Here it was – all Dr Hennock's schemes. Plans for staff changes, plans for building, plans for changing parts of the school's use, applications for planning permission, correspondence with local government about housing developments, letters and emails to governors, emails to schools in China, recruitment: reams and reams of stuff, some legal, some about the school's foundation, proposals for independence.

Once more, Dom could not take it all in; but this time he was determined to have a record of it, whatever the legality, whatever the consequences.

Where was his phone? He put the folder back in its place, stuffed the paper back on its shelf, grabbed his jacket hung on a peg behind the desk. He had time- just. He must act quickly, quickly though. The meeting! He crossed back to the cupboard, put his phone down nearby, was about to remove the file again.

Then he jumped out of his skin.

'What on earth do you think you are doing? And what are you looking at?'

Dr Hennock was standing at the door. For a split second Dom did not know what to say.

Caught.

'Paper,' he began, trying to sound calm and innocent. 'We wanted paper – a game I was playing. I'm returning paper.'

Hennock stared at him, then crossed the room, pushed past, looking into the cupboard.

'Have you been in here before?'

'No, course, not. It's always locked isn't it? One of the kids said there was some paper in here. You'd left it open.'

Dr Hennock stared hard at him.

Dom was sure he knew, must know; but he was saying nothing. Then Hennock, without asking him to move out of the way, closed, and locked the cupboard doors, pushing one of them shut so it scraped hard against Dom's arm.

He was forced to step back, angry at the man's shove.

'Sit down,' Hennock said.

Dom did not.

Hennock moved closer to him, intimidating.

'Why did you warn Waseley about me?' he said. 'Don't deny it. What do you know?' he pressed.

But Dom had had time to regain his composure. He thought of Emma leaving, Mr Royal forced out, all his pent up frustrations.

'I don't understand what you mean, but, yes, I did speak to Mr Waseley about you. Your attitude to me, to Emma. I was worried. I am worried, what's happening in school.'

Dr Hennock stared at him for a moment.

'You been listening to staff gossip, haven't you? That's what the Head thinks. I warned you when you started.'

'Actually, I haven't had time for gossip. But as you are asking, a lot of staff think there's been a lot of promises about the future without much sense of how we might get there.'

'And who's been coaching you in that, Charles Royal, I suppose, Walker, Tring? And your authority for that point of view is?'

Dom had had enough.

'The way you treat people!'

He'd said it.

'School, politics, changes, principles – it's *people* in the end,' Dom continued, trying to find words. 'Everything's personal, personal in the end. Don't you see? I'm not being rude, but that's the way I see it. Look at the way you treated me, Emma, and even Charl- Mr Royal,... what do you expect me to say?'

Hennock tutted.

'All because you're consistently pulled up for silly mistakes you've made?'

Dom shook his head.

'It's not that. I know I've stuffed up at times, but I've done my best, worked hard, tried, you know that.'

'We're not paying for people who try, I've told you before,' said Hennock.

Dom stared at him. He wasn't arguing with the man's principles, he might even respect those, even his drive to take the school somewhere else through independence, but it was something deeper. Did the man never accept he might in some way be wrong?

He shook his head again.

'I feel sorry for you,' Dom said suddenly.

Hennock laughed, made a dismissive gesture.

Dom's anger turned cold then. He surprised himself.

'Sorry for what you are, what you would make the rest of us.'

There was a silence between them.

Dom could feel his heart beating hard.

'Finished?' said Hennock, eventually. 'May I get a word in. I might just be prepared to overlook the fact that you are speaking rudely –offensively indeed to a senior member of staff who has done so much to support you, save you from your own inexperience. I'll put some of it down to the strain you put yourself under. I could even ignore your breaking into a member of staff's private property, but must I remind you that, not only are you on probation here, but that the whole future of the school hangs in the balance? That should be more important to both of us than overreactions, little upsets, grievances. Does it never occur to you that you might be being rather arrogant?'

He paused, but before Dom could defend himself he continued.

'I thought we'd have problems when you'd finished your play. Everything's about themselves for a lot of people isn't it. Let me tell you some home truths, speak plainly, as we are about to in the meeting.

'I am amazed at how much everyone thinks they know about this school, its future, how things should run, above all how they should be treated. Have you ever stopped to consider what is at stake? Have you? What about considering the school's future on which we all depend? You've never stopped to think have you – what is really going on in this school, or in the country? Our survival, prosperity, freedom even are all on the line. Meanwhile, you're taken up with little personal dramas – your own small world of friendships and loyalties. You shake your head, but it's easy to be superior, self-righteous, when you never have to get your hands dirty taking decisions. Ever heard of touchline critics, backseat drivers, Dominic? The profession is full of them, this school in particular.

'Hillview stands at a crossroads. We can go forward or we can carry on with our old ways. But there's no free ride for anyone anymore. It's survival not sentiment that counts now. There's no room for tired, moaning teachers – ones with issues, too much ego. Let alone ones who can't cope, turn to drink. Don't pretend you didn't know about Charles, but what did you do about it? Nothing. Felt sorry for him like the rest of the staff whilst someone else had to deal with the consequences, of course.

'Meanwhile, whilst staff are feeling tender about their own weak links, the school takes hit after hit. Our results have got worse, we have falling rolls, financial cuts, perhaps closure. There's little left in our foundation, the state won't give us enough money to do the job properly: never has, never will. And there are still people here who haven't grasped this. They think the school will provide whatever happens, whatever they do. They imagine school owes its staff a living, not the other way round! Then people wonder why no one has any sense of responsibility anymore. Why should they?'

Dom was about to interrupt. The man was talking nonsense, but Hennock held up his hand.

'I haven't finished. What about ideas of service and loyalty? We can all live in dreams. But someone, something always demands a reckoning. Look at the world we actually live in. Our Chinese friends – miles ahead of us. We indulge our consciences, a sense of victimhood: they stride ahead.

'You're young: you should be eager for change. This school has to fight for itself, be dynamic, forward looking, productive, not some kind of self-indulgent welfare pudding for minding pupils, or washed-up staff; having a pop at authority any moment it interferes with our finer feelings when things get uncomfortable.'

'But-,' began Dom again.

Hennock had his piece to say however.

'I admit, the way I want to take the school forward will be a shock. It'll force us all to work harder, fight for what we believe in, stand on our own feet, not lean on others, like grown up people should. We need to take control responsibility. Urgently. Childhood is over. The sooner staff realise it the better.'

'You say all that,' Dom began, 'and all the time, everything screams out that there must be better ways of doing things; without destroying what's good, twisting it away. You're putting money first, making everything a competition, a race against everyone else, to the bottom.'

Hennock shook his head.

'You *do* have a lot to learn! School is a business. Life is a business. Independence is a means to a better end, a better business if you like. I want the pupils here to grow up, be useful in life, do things, achieve things. I'm offering leadership. This school has been crying out for it for years. If people are too timid or too sensitive to take it, move aside. Nothing, nothing and no one is going to stop me from doing what needs to be done.'

Dom shook his head. Somehow, Hennock, his views, they were wrong, must be wrong: wrong answers to wrong questions.

But Dr Hennock was looking at his watch.

'We need to go. I haven't time for all this. How many times have I had to say that to you this term? But, Dominic, there's a place for you in this school, perhaps even promotion, if you play your cards right. There's money in our future – for those who are fully on board.

There was a moment's silence.

Hennock searched Dom's face.

'You know Royal will not return. You're young, you've got energy at least, and, as you gain experience: Royal's loss, your gain? We'll need new leadership in that department. Any important role would be conditional of course: sustained competent performance, but loyalty above all. When I have to, for the greater good, I can overlook mistakes, as long as we have loyalty. Think of your future, Dominic!'

For a second or two, Dom was drawn in by the man's confidence, as he had been before when Waseley had first spoken about some idea of independence. Here was someone with go, ideas, a vision, who had the big picture, knew – or seemed to know – what he wanted. And who was he, Dom, in comparison? What were all his concerns but little personal ones? A worm of contrition burrowed in his mind. Had he got it wrong, Hennock wrong, as he had got so much wrong in his first term?

But then he looked at Dr Hennock, right in front of him now, the man, with his false smile. He remembered all he had said and done to those around him, so many times. It *was* personal, had to be personal. No words of big dreams could change what he was, what he had done, would do, or was trying to.

Hennock, however, seemed to take Dom's silence as acquiescence of some kind.

The doctor continued, confidential.

'Royal was on a good salary. Maybe the governors'll want a leader of drama one day. It could all be very exciting down the line. Opportunities, Dom, opportunities. That has made you think, hasn't it?

'You'll hear the first news of big changes at the meeting. You can be a part of it all, Dom. Mike and Paul are on board, maybe Emma won't leave either. Think it over, Dom, *carefully.*'

Hennock paused significantly, then he looked back at the cupboard and at his watch yet again.

'Do remember: staff's personal property, like their personal space, must be respected, especially when you are using someone else's room. We should set the right example,' he continued. 'I shalln't take things further this time, but respect, respect for others is always important.'

-460-

Dr Hennock turned from Dom, busied himself testing to see if the cupboard was now securely fastened.

Dom took a deep breath.

'Dr Hennock, I know I am still wet behind the ears-'

The doctor laughed.

'I am sure there is plenty I don't understand or know about the school. I certainly have lots to learn. There may be something in what you say, how you have explained the school's situation, I don't know. How can I after barely a term? But I'm afraid, none of this stacks up for me: promises, bribes-'

Dom crossed to the door, and then stopped, looked back, determined not to leave without saying more. He'd gone this far.

'You mention Charles. He's given his life, his soul to this place. What's he got to show for it? He once said to me that education – it's – it should be – a search for truth; but, just as much, it's the long history of us learning to be kind to one another, find better ways of-'

'We are tired and emotional, aren't we?' sighed the doctor, busy with his keys, as if Dom weren't really there.

Dom looked back, at the cupboard, all it held, at Hennock.

After a pause, calmly and quietly he simply said: *'What went wrong?'*

The two men looked at each other for a few seconds, and then, brave or foolish, innocent or childish, Dom turned and left.

CHAPTER FORTY-SEVEN

COUP

Five minutes later, Dom was sitting in the Great Hall, sitting alone, waiting for the meeting.

He had drawn his line. Maybe all that would happen would be for him to lose by that; but you could try to be the big person you wanted to be, or get tangled up, lost in something less.

He looked round, for Emma, as other staff assembled. She was not there. She had said she would not come. Perhaps she had been right in her instincts all along.

He texted her. As he tapped away he noticed an email from Tom Rymer.

He smiled to himself. The boy was like one of the fates, always popping up, a portentous messenger of some kind.

Dear Mr Grieves

Just to say that I loved the play it was amazing. I never thought Shakespear was fun before.

Saw Dr Hennock there.he was horrible asking why I was there. Don't think he likes plays.

I wish I was still at Hillview I hate my new school. Things are not good at home to

It's doing my head in

I have something for you a sort of thanks its from my mum
really – I am seeing the twins after the carol concert so see
you then

Tom Rymer

Remembered again! Touching: weeks were years in the life of a teenager. Tom might be a disaster area, perhaps they were well to be free of him, but he felt for the poor kid.

He sighed, wishing Emma would reply.

Meanwhile, all around him, the nervous atmosphere reminded Dom of the feeling before and during inspection, but then there had been solidarity against outsiders. Now he wondered how the divisions that had surfaced before would play out.

The Head was arriving, hair wilder than ever, and greyer. Could you go grey that quickly? The man did not look well, but he was smiling, and late as usual.

How beguiling confidence was.

In was coming Dr Hennock too. Had Dom's gauche comments touched him in the slightest, or just washed off? Maybe such moments were all in a day's work, something you lived with when you got to be important. And finally, the Chairman of the governors swept in too.

It must be very serious then.

Silence.

Dom looked at Waseley, thinking for some reason of that zebra caught in its predator's jaws.

For a few moments, Mr Waseley stood at the front of the gathered staff fumbling with his papers. He puffed his lips out, looked for a moment at the floor. Dom continued to stare at him as did everyone, but then, feeling awkward, he looked away, past him, out of the window.

Darkness had fallen. The lights cast a harsh glare on the outside world. It had snowed once more, earlier in the day, but only enough to cover the ground in a thin layer, so there had been no second panic. A few flakes were still falling. A set of footprints lead up to the square of light that spilled outdoors from the Great Hall into the deep shadow and gloom beyond. There were no footmarks leading away, however: someone had played a trick so it looked as if a person should still be there, listening, by the window, the secret owner of the footfall, now invisible.

How little you knew of the very story you were in, who was really watching, understanding.

Someone swallowed, cleared their throat. Waseley seemed to wake. He looked around, composing a professional smile, hand tousling his mane.

He began to bid an astonished audience farewell in words that were not him.

'Ladies and Gentlemen, thank you for coming to this extraordinary meeting, the first of a number of meetings about the future of the school. I appreciate your attendance at such a busy time. I felt it right, in my usual fashion, to be upfront, honest to your faces.

'I have gathered this meeting to inform you that I am resigning with immediate effect as your Headmaster. It's become obvious that for various reasons, both strategic and personal, my long association with the school must now come to an end. I will, however, continue in an acting capacity until the end of term. I had been planning my retirement as many of you know. I am naturally disappointed that I am not able to complete the journey down the road to whatever the future holds for the school: independence, or whatever; and all our other bold initiatives currently underway. But such is life. These things happen. I leave with my head held high at all I have been privileged to achieve. Parents are being written to. I shall inform the wider school community tomorrow.

'I have the full support of the governors and management in this decision. Indeed, I have had their, er, encouragement. Mr, er, Dr Hennock is taking over with full effect from the start of next term as Acting Head. The school, however, will be advertising for a permanent appointment. The governors have full confidence in him and his leadership. He will be outlining over the next few days a number of changes he intends to make to develop the school further?

Waseley paused, looked up.

No one said anything.

'Thank you all for the support you have all given me over many years, the last few in particular. I know that Mrs Waseley 2, er, Jane, and I are going to miss you, and much about the job, Hillview, in the coming years.'

Waseley's voice sounded strange.

There was another excruciating pause. He resumed.

'I have always believed this to be one of the very best schools in the country. It's been an absolute honour to serve. I wish you all the very best for a splendid future. You'll need it, *deserve it*, I mean. And, finally, it's particularly sad that I won't be able to play santa any more at the usual festive party, but I wish you a happy Christmas, which is nearly here, or will be, one day, very soon now, and how glad of that we'll all be, I'm sure-.'

He petered out, standing there, blinking a lot, papers sagging in one hand, one arm of his specs in the other. Then shoulders hunched, he turned swiftly, sitting down, seemingly far, far away.

Dom averted his eyes but as he did so he caught sight of Dr Hennock, the corners of his mouth twitching up into a smile he was trying to resist.

He felt sick.

Then, at last, Alison broke the tension, standing, saying a brief public thank you to Mr Waseley. She started some clapping.

Everyone joined in.

The applause went on politely for a while- there were a few cheers – and then a little too long.

It looked for a moment as if Waseley might rise, acknowledge his staff, come back even, but at this point the Chair of the governors, who had been observing everything, nodding now and again, stepped forward.

'Thank you, thank you so much, Colin. Never an easy thing to say goodbye. I wanted staff to know just how much governors have supported Colin in his decision, how grateful we all feel to him for his, er, stewardship of Hillview over many years, the last few difficult ones especially. Colin's energy, enthusiasm, unfailing optimism, his achievements-.'

The man carried on, exhorting them to support their new headmaster as they had their old; he knew they would, would have confidence in Dr Hennock, his plans, the brave changes that lay enticingly ahead.

Dom looked at Alison. She seemed to be avoiding eye contact, twisting a scarf self-consciously around her neck. He looked at his colleagues wondering what each one was actually thinking.

The Governor was wishing them all a happy Christmas, a great New Year. This meeting would break up shortly out of respect for Waseley; but there were more to come, much more lay ahead for them. Dr Hennock took the floor, promised them details of exciting developments in another special meeting, emails to follow on this and that, then went into a short speech about the promise of independence, the prizes for the school if it took its chances now, changed boldly.

There was lavish talk of benefits, opportunities galore, a new constitution, a new philosophy, better pay, for everybody: optimism, promise, a simply wonderful tomorrow.

When he was done, staff gathered around Waseley, former constraints gone. Those who had disliked him before and avoided civility if they could, wished him well. No one could deny him the sympathy of one human to another, at least now he was out.

Dr Hennock had discreetly withdrawn; but the governor remained, seemingly oblivious to a mounting resentment in the room at the upheavals that loomed. The brutal way Waseley had been dispatched seemed, just then, worse than any of his idiocies, even the deceits of his own laziness. His affable laissez faire chaos seemed better than their likely fortune too. The staff knew they were about to be bounced into someone else's plans for their future, but no one had the heart or found the voice, the authority, just then, to protest.

The Chairman continued his manoeuvres, intruding where he was not wanted, getting names wrong, thanking people without the least show of any real empathy, often falsely or mistakenly, for what they had and had not done that term.

Still, no one openly spoke what they thought.

Dom, looked round, feeling cold, strangely detached, rather disgusted by it all, a sympathy for Waseley, he believed, the only good thing left in his thoughts. Then he joined in with those speaking to him personally, wishing him well, thanking him, aware of a certain hypocrisy in his actions, wondering again at the mixture of real feeling and pretence that came with being professional, so grown up.

*

Later he ran into Paul who was in a fervour of excitement all of his own, claiming to have inside information from one of the secretaries that Waseley had begun clearing his desk days before. Waseley was toast, the acting role a sop. Hennock was indeed, and had been for a while apparently, in real charge. Paul had already been in to congratulate, and tell him what he should do.

'Now at last things will move forward. We'll get real leadership. Waseley could not make up his mind about anything, let alone independence. Hennock'll push it through. Hennock has a plan. Hennock's Hillview! The future is secure-.'

Dom wandered back across campus towards his flat. He saw Jane, going home late: she'd gone into the choir after the play. She waved to him, smiled: he waved back. He remembered his conversation with her weeks ago; thought how far politics at school had taken them from what was important.

Here and there some of the boarders and other kids, who were still around, were trying to have snowball fights with what little had fallen. They lobbed one at him, missing the target, but spraying him on impact. He responded in kind and hit some of them with a playful puff of snow and a laugh, glad to be outside, amongst the youngsters, normal.

'Sir, will you be on our side?' groups called out excitedly.

'I'm not sure I want to be on anyone's side, thanks. Don't let Dr Hennock catch you! You never know what might happen,' he shouted back.

As he approached the door that led into the boarding house and up to his flat, he caught sight of Emma, silhouetted against a window, sitting alone in the school library, marking or typing reports. For a moment or two he hesitated. Then he went in.

*

She was sitting in a pool of light in the corner of the school library marking; it was a place staff could steal away to when they needed to work in peace.

'I'm getting this finished. I don't think I can bear to mark again this term, or ever,' she said. 'Then, last reports and I'm done.'

'How can you when all this's just happened?' cried Dom, 'and how come you missed the meeting. Have you heard?'

Emma looked at him.

'Waseley? I knew already,' she looked at him. 'You were right. I never quite believed it, you know.'

'I never really expected it, despite what Paul kept saying. Hennock for Head! How did you know beforehand? What do you think?'

Emma looked away, put her pen down.

'Hennock was never going to be content until he was Head- even if it's only temporary. We know what he's like. And we all know Waseley. I'm not sure he's ever been up to it, certainly not in a time of crisis. I've never come across anyone quite so slack and sloppy over detail. He did optimism, but the rest-. I suppose you feel sorry for him now?'

Before Dom could reply Emma carried on in full flood.

'You mustn't. Waseley wasn't a bastard, but he was up to all sorts in his way. Got away with it because of confidence, charm, if you can call it that.'

'But to treat him like that; put Hennock there!'

'Dom! He was lucky to get away with it for so long. But I agree, Darren in charge! The governors'll think they've found someone to sort the staff out, bang heads together, get money rolling in – if this independence malarkey ever takes off. Proves my decision to leave was right?'

Dom shook his head.

'Come on. You can't be that surprised at what's happened.'

'You don't know the half of it,' said Dom.

It all tumbled out then. He needed to tell someone. All the things he had seen and heard by chance, and sometimes done, secretly, since he had come to the school. Hennock behaving strangely with the governor friend the first day, seeing the file, his night adventures, the experience on the Cloud, attempts to warn Waseley, Royal, Alison, his latest confrontations everything except the strange figure he imagined he'd seen.

At first Emma looked bemused, even though he had told her some before, but as he went on, she sat back, looking at him in a different way.

'Not sure you were right to speak to Hennock like that, even if he deserves it. If it was somebody else, I'd think you were making it up,' she said eventually.

'You couldn't make it up,' said Dom.

'You have been busy! Why didn't you tell me before, do something.'

'I tried,' said Dom, 'but people don't listen. And where was the evidence?'

'I'm not so sure. If this is part of some bigger plan to change the school behind people's backs without really getting proper staff agreement or understanding-. You can't do that these days. Well you can, but when it comes out just how much's already been going on, and staff wake up to being mugged over. But, there are several things I don't understand. I don't see how it all ties together.'

'Tell me about it!'

Emma sat back.

'The awful thing Darren's right in some ways. The place has to change. It's living on its past. Perhaps independence-perhaps he has thought it through, has some plan to push it all forward, make it a success. Some staff must be in on it too, like a takeover in the business world, or a coup.'

'But at what cost?' said Dom.

'That no one can tell.'

She looked at Dom again, and then shook her head.

'As I said, makes me think I made the right decision. Anyway, I'm leaving. Not my problem.'

She started to tick and flick again, much to Dom's exasperation.

'Paul's right about one thing: you should write it all down one day. No one will read it, but you might make it interesting. Hillview's Young Sherlock, nearly.'

She was laughing, at him as usual.

Dom pulled a face.

'I don't know about that. And I'll probably lose my job, now. So much for doing the right thing! I could do with a drink,' he said, 'a strong one.'

'Give me an hour,' she said to his surprise, 'and I really will have these finished. We were talking about it anyway. Who knows about tomorrow? We may all be out. Let's grab some food too, celebrate – my liberation – the end of these ridiculous reports, your play, all that spying,' she laughed. 'It's our time now: now, or never!'

For once, they could both agree.

CHAPTER FORTY-EIGHT

THROUGH A GLASS DARKLY

Dom made his way back to his flat, giddy with everything. There were texts coming in on his mobile; his answer phone was winking at him, but he went straight to have a shower, change his shirt. He took particular care with his grooming.

He stared hard into the mirror. Where was he now? There was tension in his face, but his eyes sparkled.

As he was drying his hair, patting it down so it did not stick up – there came a knock on the door. If this were some child wanting something – some idiotic question. He opened the door, still only half dressed, preparing to give them a piece of his mind. At first he could see nothing. The light had recently broken altogether. Terry had been too busy to repair it. Then out of the shadows stepped a tall imposing figure, making Dom jump.

It was Charles.

'Bath time for the boys?' he quipped laughing like his old self, entering without invitation.

He had never been to Dom's rooms before. Dom, all apologies, embarrassment, quickly retreated to the bathroom pulling on what he could find. He caught sight of himself in the mirror again, hair sticking up already, his clean best shirt creased, clinging rumpled to his wet back. He hoped Charles would not stay long.

When he went back flustered into the little sitting room area, Charles was sitting, entirely composed and comfortable.

'You've made this nice. You should see the place I had when I started.'

He began to reminisce in elaborate detail about his job, former colleagues. Dom wondered if he should offer him a drink, then thought better of that. Perhaps a coffee. Why was he here?

He asked him if he were better.

'Coffee would be most acceptable- all those stairs, tiddlypom! I remember my days of Dorm Duty. The good old days. Twenty years. You really get to know them, then. Nice kids in those days, mostly. Little bs one or two of them, the ones who will always be with us.'

Dom made him a drink as quickly as he could, wondering if the milk was off, pondering what to say that would not be clumsy. Emma would soon be waiting and he could feel his drying hair spiking up on top, a law unto itself whenever he wanted to look good.

He tried to remember Charles had lost everything.

Soon, however, his visitor came to a point.

'I've just been in to see Walker. Exciting times! Thought I'd drop by, briefly, don't worry. You youngsters – always in a hurry over something! Rushing- but where?

'I did want to say again how much I enjoyed your play: the boys and girls rose to it- shows what they can do. Recovered? It'll take you to the end of Christmas break at least. But I came, mainly to say goodbye.'

'I'm sorry,' said Dom, nodding, trying to show he understood. 'I wish you were staying -- we've missed you. It's not the same without you.'

He wondered if Charles had been drinking. This could all turn maudlin.

'Of course you don't! But kind, kind to say it: I'm sure you're managing perfectly. I've given you plenty of practice! Everything's happening now I have left- almost a shame I can't be here to watch it all unravel. But then nothing ever gets simpler in my experience. You, you're young, you'll survive. I'll hardly recognise the school soon if all this happens. Like the world. It's left me behind. Education today! Universities stuffing them with theory, political correctness before they've learnt to think for themselves; secondary schools more interested in results than understanding, welfare than challenge; junior schools swaddling them in blankets of banalities, protected characteristics, before they can even read. Staff stressed blind. Children obsessed with a sense of entitlement and identity before they know what it means. Promiscuous tech, the final break between effort, understanding and responsibility. The age of the individual: everyone wanting to be different but the same.

'Forgive me! We become caricatures of ourselves as we grow old. Indeed, everything degenerates into parody. You find everything's a bit of an illusion in the end...But as for me and Hillview. Enough is enough! I can't keep setting things right any more, strive against all that isn't what it could be; and, well, I think I've more than done my bit. Time for others to step up-. Fight for it, Dom: the academic, the disinterested pursuit of truth, the creative imagination, the reading that opens richer minds and lives to us; or it will surely die in the true madness of the unimaginative.'

Dom did not know what to say to any of all that.

'No, I wanted to set the record straight. I feel I should have been helping more, not caught in my own troubles. That's been exaggerated. Part of our friend, the great Dr's plans to get rid of me,' he looked sharply at Dom. 'You tried to warn me, and I was less than grateful. But there's more to all this than me – you see that now. Waseley-.'

'Yes. We've just had this meeting.'

'Indeed you have. Hennock's doing, of course.'

He looked at Dom again and shook his head.

'Change is inevitable, but it's stressful. You need to take people with you or it's a disaster.... The trouble with you youngsters, you've nothing to compare things with – *you don't know any different*, and when everything happens too quickly... But no, we're not here to go over all that-.'

'I'm sorry,' began Dom again, but Charles carried on.

'Some of us put two and two together went to Waseley a few weeks back. I gather you had done the same. Very precocious, if I may say so. But we underestimated Hennock. Can you imagine someone actually logging every single thing they thought you said or did wrong day after day, month after month – stuff reported to him by colleagues, then presenting it to the Head and governors? Hennock was even planning to replace me with dear Emma at one point.'

Dom hardly had time to wonder why Emma had never mentioned such a thing to him.

'When I was young, you stepped out of line you got a bollocking, that was an end to it. Now we have all this professional tracking, inspections, reviews, formal assessments, and more busybodies, intrigue and finesse than ever. And are things any better? And where's trust gone? Management!'

Charles snorted.

'But I can see I am boring – the privilege of the old. Where was I? Yes, I went to Waseley – told him a few truths about Hennock – what was really going on in his school. Even he had to wake up. No one gets it until it's them. But too late for Waseley, and me. The only consolation is that Hennock has been forced into moving too soon before all his plans are finalised, and without enough time to fix enough staff back stage. He's been promising this that and the other already to those in favour; but you know all that. Alison's absolutely furious -the only one at the top anyone's got any respect for.'

To Dom it seemed as if Charles were almost talking to himself. In fact there was much he did not understand, did not know. He wondered if he should tell him all as he had Emma. She would be off to the pub soon.

'It's only my first term. I don't know much: what's been going on, what to think half the time. People forget it's my first time. But you. What about your future? And what's going to happen to the school – with Hennock in charge?'

'Ah,' said Charles, 'There we have it. Hennock in charge. I didn't think you would be keen. Many staff aren't: so his position is not as secure as he thinks, or you fear!'

Charles was grinning as if it were all some game. Dom felt torn: hard choices, real problems, dealing with difficult people, met with irony, puzzles, games?

But his mentor was pronouncing.

'Me? Oh, I'll grow old not very gracefully, get ill and die- but not just yet. I'm all right. In fact I feel better. I'll do some tutoring, somewhere. Somebody'll want me. I'll miss the place, I know, after all these years – I'll miss the pupils, but not the politics, the backbiting, the loss of trust. Everything in perpetual disarray. Hillview's always been a mirror of the country. No decent leadership for years. And people pretending we can have it all, knowing we can't. Prizes for all! What about hard work, service, duty, responsibility?

'I know: you're thinking: who's this old man to talk. Can't even look after himself?'

Something in Dom wanted to argue against all he seemed to be saying, the defeat in it – but the ticking clock was moving inexorably.

'Following? I suspect not. I hope not actually. You're young. The world is different when we're young. But you!

I actually think you have done very well – for a first term. You've taken some responsibility: you care, take it seriously. You might do well, if you last!'

Dom nodded, wondering where all this was going, where it would end.

'Dr Hennock, he and I – don't see eye to eye on anything much. I had a row with him. I wanted to talk to someone. I'm worried. I think I've blown it. I may end up leaving, like Emma, or be sacked.'

Dom was glad he had told him.

'So you'll both be leaving together – romantic! That would be amusing – Miss Tidy will have to break out her coloured pens. No one left in the department! They'll end up employing Dotty. That'll give Hennock a hernia or two. But, no, he won't do anything to you. He's got his hands full just now. As for Emma leaving; but then you know all about that,' said Charles, laughing.

Dom wondered what he was getting at now.

'The biggest battle in life is with ourselves, of course. Don't end up being a people pleaser all the time. And don't end up like me- all spent!'

What was this now? Part of Dom wished he would just go, leave him with what remained of his high idea of him.

'But think of all you have done, all the pupils you inspired-' Dom tried.

'Perhaps you're right. Perhaps you are. You give your all to something, then find all your life gone by and there's no use for you anymore. What is it they say, we live life forward, understand it backwards. Now, Dominic, it wouldn't do at all for you to wake up one day, find the same.'

'I think I've learnt a bit already,' Dom replied, trying to sound as if he would always be on top of whatever Charles was so uncomfortably on about.

'Perfection makes a lonely being. Things are never quite what you think they should be, and Mr Yeats was right. What did he say, *know why an old man should be mad, because no better could be had.*'

Dom had an answer to that one.

'But wasn't he just a hopeless idealist, an old misery?' cried Dom, immediately regretting it.

'Like me?' laughed Charles, his despondency seeming to vanish. 'Perhaps but he got the measure of life when he finally grew up, rather late. Beware, Dom! Look and learn. We understand others more quickly than we understand ourselves. And it's very out of fashion, self knowledge, too much truth, too much responsibility, tears in that. And *we* might have to change ourselves. That will never do.'

Dom felt resentful, as if Charles were trying to heap on him things that he should not have to deal with, understand. Bitterness was no end, any end. There were always choices, chances.

'Don't you just think it's the way things are right now that is depressing?' he ventured.

Charles laughed.

'And an old man would always answer, that today is tomorrow and especially yesterday, but enough. I came to say thank you. I have. *Kindness is never wasted.* Dickens wasn't it? I want to help you in return, tell you something that might cheer you. Some of us are doing something about Dr Hennock, his plans.'

Charles paused, savouring his effect..

'Well, go on, you can't say something like that, not explain,' said Dom forgetting the clock for a moment.

'Let's just say I think Hennock's manoeuvres, when exposed, might be of more general interest than he realises. There. Probably said too much. I'm not saying more. Wait and see. I am not quite done with Hillview, even if it's done with me.

'Now – I must go. I'm not supposed to be here! Such a bad example I've been!' he said standing. 'Tiddlypom! Don't worry. I'm happier than you suppose, happier than someone like Hennock can ever be. I've spent my life teaching things that matter: a certain good in a sorry world!'

'I wish you would tell me what you mean sometimes,' cried Dom, but Charles seemed in a hurry to leave then. 'You'll be at the staff party at the end of term at least to say goodbye.'

'Couldn't think of anything worse. And I embarrass them too much – that would never do; though that would be reason for going. Now this really is goodbye,' he crossed to the door. 'But we'll keep in touch. If they make you Leader in English or Drama, I'm always ready to give advice, on any topic. You may have noticed.'

'Thank you – thank you for all your help,' said Dom, feeling the inadequacy of what he said.

'Nonsense,' he replied. 'I've been an awkward old sod most of the time,' he opened the door, looked out. 'Ah, no Hennock spying outside, wandering about on the stairs or down secret corridors- or is that your role?'

He looked at Dom in whose head a thousand questions sprang. What did Charles know?

'A lot of people don't amount to much. Don't let them pull you down. Keep your dreams, as long as they'll last. Give my best wishes, love – to Emma. And forgive an old man his little theatrics, his sententiousness. Know what that means? I bet not. Tiddlypom. What do they teach these days?'

He shook hands, formal suddenly, stepped out into the shadows, disappearing into darkness.

For a few seconds, as he heard Charles's steps diminish down echoing stairs, Dom felt a pang of remorse, guilt even: sorry for the man, sorry for something like a friendship, companionship, an understanding somewhere, and all that might have been. He stood there trying to imagine, as he had before, some future for Charles, this time a positive one: grateful pupils returning to see him; glad to be out of it, free and relaxed; recovering some true, better self.

And then?

But he remembered he was seeing Emma, and quickly closed the door. In a mad scramble to be ready all other thoughts fell away. He thought of changing his shirt, tried one last time to smooth down his errant hair, but he was going to be so late.

Soon he had quite forgotten the old man, his praise, his warnings, hints and riddles. He was off, thinking only of himself and Emma.

CHAPTER FORTY-NINE

FRUSTRATION

The pub was busier than it had been the last time, but Dom and Emma found their place by the fire hissing with new logs recently piled on, smoking more than burning.

They had decided to have a drink first; and the place had taken on a certain significance for them, though they did not realise it. Then they would go to Wellsway to a Chinese restaurant that Emma was full of; whatever was up, teaching made you ravenous: and just going out, so intense had things been, was release.

Out of school, just the two of them, a kind of constraint settled on Dom, but in the drowsy warmth of the pub, after a beer, he began to relax.

'Do you remember the first time we all came here? Seems another lifetime. I could have done with coming here during *Dream'*

'You were in such a state – it can't do you any good.'

'It's odd,' he said, 'it made me so happy in the end, almost to the point where I did not care about anything else, but then I was sad it was all over. I know that this is going to sound ridiculous, but it feels like some great loss, a kind of bereavement. Some of the kids came up to me yesterday, said, *We're missing the play, it's days to the end of term, nothing to look forward to now.'*

Emma laughed, shaking her head.

'How can you?' she said, eyes sparkling. 'The way you went on and on about them. It was going to be a disaster, you were going to be sacked.'

Dom looked sheepish.

'Well, it nearly was: maybe I am!'

'It was awesome; and you know it, stop fishing for compliments. What's the next?' teased Emma.

They laughed.

Dom could feel his heart beating hard; but where to begin? It had never seemed this difficult before when he had been interested in some girl. Didn't you ever grow up?

He asked Emma about plans for Christmas, chatted about his. He was looking forward to going home after his time away, catching up with parents, their travels. Emma listened, nodded here and there, but her mind seemed to be on something else. Perhaps she was thinking what he was thinking: wondering where to begin; or perhaps not at all, and he was nothing. It would be easier to chat the evening away in littlenesses. But that was no life.

Emma broke in.

'It's time we went if we're going to get something to eat, I'm starving.'

They left the pub, its fire still only smouldering, drove separately to Wellsway, parking side by side. The snow had turned to rain mixed with sleet. The streets were black and wet but the little town seemed alive in a way that it never had before. High above, stars scurried in and out of fast moving clouds. There was some local Christmas market on. Outside, people in merry groups bustled to and fro on the pavements despite the blackness all around of deep winter. Christmas parties and meals were underway in little restaurants they passed, lights and cheer spilling onto the streets. In the lovely old abbey church that still dominated the main street, despite all that had grown up around, there was a carol service rehearsal going on. Lights blazed yellow through windows. The sound of music drifted out. Christmas sparkle bedecked the shops, many still open, specially. At the market, the smell of mulled wine and toast, burgers and chips, spuds with all sorts of toppings drifted everywhere, sickly sweet but piquing their hunger. Emma slipped into a different mode, lingering at one of the stalls, an expert eye sifting choices, selecting, appraising, discarding with a swift discrimination that astonished Dom.

They passed the theatre where Dom had taken that first trip. He nudged Emma.

'Remember. It seems so long ago now.'

'How could I forget!' she laughed.

Inside, little groups were chatting and laughing, drinking and queuing for coffee, quite absorbed in their world, waiting for things to begin. Dom and Emma stopped looking in.

This time it was pantomime, not passion on the moors. Terry would approve.

Just a bit further on, there was a homeless person, swathed in rags, surrounded by bits of card board, propped in a doorway. Dom wondered if it was the same one he had seen all those weeks ago. He felt ashamed he did not remember, put some money in a cap.

Emma told him off.

'It's Christmas!' he replied.

He found her hand, then, surer of himself. She looked into his eyes and laughed. He kissed her, on the lips. The rain and the sleet seemed to be coming on more so they ran quickly, excitedly down the street to the restaurant, realising they might be late, laughing for no reason.

As they stepped into Emma's Chinese, however, Dom's heart sank. There was non other than Katie Trippett, with a much older man, sitting near the window. It would be her. Emma was across the room, chatting away in an instant. Dom followed slowly, having sorted a table.

Katie looked Dom up and down with renewed interest when he approached, but did not introduce her friend as she clearly had to Emma. Perhaps it was her dad, Dom wondered.

'So what brings you two out after today's events at school? Anything special?'

'No,' said Emma. 'We just fancied getting out: celebrating, finishing my reports, Dom's play. How's-?' and they were off into some wild girly chat about a shared acquaintance. Dom hovered for a moment, nodding at the man who looked back at him without any response. Then he retreated to the table, feeling spare, started to look at the menu, 'anything special, no' playing on his mind.

Emma seemed to chat for a long time to Ms Trippett; Dom felt quite stupid, like a child.

Eventually she came and sat down but there was no explanation of what it had all been about. She was intent on the menu. Whatever had been shared with Katie he had no part in. He was not going to ask. He disliked her and, it seemed, Emma did not. He did not want disagreement.

His spirits rallied as they ordered. The food arrived quickly, sizzling and spitting in metal trays and the little waiter, who recognised Emma, began to flirt, flourished the plates and dishes in a practised little ritual, pouring the rather cheap wine as if he were distributing nectar.

They both laughed and grimaced when they tasted it.

'The food's amazing, honest,' said Emma, like a hostess keen to impress.

They chatted openly about family and friends, but then it turned serious, Dom's doing: what they wanted from life.

Dom spoke most – his hopes for his teaching. How he wanted to change things, change education no less so it all worked better, and then the plays he would do, one day, with the right casts, if he kept his job. He was excited by it – what could be, given time, chance, experience.

Emma said less and less.

It's all boring to her, thought Dom. I sound like Paul- a night out and all I do is grind on about work. He made a joke about it. She smiled absently. He changed the topic. Emma kept glancing across to Katie, as if she were thinking more about her.

Eventually the conversation came back to Hillview, what Hennock had said to Dom. He tried to sound breezy, but inside, he was worried, hoped she would register that, respond. Then there was Mr Royal's strange visit, odd warnings, riddles.

'He said you might be offered his job,' Dom recalled. 'I think Hennock was trying to offer me something, but then I burnt my boats.'

'Oh,' Emma said, but not much more. She looked preoccupied, kept checking her phone.

Dom felt confused, irritated.

He tried the idea she and Mike had had of starting their own school, doing things a better way.

'Mike was never going to be the right person for that,' was the short reply.

The cold thoughts returned. He was too intense, too boring, for her: she wanted someone cool, confident, streetwise, not serious – naive, like him. Girls always did, whatever they said.

'Your hair's sticking up on end. Can't you do something about it?' she said suddenly at one point.

Soon, Katie came across to say goodbye, her friend standing at a distance. Emma seemed to come to life moving away, talking to her, in hushed tones with Dom feeling once more just some clumsy boy.

He tried to make conversation with her partner, got nowhere.

Eventually, thank goodness, Katie was going. She gave Dom a parting smirk.

Emma sat down again, quiet, wrapped up in herself.

'Who was that she was with?' Dom said at last, having waited for an explanation that did not come. 'What were you two gossiping about?'

'We weren't gossiping. Men always think women gossip. I bet you think the same sort of things but don't say.'

'I wouldn't put money on that,' said Dom. 'Who was he, her Dad?'

'*No!* That's not very nice!' Emma tutted. 'That's her new partner, Jon: nice guy.'

Dom wanted to add then why's he going out with her, but said: 'He looks like her dad!'

'Men always judge by appearances,' said Emma disapprovingly. 'Just because he's not fresh-faced like you. You don't like her do you?'

Dom shrugged.

'I can't respect her. She's so two-faced: and she's mixed up in all this business with Hennock. Charles always hated her.'

'And the rest of us aren't. Typical Charles to hate her. School again,' sighed Emma.

'I don't want to talk all the time about school. You can always volunteer a subject you know. You're very quiet,' he said.

There was silence from Emma.

Dom felt angry – at least they could be friendly, even if she wasn't interested.

'It is nice in here. Good choice, although Terry wouldn't approve. Another sign the Chinese are taking over the world he would say,' Dom said.

Emma looked at him critically.

'You are turning into Charles you know: school obsessed, silly prejudices.'

'It's a joke,' cried Dom, exasperated,

'A joke that tries to conceal its essential cruelty, like most jokes.'

'Look, have I said – done something wrong? You seem to want to quarrel again. This was supposed to be a celebration,' he sighed. 'Can't we just be friendly, even if -'

'It's not my fault; I can't let these things go past. There's too much that goes by unchallenged. People get away with saying and doing things without thinking at all of the consequences, or their responsibilities.'

'Now who sounds like Charles! And what about your friend Katie. She says all sorts. Look what she does. I don't see people calling her out,' replied Dom, provoked.

'That's a typical male reaction, going for the personal when someone's point can't be defeated any other way.'

'And what about generalisations about men? We aren't all some evil unthinking, uncaring stereotypes. It's people's individual nastiness, arrogance that messes things up, not which group they belong to.'

'On your high horse now? You've just attacked my friend Katie because she is an independent woman who stands up for herself at work, has her own opinions and ways of doing things!'

'I attack her because she's mean and trivial and sneaks around.'

'Who's being mean now? You're just demeaning what you can't control.'

'O, come on, you know what she's like.'

'You wouldn't have said stuff like that a few weeks ago. See what Hillview's done to you.'

He supposed it must be his fault. Maybe she had stuff on her mind, leaving and all that. If she hated the place, she must resent him for staying, wanting to stay. But then why not out and deal with it instead of sniping at him.

Perhaps she was bored, tired of humouring him – hated him.

Now there was silence between them.

He pulled back.

'Sorry,' he said eventually to Emma. 'I'm tired after everything. Upset. Hennock getting his way, poor Charles, the way the school is going. I know I go on, but it's been all my life every day, every moment of the last however many weeks. It has for you. I'm angry...and sad you are going to leave. But I understand. Really. And I don't want us to keep ending up arguing. There's so little time. People never say what they should when they should but if ever things needed someone to call things out... I've tried in my own way, but, I've been so alone with it all... I hoped you would understand. Sometimes you seem to. And you're so different, good and kind – such a special person, and just-lovely. And so much better than me. I'm nothing and...I hoped we could-that we had something-. But I don't really understand what, except how I feel, and even that-.'

Dom felt so foolish. She was staring at him so intently he started laughing.

'I feel like I'm talking to my dad or Mr Royal or someone now; about something embarrassing.'

He was aware of stillness around them.

Emma looked at him for a moment, then away. Then she got up and came to him, putting her arms round him, kissing him full on the lips.

'I'm sorry, too,' she began. 'Things on my mind-.'

Then her phone pinged. She moved back slightly, his hand sliding slowly down her arm, squeezing her hand gently before she became detached again, busy reading her message, answering, fingers and thumbs flashing a reply in her quick decided way.

Dom could see the look of concentration on her face grow as she answered. He was outside her world again.

Baffled, wishing they were alone somewhere, his eyes flitted around the restaurant before returning to her. They were the only ones left. The Chinese waiter who had been hovering near, and seeing Emma standing, ostentatiously put the bill down next to Dom. It was getting late, a weekday; they wanted to close.

'I shall have to go,' Emma said suddenly.

'What? What is it?' he said. 'Anything wrong?' he said, standing up close beside her.

She looked as if she were about to say something, turned away, shook her head. She was gathering her things, drawing a wad of cash from her purse to leave on the table, busy apart.

'Can you settle. I must just pop to the-' and she was off picking up her bag and coat, heading for the back of the restaurant.

He watched her go, puzzled.

Dom sorted the cash, his thoughts hardly there. Then he noticed the bill was more than it should be, steep; he ought to dispute it. Something to do, something else to think about.

He did, but it was right. He checked the money again. The Chinese man took it, leaving change, lots, conspicuously, for a tip, Dom annoyed that they wanted even more.

But where was Emma? He gathered his things. His phone went, and he checked it.

It was a text: from her.

Sorry. Just had to leave. Can't explain now, will tomorrow, promise. My fault. Xxx

At first Dom could not believe what he read. Then a flash of anger went through him. What on earth was she playing at? Why had she not at least stopped to say goodbye if it were something serious, could she not share that?

He looked at the back of the restaurant: there must be another way out. He could run after her – back to the car park, instead of standing there, nothing.

The waiter approached.

'Lady not enjoy?' he said, looking around, searching Dom's face.

'No, er, yes, she's-, er, she's been before.'

'Lady finish,' he nodded, smiling and would have ushered Dom to the door, profuse in his thanks.

'We close after Chinese New Year for month then open in bigger restaurant, bigger, very grand. Doing well.'

He pressed a flyer with details of the move into Dom's hands.

'I must just check-,' explained Dom, making his way to the back of the restaurant. He passed the loos, moved down a dingy corridor, and yes there was a back door there. He pulled it hard. It was unyielding at first, then stiff, but soon it gave way. He stepped out into the cold night, sleet falling again.

For a moment he had no idea where he was, some rundown back alley, a slippy uneven cobbled way. Along it there were steaming, dripping vents, the backs of houses, some with broken windows running to join another way.

Behind him, the waiter nodded at him, already bolting the door. The light above the door snapped off.

Dom half ran back to the car park, texting, trying to phone as he went. He sent her several messages. Nothing came back.

In the car park his car stood alone. On the empty space by its side sleet met the black ground, vanishing instantly.

For a moment he thought of following her to her flat; but it seemed futile.

Lady finish.

He couldn't handle it any more.

*

When he got back to his flat there was a card pushed under the door, his surname spelt wrong- Griefs- as usual. He seized it, ripped it open, hoping against all reason that it was something to do with, some explanation from Emma.

It was a Christmas card, from Andy – thanks for the play. Could he, and Rachel, be in the next one? So long as they did *Fame*. They had ideas for the casting already, had spoken to a number of their peers about their parts.

Those two were an item again.

Dom sat down, turned his desktop on, then got a pen and paper out, as if he were going to write something in an old fashioned way. He put his head down, his cheek resting on a cold blank piece of paper. Then, not raising his head, he groped for the light switch, turned it off.

Fully clothed he remained there, computer screen flickering away until it went to standby mode, leaving just a faint humming in the darkness. Eventually he fell asleep, all the day's and term's experiences spinning in his head until a grey morning came.

He woke stiff and tired, cold inside, wondering if all the same things would simply resume.

CHAPTER FIFTY

IN THE NEWS

It was the middle of the morning. Dom was teaching- his favourite class of course.

Earlier, he had tried to give the twins some extra help with writing. Mr Jolson had said he had connected with them in the play; he was young, they needed support. But they had not been in the mood. He tried to get them to look at individual words, think about connotations, what they were, why they worked. They couldn't even find things on the page. When he showed them, they had no ideas, no ideas at all. After a bouncing start, they were pleased to see him, thinking it would all be fun, they had become bored, stroppy when he persisted. One of them stormed off – the cheerful happy twins, miserable because they wouldn't or couldn't imagine what he wanted.

Maybe he had to accept it: they might never see. No use brooding: move on, always move on.

*

Now he was talking about media, getting his pupils to discover for themselves how differently various newspapers and web pages would treat the same story: how life was largely people's own version, their story. He could have been personal that morning on his theme; but he had a job to do.

Most had never looked at, seen a newspaper. He didn't much. It had been a ritual at home for his parents. Some children took the opportunity to read the sports pages, ogle heroes. The class enjoyed the celebrity tittle tattle but it was tame compared to the red meat of social media.

'He's *so* good looking!' cried one of the girls, eyes only for some teenage swimmer.

'He's gay,' said one of the boys, eager to dishearten, forgetting what he had been taught.

A row.

'Is it deliberate, Sir?' came from Tim.

'Is what deliberate?' responded Dom.

'This twisting you keep on about: the sensationalising and the exaggeration, hyperbowling or what long word you were using.'

Someone else said, 'And the stereo thingy. Can't people see through this. Everyone's not shallow?'

'Sir,' groaned someone, 'making things heavy again! It's Christmas!'

Dom ignored.

'We're often sold only what looks good. People stop questioning – just buy with their eyes, go for what sounds dramatic, entertaining,' he continued.

'Can we use phones, Sir?'

'Do you buy with your eyes, Sir?' said one of the boys, smirking.

Dom gave them writing to do, knowing they would not do it, but it might buy time, to think things through.

Had he? Was he the floundering Bottom of his own story, tricked by his vanity?

'Sir, you look sad,' came from Jane. 'Cheer up, it's Christmas.'

'Ahh!' came voices thick with irony, but Jane cared less now.

'No, just tired. It's been a long term, hasn't it?'

They sighed in mock sympathy. Dom smiled a little.

Sir did seem out of sorts.

'Sir, we done enough for today. What's happened to Mr Royal and Mr Waseley. Is Dr Hennock taking over?'

'Why are staff leaving? You'll be the only English teacher left soon.'

'Shit'.

'Sir, has Mr Royal been sacked for drinking? You can tell us.'

'Best teacher in the school.'

'Not much competition in this dump.'

'Waseley was cool. You could get away with anything.'

'What's going to happen to us with Hennock in charge. Everybody hates him.'

Dom wished he knew.

He tried to wrench the lesson back to work but the big news of little Hillview had unsettled. They faced the prospect of their most important years in the school without the Mr Royals and Mr Waseleys whose eccentricities made the grind of school worth enduring, some days.

'Sir, I feel like leaving, now,' said Tim.

Someone muttered shame but then much was said in opposition to all that was going on. Feelings were running high. Dom had not the will just then to stop it.

An idea came to him.

'Why don't you get up a petition or something if you feel that strongly? Persuade Mr Royal to stay.'

The class seized on the idea as something to say they were doing that did not involve work.

One or two took it to heart.

Jane was dubious.

'Sir, can we do something like that? Isn't it against school?'

Dom could see a thousand issues, began to misdoubt what he had said, but he did not care as much anymore about personal consequences; the future under Hennock looked bad enough, and without Emma-. Anyway, knowing most of this lot, they wouldn't do anything.

But by that afternoon an online petition had been launched, led by Tim, Jane and some of their friends. Pupils and parents were signing up; even staff had reputedly added their support.

Katie found out, went straight to Hennock, who sent an email around that needed to be read instantly to the children asking them to see him if they had concerns about any minor issues over the present situation in the school, warning them, in not very subtle terms, about abuse of social media as well as time wasting. It finished with a claim that Mr Royal had resigned for health reasons: this would not be good for him.

A rather longer and more menacing email was sent to the staff telling them to calm any little fears at this difficult time in the school's history. It contained a comment about strong action to be taken in the case of unprofessional conduct, breaching of confidentiality for example.

Dom waited for another hammer blow when his part in the initiation of the petition were discovered, but the whole thing had acquired a life of its own, its instigator forgotten as all the school networks became consumed with gossip about departures, sackings, coups, all given an edge by the impending end of term. Christmas over excitement coupled with one more social media inquisition had begun, only to be swiftly overtaken with a rather more disturbingly real threat of further bad weather.

*

Dom saw nothing of Emma except briefly at morning break when she was being buttonholed by Alison, then Hennock.

He tried to catch her eye, even smiled but she seemed to be avoiding him.

So be it. Lady finish then. Not even a text.

At the end of the day, Dom retreated to his flat. He had managed to clear his last corrections to his last reports, through the blear of a tiredness that would not leave him and which Mr Walker told him would last thirty years. Tired, disappointed as he was, he could not rest, however. He fancied going out for a walk but it was bitter outside, dark already, snowing hard. He wondered if the term would end in weather chaos. Perhaps that would be a metaphor. Everything was a metaphor as he had tried to tell the twins that morning.

He wandered back down to the Staff Room not quite knowing why.

Paul was there with Katie.

They both stared at him. There seemed to be an atmosphere.

'Royal's gone to the media,' said Paul simply.

'What do you mean?' said Dom, slow in his thoughts, but then remembering Charles's visit yesterday.

'He's told the local paper that he has been forced out after thirty years in the school. It's all exaggerated, sensationalised. It's online already – in tonight's print edition apparently and, look!' said Paul. 'We made it to the front page. Hennock's furious.'

Paul waved his phone in front of him.

'Don't you see?' said Paul. 'They've got the whole story, blown the development plans out of the water.'

TAKEOVER AT LOCAL SCHOOL: HILLVIEW GETS NEW HEAD IN MULTIMILLION POUND DASH FOR INDEPENDENCE.LONG SERVING STAFF OUSTED IN SCHOOL BID FOR FREEDOM.

Dom scanned the story. Waseley had been sacked according to sources, not resigned. Next, a member of staff unmentioned by name, but of distinction and long service had also been ousted in a plan to reorganise; assertions of falling rolls and standards, financial difficulties followed. The story concentrated divisively on money, the school's alleged privileged identity with a foot in state and a toe in private camps already, then what it would cost for people to go if it became independent.

There was nothing about any sort of principle, vision.

A pupil rebellion was underway too apparently. There was even mention of the petition. A pupil strike was impending. Staff were about to down tools whilst parents were up in arms. There were hints about Chinese recruitment – priority would being given to them, changing a proud local school into a remote exclusive college. Government, local trusts had backed school funding for years, through thick and thin. Now all Hillview wanted was to grab more cash from murky origins in a mad dash for its own selfish independence.

For a moment, Dom had a fleeting sympathy for Hennock, the school's masters.

'How can they write this. I thought the editor of the paper was some old boy?' said Dom, remembering something half heard one day.

'He is. That makes it worse. Royal has obviously gone to work on him, decided to pull the whole place down as a kind of revenge. How f-ing childish is that.'

'I can understand why, but he wouldn't have meant this,' said Dom.

'It threatens to destroy the school's reputation completely, never mind any future!' said Paul.

'And our jobs, yours included,' cried Katie.

'But this is all got up in a way-, 'cried Dom, remembering all too clearly yesterday. 'Are you sure it's him?'

'Of course it is, the bastard. Who else would do such a thing at such a time – who else could get the media on to all this?' said Paul.

'And you stirred up the pupils to start a petition,' cried Katie, who had been waiting to say it.

'I don't know about stirred up. They were upset. I am, about him going and all the changes in the school. Frankly I don't blame them for that. The place'll be wrecked if something doesn't happen.'

'It's wrecked already. Totally unprofessional,' pronounced Paul.

'What about loyalty to the place that gives you your job? Biting the hand that feeds you? You would risk everything, like Royal – how selfish can you get?' continued Katie.

Dom remembered Alison's comments how they all owed everything they had to the school.

What a mess! But whose fault was it really?

'You can't tell me the shenanigans going on in this place weren't bound to lead to something like this. And you can't treat people, all they've done, all a school should be, like this, and get away with it.'

'You approve, don't you? You're defending it. You think because you're new, young, you're immune. You can swan off somewhere else if things crash. I'm going to see Darren. At least he genuinely cares about the school,' cried Katie.

'This is ridiculous,' said Dom. 'Either way, independence or state, look how the way it's done is dividing us already, setting us against each other. You see what I mean, Paul. This is where all this silly school politics – intrigue has led us -to be the local laughing stock.'

'There's an emergency governors' meeting. Who knows what will happen? No, I don't see it at all. I think you'll find it's a simple question of loyalty and principle.'

'Loyalty? Loyalty, to what! To those whose snouts are deepest in the trough?' cried Dom.

Then, feeling falsely accused when he'd tried to find some thread of principle, a surge of frustration took him too.

'And talking about loyalty, I thought we were supposed to be mates, starting out together here, helping each other out. You – you've sold out completely.'

'Sold out? Ah, so now we see where your loyalty really lies- to yourself. Setting yourself up on the moral high ground whilst supporting someone who wants to wreck the school?' replied Paul.

'There are more important things than the bloody school, or our jobs for God's sake. What are we here for?'

'You don't understand. It's not some little personal matter, Dom Greaves's little world.–All you're doing is damaging the place, like Royal.'

'No, *you* don't understand! All you're doing is kowtowing to authority because it suits you, not because it's right. You've sucked up to Hennock from the start. You can't see beyond yourself!'

'Ah, now we see what Mr self styled Nice Guy believes in- himself! I'm fighting for my school, my future and my livelihood. So should you. You think you're better than the rest of us, your opinions better than anyone's, don't you?'

'*What?* No, I don't – all I want is to do the right thing, that's what we're all here for isn't it- to teach the kids that? Just explain to me, if you can, how going along with bullshit is going to make education here or the school better for any of us?'

He suddenly realised Emma was standing just inside the room.

Even after all that had happened, a jolt went through him.

'If you two have quite finished World War Three, I would

like a word with Dom, please Paul. Like you, I rather think I owe him an explanation. Perhaps you do.'

Paul stared hard at Emma.

'What do you mean?'

'I think you know exactly what I mean. Have you told him about your promotion?

There was a moment's silence. Dom stared at Paul.

'I don't know what you are talking about.'

'Does Dom know that you've been lined up for a better job, and a hefty pay rise? Well done for toadying up to Hennock, and Katie. Thanks for betraying your friends!'

'You're talking nonsense. You two in league? I've never betrayed anyone. What ridiculous language.'

'You're lying, just as you did over that stuff posted about me on social media.'

Paul began to protest his innocence, loudly.

'Where's his information come from? Tell him, Paul. Tell him about you and Katie for a start.'

Paul went red in the face, but fixed his eyes on Dom.

'She's lying, just as she did to Mike when she was cheating on him. Ignore her, Dom. I don't have to stand here take this shit. Don't listen to her: she's a fucking, twisted liar.'

He walked off pushing past her. At the door, he stopped, turning back to Emma.

'Good job you're leaving of your own accord, saves Darren the trouble of sacking you. Or have you changed your mind again, like over Mike? Interfering with anyone else yet? Everyone knows you know.'

And he turned and was gone.

There were a few moments silence, then Dom spoke quietly.

'Would someone mind telling me what is going on?'

CHAPTER FIFTY-ONE

EXPLANATION. EXCURSION

Half an hour later, he and Emma were sitting once more in The White Hart. She had insisted on driving. The journey had been mostly silent. Dom was determined to sulk.

'There's something wrong with the car,' he told her at one point, alarmed at the noise it was making.

'There's nothing wrong. It's your imagination. It's fine,' she said brusquely, staring hard into the dark countryside, passing sixty miles an hour. He could not help watching her, her face lit up by the glow of the dash board, but he let her concentrate. She powered through the night, too fast for him.

*

'Don't you do any work at that place? Broken up already?' commented the landlord. 'Dramas up there, I hear,' he said, keen for gossip.

Dom and Emma smiled diplomatically, took their places.

'You wanted to come. If you're going to leave, can you give me a little warning this time,' said Dom, hoping it would hurt.

It did.

'Well?' he persisted.

For a moment, her eyes almost seemed to fill with tears.

'I can tell you some, Dom. I'm sorry – leaving yesterday,

honest. I care what you think despite what you might-. That's why I had to go, yesterday; why I left. But if you don't want to listen-.'

'Is there any point?' he said after a pause.

'Anyone ever told you how difficult, infuriating you can be?'

'*I'm* infuriating!'

Emma looked at him again, and then, away at her glass, her fingers twisting round its rim.

She shook her head.

'I told you before: you have some idea of yourself, and of me-. Listen, please listen... Before I came here, Dom, my last boyfriend, guy called James, not counting whatever that was with Mike- he was older than me. He was in marketing too. I looked up to him. The way he handled things, people, his confidence. He made me part of his world, made me feel-'

Why was she telling him this, to rub things in?

'I thought we had something, even though, when I was alone-. Part of me had convinced myself I was happy, in his world. But something wasn't right. I thought it was marketing at first, not me, but no; it wasn't that. I felt I was always playing some part when I was with him. I wasn't really myself, me. Dom, what I'm trying to say, I came to Hillview on the rebound, to sort myself out. It's been hard, made me realise things, what I want myself, not just in a relationship: not somebody else's me. I've always been independent, bit of a free spirit. More me on my own than me when I'm with someone.'

She looked up at him.

'It's so much easier for men, even today: things a woman would understand.'

Dom wanted to argue with that at least; but knew where it was going now.

'He had someone else. Not at first, but later. I found out, in the end,' Emma paused. 'I'll spare you details. It's an old story. There were money issues too. There always are. We were about to put down a deposit. That's still dragging on. Anyway, I'm over all that now. Moved on. So you see, I'm just some ordinary girl, carrying her share of baggage, screwed up by... expectations- my own most of all. Mixed up, like everyone: but not very romantic any more, Dom. Depressingly selfish, and very first world, my issues, I'm afraid.'

She smiled for a moment, then looked at the fire.

'I threw in the job, I wanted out of all that; thought it would help. Friends, family, said I'd find somebody else: Mr Right next time. That's still the dream most parents have for their little girls, even when everyone knows there's no such thing, except in stories. My fault. Perhaps this explains some things? It's an explanation, not an excuse I'm offering. You know me.'

There was a long pause.

'A friend I was at uni with, she suggested re training as a teacher, a different life, a new start. It was partly paid for. Something appealed. I'd never really used my degree, but I'd enjoyed it, when I wasn't having a good time. So, I did teaching practice: quite liked it. It helped to be busy. I had two good placements. Lucky. Before I knew it, I'd applied for jobs, although my change of career put people off, until I got Hillview. They liked my background. I can see why now; I should have seen that one coming.

'You know the rest: most of it. All the things happening here. Mike. Because I was lonely and he was free too. No, don't shake your head! Lots of couples- love at first sight! It's not that deep really; sometimes it grows, but most of the time, things happen and then-. Someone like you would say sounds like people using each other. You said something like that to me once,' she continued but then as if to herself. 'But it is what it is. That's the way things are. You have to compromise in life, or you can hold onto some dream, some idea. That's the choice.'

He realised completely what she was saying. He'd half expected something like this all along. No, he had known it from the start if he only he had been honest with himself; and after yesterday especially.

'Hillview. I wanted to do well, I'd always made a success of things before. Then all the stuff on social media; getting run down, flu.'

She paused, staring into the fire.

He looked at her wondering again why she was telling him all this now; but he couldn't not feel pity, not make some effort, whatever hopes he'd had. For a moment, he forgot to be unkind.

'When I was home half term, Dad says to me most jobs are largely bread and butter stuff in the end. There's stuff in everything you just have to put up with, get through.'

'Dom! There's got to be more out there than here, something better.'

Dom thought how ironic such words could sound, his own secret words so often spoken to himself.

'I got into such a state at one point on teaching practice. My dad- I nearly gave up. There. I've never actually told anyone else that before,' said Dom, with feeling, despite what he felt.

Then he pulled back.

'I'm not being unsympathetic, but everyone has things in their past. And you say about being practical about everything. Didn't you realise on teaching practice?'

Emma just looked at him.

'But I still don't understand-.'

'What's there to understand? I'm selfish – always have been, Daddy's little princess – expecting too much, things, people to be more than I am myself. But when things aren't good- job, relationships-I can't wait for life to happen like you. I can't spend my time preparing to live, or preparing others to live, putting up. I wanted to say this to you, wanted to say it for a while. I don't completely understand why. You are so different in many ways, young —and I know you don't like me saying that but it's true. At least you haven't got an agenda, the same agenda most people have.'

'Are you sure? And thanks. All that makes me feel great, even more of a prat. I wish you wouldn't keep saying how young I was: there's only a few years' difference. It makes me feel like some kind of retard,' replied Dom.

Emma laughed at least.

'And, whatever's gone on, as for maturity, what about yesterday, walking off.'

For a while there was silence; but Dom felt he had something to explain too, however hopeless now.

'Everyone seems to forget, when you do something, feel something for the first time, really feel it in your life, there's no script, not just with a job, but everything, all the important things. You seemed so – so confident about everything, when I started. I was a bit in awe, as well as-. I looked up to you. I tried to be friends. I'd be happy with that if I felt it meant anything at all to you. No. No, I wouldn't. I cared. I care. I-you've, you've confused me.'

'Never deliberately, Dom. Haven't you been listening. Whatever else, I'm not that.'

'And talk about me being different, difficult! You been so distant a lot of the time, then at others. I don't understand-what you really think of me.'

She pushed her hair back, looked at the back of her hands as if not sure what to say.

'I thought you'd posted all that stuff on social media about me and Mike. Remember? Paul encouraged me, although I wanted to.'

'Paul? What do you mean wanted to?'

'Paul doesn't like me. Hates me. He asked me out at the start of term. I said no, not my type – but he kept on until I really told him. It's as simple as that. And then I found out about him and Katie, and he knew I knew.'

'Paul asked you- Katie? *Katie Trippett?*'

'Yes, Mike told me. Hard to believe isn't it? She's moved on quickly enough, hasn't she? Paul's got a bit of the Hennock about him, when it comes to what he wants. I think that was his appeal to her. And Dom, I'm like that, or like to believe I can be: that's part what I'm trying to tell you, Dom.'

'You're not really like that. You couldn't be. It's not the real you, it's a front,' he declared.

'I wouldn't be too sure of that, Dom.'

'You should listen to yourself, what you're really saying, what you really want. You're too- too nice a person to-'

'*Dom!*'

'And as for Paul! Is that part of the reason why you were arguing earlier?'

Emma nodded.

'Yes: what he's posted, still posts sometimes: showing off in some way. Guys do, all the time. The way he's relayed stuff to management, all sorts, and then you seemed to stick the knife in too when you said about Mike, being hurt, me being unworthy.'

'And I thought I was the one who imagined. But you believed all that of me.'

'For a while. I did; and didn't want to. There's another admission for you, Dom, if you're listening. And part of me was jealous, I suppose, because you all fitted, and I, I who never had a quiet five minutes in London even after I split from James, shut in a dingy flat in Wellsway, dying with flu, marking till the small hours, watching life disappear.'

'I wish you had said this before. At least you can't think so badly of me now, even if you don't-' said Dom, trying to take it in, 'apart from me being Mr Serious and Mr Pompous, and Mr Totally Naive.'

He smiled suddenly, feeling lighter of heart for no sensible reason; perhaps it was some relief they were both being more open.

'I sometimes feel as if I live my life half asleep like I'm half in and half out of a dream, especially the few last weeks. I'm an idiot! I get things so wrong.'

'Like now, me!' cried Emma smiling, searching his face.

But Dom felt she was only laughing at him again. He remembered he wanted humbling explanations, petty revenge by hurting her feelings as she had hurt his.

'And yesterday? I'm still waiting, for all you said. And I thought you and Katie were friends?'

Emma was staring intently at him, but then looked away, almost it seemed disappointed.

She continued, sounding rather tired.

'O! *That!* Katie and me? We are in a way. A girl needs her girlfriends. No flies on her; until I found out everything I said to her went straight to Hennock, personal stuff. Do you remember when he found us arguing. She'd heard, knew; but I've kept in with her. It's been clear since the start of term she was to be the next deputy head. I thought for a while that that might change things. Stupid me. She was trying to persuade me to stay yesterday.'

'Katie, *deputy head?!*'

'Yes. In fact, I've been offered a big job too – Charles's job. Subject Leader for English. Yes, Dom. The formal offer, with a big pay rise promised, arrived last night from Darren whilst we were having our meal.'

'But-' began Dom, shaking his head with a thousand questions in his thoughts.

'Hennock is to announce further staff changes tomorrow. He wants my name on the list – retaining new blood, new world, all that. I'm sorry, Dom: that's why I had to leave yesterday. I was sent another offer whilst we were out, an ultimatum in effect. It would have been wrong to have stayed, not said anything, you must see that, now. I had to go, think it out alone. For me. I've told you why, at length, been honest with you.'

She paused, looking at Dom, almost as if she really cared what he thought.

'And I had to go and think- about you.'

'Me?' said Dom simply confused once more. 'But why couldn't you say anything to me. I don't understand. You were definitely leaving, and you hate the man! What's it got to do with me?'

Emma stared at him again, shaking her head slightly before she replied.

'What am I going to do with you?' she said. 'They were offering me shed loads – God knows where or how. In fact they still are. Talk about desperate! Agency staff cost the earth; but their real reason is marketing, getting more people through the door whatever happens to the school. I still haven't answered definitely, only that I am giving it serious thought. It would be marketing, plus organising the teaching in the department- more admin than teaching, until things settle. And for that much money, for a few more months, terms; but none of that's the main thing.'

'But I still don't understand why you couldn't say something to me? And how can you think about staying after all you've said.'

'You see your reaction. But it's not the job,' Emma came back slowly.

There was silence on both sides, Dom quite lost. He tried to get his head round it all.

'You mustn't condemn me. I was honest: in my silence to you, Dom. You see I was. I kept in with Katie, but-.'

'You've played along with things.'

'No I haven't. You weren't listening. I'm only *considering* it. It's an extraordinary offer, but the job, that's not the important thing. Anyway, look what you've been up to all the time and didn't say a thing to me!'

Emma sounded different now, almost frustrated with him Dom thought. How upside down could you get?

She looked at him once more, then sighing, turned away.

'Well-. But I will leave, I've always told you that, if not immediately.'

So that was that, after all the turmoil. At least things were clear.

He sighed in turn.

'All this going on in a school, teachers, us behaving in one way or another like-.'

'Oh, come on, Dom. That's where we're different. What do you expect? People are just people whatever they seem.'

'Things don't have to be just so: things shouldn't be all this,' he cried.

'Of course they shouldn't, but they usually are.'

'I can't accept that. You don't mean that, or you would not be thinking about leaving, after something else. You know yourself it's not just money.'

'No, I suppose not. It's not just money, staying or leaving, Dom. That's what I'm trying to tell you. But now all I've done is made you miserable again. Poor Dom!'

'Please, don't feel sorry for me, that's the worse thing!'

'What do you want then, praise? I respect you, trust you even, up to a point. You're certainly too good for this place, I've told you that, if you'd been listening. That's a lot for a girl to say, even these days, especially when a man thinks she's unworthy.'

Couldn't she just leave things?

'Emma! I don't think so little of you at all; but I don't want respect, praise, thank you!'

'I see. Well, that's that then. But you *haven't* been listening! You really can't see what this has to do with you, can you? I thought, goodness knows why- but-. So I was wrong too. I thought you might have cared a bit about – even be pleased, for me. Well, I hope we'll stay friends at least. And don't change, even if you are odd, and Mr Serious. I like you anyway, whatever. I'm glad I've told you things, even if I'm not sure that you know that, even now. Friends?'

'Friends?' said Dom after a few moments, feeling that was the safest word to land on without crashing. Suddenly the word seemed disappointing, despite all he thought he now knew too well.

'Yes, friends! Do I have to hit you over the head? Can't you see what I'm saying? Well, friends at least, Dom.'

There was much that, Dom being Dom, must still perplex, even baffle, but even he could begin to register something more then.

'Friends!' he repeated, like one of his pupils puzzling dumbly over a completely new and difficult word they'd never seen before. But not completely without hope of enlightenment.

'That it then?' he said rather brusquely, as if reaching the end of something banal he wasn't interested in, was hoping now finished.

Emma smiled at him in her way.

'Why, what else are you proposing, Mr Greaves? You surely don't want to get mixed up with someone like me, a deeply unworthy, cynical woman on the cusp of the horrors of early middle age? I've told you – life is not a dress rehearsal, even if Hillview seems like a very bad play most of the time.'

They looked at each other. Dom could see then, just about anyway. She liked him.

She liked him.

The landlord who had been tacking back and forth across the room ostentatiously stacking glasses, clearing, chose that moment to barge between them.

'You two finished or y'going to be stopping the night? It's time, especially for young Romeo here!'

They both burst out laughing as he disappeared with their glasses into the space behind the bar where a television boomed out even older news. Dom was surprisingly eager to help her into her coat, even put his arms round her as they left, pausing in the porch.

'I thought-. God, I am a fool. Me being so very young, you see. I don't know anything anymore. Except, it's the end of term! There's only a few days, and then Christmas, another year beginning, a whole year gone. Who knows the future? Now is all there is – especially after a drink. Maybe Hennock'll spontaneously combust with all his schemes, like the guy in that book I never finished at uni; but just now I don't care. There's more in the world. Come on!'

They ran to her car, slipping and sliding but laughing again despite a freezing rain and the cold blackness of a winter night. All the heaped up challenges of Hillview, its promise and failure, its friends and foes, the endless shifting alliances and authorities, successes and disappointments, even its unwritten future, had lost substance. That world lay smoking into the darkness around; theirs leapt, for now, vividly to life.

Dom hardly dared think what might happen next as they got in, suddenly intimately alone together, excited, confused, apprehensive all at once.

But then Emma's car would not start.

It seemed helplessly funny to them both.

'I told you there was something wrong. You see, you never take me seriously!' cried Dom as they sat in the cold interior, dripping wet.

'There's nothing wrong!' she protested, all playful indignation at his impudence.

She turned the key again and again, a disturbing whirring and grinding sound becoming increasingly more feeble.

'It doesn't sound good, does it?' she said, solemnly for a moment.

They looked at each other and burst out laughing.

'What are we going to do? I suppose we could get a taxi, but it'll cost the earth. And I'm not going to wait ages,' she said, her brisk self back in charge.

Then more slowly, feeling his heart beat, Dom spoke, hearing his own words.

'Come back with me. There's a last night bus that goes past here near the school. I noticed at half term, takes you almost all the way. It's a bit of a roundabout ride, but gets there in the end, and then I can- run you back. We'll have to hurry. It's almost too late.'

They looked at each other for what seemed like the longest moment of Dom's very long first term. Then he kissed her.

Soon they were chasing along the road to the stop, arm in arm, giggling like a couple of kids.

They made it just in time, much to the driver's annoyance. *Don't normally do this stop this late. Puts me out. Don't want any hassle this time o'night, no trouble like as what they put me through last week.*

The few rather elderly passengers, muffled in coats and scarves looked on disapprovingly at the young pair, laughing away too loudly. Some nonsense or other.

Kids today.

The bus lurched off, before the driver let them find a seat, so they scrambled upstairs to get away from him, everyone else, sitting down first at the front, then at the back because of a window jammed open that let the rain and cold air spray in.

They were laughing still as a wild ride began, the bus careering through the plashing night. Soon they were the only passengers. The driver sped manically through the darkness, almost forgetting his two last charges completely, keen to get home, stop start on his rollercoaster route.

Upstairs, it became almost hysterical as they jolted and bumped and skidded around, bouncing out of their seats even though they were holding onto each other, as the bus hurtled along the pothole-pitted country roads. At one jolt, Dom came off the seat completely, slid down towards the front. Emma was in tears of laughter, but she got him back in place.

Eventually they settled into a smoother rhythm clinging to each other, their hearts light, free for the rest of the ride.

They reached a main road stretch, not far from the school, speeding along even faster, but smoothly and steady at last. For a few frail moments, it became almost dreamlike up there, alone, silent, entirely happy in each others' warmth, a small boat on a vast black ocean stretching out all around.

To any roadside watcher the bus passed swiftly, quickly becoming a tiny thin dash of light, a punctuation mark in the night, then vanishing from sight and sound completely, leaving only wind and sleet, darkness behind.

They nearly missed their stop.

As they walked the last half mile together the sleet turned again. Large snowflakes fell, settling now, the cold all about them. But neither of them minded, intent only on each other.

CHAPTER FIFTY-TWO

VOTES FOR CHRISTMAS

It seemed strange to be back in the classroom. With only three days left, it was final lessons. The following days were dominated by a Christmas Carol Concert, all the protracted formalities of end of term. Both sides, pupils and teachers, fortunately, were decidedly on auto pilot that day.

Superficially Dom felt unchanged. Deep down he was a different person: back in the centre of his story. He'd found space for himself, and for Emma, despite all the misunderstandings, turmoils, much that was still uncertain. He was even surprised at himself.

Looking about, he was unable to see people around him in quite the same way. He half wondered if they sensed something, could tell, and he would suddenly feel shy, although it was no first experience. He thought wryly of past adventures, passionate beginnings, sometimes slightly drunken fumblings, even embarrassments, remorse. This was different: all broadening feelings, dancing spirits, exciting possibility. He couldn't work out if what he felt and knew now he had never really felt before, or if it was something long lost, finally recovered; but, *something had happened*. Now the day felt alive in and for itself, not buckling under considerations, dissipating in triviality. It was a real beginning, itching for ever more exploration.

Of course, Dom was still Dom. There was apprehension –
the future: where, what now. There were shadows in what she
had told him, done: there was her beguiling independence
of character. Perhaps she would always remain further on
than him. But they had spanned a divide, crossed together,
gone somewhere beyond. There would always be that now:
a dream real as touch.

*

Meanwhile, the harsh strip-lights of the classroom bore down
on thirty less abstracted souls trapped in a more prosaic
dimension, digging away at the vagaries of words.

Under Instruction!

There ought to be a warning sign:

Education: Danger, look out!

In his present mood Dom felt almost sorry he would not
teach again until New Year.

'What you doing for Christmas, Sir?'

'I hate Christmas, Sir. There's always rows. My parents
split at Christmas.'

'We got flooded last year.'

'Our loo got blocked. Dad went mental.'

'You've survived your first term, Sir!' came from Tim.

'Have you enjoyed it?' came from Jane.

Dom smiled broadly today.

'It's been, well: I didn't at first. And you guys weren't –
aren't easy.'

'Sir, at my sister's school, they shaved one of their
teacher's hair off.'

'At my last school, one of the teachers got beaten up by a
parent.'

'Have you heard of Pig, this psycho who used to teach
here, Sir. He used to pin kids up against the wall if they didn'
do their homework.'

'And Sir, Sir, he ate with his mouth open – you could see all this stuff working round and round, and he dribbled, it was disgusting This one time, a couple of Year Eleven waited for him in the dark and emptied the contents of a wheelie bin on him.'

'Sounds like kids like you lot,' Dom replied, wanting to laugh.

Even if they pushed boundaries, they must say what they felt sometimes, even if a lot of it was daft, wrong. Otherwise it was all only pretend: like grownups.

It was a matter of trust. It became real then.

'You've changed, Sir,' came from Jane regarding him.

There were sucking noises as there still were when Jane spoke.

'We've Hillviewed him,' came from one of the boys. 'He's not so into his hidden meanings.'

'You're almost cool now, Sir,' said another.

All the class laughed then. That encouraged more openness.

'Sir, what's going to happen to us if the school's going independent?' said Jane.

'Everyone'll leave and we won't have to go to school anymore,' came an ever hopeful voice.

'My Mum says if the school closes and I'm home more, now Dad's left, she's going to kill herself.'

The class laughed again, and the bell was ringing and they were off, forgetting. But they had been listened to.

Soon all but Jane and Tim were gone.

Those last two came forward, awkward.

'Thanks for teaching us this term, Sir. We bought you a card: it's not a very nice one. Happy Christmas, Sir. Don't get too p-, er drunk.'

'Sir, is it true you're going out with Miss Oakley?'

How on earth?

'We're all friends on the staff,' he said grinning more than he could help.

They laughed. Their minds snapped to something else.

'Happy Christmas, Sir! See you next term! You'll be at the party?'

He remembered his first day – those two, last out.

*

He had persuaded Emma to go and see Alison with him that afternoon. Neither felt they had anything left to lose in saying their piece, given their respective situations. They felt more confident together, united in their dislike of the doctor, even more at what had been going on. Alison was the only one left whom they felt might usefully listen. Both together could not be brushed aside, even if she too were some agent herself.

Rumours of all sorts were flying: promotions, new jobs, better facilities, replacements, cuts, restructuring, redundancy. Emma's experience, it seemed, was only the tip of some iceberg of promises for those trending: for those not, there was a fist of anxiety in the guts.

They could not get to see her. The governors' meeting precipitated by Mr Royal's disclosures to the press, the petition, its fallout were still commanding the attention of the management. Mrs Tenace was 'out of office'.

Outside more snow fell. For a while it looked once more as if the school could be cut off and tomorrow's great carol concert in the afternoon in Wellsway would be cancelled for the first time ever. Mr Walker returned to his theme of universal apocalypse. Terry cursed. Mrs Dot brought in some homemade cake for staff in case they all got stuck. They did, on her cake.

No one seemed to be in charge that day. It could be felt everywhere in the school. Lessons limped on. For those few who had not got in, blended learning was once more the order of the day as it had been during the flu, driving exhausted staff to the last reaches of patience. Mr Tring tried to rehearse missing choir members on line and was seen crossing the campus tearing his hair, shouting Christmas was cancelled, and promising death and torment to anyone or anything that obstructed another practice.

About the middle of the afternoon, staff heard that another governors' meeting had finally finished. Then an email arrived asking all staff to assemble in the great hall for the meeting with their Head, Dr Hennock, for important announcements. The Acting Head label had been dropped.

Mr Tring went mad again because his rehearsals for the next day's celebrations were being further ruined. Alison got to him, begged him to see sense, the supreme importance of the school's future, promised him the thin comfort of more time tomorrow before the service. Tring assented reluctantly, but went around denouncing the tinpot dictator Hennock to anyone brave enough to listen, saying they could stuff any plans or proposed votes up the new Head's arse.

Although Emma and Dom still could not reach Alison in person, just before the main staff meeting was to begin Dom received an email.

Apologies. I know you have been trying to see me. I hope nothing urgent, but will try to catch you first thing tomorrow. As you can imagine, today has been impossible.

Alison

PS. Bit of a long shot but did you ever hear any more on the grapevine of that boy Tom Rymer who left? He thought a lot of you, wanted to be in the play, etc etc. Apparently he has run away again. He is still in touch with friends here, you know – the twins. Mother anxious. Let me know if you know anything at all.

AT

Dom knew nothing, but he had not forgotten Tom, nor his own recent mysterious email. He wondered what the poor kid would think now as Hennock bestrode his world in triumph.

*

Emma was at the meeting this time. Dom had persuaded her, but even she was curious today. Dom hoped she would stay now, of course. He felt confident he could persuade anyone to anything just then, but he knew she was still deliberating, desperate not to upset what they had, so late in the day, found. They had agreed to keep what was between them secret. It seemed easier that way, especially, without exactly admitting it, whilst they were finding out themselves. It gave them some control, tightening the excitement of intimacy.

Dom sought her eye across the crowded hall, once they were assembled, but she was not looking for him as he for her. For a few moments, apprehensions returned. He felt a sudden sinking feeling, the high he'd be on all night and day suddenly tumbling away. Mrs Trotman, who happened to be sitting beside him, everyone had been commanded there, spoke to him.

'All right? It's the end of term! You've got through. First term. It'll never be as tough again, whatever this brings.'

'I'm all right,' he replied. 'Just wondering where everything's going.'

He looked across to Emma again. She caught his eye this time, smiled back.

Mrs Trotman saw the glances, read the looks, shook her head; but Hennock was about to deliver.

Darren Hennock looked quite unperturbed by the petitions, the meetings, the controversies – even Dom's little tilt at his windmills, with which he must have been dealing.

Sitting next to the Doctor was his governor friend today. He kept looking at his watch, then staring round hard over the rim of his glasses at the staff assembled, fixing his gaze on one or the other. Slightly apart, it seemed was Alison, looking tired as ever. Almost everyone looked tired. How different it all appeared from the start of term, Dom thought, when he had been in quiet awe.

But he was no longer alone.

He caught Emma's eye once more, could not help his smile.

It began.

At first, from the new Headmaster, came only old Waseley like platitudes about how hard everyone had been working, what a busy but successful term everyone had had. There was no mention of the petition to save Royal or anything more about the former boss.

He soon got on to what he really wanted to say, and do.

'Now, I am pleased to announce that I have secured the governors' agreement to make some very important announcements. We intend to move ahead with the final planning and indeed action on some exciting shovel ready developments at Hillview. I wanted you all to be the first to know, and to give you a chance to cast your vote for your future, in an advisory fashion of course, as we promised.

'I am pleased to tell you today that, following the proposed sale of some of our land, and the swift granting of planning permission under new laws for housing on the Wellsway side of the Cloud, plus some modest borrowing on the back of our trust, funds to redevelop parts of the entire school site, improve our facilities and provision are being secured.

'I can't go into details. There are still parts of the process being formalised; and, at the moment it's still constrained by our status as a state school. But you will all be sent an email attachment shortly after this meeting with more information, details on transitional arrangement, further proposals for independence and so on. Several much needed new science labs, a new IT centre, upgrading of boarding facilities and welfare provision are all included in this. We all know how the welfare side of our work has been growing. This is all set to happen, dependent of course, in large measure on the progress of our plans to become, once more, an independent institution.

'Discussions with staff directly affected have taken place. Meanwhile, we are determined to begin planning and initiating, with your approval, the process of transition to independence. In conjunction with a link school in China that I have established, we also plan to open a summer residential international language centre both in its own right and to encourage more foreign boarders, a growing and vital market for New Hillview's future.

'The oldest part of the school at the top of the boarding house which you all know has been disused since the last inspection will be restored and form part of this centre with upgraded sleeping accommodation serving our pupils better, and these summer lets which should be partly self funded. It is also proposed that some of the land sold off will be used as a business park securing further cash resources for the school on a long-term basis.'

Incredulity.

Dom nodded at Emma, beginning to understand much of what he had witnessed in secret. She smiled back, shaking her head.

'One more thing before I take any of the million questions or comments, I am sure you are all bursting with, and this is very important.'

Hennock seemed to do a little shimmy on his chair before settling again.

'I'm sure you all understand that these plans have necessitated a thorough series of proposals for restructuring, a shaking up of staffing responsibilities. Many of you have longed for such a comprehensive review for many years.

'The governors are keen to emphasise that no one's job is currently under threat. Indeed, such restructuring comes with significant opportunities for many for career development and commensurate remuneration. These discussions are naturally ongoing.

'But one other thing I can announce today, here and now. Our support staff – we all know how much we owe them – will benefit too. It's always been a bit of Hillview oversight, I am afraid, never to properly recognise the contribution of some key workers. This will change if plans for independence go ahead: across the board pay rises; the granting of proper privileges; access to Staff Room facilities; proper pensions and so on. I think we'd all agree, in the modern world, that education and Hillview in particular have long past the feudal stage.'

The dam finally burst.

'Restructuring, my arse,' came from Mr Tring who had been boiling away all day. 'That means the sack for some, less money for others. Who the hell's going to pay for this? –Vote! It's been settled already!'

'Where's all this money suddenly coming from?'

'And who's allowing us do all this? '

'How the hell are we going to fill places with fee-paying pupils? We haven't even begun and you're spending the money!'

'I didn't sign up to teach in some private school.'

'Whose jobs are on the line amidst all this fantasy and snake oil stuff?'

'How the hell has the school promised to sell that land. It's an SSI on the slopes of a beauty spot.'

'Or get planning permission.'

Waves of consternation and protest swept in tides of dissension and outrage; but, as before, counter-voices began to sound.

But before argument could rally properly on either side, Mrs Dot began.

'All this building! How exciting, Dr Hennock! Where will my new cookery club go?' she began, quite in her own world.

There were groans from some of the staff, but she was off, wild enthusiasm as ever and a cascade of fantastic ideas about refurbishing the old part of the school especially with a fabulous new cookery suite.

'Round the f-in bend,' was heard emanating from Mr Tring's vicinity.

All lock on seriousness was broken as almost everyone got taken up in obscure debates about what could be done, with the old part of the school in particular, its unique heritage, now that money was magically to appear: and as long as everyone voted the right way of course.

Dom sat there reflecting that he'd been right in some part in some of his own stumbling discoveries and suspicions. But the scope of Hennock's plans and ambitions, dreams even – were staggering.

Meanwhile, the doctor nodded to himself, apparently happy with diversion into speculation about all the good things that might happen, rather than hard choices as to what really would.

But then a wave beat back.

'None of us know enough to make a proper decision. There's too much to take in.'

'And what's the point of some proposed vote when no one knows exactly what they're voting for? And if you let everyone else involved in the school decide – promise them all money – who's going to vote rationally?' came from Mr Walker, taking Charles's old role.

Arguments about identity and status and money and fees and jobs *and who knew what, and what were education, teaching really all about* rose just as in the last meeting in a wild tangle and ill disciplined crescendo.

Confusion. The people were having their say, but there was more division than understanding.

Hennock let it ride, for the people must be allowed a voice, for a while at least. Then he held up his hand for silence.

The governor stood – bang on cue.

'Please could I reassure you on behalf of the governing body that there is no *immediate* threat to jobs, pensions at all – just *repurposing for the future*. We are a business, in or out of the current system. Trust us, we have been working hard on the details of all this, from transitional arrangements to specific outcomes morning noon and night, many weekends if I may say, when most of you have been off relaxing with partners and families. We may be finding a bit of money to bump up staff and support staff salaries. Pay you what you always say you deserve. That's high on your list of concerns. What could be a better plan?'

'Bollocks,' muttered Mr Tring.

Another wave of staff anger swept through the hall, seething at the governor's insensitivity. Ignoring him, they flung questions, comments at Hennock, many solid only in a feeling of victimhood, spiked by the governor's mention of his own hard work, and unable to imagine change that did not come without grim cost. General frustrations mounted, and, a feeling of grievance at the way things were, as before, only escalated the tension and bad temper, muddied the waters.

Skilfully, Hennock continue to ride each wave, by articulating promise after promise

Better a promise of broad sunlit uplands than living with the mess that was.

And they were being given a vote. How patronising to assume they could not use that wisely, take back their control. It was not the spirit of the age to ignore the individuals who alone would decide.

Eventually, Dr Hennock quite unruffled, called for order, asked all staff to complete an 'options for change' form, a real advisory vote, no less, for the first time in the school's history. That would be in their inboxes imminently. This was *their* moment, *their* opportunity to decide, they were told; as long as they did the right thing. Dr Hennock's only constraint, he averred, was that speed was now needed, given all that was happening in school, county and country. Indeed views needed to be expressed *by tomorrow morning at the latest.*

Meanwhile, he was keeping them all informed by announcing some immediate changes and appointments. Amongst those mentioned, Katie Trippett would be one of the new deputy heads with special oversight of the changes pending, Deputy Head Director of Transition, and much else no less. Paul Workman was also being promoted: to a place on the boarding house team, bringing welcome new blood and fresh ideas.

Dom saw Mr Jolson looking surprised.

Dr Hennock saved his final blows for his last remarks.

'There are, of course, a number of other posts that will become vacant or be reorganised or repurposed. All current staff are invited to apply for these – indeed their own positions if they fall under the restructuring. We need you all to sign up to new contracts, of course, too, but please feel free to have a good look at these first – discuss them with one of our enhanced management team.

'Now, we felt you would all like time to discuss this amongst yourselves without the leadership team exerting undue influence. We invite you to stay behind so that you can consider, even debate, all that has been said, before completing the advisory ballot of course. Mrs Dot is as ever kindly providing refreshments.'

Mrs Dot bowed, entirely happy.

The staff remained behind.

Someone started saying that unions must be contacted, as if they were the cavalry who would magically appear over the hill to save them. They claimed new contracts were a con, you couldn't abolish jobs just like that. They wouldn't let that happen.

Then a cold but knowing voice said they could abolish jobs and roles if they changed their descriptions. *They* knew that.

Eventually a delegation was selected by staff to voice their disparate opinions, worries at the way this had all been burst upon them, all the concerns, whichever way things swung. There must be delay, more discussion, before even a vote or they were all going blind into the night.

They would go to Alison first, then brave Hennock, and the governors.

But a lot of people left keeping their own counsel, plenty thinking only: things ought to be better than they were; some few of promotions, money in their pockets.

And what was the point of freedom if not to exercise it to set themselves free?

*

Mr Walker trapped Dom as he was leaving with Emma.

Disaster any which way he asserted.

'Restructuring, repurposed! God save us from our words. But it's our own fault. We've stuck our heads in the sands for so long, clinging to Waseley's and the like's half-baked complacency, and now ill judged promises. And look already: a community divided who had no division before. Whatever happens, it's the end of Hillview as we know it. Charles was right. Independence! An illusion! Finding out what it means to be on our own in a cold hard world more like. Time to retire.'

Gradually, all went home. Perhaps independence would sort things out, or Christmas, or something.

Next term must be better, somehow.

CHAPTER FIFTY-THREE

NO ALTERNATIVE

Later when Dom and Emma had been back at his flat some time, carefully avoiding others on the way, Dom, feeling confident, inspired, must think through all he had heard: try to square the human personalities involved with both common sense, and the highest of principles.

'At least we know now what he's been up to all the time! Surely you can't do all that without involving colleagues more. He can't just get rid of people?' said Dom to Emma.

'He can if he abolishes their jobs or titles, he can try to, that or undermine them so that they lose confidence: that's happened already. And that's why all the secrecy. It's not just a coup, it's a revolution. Think of all the deals, and scheming and planning – all done behind most people's backs. You've got to hand it to him. Shock and awe, no less,' she replied.

'But what a way to operate: to use people, hide things from or deceive so many close colleagues. I bet Alison is furious.'

'Apparently she knew little until yesterday, so Katie told me.'

'This talk of independence doesn't always seem to have much to do with what's right educationally, changing things: selling off assets, land – business parks, housing developments, international schools. It's about making money, not what, how we teach. That's the important thing: how we treat them, and each other.'

'You're quick!' laughed Emma. 'Why didn't you say any of this in the meeting?'

'Can't people see what Hennock's like, what he's up to, what's gone on? And what he'll do if he gets his way. What's the matter with us all? We should just kick it all out, him too. Start over properly. Surely no one's going to vote for all that.'

'Dom! Calm down! And anyway, I said – what's the alternative? And perhaps he's right: at least he has a plan, a vision. The school isn't going anywhere without change, some vision – more money.'

'I hate it. I hate it all- all the politicking, this behind the scenes stuff, pettiness, the whole lot! I s'pose I can always leave at the end of the year, if I'm not sacked first.'

'O stop worrying. Hennock has bigger concerns than you just now. Royal told you that. We're nothing. And it's too late. They've got their plans sorted, you can see that. The meeting won't have helped – people like Tring and Walker sounding off. People reminding everyone what a mess things are. A lot didn't say much at all. They're frightened about their jobs.'

'It's all so wrong. Why do things have to be this way?'

'Dreamer.'

'But it's not fair.'

'Happens all the time in the real world.'

'Then I don't like the real world, very much.'

'Better stay here then. It does not get better outside.'

'And I don't want to teach only kids who can pay.'

'We all pay for things, one way or another, Dom. Hennock's right there. Why shouldn't people try to do their best for their kids, use their money as they want. There's no free lunches in life.'

There was a pause.

'So what's your answer to it all. What are you going to do?'

Emma said nothing, just shook her head.

'I wish we could stay here; slam the door on all the rest.'

Emma looked at him.

'What am I going to do with you?' she said once more, laughing.

*

Later Dom must continue. He wanted to talk about their future too, but it was easier to find the words to say other things.

'I can't ever vote for Hennock, even if this place needs change. The change won't change the things that need changing. It's people you need to change. What we're about. It'll leave us worse than we are now.'

'You're starting to sound cynical, good.'

'It isn't good. Neither choice puts the things wrong right. The alternatives are wrong. The place deserves better. The kids deserve better. They're blameless.'

'Are they? Are any of us? Who's got us into this position. People like us, I expect, who want our own way, don't care enough, know better. The children- they'll be all right. They're young; they'll survive. Look at the Jameses of the world.'

'All right isn't good enough. You only live once. They aren't challenged enough. Half of them just want fun, to enjoy themselves. They don't want to think about serious things ever – neither do half the staff. They'll just let it all happen. Perhaps they're right.'

'Dom, no! Even I'm not that cynical. You have to use your time, make it work for you, or your life just slips away.'

There was silence.

Dom looked at her. The big world and its ridiculous tangles! Why couldn't you just stay separate, apart from it all.

He caught himself, smiled at the whole situation.

Soon Emma was fast asleep, but he was restless, full of life, happy as he had rarely been all term, charged with a passion to change things as he had changed himself: make the world beyond his own feel what it could be.

His imagination teemed with thoughts of possibilities if you asked the right questions, had courage, confidence. Maybe you should just teach that; but then people would worship only strength, the strong, and back you went into some jungle.

Eventually he got up, careful not to disturb Emma, crossing the cold floor to the window.

He stared out. Snow was falling outside. It had begun again, secretly it seemed, dropping soundlessly out of the endless blackness all around. Everything beyond lay still, silent, muffled.

Here's just us and darkness all around, not frightening but like a blanket. Our own wrapped up world, he thought. He looked back at Emma. Then he was remembering another Dom, a Dom staring out into the night at the end of his first day when he'd seen Dr Hennock and the governor.

You imagine one adventure, life becomes another.

He'd been quite alone that night, but not unhopeful.

He thought of all the dramas playing out at Hillview, his own happiness. He tried to understand.

Perhaps it was that when people grew up, had to work, get money, the business of everyday life, getting on, just trapped them: then they were lost in what they were doing, getting on becoming getting by.

He knew that Hillview's troubles were no troubles at all in the great action and spill of time and space, but even here it was impossible, the way small mean things seemed to twist the good away.

But so, too, was all this impossible in a different, wholly positive way, he thought, as he looked back at Emma; what he felt now in this room, in this moment of time, even as snow fell outside.

Who could say what was mere dream, what one day might become real.

CHAPTER FIFTY-FOUR

RESULT

That night it continued to snow all through the long dark hours. Emma and Dom woke to a silent white world whose stillness and chill came inside the room, rousing them early. They looked out, shivering, on a Hillview sculpted in white, and blue grey shadows. Thick snowflakes were tapping the window, mostly melting, some settling on the sill. Soon the dawn broke spreading a strange light across campus.

They washed and dressed, returning ever and again to the window scene: pristine, innocent, untouched.

Before long some boarders were up, cautious, reverential, hushed at first: a fresh new world outside, primeval, awe inspiring, mysterious. All too soon they were excitedly pelting each other, hardly able to believe the freedom, the absence of control.

But Terry was upon them almost at once, swearing and cursing to little effect, and then came Hennock bringing rule, halting fun, and fights, spoiling their play.

The pupils, disgruntled, were ordered back indoors to chores, cleaning up, routine. Arm in arm Emma and Dom continued to regard the scene outside, fascinated, suspended, wishing they too could run out, join in, get lost in it all.

The snow turned thicker for a time, but that heralded warmer air, and soon a thaw began. Around eight-thirty a weak winter sun finally broke through, the light dazzling all observers, blindingly bright, showing a thousand footprints, heartbreaking beauty in a million sparkling flaws.

*

The plan had been for Emma to return very early to her flat, but now, if anyone challenged, they could claim that she had been forced to stay over because of the weather. No one would notice, all thoughts were on the snow, the carol service, the end of term, the big future, whichever way it swung. All the school would be bussed to Wellsway in the afternoon for carols.

The first news on campus, however, sent round by Ms Trippett, already consumed in her new role, was not propitious. It looked as if the snow, although melting, was enough to disrupt the service. There was palpable disappointment: the concert was a bringing together and celebration, that offered all but the most stubborn of souls something.

Katie, discovering the scale of her responsibilities as well as duties, wanted it cancelled altogether.

Mr Tring, still livid after yesterday, shot off to see if he could find her, kill her slowly, or saving that, inflict terrible new tortures on any members of the leadership he could lay his hands on.

In fact, the joyous Christmas confection looked in doubt for only about half an hour. By nine o'clock a rapid thaw was gathering strength and melting all trace of the early fun and fight; morning lessons would have to be taught, even if some pupils would be late; routine would prevail. Ms Trippett sent email after email with contradictory instructions, trying to look as if she had really known what she was doing all along.

Staff got on with things. They always did.

Then came an email from Dr Hennock encouraging those who still had not completed their options for change form, voted, to please do so by lunchtime so the result could be sorted before the concert. *It was only an advisory vote, to gauge support in proceeding with planning and further exploration of options* read the email. *Far more detailed consultations would of course follow.* There seemed to have been a bit of a pull back there; someone or somebodies had got to Hennock, but a vote was going ahead; and a vote was a vote.

By morning break, Dom and Emma finally managed to get to Alison, following a long queue of either outraged or deeply worried colleagues, upset from yesterday. She did not say much as Dom and Emma told her once more their concerns about the school, the uncertainties over independence, even its very future; and the agency of Dr Hennock.

Dom did most of the talking – but Emma was ready to speak up too. They both felt they had a valid theme in the lack of real consultation and information, whatever the vote – the secrecy with which this had all been surrounded, the vagueness about the radical implications of the changes proposed. Above all, better alternatives must exist.

At first, Alison was defensive. The school had reached a watershed; staff did not appreciate its current financial straitjacket; the state would not sustain it in its present form if the school went down. It was clear, however, she cared about the people and personalities involved, the Hillview that was, at its best, something special. She tried to persuade Emma to stay once more, Dom's heart leaping in hope.

'I am not unsympathetic to what you're saying. Quite a few staff have been in- yesterday – today – similar concerns. I will tell you that I am meeting with an independent group of senior staff and governors at lunch time. I have undertaken personally to report back to staff on what we discuss, but room for manoeuvre, it's dictated by money. We can't overlook the benefits to the school of some of the proposed changes. All the issues, plans raised, have been rumbling for years. Perhaps now at least we can take some steps forward.'

Before they left she did, however, step out from behind her professionalism for a moment as she was ushering them out.

'Sorry you've both had such a torrid time this term. Dom, I don't think you need to worry about your future. Dr Hennock's been under such pressure – we all have. And I'm sorry you're still undecided Emma. You know what I want. The offer is still open, but we can't wait longer. Please think carefully. You're both a force for good in the place in my opinion. I'll raise your concerns, but between us and these four walls, my voice is not always listened to. Things are happening at pace. Sorry I can't give you more time: it's a big operation getting everyone into Wellsway – one thing the school does well, the concert. Let's hope the goodwill celebrated spreads a little light. Oh, by the way, Dom, did you get my email about Tom?'

They left the meeting mollified that they had at least been listened to. They had both cast their vote against the changes, but not, they agreed, against change. That was genuinely needed.

Before the school left for Wellsway, there came, an exultant email from Dr Hennock announcing that the advisory vote had been close, but decisive. He was disappointed that some had not taken part, but a big majority had, and of those who had, a significant majority had approved. Dr Hennock was delighted with this brave and forward looking resolution. The school now had the moral authority to pursue plans, he declared, take on the state; and staff, support staff, governors, pupils and parents would all go forward together, quickly and united, embracing a new dawn for Hillview. And please could staff sign their new contracts before the end of business on the last day of term.

Despite all the passion of the last few weeks, the fierce debates of only yesterday, long festering issues, years of swelling discontent, all the hot air, somehow, no one had quite imagined an actual outcome, a decision. Something tremendous, with incalculable consequences, had taken place almost by accident. The shock of a real result, a verdict no less, gave everyone some kind of surprise.

Dom could seemingly find few who had actually voted for, now it had happened. It was believed by some that many had voted simply for the hope of change or more control; they would at least be making their own mistakes they believed. A few, the few who dreamed they had most to gain, were, however, triumphant.

Mr Walker, and an apocalyptic Mr Tring, asserted that support staff, flush with promises of being listened to at last, better pay, and keeping their jobs secure from an invasion of cheaper younger recruits, had swung it in the end. The truth was more complex, and involved a lot of people who hadn't been listened to for far too long, even if they might be disappointed, shocked at potential consequences far beyond current dismays and indeterminate dreams for the future.

'Turds rise and float,' declared Mr Tring, rather more simply. 'Damn that conniving, stirring bastard Hennock, damn that idle fence-sitting complacent Waseley who's allowed us to drift into all this shit, and damn the stupid thick moronic staff who did vote for it. You'll see! It'll be strike action next!' he shouted, before he stormed away.

Mr Walker was more philosophical, telling Dom for the millionth time that he was glad he was retiring, certain that all would be let down, end in tears: 'What a world. One to be well out of. Even turkeys vote for Christmas here.'

The general mood became one of resignation, mixed with more confusion over exactly what had been decided, or even if the vote was real, or would be called again, and how on earth they would ever get permission let alone money to go ahead with any of it. But Hillview was preparing its best face for the world. Everything else must wait whilst school business proceeded. Whatever turmoil was to come, the show must go on.

CHAPTER FIFTY-FIVE

CAROL CONCERT

The Carol Concert – the religious side of it had diminished over the years – always took place in the old Abbey Church of Wellsway. It was indeed a big event in the life of the school, so grand a setting as to lift all out of themselves, even in current circumstances.

Dom was particularly stirred by it all. He'd never been in the place before, and looked with awe around the vast nave, with its smell of stone and the dust of time, its towering Norman columns, seemingly so solid, beyond all merely human frailty; its grand monumental graves, names polished almost to nothing by centuries of irreverent footfall; its impossible vaulted ceiling with all that weight of stone gracefully held up to heaven as if by magic, a reproof to any cynicism, even if there were odd stains and leaks. It was dark inside after the blinding white of melting snow outside, but the bright afternoon was streaming through glorious stained glass windows, mixing with the calm glow of candles to shine a romantic fire of living light into this old cavern of timeless time.

Dom could now simply watch and wait, as if indeed in expectation of something, some advent. The slush and mud and melting snow outside and the tramp from the buses had left his feet wet and cold. He could feel walls and currents of chill air moving around the building, but the silent drafts that brought a scent of incense, of fire and smoke and ancient stone, the hush and the waiting stillness all around (except from those still coughing with the flu) was real enchantment. The waiting congregation shared the spell: Christmas was really coming.

Officiants fussed and rushed about. A few parents bustled in late. Some were seated already, as near to the front as they could possibly be so that they could share in all this, celebrate their child, their gift, their school. The tired faces of smart suited staff ushered the latecomers to their place. Mr Tring tore about, his gown at half mast, sheets of music spilling from his grasp, deploying his forces in different parts of the building, a practised professional, knowing exactly how to use his cast, his set, to perfect effect. He was all smiles, delighted to be busy, centre stage at last, doing what he loved in the way he loved for the school he loved.

Some of the choir up front were laughing and chatting until admonished by Dr Hennock, temporarily drawn away from unctuous attentions to the more important official guests. A bit further down the nave was Mrs Dot directing the wrong people to the wrong seats, unknowingly handing out last year's programmes to those who were not already wary of her through experience. Just by her was Emma, busy salvaging Alison's seating plan from the depredations of Mrs Dot, and looked as if she had done it all for years and this was not her first, and last. She was standing tall and elegant, her striking figure, intimately familiar in all its movements making Dom think not so reverently for a moment.

But as he watched, waited, Dom felt a kind of peace and quiet settle. There he was, calm and content, open-hearted, taking it all in, letting it all in. His simple tranquillity matched the stillness that fell on all in that twilight December afternoon, when eventually they stood, humbly, in hope.

A solo treble voice began singing, perfectly pitched, heart breaking in its purity, its innocence.

It was Rachel. Dom smiled to himself at the battle she would have fought and, no doubt, swiftly won for another moment of supremacy. She was singing Away in A Manger, finding all alone a Christmas note that cut through any winter of the soul, a sword of light in a dark place, setting all the abbey aglow with the spirit of innocence.

It seemed to him then as if he were in some perfect Christmas tableau, promise fulfilled. All the sad things in life, the petty frustrations and littleness, and even real leaping evils were suspended, overmastered. Everyone was good after all; everything would come right in the end. Triviality, meanness, nastiness might beat back, wickedness have its day, but nothing, nothing could finally take this away for good.

To his embarrassment, Dom felt tears prick in his eyes. From what mixture of joy for good things, or simple relief that he'd got through, exhaustion, uncontained wonder at all that had happened and was happening around and to him, he could not quite work out, and never did; but none of that mattered.

*

Outside when the service had finished it was colder. Sleet was falling lightly as even the short December day's feeble warmth died. The congregation became staff and kids and parents and guests again, going their own way. The huge fleet of buses that had brought the children to the abbey were revving engines, steaming in the twilight. As soon as they were full, they roared off one by one in some precisely calculated order, headlights blazing into gathering gloom and rising fog.

Hennock was snapping at a child in the choir who had been talking and laughing during one of the longer hymns, but Mr Tring was everywhere beaming pride and satisfaction, whilst Rachel basked in the limelight she deserved. Even Mr Waseley had been there, turning up at the front, relaxed and ruddy-faced, hair under orders, seemingly relieved he had no more part to play but that of honoured passenger.

As he waited for his final charges to reach the coach, Dom could hear Mrs Tray talking at Ms Trippett. Both looked stressed.

'Yes, lovely of course, always is, though not quite as good as in 20-. Rachel. Wonderful. Pity not all staff appreciate her. I told you about that, didn't I? But we were all sitting too far back to see properly. I really think you should give more thought to who gets to sit where. There's one or two other issues I need to raise with you: now you're in your new role.'

Mr Walker, who happened to be standing next to Dom, was looking around with the air of a man who had seen this a thousand times. He too smiled when he heard Ms Trippett.

'When they finally take those two to the incinerator, they're going to find the jawbones completely worn away. No doubt Mrs Tray's next request will be to ask for the Abbey to be moved a little bit nearer her home so she does not have to travel so far.'

Dom, light of heart could not but laugh and was rewarded for his seeming encouragement by Mr Walker telling him in great detail just what a disaster Hennock and Trippett would be for the school and, once again, how glad he was he was not to be Dom's age, facing decades of a slow car crash, whatever he did, wherever he went.

Just as his last charge, none other than James, hurried on to the bus he was supervising, arm around yet another girl (they were late – duties he claimed), Dom heard a once familiar voice call out to him.

It was Tom Rymer. Dom remembered his email then.

He was clearly pleased to see Mr Greaves, had been looking out for him.

'I saw the coaches – wondered if you would be around,' said Tom, a little shy.

Ignoring the voices inside the coach, the driver's impatient revving of his engine, Dom stepped down and rather formally shook his hand.

'All right? How's it going? What are you doing here? Behaving I hope? Mrs Tenace's worried sick about you, running away or something?'

Tom looked sheepish for a second shaking his head.

'The twins said it was something today. Did you get my message? Home's just the same. Didn't work out at Abbey Academy, Sir. I think Mr Hennock saw to that, telling them about me, before I had chance. Is he here?'

'He's our new Head now,' replied Dom drily.

'You're joking? The twins said Waseley was going. I liked him, he was easy. Hennock'll have it in for you all. Never mind, Sir, you can always leave, like me!'

'Right,' said Dom.

'I bet he makes all teachers' lives shit. Staff have it worse than we do, don't they?' laughed Tom. 'How's Miss Oakley?' came next, in a way that implied more.

'Sir, we're ready,' came from the coach and a raucous chorus of 'why are we waiting?' struck up as the driver revved the engine once again.

The sleet had turned to rain, was coming down in thick drops, punching little holes in the once magical snow.

'Look, sorry, it's good to see you – but I have to leave. Why don't you come back, see us sometime, tell us what you are up to?'

'I don't think school would be happy to see me. I haven't got your address, Sir, only school's.'

'I shouldn't think that would cause you much of a problem,' said Dom, remembering. 'You still online king?'

Tom smiled, then looked serious, sad.

'It got me into trouble again. Hennock made sure they knew. He tried to get the police involved – he's such a nob, that guy. It was just a laugh. I haven't forgotten what he did to me, my mum. I'll never forget. He'd better watch out. Good to see you, Sir. Happy Christmas an' all that. Sorry for being a pain – and –yes, I will be in touch. I've got something for you, remember, Sir.'

'Same to you, Tom. Look after yourself. Forget Hennock. Let your mum – people know where you are. I'll tell Mrs Tenace. Where are you staying now?' replied Dom.

'With the Feltons. The twins know. She used to work at Hillview. She got out, Sir-.'

There was a moment's awkwardness. Tom looked lost, rather hopeless, but clearly did not have anything for him just then.

'Make something of yourself. Make a difference, Tom. Use your talents. But don't go hacking stuff – you'll get into real trouble.'

'Yes. Who knows what I can do!' said Tom, seriously. 'I'll be in touch – as for Hennock. I'll send you-.'

But before Dom could say more, the driver whose patience had worn as thin as Christmas tinsel, took matters into his own hands and the coach was lurching forward, doors still wide open. He had to grab at the rail, mount the steps quickly.

The last thing Dom saw as he took the last seat at the front was the frail figure of Tom standing there, caught for a second or two by sweeping headlights, then gone, vanished into darkness amidst the roar of the motor, the splashing of slush. Soon the coach was tearing past lingering shoppers and dancing lights, and then out in the countryside crossing the few empty black miles back to school.

CHAPTER FIFTY-SIX

WAITING

The last full day of term. Tomorrow was a half day of admin, clear up and goodbyes, but today remained to be filled with activities, odd meetings to be got through, films seen before, games and quizzes that just about kept the clock from stalling completely.

Dom was showing a film, but had promised the class games later, if he had the energy, when Alison knocked at the door, asked for a private word outside. He wondered what now.

'Sorry I could not be more supportive the last time we met. Some senior staff and I have been meeting with governors. They would like to see you – lunchtime – one-thirty sharp. Nothing to worry about. They want to hear what you have to say, as a new member of staff.'

'About?' said Dom.

Alison hesitated a moment.

'About how things have been done in the school, from your point of view, a beginner; mentoring, and Charles, the publicity we got in the local press. Whatever the rights and wrongs, it's not helping the school. They're still on the story. There may be more for them to dig up.'

'What do you mean?' said Dom.

'I'm not sure. The Acting Head is concerned.' She spoke the words Acting Head in a way that was curious.

Dom returned to the classroom, his mind even less engaged with the class. Surreptitiously, he checked his phone. There was a text from Emma that could only make him smile. There was also an email from Tom Rymer, this time on his private email. Dom wondered if he had been too friendly.

The message was short full of mistakes, disconcerting.

Nice to see you sir yesterday

am now staying at a friends so miss Tenace cant worry

happy Christmas

doc hennock's in for a suprise later…

Dom did not like the sound of that, wondered what Tom was up to, what trick was coming. Poor kid, but little fool too if he was really going to do something. He thought of Pig and the wheelie bin.

Dom wanted to hang onto his job. Dr Hennock would not be slow at tracing back links to him. It sounded as if the boy had run off again as well. He must let Alison know as he had yesterday. He emailed back, copied Alison in on it all.

Then, almost instantly, came one, much to his surprise, from Mr Royal.

Dominic

Hope the end of term jollies not dreadful. I could never bear it.

Walker is representing me at the meeting but I have presented evidence, caused quite a stir.

I think we have our friend.

CHMR

What was Charles up to as well he wondered?

Mad place.

The rest of the morning could not go quickly enough. He caught Emma briefly at lunchtime, brought her up to date.

'They didn't ask me,' she responded, momentarily put out, then, 'I suppose they've given up on me. The intrigue continues,' she smiled, then looked serious. 'Our secret is out. This place, honestly. Text me. Watch your back. Remember, last man in-.'

Dom bumped into Mike.

'Paul told me about you and Emma. Who'd have thought it? Still waters, eh? It'll never last. Good luck, mate.'

*

There was a large mirror outside the meeting room he had been summoned to, so Dom remembered, just in time, to tuck his shirt in. He could see an ironic side to it all despite the gravity of the school's situation, perhaps his own. Before you knew it, you were part of it all, but then probably too late, he thought, far too late to do anything.

Inside were Alison, Mr Walker, Mr Tring and Mr Jolson, two other senior staff, four men and one woman who must be governors. They were all sitting around a large table with a tray of sandwiches, a pot of coffee bottles and bottles of expensive spa water. The atmosphere seemed oddly relaxed, but Dom felt as if he were come for some kind of interview.

Mr Walker was holding forth about the hasty way some recent appointment had been made. He looked at Dom, lowering his voice theatrically.

Quickly Alison spoke to Dom aside, thanked him for his note about Tom, asked if he had heard any more. Social services had been in touch with school, his friends. The boy had disappeared once more. Alison said, business like, there was not much they could do.

Mr Walker had stopped talking. One of the others present was murmuring, 'This seems to be the pattern.'

Dom thought the governors didn't look terribly interested, given what was up.

Then Alison introduced him. They asked him about his experiences and concerns as newcomer to the school. They seemed to know a good deal, probed him hard on his mentoring, his Head of Department, visits to Waseley and Hennock. They even asked him what he thought about the proposed changes in the school, how it was all happening. He tried to be fair, told of his own mistakes. He made light of some of the things he had overheard, his suspicions, glossing over his more remarkable expeditions. Somewhere in it all he was trying to talk about not being listened to, about how people were treated, a need for better communication, wanting to be involved actually, disturbed at the speed and direction of what had been happening too fast, in the dark (literally he thought).

When he got to the end, Mr Walker nodded as if in approval.

'Thank you, Paul,' said one of the governors.

'Dominic,' corrected Alison with a roll of her eyes towards Dom.

'This all helps us build up a picture of staff morale in the school, consultation, what has been going on. All a storm in a tea cup, I suspect, but I wonder if you would mind answering one more question. It may seem strange, but we are asking everyone we meet out of, er, general curiosity. Did Dr Hennock offer you any kind of job or promotion at any stage of the term?'

Dom actually laughed.

'No!Although I suppose Dr Hennock did sort of offer me something when I last spoke to him.'

'What do you mean?' came back from several voices.

'We were having an argu-, disagreement. But I think he was on about a Leader of Drama.'

'And this disagreement, about-?'

Dom remembered Emma had told him to speak his mind.

'The way school was going, being managed, sometimes. Losing its heart, and soul. But I'd rather not say more. I feel bad talking about all this, behind people's backs. It's my first term. I'm not used to this. It's not what I expected in a school.'

Someone tutted. Someone cleared their throat.

The group looked at one another. Dom was gently and firmly dismissed.

As he was leaving, Mr Walker rushed after him into the corridor.

'Thank you, thank you,' he said in a loud voice and then much quieter looking around. 'Charles has told you we think we have Hennock. He's been up to all sorts – unprofessional behaviour, offering people jobs before he had been properly appointed, promising this and that, reading staff emails, negotiating behind Waseley's back. I can't say more – we need more proof, but there's all sorts. As long as this group of governors stands firm and we can prove what's been going on...'

'But-' began Dom.

'No time. Charles'll contact you. Hennock suspects what we're up to. We need to convince the rest of governors staff won't stand for it. Quite a few are on his side you see- money. Fools! It's always money in the end. Glad I'm retiring!' he ended.

Before Dom could say more, he was off back into the meeting. The door shut on him.

Dom wondered what authority the group had, how they could convene behind a new Head's back, only just appointed. He had no time for Hennock, but it all got worse and worse. He was glad to get out. The way things were developing did not please. He looked petty himself. No one looked grown up. And he was part of a school tearing itself to bits. And if the media continued on it-.

*

Emma was curious as to who had been there.

'That lot won't cut it! Jolson! They need more on Darren – not just a lot of people who feel put out, not listened to, or have long-standing grievances. Some of the governors have obviously been backing him. What are they playing at now? I bet they're just letting people let off steam. At least Alison takes it seriously. But Hennock, he won't waste time.'

Dom could only yearn for the end of term, but that meant a parting from Emma; and that mattered more than anything.

*

At last it was his final session of term! But just as Dom was about to begin some games, an urgent message arrived in his inbox, not from Charles as he hoped, detailing some successful outcome to the meeting, but from Katie. She wanted to see him immediately. She was sending someone to cover his lesson.

Yet again, nothing to worry about of course.

Dom thought rapidly. Ms Trippett could only be acting for Dr Hennock. Dom's name would have featured in reports, and with his track record, recent argument.

He told the class he was going to have to leave, another teacher would come but he was sure they would do something fun too. They were to be respectful, remember themselves.

Groans.

'You been lookin' at your phone, Sir, we get done for that.'

'You been sacked, Sir?'

'Sacked, again!' came the inevitable cheeky retort.

'With a bit of luck, then I don't have to listen to you anymore.'

But then Mrs Dot was arriving. Who could possibly be deploying her in actual academic lessons, especially at this stage in term, and in Dr Hennock's lair? Was there no one else?

The class were divided between realising that she would never be able to control them so it would all be a waste of time, and a sense of opportunity for some well earned end of term sport.

Just before he left her, or left her to them, she asked for a quick word outside.

'I've been asked to resign,' she told him.

Dom suddenly noticed how pale she was looking, her eyes red.

'I wanted to tell you. You've always been so kind, nice, even when you were doing your play, and I went a bit wrong. I shall miss it all, am sorry to be going, loved it here. All these years. But Dr Hennock has to make changes, for the good of the place, the good of the school; yes that's it, the good of the school.'

There was a huge crash from Dr Hennock's classroom. She shot off to do her duty, which she always did, however much they ragged or taunted. Battle was swiftly joined. The door, now in the control of the class, slammed and locked shut on chaos.

Dom stood for a moment feeling wretched, for her, for what he guessed must be following for him. He wasn't so consumed with his own likely demise as to feel a deal of remorse for his colleague. He thought how they all mocked her, himself included, trashed her simple kindness, good intentions, delighting in her mistakes. But then he was off, speeding down the corridors in search of Ms Trippett. Mrs Dot had forgotten where Katie said she would be.

He rushed across to the admin block, suddenly hot and stifling despite the nipping air outside. He had thought all his experiences might have taught him some equanimity. But he could feel his heart pounding, his face flushing, a thousand anxious thoughts attacking, as he mounted the stairs to Hennock's old office.

When he reached the top, Katie was waiting to lead him on. Dom was ushered in past a new gleaming sign: a new title for a new age.

Dr Darren Hennock.

Master

Katie closed the door firmly behind him, smiling.

He was in the lion's den once more, knowing too much, nowhere to hide. This must be it now: not even time to finish his very last lesson.

CHAPTER FIFTY-SEVEN

SAYING NO

Dr Hennock was standing with his back to the door, looking out of the window, and for a second when he turned around, he looked different, drawn, even worried Dom thought.

Then he smiled his smile.

Dom thought of all the miles he had gone since they had first met.

'Ah, Dom,' began Hennock. 'Good to see you.'

He crossed to him, patted Dom on the back.

'You must be tired – end of your first term. Sit down, please.'

Dom nodded, wondering what game Hennock was playing today.

'I think you understand that we are all, and have been, under a certain degree of pressure at the moment. We face many challenges-.

He paused. Dom kept silent.

'I have spoken a few times to Alison in the last day or two about... staff morale. I think you know. She feels, strongly, that some of us carrying the burden of leadership have, perhaps, had to be-. You can imagine the decisions needing to be made, efforts behind the scenes. The Head being-leaving, and so on. No leader facing such stark choices, such a difficult scenario, could have behaved in any other way at such a time. People have had to be challenged, upset even; conversations had, some that should have happened years ago, to move things on. You understand. But, well, I wanted to see if we, at least, could, somehow, find a way forward. The school is moving on. We – both, need to move on.'

Dom was confused, bewildered by the tone: what was really coming?

'However much you have been at fault, all your mistakes, we have come to value your contribution, aspects of it – for all it's been a shaky start. We have made allowances, held back because there have been signs of *potential*.

'Indeed, in some areas of school, particularly with some of the oddballs we attract here – you have, Alison believes, built up something of a following.'

Dom wanted to laugh, especially at that. Hennock was struggling to say something nice; perhaps that was the way you prepared the ground for dismissal. Alison had got at him, or the governors. When, however, was the sting in the tail coming?

'What are you doing over the break, something nice?' continued Hennock.

Dom found this harder to deal with than anything.

'Well, going to my parents for Christmas. Then seeing friends and, er, I hope, Emma.'

'Ah, Emma!' said Hennock. 'I'm glad we've had the benefit of her this term, even if, like you, she has taken time finding her feet. I'm sure she has helped you. In it together; sharing each others' little woes. Her business like attitude to things is an example to learn from, Dom, in the world we find ourselves.'

Dom nodded, wondering why this hypocrisy was worse than his unpleasantness, but he made no reply. He had begun to learn the value of silence in adult games.

'Now Dom, our school faces tough choices. If we play this right, seize our opportunity for independence, my plans materialise, we have a bright future. But in the short term. We have to make choices – staffing. To put it simply, we need to let some staff go, enable them to move on, develop careers, elsewhere.'

Here it comes he thought. Perhaps all his niceness was another form of bullying, savouring someone's discomfort.

Dom knew already how he was going to reply.

'We also still need to fill vacancies. This is why I wanted to see you. I hinted at things before in our last conversation. Now I have a specific proposal. I offered your friend Paul a special role in the boarding house. I wonder if you are up for a challenge too, to take on an enhanced role – beginning this very next September in your case, filling Mr Royal's shoes in part.

'In short I want you on the team, Dominic, but fully on board. I'm not a man to dwell on past idiocies. To get to the point, I think you could fill something of a role as subject leader in drama. Not exactly an important one you understand, you're so young – but we need someone to give that side of things a lift. You've got energy, some talent. With more experience, organisation...There will be money for better facilities one day if things work out. More in your own pocket too.'

'You see, our intention is to not to have to replace Mr Royal at all, but get other staff to take on a few of his little jobs. There'll be more teaching for you anyway, but you're young.

'We would normally advertise, but, you of all people know how trying it is to take on people with limited experience at this school.'

Dom continued to listen, bemused, mistrusting every word.

'Pleased? I can see you are. You looked interested last time, but you were- emotional then... one of the things you've got to learn, Dom. Things are hard when we get ourselves overtired. The stresses of term, something you need to learn to cope with. And upsets over Charles. He let you down didn't he? But you've put all that behind you.

'Now, whilst you take my offer in, have a think. It's only fair that I say that there are things we would hope for in return, expectations. You know me: completely straightforward, telling it as it is, as I have done with the staff. Loyalty, trust: those are our secret weapons in business, in school, in life – with children, with staff.'

He fixed his gaze, his smile on Dom.

'I must have the complete support of those who work for me.'

Dom found it hard to believe, even with all his recent experience, that someone who had worked covertly to undermine the whole basis of the school, got rid of some of his colleagues in an underhand, brutal way, apparently proposed deals to anyone who would dance to his tune, was now preaching trust.

But Hennock continued.

'My only interest is the good future of the school. If we are to succeed-.

Hennock paused, searching Dom's face. Dom said nothing.

'If you come with us, Dominic, the sky's the limit, for the school, for you. But, I repeat, absolute loyalty is key. Now, if, for example, if I needed some informal information from you on a member of staff, or pupil even-. Not that I ever would really have to employ such a procedure if the loyalty I talk of was understood. But if, *if* I did-. Let me give you an instance. Remember that boy who left here, what was his name, Rommer, Rymer? Yes, Tom Rymer, an IT geek, but talented if a pest – you remember. He hacked your emails, didn't he? Well, no one's bothered about that, but I recall him looking at important staff emails,perhaps even mine. I can't quite recall what. The point is, in such instances, we would know where your loyalty lay, if he had had, purely accidently, access to some confidential school data, for example?

'You would know which side you were on wouldn't you? I'm sure he didn't or would be too young, to understand what he had found, its significance, but I would know where your loyalty lay if I needed to know something like that?'

He smiled, his repetitions speaking volumes. Dom nodded, but in understanding not agreement.

'Good to see you taking this in a more mature way, Dominic. *For the good of the school.* We all have to remember that.'

Dom stared back, clear that Hennock, for all his talk, was wondering what Rymer might have found all those weeks ago, what he, even Dom might know.

He spoke at last, carefully, nonchalantly, feeling his way, quite grown up, himself, in approach.

'Tom Rymer? Alison was worried about him. He keeps running away. I saw him briefly at the carol concert, but – he did not say much, except he wasn't happy – his new place. I don't know much more than that, poor lad.'

'I'm not interested in the boy's welfare: he's off our hands, not our problem anymore. No-,' said Hennock, suddenly impatient.

'No, no. It's a question of – that hacking business – what may damage the school's future. That's all that concerns me. I-, we've had problems with Royal, Charles, getting emotional, talking to the media. Very unprofessional, very bad for the school. Disloyalty after all those years. Unbelievable really, after all my support. To be so petty...

'But, to get to the heart of the matter, if you could help, with Tom: what he knows. You know what these media hounds are; well, I would see that as a sign that you were up to the task of taking on more responsibility. That the school could have confidence in you, where your heart lies. I would do all I could to ease your way to promotion. One good turn-

'If, however, on the other hand, you could not help in such a matter. If we felt your loyalties lay only to some idea of yourself.We have to make cuts, in staffing. I prefer to call them savings. Savings is our real end, saving to tide us over our period of transition and then spend on better things, investing in a better future: your department, perhaps. You'd like that wouldn't you? I had hoped Emma- but, well you know all about that. Who better?'

Hennock laughed.

Whilst Hennock was talking away, Dom's mind was working. Hennock's file had been a chimera. The real truths of Dr Hennock's plotting and plans must be recorded in some form in email trails. And there must have been many things that Hennock had wanted to keep from his colleagues as he schemed and planned. And Rymer had had access. What might he have found? Was Hennock trying to bribe Dom into silence over something, or imagining what he knew was incriminating in some way?

The risible thing was that Dom did not know exactly what Tom might have seen, had or knew, or quite what Hennock feared. If he'd had time, if he'd been a different kind of person, he could have used this position of advantage, could still maybe use it. But amidst a tumult of thoughts and feelings, Dom felt mostly simple recoil and disgust. The boy had been a pest, pathetic really. But it was a mischief born of frustration not malice, not some deep plot to steal information about schemes which he would never be interested in, begin to understand.

Hennock, however.

'Dr Hennock,' he began.

'Oh, please,' said Hennock with that smile, 'first names now, after all it's the end of term.'

Dom took a deep breath, standing up as if to leave, emotions welling, but determined.

'Agreed?' cried Hennock, misunderstanding Dom getting up. 'Let's shake on it!'

'Darren, you have had a difficult time with me, and other new staff, and all the stuff you have been dealing with. I am sorry about that; but as for your offer, I think I owe it to Mr Royal, at the very least, to say no. I'd love to do something like that one day, but I'm not ready yet, you know that, better than most. And I think I know why you are doing this, asking me. You talk of the school and loyalty but it's loyalty to you you want, isn't it, whatever's going on. What about trust, real trust? Isn't that the important thing?'

Hennock broke in, irritated.

'No, no! Here you go again. You throw back words loyalty, trust, as if they're abstract concepts, detached from circumstance; some moral token you think you and only you wear. I'm disappointed, disappointed, Dominic. Your generation! Moral posturing, self indulgence. It's arrogance. I know things about the school you can never know, never understand. I've warned you before, if you take your own line, go your own way, if we all do that, we just weaken the school, trash plans for its future, turn our back on the facts of our situation.'

'Plans?! Facts!' Dom interrupted. 'Look at this independence idea! Isn't it a delusion in the world we live in today? Setting people against each other. Beggar my neighbour! Some ridiculous race to the bottom. Just look, look outside, beyond all this. Selling the Cloud for housing for example. That will destroy something that can never be replaced. Is that really a price worth paying, what education is all about, money?'

'A nimby! At your age! So that's all you're concerned about: the picturesque! That matters more than homes, some scrubland more than our school's future, or real, practical opportunities for children?'

'No. You know that's not what I mean,' cried Dom. 'It's respect, respect for the world around us, nature, the way it is, the way people should live, be. You talk of things like trust and loyalty, but look at your plans, your *facts*. It's all about money, isn't it. It's not what matters most in a school, or anywhere. It's what we do in it, what we make of others, ourselves, better ways of living our lives, a culture-'

'I'm afraid you must leave student politics, the school boy behind.'

But Dom was not listening any more.

'And as for Rymer. There's a good example, a perfect example of what matters, and it isn't money. Isn't our first duty to try to help, protect a lad like that who did stupid stuff, probably because he was never supported enough. Never shown anything better. It's caring, really caring that matters: can't you see? Do you care about what's happened to him, or just what he might do? I've never seen any of the emails he hacked from you: that's what this is all about isn't it? I've no idea what he has or where he is, what he knows. But if I did and he had found something to your disadvantage, or mine or anyone's –'

'Now just a minute-'

'I've said I'm sorry, a thousand times; and I am: sorry you think so little of me, my generation as you call it. Perhaps we are selfish, a my truth first lot, but I was brought up to believe that life was about trying to do the right thing, even when we can't know it easily. You talk trust and loyalty, but the words mean nothing to you. Frankly, I'd rather leave school than it continued like that-.'

Dom stopped, out of breath, his face flushed.

Hennock looked at him for a few moments. Then he spoke, slowly at first.

'And this is the response I get after all my generosity to you!'

'So. My instincts have been right all along. You do need to grow up. As for the rest of your comments-.You could have said yes – easily, Dominic, made something of yourself. You still could. But choose your own way. So be it. As for Master Rymer, it may well be that the police become interested in his withholding of information, stolen data; and yours. What about your potential complicity in such a crime? Hadn't thought that through either, have you? How would that look, a criminal record for him, and for you.

'Go away. Calm down! I'm leaving the door open, despite your attitude. But this will be your last chance, your very last chance As for your concerns: *A bit of building on the Cloud.* Dominic!'

Hennock shook his head.

But Dom would hear no more. He drew himself up. Another car crash, but better to lose it all than continue like this.

'I've said my piece. I'm sorry if I'm rude, and you think so little of what I'm trying to say. But no, *no* to whatever you are on about; and no means no, in my world, to my generation, even if, thank God, it isn't a very grown up one.'

He turned, walked out.

He found he was shaking slightly, but he kept on walking, walking away. He'd done it now, he was sure; but there were more important things in life. *No!* That much he'd learnt at least.

His phone pinged. It was the long awaited email from Mr Royal. Dom's eyes shot through it.

Meeting ended without conclusion: not enough evidence for governors to pin anything of substance on Hennock re his handling of staff etc.

They lack the balls, not the proof, to do what is right. They can't afford more divisions in the school. Upside down world!

Some talk of financial compensation for me at least. I'll take it, I need to, but I would prefer my self-respect back.

Sorry about all this, for the school, for Hillview, for you more than me, and for those who come after. Watch your step in these hard times. Better to have a job than none at all.

Hennock and his like won't succeed in the end. They can't. They haven't imagination.

*

All Dom had left was nothing but a faint hope that some kind of further revelations as to the nature of Hennock's character, the lengths he was prepared to go to get his way, lay out there – in a file, in something. But it was the slenderest of chances, and would anyone ever act?

Bitterly he registered a sense of frustrating helplessness before injustice. Maybe this little play in this little place was all overblown, but the greedy ways of the world drove hard and arrogantly by whatever made up the better side of human nature here. And he'd been told to grow up.

He began to descend the steps that led up to Hennock's office: down, down, down, back to his first day, his first steps.

Katie, who must have been on watch, came running.

'Did you accept?' she cried after him, smiling, coming close, searching his face as ever. 'I knew you would, now that Emma is staying.'

'*What?*' cried Dom.

'Working under Emma as your subject leader, you wouldn't say no. I knew she'd change her mind, change yours. Surprised? Don't say you didn't know about Emma. She would have told you.'

Then, as she became sure he did not know, her interest seemed to increase.

'Didn't she tell you, Dominic? Emma is your new subject leader. She's staying on. I knew she would in the end. Her former boyfriend is relocating to the area, but it's the offer that's turned her.

'Why, Dominic, we thought you would be delighted.'

CHAPTER FIFTY-EIGHT

ONLY SKY ABOVE

'But is it true? Why didn't you tell me?' Dom demanded.

Whether it was some inevitable drop after all the excitement of the last days, or a feeling of disappointment, even betrayal, Dom did not know; but he was his feelings.

'I *was* going to tell you. I've not signed anything. I need to think about it more. I thought you would be pleased, really pleased,' cried Emma, upset.

'Of course I'm pleased. I'm over the moon for you, for me, if I've still got a job, the school. But it hurts – I found out from, from someone else.'

'I did say I'd had an offer. They came back again, an even better one. They're desperate for someone with experience, who's here now, who could start work straight away. It was Alison in the end – not Hennock's money. She practically begged. They needed a verbal decision, but I've not signed anything. I'm still thinking.'

'You could have mentioned it, discussed it with me, talked to me about it.'

'I wanted to tell you, but, I'm not definite yet, honest. Oh, come on, if that's all it is. You're not jealous are you?'

'*Jealous!* Oh for God's sake, Emma. Hennock's just been trying stuff on me, offering me something – until I realised what he was up to. I'm not ready, even if- and the more I see of things. But you, you've gone against everything you said just as I've thrown everything away.'

'Oh, Dom, don't be ridiculous. Even you can't get sacked twice in the space of two days. You heard Alison.'

'You weren't in the meeting.'

'What have you said now?'

'It doesn't matter,' said Dom wrenching a chair towards him noisily, and then sitting down, putting his head in his hands. After a moment he spoke again, not looking at her.

'What's the real reason you're staying? Have you told me everything?'

'What do you mean? I've told you. What more is there to say? I said, I thought you would be really pleased.'

'It doesn't matter now,' said Dom, all the turns of the term twisting inside him. He paused, fighting words he wanted to say. 'But it seems I can't completely trust anyone.'

'O, Dom. Don't be silly: making all this out of nothing. Just because-. The odds are I won't stay, you know that, better than anyone. We talked before.'

'Then why trust Katie with your decision first and everyone else but me?'

'I didn't say anything to her! You can't turn this into something about trust, that's absurd. I made it clear to Alison, Hennock too, that if, *if* I stay things would have to change. I'm no push over, Dom, you know me.'

'Do I? We are more than just friends, aren't we?'

'What do you mean now?'

'I've always had your back. All the time I've been here. I'd like to think -. Is there anything else I need to find out the hard way?'

Emma turned away, angry then.

'Stop feeling sorry for yourself...just because you think the world we live in should be something it isn't! Don't *you* trust *me*, isn't that the problem? Anyway, none of this means

I won't take my own decisions, I have to run things by you all the time. I said that to you, the other night. And I don't want you to rely on me,' cried Emma.

'I'm not saying that but, well I thought you hated the crap that was going on. I thought you meant it, meant what you said, *cared.*'

He ran his hands through his hair putting his face in his hands once more.

'I wish-'

'You're overreacting. If you could see yourself. You've had a bad time with Hennock'

'No, loved every minute of it.'

'And now you're being sarcastic, very clever.'

'I expected it, from him.'

'And what's that supposed to mean?'

'Hennock wanted me to be some kind of subject leader for drama. *I* refused.'

'Refused?'

'Yes, refused. It's all wrong –. It's Charles too, after all he's-. It's some ploy to get people on board that don't dare rock the boat, approve his plans and schemes, be completely loyal whatever, not that I've exactly been Mr Revolutionary so far in this crazy place.'

'You've got some ridiculous idea I've betrayed my principles, any principles, I suppose. I'm sorry if I've upset you, but you're being silly. The offer was exceptional, especially after all my hesitations, right at the end of term.'

Dom looked at her, turned away again. Only resentment made sense.

'Meanwhile, I get the sack, or threatened with it.'

'Is this about me or you? It wasn't, isn't how you think. Things are never black and white, you have to compromise. I told you that too. We need to accept that both of us.'

Dom looked at her for a while.

'How is it then?' he said quietly.

There was a long pause.

Then he stood up.

'I need to get out of here, clear my head. I'm sorry. I know I'm being silly, naive, or whatever you call it, but-. There's this end of term party thing later. If you're still going I suppose I can see you at that. Before we go our separate ways tomorrow.'

'Oh, Dom, don't be silly. Don't go, Dom, I want to hear what happened.'

'Not now, not here. Give me some space, time. I must think things through. And you don't need me.'

'*Dom!* Aren't you being-'

'Immature?' he shook his head. 'I don't think I'm alone in that in this place. What was it Alison said all those weeks ago: we never leave the playground.'

Emma paused, then coldly continued, turning away.

'Mrs Dot was looking for you. She was covering a class: yours – Hennock's room. There was some incident – damage. Usual Hillview classroom management. I couldn't get much sense out of her. You know what she's like.'

'That's all I need. She can't do anything right. She's a complete f-ing nightmare,' cried Dom, then remembered she had just been sacked.

Emma looked at him for a moment.

'That's harsh. You've said yourself she's a kind soul. Isn't that what matters? I thought it was all about sensitivity; or is it only yours? You've changed. You wouldn't have said anything like that a few weeks ago, about her, or Katie. Or to me.'

'She's been sacked actually. The way of business. I assumed you'd approve.'

Dom looked at her, and then turned and went out, outside, into the failing cold December day, all the events of the term whirling in his head, not knowing at first where he was going.

After a while he found himself making for the Cloud.

His feet were soon slipping and sliding on patches of thaw and frost as he made his ascent, the chill air biting, the cold water seeping into his shoes, his work shoes; but he was oblivious, quite separate from everything, wrapped up in his little storm.

Eventually he reached the top. As so often before, exercise steadied him.

Finally, he stopped, as the last light of the sun slipped over the horizon. The frost was winning its battle, fastening its grip once more on a feeble thaw.

He shivered at it all.

He wondered if there really had once been a settlement on top of the hill. He remembered the day James had showed him round in September sunshine, his thoughts of buried treasure, – romantic stuff. He didn't believe that any more. The real mystery was how on earth its ancient inhabitants survived the cruel winters in the past. How had they endured, the struggle to keep alive, the fearful scanning of horizons for enemies hungry for what they had, the illnesses that beset them, and for those who survived that, the hopeless attrition of age: how tough life must have been, how cruel its way.

He told himself he had nothing to complain of in comparison, but confidence had gone. Embarrassment at his own dramatics hurt too. He wasn't making much of a hero, stropping off. But what he'd seen in his own little world was disturbing, even if he was just another of Mr Walker's snowflakes.

He looked around again, wondering if much made any sense. The ancient struggle to understand might endure, but beyond that? He looked up at the vastness of the night, the wide dark empty skies weighed down with unanswered questions, a few hard stars beginning to appear, twinkling – promising what?

Stars! The broken glass of heaven someone had called them. Beyond that – darkness, silence.

He was shivering even more. The light was so quickly gone and long night stretched forever at this time of year: how many hours of darkness there were. He scanned the land around. There lay the distant suburbs of Wellsway, lapping greedily up the lower slopes. Soon they would advance further under Hennock's plans, a symptom of malaise, not progress. Greedy humanity living the wrong way. They would spread right around, all over the hill, smother nature, identical little houses, the same identical, disappointing lives boxed in.

Hennock had mocked his little cares for the natural world, but it was all of a piece. Didn't he see what he was doing was only the mean part of bigger evils?

He might be moody, naive, immature, but there was substance in the wrongs he saw at work, not just personal grievance, delusions. There had been from the start.

Education. It was supposed to inspire, uplift– but even here, in Hillview, a cradle of futures, of understanding and knowledge, how easy came the falls: distraction from what mattered; feeble focus on the right, the good things; authority that never clearly called out better ways. It didn't need big evils to do harm, twist everything good into less than what might be.

He thought of the zebra, caught in the jaws of the lion. He felt helpless, the naive young teacher fronting a bad class who were all your world: first ragged in discipline; then pushing boundaries idly for the sake of it; finally driven by some collective force you could not control, grasp, into sheer unreason, a will to disintegration, blindly intent on self-destruction.

He looked out longingly towards the distant sea, but it was a darkening grey shadow on a blurred horizon, cold and bleak, even apocalyptic, in the December twilight.

Nothing came that way. No comfort there. In his tired heart, people, him too, had become mere egos, silly selfish animals; promises of perfection, something better- vanity, stupid illusions.

*

It was his job, his charges, the children, perhaps, that pulled him back, out of himself, as they had often before, from that first day on, without him quite realising. That and thoughts of his family, friends, Emma.

He had his duties, his mission, his responsibilities, directly in his case to those he taught – whatever school, whatever world. The children: however much some, sometimes, were maddening, thoughtless, stupid, lazy, cruel, they should have better. They were young, needed to be allowed to grow and flourish, persuaded to take their good chances. Their passions burnt for a better world. They deserved something more.

*

He started to make his way home, slipping and sliding, shoes caked with mud and snow, laces trailing – like some weary school boy. He stooped to tie them, noticing he had odd socks on again – how many times this term, despite all admonition.

Mismatching socks! Feet of clay!

That made him smile.

He thought of Mrs Tombs struggling eternally with all that laundry, her relentless, nagging cry, not just to everyone else but to him too: *pin your socks together*. And despite everything he had built in his mind he laughed then, laughed out loud as the picture in his fancy grew until she became a crazy symbol, a refuge of reason and sense, battling away to hold things together whilst everyone else, him included, carelessly let all slip, unless forcibly stopped.

Gradually he thought more kindly of things, and himself. Dom, the fearful September child, full of wild but hopeful dreams, how tested he had been, yet resilient too in ways he could not have imagined, believed once, become almost another person now.

Be your own redemption, at least in part, or be nothing, he told himself. Context was part excuse, part explanation, part cause, but never all. No God, no state, no utopia, such as Joe might envision, would deliver if you did not try yourself.

And work *was* that. Education: to empathy and kindness, big and small, or the world become only Hennocks, or only Doms; monsters who drove arrogantly their own way, blind to everyone else, thinking they were what the world was about. And if kindness would fail a million times, because of what we were, it could still triumph in the end because it was the only truly creative thing.

But empathy was only part, perhaps the easy part – because education was responsibility too – *response* for those around you, but equally from yourself, what you were, good and bad.

So – *Pin your socks together.*

His thoughts enlarged. All these characters on his stage: they were himself in some way, his imagination. They were him: the good, the bad. In some way, he had made them as surely as he made himself: and if that were so, there were choices, possibilities, always.

*

He had his thoughts better marshalled now, confidence returning. Even if things would always fall, like on that very first day, or today, they could come back.

He must go – back to work, for all its ups and downs; back to the life that was, not a dream that wasn't, not yet anyway. Back too, to Emma, who spanned reality and imagination so perplexingly, unfathomably, and was for always in his feelings.

He hurried then. The woods were too dark and deep for him now, thinking about the last time he had been up there at night! That strange encounter he had had on the hill the night he had tracked Hennock. That imaginary figure – the shock! It might have been real. Perhaps it had been, in some way.

Like a flash forgotten in his self-preoccupation, came back to him the thought of Rymer and Hennock's fears. If he had really hacked significant information, as Hennock seemed genuinely to fear, there might be possibilities in that. The boy had been in enough trouble already in his life. Dom would do nothing to compromise him in any sense further, but what he may have found...

He tried to remember all they had been told on teaching practice and induction about emails, a school's rights and ownership, and slowly, the makings of a plan began to stir. If only he had had his phone with him as he usually did.

He raced the last mile back to campus.

So, the staff group had failed, but there were other trails. Something out there.

He must find Alison immediately.

Would he be in time?

CHAPTER FIFTY-NINE

CHRISTMAS PARTY

Dom could not find the words he really wanted to say to Emma when back with her; but he needed someone to run his plan by. It was an excuse to see her, be with her, at least for a time, whatever the future, whatever was happening.

'She'll never agree,' said Emma.

'I don't see why not – she was part of that committee. It keeps Rymer out of things – gives her leverage. It's all school practice.'

'Are you sure? Is it legal?'

'No idea. But I think so. School emails are ultimately school property. The problem might be if Hennock has used a private email. You're not supposed to. He's not stupid; but he is arrogant. Probably thinks he's above all this. He's worried about something.'

'Won't he have deleted them?'

'They're all automatically copied here for the leadership team – someone said in a safeguarding meeting; and then there's Rymer; he accessed them without knowing what he was on to. He has something. Hennock's scared.'

'Don't underestimate Darren, he'll know that too.'

'He can't wipe Alison's emails.'

'Sure? And who's going to have time to wade through all that and why hasn't she anyway?'

'Too many, too busy. Not sure someone of her generation would think of it, or think to do it. They may have been searching for other stuff, more recent – him offering jobs to some, not others, before his appointment, contracts, bribes. Not plans weeks ago.'

Dom paused a moment, looking at Emma; she looked away.

'I have a rough idea of when he hacked them. If there's something-.'

'It's a wild shot. He's unlikely to have left anything of importance she could see at any point. I suppose there might be something. Young Sherlock again.'

'Hm. If there's anything, it might slow Hennock's progress at least.'

There was a pause.

'But you Dom? Is this you? And me, if I decide to stay, or go? I don't want Hillview to come between us, but-.'

What could he say, a thousand things, leaping hopes, twisting doubts, embarrassment at himself, nothing.

'You can't mess the school about any longer. I'll respect your decision; but I do care, care very much what you do. I'm sorry if it didn't come out-. It's all confused. I must see Alison.'

He paused a moment, passion and resentment hand in hand.

Then he remembered he needed to grow up, school himself: this was what was.

'You're still coming to the kids' do this evening, aren't you?'

'Why not?' she replied.

They parted, nothing resolved.

*

Alison was annoyed, upset.

'Dom! What are you asking of me? It's extraordinary – even by the standards of the last few days. What are we all becoming, getting ourselves into? This is supposed to be about the future good of a school. I'm astonished, shocked such a suggestion should ever come my way especially from you.'

Dom had managed to get in to see her, heart in mouth, although she was so busy. She was wearing specs. He'd never seen them before. Here he was heaping more on her.

'And even if I thought it right to do, do you know how many emails this place generates, even when you know what you're looking for.

'This is all highly irregular – to put it mildly, hunting through a colleague's past emails on the off chance there is something there that might reveal unprofessional conduct, illegal dealings all on the basis of something a boy, a known liar, might have mistakenly seen half a term ago. Are you sure imagination isn't running away with you again? We did talk about gossip earlier this term.'

'And look what happened!' Dom interrupted.

'That was all the result of a long and difficult inquiry into Charles's unprofessional conduct, not wild speculation about a key member of the management team.'

'Then what was that meeting all about?' Dom came back.

Alison paused, looking awkward.

'Are you sure this is not just personal, the end of term in this hothouse, your first term? It's not been easy for any of us. It's like one of those novels you teach. And there is something else, too, a protocol that we sign up to – if someone needs to access others' emails, he or she has to inform the team. It's safeguarding, protecting ourselves, our professionalism, privacy, what's left of it.'

'But if we don't try! At least buy time so we can think this through properly. You know better than most the consequences.'

Alison sighed deeply again.

'I am not used to this. Look what progress has brought us. Technology making monsters of us. And Dr Hennock, I can't believe-' she pulled back. 'He'd know I've been investigating. Places like this work on trust. And must we resort to this, trust stuff that is just loose without real ownership or control, something said, written yesterday, now forever as if it's some Gospel? I spend half my time dealing with crap on social media, what it's doing. Look at what you'd have me do! Look at poor Rymer, lost to our brave new world already. We don't want him involved.'

Dom, remembering his self-righteous speech to Hennock, felt her words keenly. At least he still cared what she said, he thought, but this course of action seemed a lesser evil.

There was a pause whilst they both looked rather helplessly at the other.

'But hasn't Dr Hennock damaged trust, loyalty already; and there's loyalty and loyalty,' said Dom finally.

Alison looked at him.

'You know I can't comment. I didn't somehow think you were-. You seemed so young, so innocent when you started, a refreshing change. And if I'm honest, you have little to lose, I – a lifetime.'

Dom weighed her words: but he was sure now of himself.

'If you must know, Dr Hennock has already hinted my job is on the line.'

'Oh, nonsense, I told you. That's just Darren, stress. *He never meant all this,*' began Alison.

'But the school?' pressed Dom. 'My job, I don't matter that much, but If we don't do something, you must know where things will end. You told us how much we all owe this place remember.'

Alison looked at him. She shook her head.

Then she took off her specs, rubbing her eyes, sighing.

'Give me the dates. I'm not committing to anything; and this conversation has never taken place. As if I haven't enough to do, young man. I wouldn't even know what I was looking for, or want to. I wish it would all go away.'

Then Dom could only wait and see.

He wandered back to his study through the dark feeling slightly sick, all that grim nonsense on the hill, his meeting with Alison, and the thing he most cared about, Emma: everything muddle again.

There were a few pupils about. They would be preparing for the Christmas party: a meal and a dance, all staff invited. It would have been fun, they had put him on a table with Emma, but-. He would get through the evening, and then school would be done with, whatever its future, or his and Emma's.

Time dragged. No news from anyone, except his parents back from their trip, wondering when they were going to see him home again.

He washed, showered, put on his best suit. The kids wanted it formal, 'grown up'. He looked hard at himself in the mirror. There were no more grey hairs. He could still pass as one of the sixth formers. But he felt older, much older.

He stared for a while, wondering for a moment who he was playing now, how life had taken hold of him. But he must keep schooling himself. Now he was in there, with all the rest, pitching and tossing like some boat battered around by seas of things imperfect. And no better than the rest; and why should he be? Mr Royal had said something to him just a few days before. The biggest battle in life is with ourselves.

But what was was.

Best just go and enjoy himself he thought, see what happens. He'd done all he could in his own world and in the wider world of Hillview to set what he could right. Things must take their course.

*

The Christmas Feast as it was known, open to the top end of the school, turned out to be a surprising tonic to all the staff who were there. Younger pupils went on an outing to a panto accompanied by staff armed with arrays of painkillers.

The children put their best feet forward and, with the promise of Christmas and freedom, were determined to have a good time, mostly behave. The food was unusually excellent. Mrs Dot had been banned; Mrs Tray, interfering to the last, had insisted on professional caterers. It was a real Christmas meal just right for winter, replete with satisfying choices for all, even a delightful vegan only option. Mr Walker nearly spoilt that by labelling such delights culinary *wokery; insipid vegetable vomit fit only for anorexics* he was overheard saying. Rachel led a move to cancel him. Mr Walker swiftly claimed he was the real victim, however: his contexts, his age, gender. He needed sympathetic understanding, he claimed, having grown up at a time when such delicious novelties were only available to the privileged few who could indulge in fussy food.

The argument boiled ferociously and absurdly away across campus and on social media for quite half an hour. There was nearly a boycott, but he was forgiven in the end when he promised to go vegan for the evening. Rachel, however, continued to demand further action, until Alison was summoned. She told her that everyone's views deserved at least a hearing, that people did not always mean quite what they said, and that anyway, there was a huge difference between always taking things personally and a deliberate personal slur. Rachel replied that he was a bigoted old man who was not fit to teach – and he smelt, only settling to her meal when charmed by Mr Tring plying her with more wine than was strictly allowed.

But whatever anyone ended up eating or drinking, there was more than enough to absorb everyone happily for a good while. Crackers were pulled, whistles screeched out, party poppers exploded and silly hats were stuffed on heads, particularly hard on teachers' who looked suitably ridiculous, if half human, for the rest of the evening. There were so many cheap plastic instruments in the crackers that a cacophony of sound soon threatened to deafen all the over twenties until Mr Tring, increasingly unable to hear anything at all, even from his beloved Rachel, finally blew a fuse for the last time that term, insisting on them being set down before mass insanity overcame the poor bloody staff.

Increasingly raunchy versions of famous Christmas carols took their place until Dr Hennock ordered a halt. To make up, there were several food fights largely undetected by senior staff until Hennock once more intervened before departing. He was quite unaware of a crushed sprout, splodge of rich gravy,and bread sauce adhering to the seat of a pair of expensive new trousers and jacket. He swept off early leaving others to take charge, do the clearing up.

Of Alison there was no further sign. The whole thing was managed by Mike. He had been clobbered with the organisation before he remembered to say no. But, young and sporty he had a natural following and enough laissez faire to make him a popular master of ceremonies. Dom was grudgingly impressed; he really knew how to do it, for a sports teacher.

Paul was there, too, on a table with a crowd of earnest pupil admirers. He had been having meetings with

Hennock, instructing him on what he should do now with their school – rather to the older man's surprise. He'd hoped his appointment would ensure he shut up, got on with it. He was now happily soaking in as much gossip as possible from the school's deep state, but also being teased mercilessly for his continuing enthusiasms for deputy heads, past and particularly present.

For all the high spirits however, behaviour stayed on side. Only Andy smuggled in extra alcohol, and some illegal vapes. No one found out until afterwards, when he was sick in the loos, bemoaning another break in his long running saga with Rachel who had gone off with the ubiquitous James.

There were sketches and skits on school life, largely incomprehensible to anyone who had not written them, sometimes to those who had; some with crude references and jokes at the expense of pupils and staff. Alison would have objected, but most of the teachers, luckily, did not get it. They gave delight to the pupils, real pain to only a few.

Dom was sitting on a table with Emma and Mrs Trotman, there in an official capacity in case anyone had a little too much of anything. Perhaps it was fortunate that they were not sitting directly next to each other. They chatted with others on the table. The pupils were delighted for them to be there (for fifteen minutes or so), but they were quickly back to their own circles. Soon he and Emma and Mrs Trotman were left alone with all the detritus of the meal strewn on the table, spilt drinks, splodges of dinner and pudding, streamers dipping rather forlornly in it all, the inevitable mobile phone or two, for once allowed out.

Everyone else was up, dancing. Even some teachers began, very embarrassingly, to move around, much to the amusement and consternation of pupils shocked to see staff as dangerously mobile flesh and blood after all. Only Dom, Emma and Mrs Trotman sat out, sipping drinks, making polite conversation. Even that became impossible as the music grew too loud.

Soon Emma made some excuse, went off somewhere. Dom sat for a while with Mrs Trotman. They watched the world strut, fling and flail about.

Mrs Trotman looked at Dom as Emma left.

'Like her, don't you? Pretty girl. Knew she'd never settle here. Face doesn't fit. Been up to welfare a few times to chat. She likes you. Ships that pass in the night?'

She paused, looking at the dancers, at Dom. When the music stopped for a moment she continued.

'Youngsters! Funny lot. They have it all today; but they see too much too soon. My husband, Steve, says it's all America's fault: spoilt rotten there he says, but still don't know what they want, who they are. Too many choices. And they miss what life's really all about when it's right in front of them. Not prepared to work hard enough at things, a lot of them: that's the problem. You're young still. Don't you think everyone expects the world and his wife on a plate today?'

But just then a message arrived saying Rachel was ill, and James and Andy had had a fight. Blood had been drawn apparently.

War now in Hillview thought Dom, glad that Mrs Trotman's duties drew her away. She was quickly off to deal with it, and Mr Tring who also needed attention for drinking too much. Dom was left to ponder Mrs Trotman's words. Was she trying to tell him something? Why was it that everyone, particularly older people, always had opinions on everything all the time, however random. They hadn't exactly got the world right themselves.

Suddenly, he felt a tap on his shoulder. There beside him were Jane and Tim. For a second he was taken aback at how she looked: years older, glamorous, mature. He remembered the girl with the mousey hair on his first day, all tears, all lost: the girl who had told him she would never be anything.

'You look- stunning,' he said, forgetting himself.

'Sir, come and have a dance. Please, Sir.'

'Oh, no, that's kind, Jane, but, well, I'm rather tired and-'

'O come on, Sir,' Tim joined in. 'Don't be shy! Even Mr Workman is dancing with Ms Trippett. How gross is that. You must see!'

So they were, Dom observed, together again. They looked, laughed. Mike was flinging himself about too. He'd managed to get his partner in, but was still an attraction for some of the girls. Dom smiled, wondering what Alison would say were she there: but no one seemed to care too much, and for once, that was a good thing.

Jane persisted, would not give up. Dom advanced, a little shy still, a little unsteady too. Tim and Jane propelled him on to the dance area, a vibrant, pulsing, sweaty, heaving mass of very happy youngsters, and a few rather breathless staff, doing their best.

'Here you go, Sir,' Jane shouted in his ear, and, before he knew it, she had steered an attractive young figure away from the group, drawing her over to dance with him. For a moment he wanted to pull away. It would be easier to walk off. But she was especially attractive, this figure, smiling at him now; and soon, really forgetting more than he remembered for once, thinking little what he was doing or where he was going, he was jiving away with this lovely partner, not too much to his disadvantage.

It was Emma of course.

A raucous cheer went up. Emma and Dom found themselves centre stage, dancing away, part of the scene now, united, vexations buried in the beat of music, the young life all around. It carried them over, hearts on holiday, good times here, sorrow before and to come, all forgotten and forgiven. Conversation was impossible, thought was almost impossible, even for Dom. Only enjoyment in the moment was possible. That was enough.

After a while they went outside. It was so hot indoors, and the music really had taken over. They wished to be alone.

Staff were allowed to drink a little more than the oldest students. They both had.

Dom kissed her.

'I can't be cross with you – you know that.'

Emma looked at him, in her indefinable, marvellous way.

'You let things become more than they ever are, in that head of yours. Part of the reason for me wanting to stay was you. Do I have to say it?'

'Katie said you were staying, because some boyfriend was relocating to the area.'

Dom had said it. Emma pulled away for a moment.

'James? So that's what's bothering you. Dom! Men are hopeless. God, she's such a stirrer. He might be moving to Bristol, if the company relocates. I mentioned that to her weeks ago. Dom, that's over and done with.'

'Then why did she say it?'

Emma looked at him.

'Because she's Katie, just like, Hennock's Hennock. And you, you! How you imagine!'

He smiled, shrugged, embarrassed.

'I'm sorry. I'll never understand you. I'm not sure you'll ever understand me, or me me, if you see what I mean. I've had a bit to drink, or, well, I wouldn't be saying much at all, just... sulking, but it doesn't matter – we're together now, even if it's ships that pass in the night.... What will you do?'

'I don't know Dom, but, whatever, it's not you. It's me.'

In a few moments they had made up for there and then.

'You're one in a million,' he slurred.

She laughed.

'Flattery, Mr Greaves? No, I'm not, I'm selfish and most unprofessionally pissed. What I can't understand at the moment is why I can't decide finally. Not me at all.'

There was only one possible answer to this.

Dom spoke then.

'I wanted to walk away from it all this afternoon. Mike was right.'

'Mike? *Dom-.*'

'No, no, I mean – going off, starting a sort of tutor college, where it was on a scale you could manage, not like this place, do the things that matter.'

'I'm pretty sure we'd end up with another Hillview sooner or later,' replied Emma.

Now his confidence was back, he told her some of his ideas then, when he'd got more experience, before they got lost in it all. It wasn't very coherent, barely worked out, but they'd be an ideal team, one day.

She didn't say much. She was probably still laughing at him; but she caught his enthusiasm, his excitement.

He looked at her, thinking of what was only just beginning.

'When we leave, tomorrow, go our separate ways – the holidays, whatever happens, whatever you decide, we will stay-.'

'I can't say, maybe can't ever say. These last days, it's been lovely – it's – everything else, Dom, all this here. That's what I meant when I said I don't want you to rely on me. But, yes, I hope we'll stay friends, friends at least, always.'

Back inside they went. The party continued. They and most of the rest of the staff and pupils stuck it to the end, eschewing the high dramas of Rachel and Andy and James, happy simply to share everyone else's company. They relished their Hillview moment, before it began to change, before they would leave it, return to their home selves, tomorrow.

All too soon it was over. Everyone was happy and sad, wishing anyone they saw a Happy Christmas, and then it was a coach to Wellsway, or parents, some fuming at the lateness of the hour again. What was this, a school or bloody holiday camp? A final few drifted back to the boarding house, staff chasing. Everyone agreed it had been awesome, the school at its best, despite recent dramas.

Dom dutifully had to help clear up. Emma stayed too although she was yawning, clearly done in by the day, the week and term. They slipped away as soon as they could, sneaked up familiar stairs, unsteady, stifling giggles.

Of course, one of the twins appeared, grinning all over his face to see them, eager with bad news. Someone had been sick, drunk at the panto. Dom rolled his eyes wondering how, then manfully sorted that, remembering his first day, just like his last he thought.

When he got back Emma was curled up in bed.

'I've never felt this way-,' Dom began.

*

He woke later, and, careful not to disturb Emma, checked his phone.

One-thirty.

There was a message from Alison.

Dominic

Thanks for coming to see me earlier. I could see your concern. I did follow through on your suggestion. I'm afraid I have drawn a blank. There are, shall we say – anomalies and deletions but no evidence at all to support any of the issues raised by you or others in the last few days. I am inclined to put much, if not all, down to an understandably febrile atmosphere in these last few weeks here at Hillview which have been extraordinary for all, let alone those new here. Truth is stranger than fiction, but the imagination sometimes easier to believe. I hope we can both agree on that.

No need to worry about your personal future. I will speak to Dr Hennock- have been trying to contact him this evening. Whilst no one can know the outcomes of all the initiatives currently under consideration, who can ever know the future, the school will go on.

Hope you enjoyed the Feast. I have to write a long email to Mrs Tray about Rachel, James and Andy. Both boys will have black eyes tomorrow. Had to read the riot act on the last day. No one listens for all our advice! Wish parents would remember their responsibilities, staff what they can and can't do.

Things carry on, you see.

AT

So, Hennock had won.

CHAPTER SIXTY

DEUS EST MACHINA; GATEKEEPER OF TOMORROW

When Dom woke he wondered where he was, a beautiful woman in his bed, discarded costumes on the floor. Bewitched lovers waking to a cold dawn in the *Dream*?

But they were together, whatever was to be.

So.

Now there were things to be done, and said, their jobs. They parted briefly, who would part for longer soon. He was taking her to the station again later; her car was not back from the garage. He would leave his at Hillview too when he went home. It was quicker, all that way, by train.

Home, at last.

They tried to keep off the subject of what she was finally going to do. She could not believe she was still thinking about it with all that had gone on. The spirit of goodbye and going away, the hope of Christmas dancing confusingly all about them, his feelings – hers – were all running first one way, then another, but parting, uncertainty, for a time at least was inevitable.

*

Came at long, long last the final hours of the last day. Dom made his way to the Staff Room, remembering his first day, heart in mouth now over leaving, as before it had been over staying. Pupils he scarcely thought he knew wished him happy Christmas, happier hols, some properly cheerful for the first time in weeks.

Even teachers deserved a goodbye that day.

More of the children had left presents on his desk in his classroom. He'd never given any of his teachers a thing. Mrs Dot had left him some cake. He wondered what to do with it: he hadn't the heart to throw it away. Mr Tring had left a bottle of wine, a card that read:

GET OUT OF THIS PLACE WHILST YOU'RE STILL SANE.

Mrs Tombs had left him one too, with a more familiar message.

PIN YOUR SOCKS TOGETHER IN 20-

The maintenance staff were everywhere already picking up the stupendous tale of all the things left behind the night before, preparing holiday tasks. Oddly, there was no sign of Terry.

Then Mrs Dot ran into Dom, literally, carrying a huge tray piled high with mince pies. She had baked, for all staff, despite everything. She was clutching some files too. Dom remembered Emma had said she wanted to see him. She sprayed him with a galaxy of words, unconscious of the fact that mince pies were dropping from her clutch, bouncing around the floor with remarkable resilience.

'Yesterday- needing paper – in locked cupboard –children helping – forcing doors -unable to stop – Dr Hennock's cupboard breaking open- rifling – their school – their paper -shelves overturning – ransacking – stealing folders- one of the children running off with- bell going –all children running -excepting Tom and Joan? – helping – but boy with files hiding them-she hunting and hunting-terrible state-one of her migraines-Dr Hennock's files- not remembering boy- all given each others' names – joking- lovely children really-hours searching-found in the end-with kipper behind heater- bad smell – aren't they inventive?- trying to see Dr Hennock- next morning-files to his office – she not wanted – her ramblings-bad any time-not now – serious-dreadful things happening -secretary crying – offering mince pies –no one listening-everyone upset- Dr Hennock not there -gone home –hoping he was all right-poor Dr Hennock – having to deal with her – everyone -such a nice man -always doing best – prank – not get Dom in trouble-his class-perhaps he could set things right-with Dr Hennock-they got on – what was he doing for Christmas-coming and staying- long as he liked-Roger-preferring company-always asking people round-not always asking her – handing files to Dom-unpleasantness over- hoping- better New Year.'

Before he could really understand what had happened, she had pressed some of Dr Hennock's files into his hands, including, yes, *the file* he believed, and, the occasional mince pie still cascading from her tray, words from her mouth, she was off, still talking.

Dom stood there beyond any words himself.

If you wrote it down: the way things turned. He pulled out the familiar looking file from the pile she had thrust into his hands, scanned briefly through to see if it was what he believed, and there it all was, in his hands at last, *evidence*, something that yet might, just possibly, stay their futures, give them a chance. This wasn't imagination.

After all that.

Unbelievable.

He weighed the folders in his hands for a moment, then set off to find Alison as quickly as he could.

But things took another turn, before he could get anywhere near her. He was intercepted in one of the corridors by Mike.

Even he seemed beside himself this morning, breathless with news.

'Checked your messages, recently?' he cried.

'No, I need to find Ali quickly.'

'She's dealing with it all, the latest crisis! Forget other stuff. Look, look!' urged Mike, and flashed his phone at him in proof.

It was all round the school already, apparently, but no one had expected what was now literally unfolding moment by moment.

Just before a last whole school assembly, that was the traditional general goodbye, a message had flashed around that Alison was to be taking this final school meeting. It contained stunning news.

Dr Hennock had been called away. He'd gone, left already.

More. There was rumour circulating that he would not be back, *not this term, not ever!...* Dom could not take it in; but Mrs Dot's tangled absurdities had told him, if he'd been listening, that something was up.

Still clutching the files, feeling ever more as if he had indeed woken to some crazy dream, he numbly followed Mike, diverting into the Staff Room nearby where a few teachers were gathered. Now, all were astonished, bewildered, shocked, agog to know what was going on – what wild last twist in the plot of the term things were taking.

Almost instantly, Paul bustled in, divided between excitement at carrying more bad news, dismay at what was happening.

'It's all over social media,' he began, out of breath as well, 'the local press are on it. *Disaster. Hennock has resigned.* Scams to do with the housing scheme, selling land, all sorts. Look!' he waved his phone in front of some of his colleagues who resumed their own hunt for news.

'Hillview is finished.'

'What do you mean?' said Dom, hardly daring to believe anything anymore.

'An end to cushy promotion prospects for some, a return to sanity for the rest of us,' chirped Mr Walker who happened to be there, as he always was. He looked more cheerful than he had for weeks.

'That reminds me, I must tell Charles,' he rushed off to phone.

Paul swore at him behind his back and dipped back into his mobile.

'This place always was a looking-glass world. Now it's a total bloody farce,' boomed Mr Tring who tore in looking for some lost music, and then shot off to lambast his choir who had one final turn that day.

'Anyone for a pie?' said Mrs Dot who was also there by now, wandering around curiously oblivious to the main event. She was not wearing her glasses. Suddenly, she started talking to an inflatable Dalek model that had been topped with a life-size photo of the head and face of Dr Hennock during some of the traditional tricks before last night's revels. It had been removed there for safe keeping.

Dom could hear her, see her vaguely puzzled that the exterminator arm was not reaching out for one of her delicacies. Surely she could see, must see what she was talking to? There were tears of laughter in his eyes, and relief, hardly daring to hope that this was all true after all.

He fingered the files once more, wondering what to do with them – it, now.

But no one was really paying any attention to him, or Mrs Dot's insane antics. It was all Hennock, what was going on?

At that moment, another email pinged into everyone's inboxes from Alison and the Chairman of Governors this time. Everyone was hanging on every word.

The news was staggering.

Dr Hennock, it read, had had, unexpectedly, to step aside from the role of Acting Head for pressing personal reasons. Alison would be acting as temporary Head for the next two terms. Parents and staff would learn more in various letters and emails urgently being prepared. Dr Hennock was thanked, cursorily, for his service to the school, his passing noted with very curt regret. But he would not be returning. *He would not be returning*; and that was that.

Shock lasted two seconds. Disbelief followed. Everyone had to read the email, several times, unable to trust their senses. It was a prank, like the Dalek, the kids had got into the system, some such. They must see it themselves. Was he ill? Terminal? His departure could not be real.

But it was.

Then there was – mostly- an ecstasy of relief, delight and joy such as had not been seen in the Staff Room for most of recent history.

Slowly, slowly, hard to take it in, but then conviction at last: a Christmas miracle!

All the little conversations that broke out were repetitions of each other. Someone steered Mrs Dot away from the Dalek, explaining what had happened several times to her, and Hennock, but she still did not understand.

'What a nice man he was- not at all a Dalek -always losing glasses- sorry- perhaps gone away to dress as Santa Claus, like Mr Waseley- files – she not flavour of the month- wondered if she dropped pies round to his house- would it cheer him up?'

Everyone was talking at once, wanting to know exactly what had happened, or claiming in some cases to have predicted it all along, but finally, just before the whole school gathered for the last time, Alison herself appeared amongst them. She was beyond exhaustion, *looks like a corpse*, said Mr Walker not very sotto voce, but she was not pretending anything anymore, struggling to be professional in the face of all that had gone on. Her smiling face shone for the first time in who knows how many weeks: confident, happy, liberated even; and certainly relieved.

She began an informal meeting, but first, nothing must delay the end of term she declared; the children were coming first, not plans or schemes or politics, but them. A spontaneous cheer went up when she said this, but she waved it aside. Someone even started clapping until she frowned it to stop.

'Can't say too much but yes, yes, it's true Darren has had to resign from the post and step back from his roles in the school, temporarily at least. All very difficult, but-.'

'All developed very early this morning. Still supposed to be confidential, but obviously a terrible shock. We send him our best wishes. Things moving fast. Staff will be given more information after the assembly. Please bear with me – hectic morning – everything happening at once. First job is to steady the ship-pupils not told just yet. But we must now all to our final assembly. I know – a million questions, but all will be answered. I'll email everyone after the meeting.

'The important thing is, we do the right thing for the school, get back to our teaching next term, not all this. There are more important things than money.'

A cheer went up from most in the room.

'I hope it's nothing to do with me that wretched cupboard and my piles,' announced Mrs Dot quite unaware of what she had actually said.

But Alison was gone in a whirl, leaving a Staff Room behind that was almost all summer, except for those who had had something to gain during Hennock's brief ascendancy, some of whom were now claiming that they had never really believed his promises anyway. Those who had hoped to, or who already had made most profit from his rise, slipped quietly aside to lick their wounds together, or hang on their phones hoping against all reason for some sudden reversal of dearly bought misfortunes.

Mr Walker, however, not known for his movement, did a little dance.

'Got the bastard, at last. This is the best day of my life!'

None thought of darker consequences just then, unsolved problems, gaping holes, not just in finance, but as to what the future might unfold. Maybe Alison's few words suggested the school would at last be run well, or at least run for the things that mattered. Whatever, for now, for many, *That man* was gone, one dragon slayed. With him out, all must be well.

All through this, Dom clung to the files he had in his hand dazed. At each twist and turn, as Alison came and went, he gripped them tightly, until at last his gaze dropped down to what he held, smiling to himself, wondering what to do with them all now, so long sought, so long thought about, and now nothing.

But one other thought rose, wouldn't let go. With this news, it could only be the case that Emma would definitely stay. Hennock gone, she would not need to leave. He knew that for sure: yes, there would be loose ends, a few confusions, even a bit of a feeling of much ado about nothing after all that tumult but a happy ending.

What was, was!

Quietly, just before they all rushed off to assembly, ushered by a very subdued Katie, he crossed to the pigeon holes. He deliberated for a moment or two, looking at both Mrs Tenace's and Dr Hennock's..The first was bursting with papers, Christmas cards, some almost falling out, even some of Mrs Dot's pies in some greaseproof paper (she forgot no one). The second was completely empty. Dr Hennock never left anything to chance, wandering hands, or eyes.

Dom thought of all that had happened, was still to happen, and then placed the key file safely back in Dr Hennock's pigeon hole, leaving the rest on a table below.

*

Staff must smarten up, sober up: a final performance called. Routine took hold. It was the school's final assembly, the life of the school resuming as if nothing had happened.

There was a rather drearily factual account of all the big events of the term. Dom thought of the version he could write, would write one day. Then they all must watch the doling out of shining awards to a legion of deserving hands, and eventually attend to rather more tarnished warnings about the terrors of the earth that would befall if pupils did not work for the multitude of forthcoming exams that lay as a rich delight all before them.

The pupils sat still for once, even Rachel, James and Andy, very sheepish and bearing black eyes and pale faces. Amidst all, Alison had insisted they were there, at the front, on display amidst all the younger children: part of their punishment.

Some of the boys at the back, nonetheless, Dom observed, seemed to be gaming on their mobiles. He frowned at them; they smiled back, carried on. He went across, quietly admonished, took their phones away.

'Happy Christmas!' he wished them, cheeky as they, just as Alison was bidding all the rest a wonderful holiday.

Then it was over. School was done. Next term, well that was years and years away – now all that had to be done was to savour those most precious moments, and do their best to forget as much as possible of what they had learnt.

Still the staff who did not know the truth had a mind only for one question: come on someone, please tell us – what has really happened.

It was Paul, not surprisingly, who had the story backed up later and much more discreetly by floods of emails from Alison, though he was less eager today to impart this tale. Dom, for a moment or two, felt sorry for him. Emma, who seemed rather subdued and quiet at all the news only said that he had got what he deserved, but that Paul had already been in to give Alison advice on what she should do now. Dom met Paul later, coming out of Alison's office when he went to see her himself.

'She's asking for my advice as a new member of staff. I'm to be some kind of representative – improving communication with young staff.' He was delighted, already bigging up his new role. He wished Dom a happy Christmas. After all that, Hennock was already history.

But Dom had no time to mull on that one, as more of the truth spilled out, and the agent of Hennock's spectacular fall was at last revealed.

The reason for Dr Hennock's departure had, apparently, come from the most unlikely of sources, but one that Dom knew well. The Christmas miracle, owed all to, and nothing less and no one less, than an excluded child, mostly forgotten by all: Tom Rymer himself.

This, Dom learnt, was what had happened.

Hearing news of all the changes at Hillview had set young Rymer thinking. More telling than that, was remembering how he had been made to feel. Bumping into Mr Greaves had jogged memories, of one or two who had tried to help in ways so little as to be all but forgotten. Texting the twins, his eyes and ears, he had learnt more. He saw much, too much for someone his age, more than anyone believed he could, including Dom who vowed, when he learnt all, never to underestimate the capacity of youngsters for good and ill again.

For Rymer had acted.

Yes, he had acted: mostly out of feelings of revenge, but also with a rather impressive if frightening degree of imagination, and perhaps for some kind of justice. Hundreds of his store of hacked emails went variously to a local media newsfeed, the Wellsway press, council staff and, amongst others, the school solicitors – all easy objects for someone with his range. He included enough of a covering explanation, however badly written, to whet the appetite of those who received them, especially with the school much in the news locally, amid a groundwork of controversy already devastatingly laid.

With little else on the regional menu but the usual dreary economic shambles, the story was irresistible. Some dodgy dealings in the setting of a school where money, independence, identity and the idea of privilege were all knotted together was manna from heaven.

'Grownups' had done the rest. The consequences had been building all through the penultimate day. Eager for bad news, emails had been sifted, a trail of what looked at best dubious, at worst illegal activities connecting Hennock with local council officials, the planning department, and even suggestions of various kinds of 'sweeteners' unearthed. There were further suspicions of backhanders and money to speed up the planning process and approve the sale of part of the Cloud, violating its protected status on the specious grounds of precedents set by new planning laws. Added to that were possible links with money from Chinese sources being used to circumvent normal procedures altogether, all enough to stoke tragically robust local prejudices even higher. Rubbishing foreigners was good sport for all everyone's supposed liberal education. Most importantly, Dr Hennock's fingerprints seemed to be all on all sorts. The exact details of any criminality were hazy, but the idea of bribes and corruption mixing with privilege was an old and potent theme and soon took on a life all of its own, so that any redeeming idea of noble motivation was quickly lost in the glory of a dripping scandal brought to light.

Dr Hennock had slipped away from the feast to write an address to the whole school, celebrating his own coronation, only to discover the media were trying to get hold of him. There was a car parked outside his house early the next day, before light, cameras ready, watching everything, everyone inside, despite new laws about personal privacy.

They got their pictures.

There was not much left of him by the middle of the following morning. The pack had their day. Meanwhile, sources had been checked, surmises drawn, so sensation could be whipped, torment inflicted and all the darker arts of journalism enjoyed. Self-righteousness, always intoxicating, was particularly piqued as children were involved. A sex scandal would have been better, but for now, there was meat in this for a good few days. And this at Christmas time when everything spoke of innocence and redemption.

Whilst precise legal crimes remained vague, enough mud had been thrown to ensure Hennock's reputation was finished, certainly at Hillview. Many, but not all of the governors had judiciously kept their hands clean. They were quick to offer him up as sacrifice.

Hennock made his escape, convinced of the sanctity of his ends, asserting, as he always had, that the good of the school was his only motivation, dismissing his means, any slight evasions of strict proprieties, as mere brutal necessities. And there were some who believed him right, enough to give everyone pause for thought. And not just those who had been promised the earth, or had voted a particular way, even if believing, knowing and understanding were, as ever, very different things.

He and his wife drove off in silence, leaving behind an empty house, curtains drawn, full of unwrapped Christmas presents, escaping to stay with friends in France. Shortly afterwards the house itself was on the market, Dr Hennock said to be teaching in some small private school abroad whilst awaiting further investigations, questioning by the police, possible extradition.

Management and governor emails and phone lines were jammed before the day had properly got going. There was some question as to how seriously any actual case could proceed – and it was based anyway on 'stolen' evidence; but those governors who had so advanced his plans could not slip entirely free from the shenanigans of which he, and they, had been part. Resignations, further turmoil followed. Even the Secretary of State became involved it was claimed, though she was proud to say she had never heard of the place.

Dr Hennock's particular governor accomplice got the chop, but he was, so stories ran, too wealthy and too well supported by a law firm to face anything like a coming to justice. Dom would have been appalled to learn how various corruptions uncovered, major or minor, were only ever partly confronted and corrected. Perhaps he would no longer have been surprised.

None of the staff ever knew how close the school came to some kind of collapse, but Alison, whose steady worth and integrity had always been such an understated asset, and its own real merits, built simply on years of good teaching and trust, saved it.

And children had to go to school somewhere.

Loyal and grateful parents rallied. The actions of Alison, some of the more sensible governors, persuaded the authorities to give it a temporary financial breathing space whilst it sorted itself out. The state would keep it under its wings, but on its terms and with cuts, its control strongly reasserted. Independence, one day, remained for some an option, a dream, but as confusing and uncertain a reality as it always had been.

If they had known about it in full, Tom might have been a hero to some staff and pupils but they did not, and never did get to know all. The hand of the law and the necessary protective discretion, or evasion, of the adult world descended.

There was a sting in the tail for those few who knew the real cast of this play, who cared.

Tom disappeared.

He was no longer at school anywhere. He was no longer at home or with friends. It seemed as if he had vanished into the virtual world he believed he so commanded. He could still be found, 'live' on line, podcasting, tweeting, gaming. There was no limit to his haunting there; but he seemed to have become a ghost, a shadow enlarged in the imagination of a few pupils and staff into some mythical agent who could wreak havoc, then vanish, temporarily at least, without physical trace – into his own kingdom.

Dom's delight at the turn of events was mitigated when he discovered its agent. He was disturbed at what the boy might have landed himself in now. In his way, he saw the boy monstered by the machine, turned into some gatekeeper of a future that no child should have the power to summon. He bothered that the kid would never find a way back but soon learnt that, amidst all her concerns and her dawning realisation of what she had always instinctively felt about Dr Hennock, his ways, Alison was helping with Tom. All the safeguarding issues were in her capable hands. The local police were on it too.

Even his parents seemed roused to something like conscience by this twist of his story.

Alison's other immediate and necessary mission was to reinstate as many people in their jobs as she needed to, even Mrs Dot, on strictly circumscribed terms which took a deal of explaining to her, and came with no certainty of compliance. The new head's work included conceding that Mr Greaves's imagination might not have been quite as wild as she had believed, and, more modestly, reassuring Dom that his job was not in question, never could have been really. Indeed she would be keen to promote him one day, when he had a little more experience, when I've grown up more, thought Dom rather wearily recognising a theme.

Dom vaguely wandered if he had not travelled a lot further in his first, than many of his colleagues in all their many terms; but he was not sorry just then to have to take some time. Looking back, he wasn't entirely convinced by, or comfortable over, some of his own actions and assumptions that term. He even wondered at his own arrogance, what he had done or nearly done. He was content to fall back – for now – on his natural diffidence, especially as he saw what happened to some who climbed the greasy pole. Perhaps deep down he realised too that he needed a larger dose of humility than even one term's teaching could furnish to make progress.

Mr Royal, however, could not be lured back by any manner of promise, or bribe; his world had been too damaged by Hennock's. It pained Dom to see how some of his colleagues had already forgotten Charles. Professional life and fortune were a fickle business it appeared, as simply mortal as the real thing.

*

All this could not happen, be learnt, fully taken in, in the hours of term left, but by lunchtime most of the pieces of the jigsaw were in place, enough food for endless reflection, even for Dom.

There remained, as ever, Emma.

He knew she was going in to see Alison at lunchtime, one o'clock precisely, one of the long queue of staff who needed to be squared, mollified, or just reassured. She had promised Dom her final final decision when they met shortly afterwards. She owed it to the school to tell them first; he must approve of that.

But with all that had happened, his doubts had vanished. His hopes rose high. Emma would 'give it another year, then see.' They would be together at Hillview, whatever else.

As for the future of the school, which way it would go, where it would land, you needed to look closely at what people actually did, what you did, Dom had decided, before you jumped too quickly to change. People saw ideas, too easily, rather than the people behind them. Ideas were actually dangerous things. Perhaps, given his own experiences, his youth, he should be forgiven for excluding from that his own better imaginings: for, if he had learnt a little about what not to do, he was more convinced than ever that there was so much more that could be done. Maybe life would never quite be the perfect art he hoped; but he would keep his dreams.

It was true, however, that he wondered a little more at the end of his first term than at the start, about the power of the imagination. It so drove things to make believe, could be uncomfortably childlike, capable of good and bad, knowing, not knowing.

Meanwhile, and he included himself here, it was Christmas, and in the best British spirit, any difficult decisions would all be once more put off, as perhaps they always had been, until the new year, January 4th, to be precise, for Hillview. By goodness, they all deserved Christmas after the term they had had; and the Christmas spirit, everyone agreed, (well, nearly everyone, Mr Walker hated it), should last all year.

CHAPTER SIXTY-ONE

HOME

The speed with which the school emptied surprised Dom, as it had before. Soon corridors rang to the sound only of silence. As he returned to his flat, he thought of the dust settling in those rooms down the corridor that had once held such fascination for him: old photos of old teachers, years gone by.

Things had enlarged during term so much into something more than themselves, even the littlenesses. And there had been all that sense of heading somewhere, to a crisis and climax; but now, that strangely melancholy emptiness. Once again, school was become a stage after a set had been finally struck, the last act done. Yet the school had become like a person to him too, someone you had lived intimately with, now suddenly gone from your life. You wondered where a familiar voice, from its urgent demands and calls, to its prosaic moment to moment little concerns could possibly have disappeared to, swept away completely, utterly, replaced with only stillness, almost a death.

What's in a life, he thought – what had it all been about: so much, come and gone in the blink of an eye, part pantomime, part fantasy, part tragedy. Trivia, absurdity, something more?

But there were still surprises.

Despite his absence earlier that morning, Terry was about. He caught Dom on his rounds, his final round.

He was leaving. He had had it: all the chops and changes, being taken for granted, taken for a ride.

'I've just told the latest Boss, I'm off. Place'll never change. Them at the top, whoever they are, always wantin' somethin' more, usually for nothin'. An' doin' f- all about it. Jus' told her where she can stick her desks and chairs. Pay rises, includin' support staff, levellin' up-... Promisin' stars, leavin' us to shovel shit, short handed, no f-in tools. Only a load of teachers'd fall for that.'

Royal, Waseley, Hennock, Terry: the rocks of the place! Dom couldn't believe it. Terry, like Walker would always be there. Was this the revolution Joe dreamed? Perhaps the school should have seen this one coming too; or was this another of those things it had turned a blind eye to?

'Don' you worry,' Terry smirked. 'Little bastards'll be back before you know it. Ain't there anywhere decent could take you and your girl?'

He went on at some length, before making off.

'Teachers,' he tutted, shaking his head. 'Schools! They'd be better off without two things: staff and kids.'

'Happy Christmas!' Dom called optimistically.

'Happy Christmas, happy New Year: happy same old same old, you mean!'

*

Dom returned to his study. He was spent: you could only take so much. And it all just rolled on anyway, regardless as Alison had said it would: up and down, up and down, like a life.

At least Emma was staying.

On the door, to his irritation, he had found one sock dramatically and prominently fastened. It had not been washed. There was a large note by it.

PIN YOUR SOCKS TOGETHER!!

For a second he felt a surge of annoyance. Didn't she ever give up?

Then, he smiled, remembering his recent resolutions, cheesy or not.

On his desk were two more cards, a bottle of whisky. They must think he was alcoholic now. Perhaps he would be by the end of another term.

And how the hell had they got into his flat whilst he was out?

He tore open the envelope:

Thanks, sir. Your the greastest teacher really. Sorry for being no good in lessnos. See u in the New Yer.

Lessnos!

It was from one of his more challenging pupils. It meant a lot, clearly more than he had been able to teach.

He opened the other one.

Happy Christmas, sir. Told you had something for you. Hennock got what was coming.

One of the twins followed you onto the Cloud one night. It was a dare from the borders. I organised it and won a mint of money. sold that school piano too online.

Good luck with miss.

I'll be around.

Tom

So there had been someone there, that night. It hadn't been imagination. But talk about nuts, weird! And the piano- more problems for Alison! The boy was a monster. Crazy, like the place! What weren't they capable of... where would it end?

But around? He must let poor Alison know all this. Didn't his duties ever stop either?

*

She wasn't going to stay after all, but leave.

Emma was going to leave.

When she told him, a world of hopes went. He thought he'd schooled himself in compromise, disappointment – come through.

'It's not you, it's not even Hillview,' she repeated over and over. 'I told you – it's me. It's just: it's not me.'

Not me.

The words went round and round in his head as she spoke on, things in pieces.

'But you'll never get another post. You've let them down!' he declared at last, desperate what to say.

She looked at him, turned away.

'It's a job, Dom, only a job. If I stay, it just takes over, empties you out. I'd be lost in it, never escape. Old one day, full of regret.'

He could never agree on that.

There must be something else; but she was adamant.

'It's because of you I took staying seriously and because of you I take going seriously. Don't be silly, Dom. This isn't the end, Dom; it's just, there's so much more out there.'

'You sound like me now,' Dom replied sarcastically.

'Please. Let's be mature about all this. Practical.'

'It's all right,' he said, eventually, not meaning it. 'I'm getting quite good at this grown up thing.'

They argued, but time was up. They had to leave.

They made conversation on the way to the station. They were hardly short of other things to talk about, given the day's, term's events: Hennock, his demise; Rymer's Revenge; the future; even Terry's dramatic exit. But everything seemed hollow.

He told Emma about Tom's card, the twin following him in the dark, the piano.

'He's a headcase. Perhaps he's got some mancrush on you.'

'No. No, I don't think so. I'm some imagined father figure – someone magic we all hope is out there somewhere, to sort things; but isn't really. You're on your own in this world.'

She looked at him, turned away.

They passed The White Hart.

'Look!' cried Dom.

There was a For Sale sign on it.

'What next?' he muttered.

As he drove along, she seemed abstracted, unreal beside him, gone already.

He could not take it in.

'I hope Rymer turns out all right. I suppose he won't,' Emma said eventually.

She spoke quietly, almost as if to herself, but then added, 'Lucky you picked his fish and chips up that day.'

'I can't help feel, somehow we've all made him that,' said Dom, solemnly.

'What do you mean?' said Emma.

Dom shook his head.

There was silence between them for a while.

'You're wearing odd socks!' she said suddenly at one point, laughing.

Neither of them spoke for a few minutes.

'I wonder what will happen. The school, independence,' muttered Dom; something to say as they waited at some traffic lights, the outskirts of Wellsway already.

'Something has to happen. But independence is always someone being selfish somewhere along the line, wanting their own way. Like me I suppose.'

Dom did not reply.

'At least Hennock won't be in charge. He'll wriggle out of things, like Waseley – his sort always do,' Emma said.

Houses, shops, people. They all passed by, somewhere else.

The station was much as before, except even colder. There was that added sense of Christmas hurry, anticipation in the air – everyone rushing, everyone determined to get to their somewhere.

They stood close to each other for a last few minutes, thoughts and feelings pulled all over the place.

'We'll still meet after Christmas as we planned?' said Dom.

Emma looked into his eyes, tears in her own, said nothing. Then they hugged each other tightly; the turmoil of the past, time unwritten.

Once more, a cold wind blew hard, litter scuttered down the platform, and the metal rails flashed in a dying sun, but this day the train was on time, perversely punctual almost to the second.

They said goodbye in a way that could not be mistaken.

All too soon Dom was back in his study, alone.

He was missing Emma already, more than he could bear.

He messaged her, then spoke to John for a long time, trying to tell him of all that had happened in the last tremendous days. John said over and over, *People are only people. Don't expect too much.*

Maybe some kinds of understanding only came with loss.

He was missing the kids, too. He'd found a purpose in them, but it was a poor sort of place without its beating heart; and they were come and gone, always would be.

He needed fresh air.

*

It was three-thirty and campus looked empty and forlorn. Light was failing and clouds were moving up from the south west as he climbed the muddy hill where the wind still danced, stirring the long grey grass, shining when it caught the sun. In the hollows of the hillside, patches of snow lay, grubby and grey, melting fast. He reached the top and felt the wind blowing stronger, warmer with splashes of rain to come.

For a moment, as he stood up there, the distant sea turned silver, then became a gold bar as the slipping sun, sea and sky coalesced in some vision that would have seemed impossible had it not been real. But all too soon, the sun snapped out, the sea was grey metal again, the horizon a ruled line hardening across miles of shadows.

The idea of writing it all down came back to him, then, of trying to get down on paper his efforts to get his head round it all. No one would believe it he was sure; or they'd dismiss as all just being in his head, his imagination, as if life wasn't exactly that. He'd given up on deep meanings, some revelatory theme, some cohering thread that would astonish the world – for today. Maybe there wasn't one. But perhaps they would find it interesting.

He turned around and looked back over the campus.

It was a matter of honour not to be last gone, on the parts of pupils and staff alike. Mist and darkness were coming up. The lights of a few cars that were still pulling away shone, but most of the buildings were silent now, their glass windows like eyes with no light behind them, cold and dark.

He thought how many times things had seemed impossible there, still seemed so. It was easy to think yourself out of possibilities when you came up against it, to accept.

But life was possibility.

He looked across to the sea for a last time. A hard gust of wind brought a sudden rush of rain, but down the hill, he went.

Then he spoke to Emma.

*

Two days later as another December dusk was gathering, Dom was glad to reach home after a slow train journey. He was cold and shivering. The heating had broken down in the coach, but Dad was waiting for him at the station. Soon he was sitting in a rather humble but warm family kitchen surrounded by long familiar cooking smells.

His parents had been quarrelling he could tell. They always did, mostly over something ridiculous, trivia. But they got through.

Mum was minding the stove, pleased to be Mum again. She could tell a lot without asking.

'You look more grown up,' she said, 'more mature: it's done you good.'

'*Mum!*' groaned Dom.

'bout bloody time,' his Dad replied, pleased really.

She would find it all out soon enough, whatever he said to the rest.

Dad poured some over generous drinks, proud of his family, determined not to show it. His younger brother chatted endlessly, rather too confidently about his first term at university. A whole host of names, particularly girls', were strewn in his tale. They meant little to anyone else, everything to him.

Dom had to tease.

'Don't start quarrelling like kids as soon as you come home!' cried Dad.

'Dom's been up to all sorts in his new job. They wanted to sack him!' his brother could not resist; but Dom would not be drawn, yet.

His parents were as eager to hear his news as they were to tell of their adventures to the other side of the same world. Each had their story. Soon they mingled becoming, it seemed, part of one and the same tale.

Eventually they turned to Dom.

'We met a lot of retired teachers on the trip. Some of the going's on! We thought of you,' said Mum.

'Sorted them out at school yet?' asked Dad. 'What's happened to this Emma? No good if she doesn't stick things.'

'Emma's left, dumping him,' anticipated annoying younger brother.

How did you answer, explain: a term, characters, a love, a life, all the things that had been good, crazy?

Dom thought of his colleagues and pupils, all that had happened: high dreams and abiding littleness; of getting people to listen at all sometimes, trying to get them to think, work hard, be responsible. He thought of empathy, and understanding, then egos ever striving to be first, how selfish everybody could be, himself included. He thought of duty, doing the right thing, service; and the simple need for infinite, infinite patience with everyone, yourself most of all. He thought of the fruits of trust, the realities of betrayal; of keeping a smile on his face, taking all to heart.

He thought, humbly, how much he'd learnt himself, had to learn.

For a second or two, to his embarrassment and shame, he felt himself welling up.

He'd failed on quite a lot, but not altogether. He'd never stopped trying, expecting, having high expectations, of others, of himself: not what you had, but what you could do, become. Everyone deserved that. *Something better*, even if it might not come quite as quickly as once he'd dreamed.

He thought of Emma.

'Oh, shut up!' he said to his brother.

Then he laughed.

'You don't know what you're talking about. It's not that simple, nothing's that simple! Actually, we've been talking, talking about starting our own school, a kind of tutor school – one day: doing the right things, doing right by the individuals it's all about, in the right way!'

'No wonder she's off!' declared brother.

'Who the hell's ever going to pay for that?' demanded Dad.

'I should get more experience first,' suggested Mum.

How far out at sea he had been Dom thought. I will write it all down some day, do my best for now, be as honest as I can.

And there he is.

He – the teacher!

What is, is: except for the imagination.

'Listen!' he begins.

THE END

ACKNOWLEDGEMENTS

'Are we in it, Sir?!'

I have taught EFL, at university, on exchange in various schools, at a tutor hub for those who don't fit in conventional education, been a school inspector, worked as a private tutor. I have had the good fortune to spend much of my teaching career in two superb schools, Rendcomb College and The King's School, Gloucester both led with vision and humanity, well managed, successful in the ways that should matter most. I've been lucky enough to encounter many delightful pupils in all these establishments.

When I began full time teaching, unlike the protagonist, I was ably supported by colleagues, especially the late Mr John Holt, his lovely wife Anne and family, a man of great wisdom and complete integrity. Likewise, most of the Heads and Deputy Heads I have come across have been good people, unlike the slipshod Waseley, or the scheming Hennock, all of them working incredibly hard, some quite wonderful.

Hillview School, its leadership, especially, is imagined rather differently. No such school or such type of school quite exists, though I hope there is enough about schools to celebrate, laugh or sigh over, recognising in entirely fictional characters and situations typical scenarios. Actual truth remains, of course, always much stranger than any fiction.

Hillview's character, its hybrid identity, was conceived in part to reflect in broad terms recent turbulence in our country as much as any school world. Indeed, Hillview is meant to be an image, on a very small scale, of aspects of our country at a pivotal point in its history. Its leading characters are imagined ones, but some situations draw inspiration from 'real' historical events. Whatever parallels, the story suggests, as a novel should, how so much comes back to people, personalities.

I'd like to thank all those who have looked at parts, or even all of this, and given me advice, particularly members of the Painswick Writers' Group, Christine and Edmund Green, Ben Sandell, Lorraine Harrison, Michael Amherst, Peter MacDonald, many pupils and colleagues, all who have shown interest, offered encouragement. I have learnt so much writing it, not least just how almost impossible writing is.

I must acknowledge one or two broad echoes of a number of plays I taught and directed a few times when I began teaching: John Godber's excellent play *Teechers* and Willy Russell's *Our Day Out* and *Educating Rita*. In a rapidly changing world, one in which sensibilities have changed much since the 70s and 80s, minor things have dated, but their themes, especially *singing a better song* are enduring ones. I owe an incalculable debt to many texts I have taught and read over the years, ones as diverse in tone and theme as *Frankenstein* and *el Quijote* itself, the story of which I have recalled ironically many times when 'doing' literature. School and education are the subject of many modern media representations. I freely confess I am shamefully ignorant of many of those. But then I believe that writing can still be a more potent form of art, more independent somehow, and closer to, more authentic about, all the strengths and weaknesses of what is fashionably called 'lived experience'. Whatever the merits of this tale, reading preserves (potentially) special virtues if we want to try to go deep, really understand.

IT plays an imagined, perhaps far-fetched role in the plot. It must. Like everything, teaching, education are in an enormous whirl of change, maybe improvement, because of it. We haven't yet even begun to imagine the scale of that. Maybe some of the old ideas and practices of school will be left far behind. As one of the characters in the story says, school is still a bit nineteenth century in its ways, its ideas, not that that is necessarily wrong. But as another character says, I rather expect the more we question or discard past or even current ideas of school, the more those ideas will come back, especially in this age of rather unsociable social media. What goes around comes around. Now which colleague used to say that?

When you have taught for a long time you unconsciously absorb so much from the pupils you teach, the colleagues you share that experience with; but if some episodes draw inspiration from historical events as I noted above, my characters' and situations' resemblance to any real places or persons is entirely coincidental. It's a work of fiction, and no imitation of people I taught with or pupils I know or knew is intended. I have too much respect for those I have come across, and, anyway, imagining is curiously liberating. There are two specific minor exceptions. Firstly, I have always been taken by the idea that a narrator lives in all his characters. Secondly, the character of Mrs Tombs – and the book's title, are based loosely on a real Mrs Toms, in truth a kindly, good-natured heroine who worked tirelessly for years washing not only boarders' clothes but those of resident staff in days long past. In her own way she was a saint, and yes she did have to remind me (gently in her case) many times to pin my socks together when I submitted laundry- to save her laboriously sorting and pairing up my old socks. It took me a long time to remember, but she persisted. Eventually, slowly, I learnt.

From that sprang a title, and much more; but that's a different kind of story altogether.

Michael Craddock JUNE 2024